DEEP GREEN COVER

BOOKS BY JOEL W. BARROWS

The Deep Cover Series
Deep White Cover
Deep Green Cover
Deep Red Cover
Deep Purple Cover
Deep Blue Cover
Deep Orange Cover

Other Titles
Poisoned Waters
The Drug Lords

JOEL W. BARROWS

DEEP GREEN COVER
THE EARTH MARTYRS BRIGADE

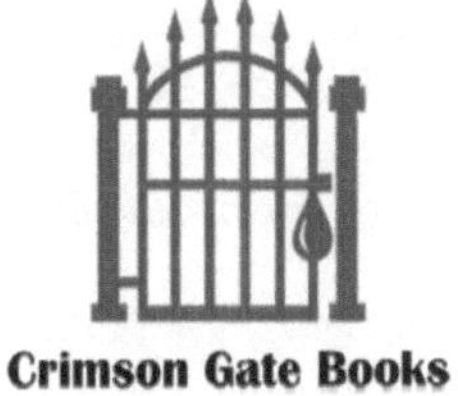

Crimson Gate Books

AUTHOR'S NOTE

The views expressed in this novel are those of
Joel W. Barrows alone and do not reflect
those of the Iowa Judicial Branch.

To those conservationists and environmentalists who persuade us in the marketplace of ideas.

CAST OF CHARACTERS

David Ward (alias, Joshua "Josh" Young; alias, Lightning), the ATF undercover agent

Tommy Stafford and Jim McNeal, the retired Missoula cops with whom Ward jams

Battalion Chief Reggie Turner, Park City Fire Department

Brooke Talbot, Reporter KSKI TV

ATF Special Agent in Charge Leroy Wheeler, Denver Field Division (Ward's SAC)

ATF Assistant Special Agent in Charge Mike McKenney, Denver Field Division

ATF Special Agent Toby Combs, Denver Field Division

ATF Special Agent Ian Maness, Denver Field Division

Troll, member of Spokane cell

Andy Garner, Tahoe Douglas Fire District firefighter

Alan Hess, reporter KTRT TV

ATF Special Agent in Charge Alex Burke, San Francisco Field Division

ATF Assistant Special Agent in Charge Bryce Warner, San Francisco Field Division

ATF Assistant Special Agent in Charge Wesley Birch, San Francisco Field Division

ATF Special Agent Cesar Cruz, San Francisco Field Division, case agent

Wolf, leader of Portland cell

Skye, member of Portland cell

Sequoia, member of Portland cell

Fern, member of Portland cell

Cobra, member of Portland cell

Firefly, member of Portland cell

Mouse, member of Portland cell

Rabbit, member of Portland cell

River, member of Portland cell

The Electrician, leader of the Madison cell

Badger, member of Madison cell

Greenhouse, member of Madison cell

ATF Deputy Director Tyson Gifford

FBI Special Agent in Charge Ramsey Kirkpatrick, Las Vegas Field Office

FBI Special Agent in Charge Susan Ellison, Salt Lake City Field Office

FBI Deputy Director Stuart Woods

FBI Special Agent Bradley Royer, FBI Headquarters, case agent

Matthias Peavey, the informant

Robert Neville, FBI Executive Assistant Director for National Security

Maureen Tully, FBI Executive Assistant Director of the Criminal, Cyber, Response and Services Branch

Etherlord, FBI White Hat hacker

Incubus, FBI White Hat hacker

President Samuel T. Buckley

White House Chief of Staff Michael Cooper

Secretary of Homeland Security Donald Page

National Security Advisor Brent Dixon

Attorney General William Bradford

White House Press Secretary Elise "Ellie" Drake

EPA Administrator Elizabeth "Liz" Keefer

Bud, member of Boulder cell

K2, (Eric Harper) member of Boulder cell

John "Jack" Olin, Special Agent in Charge, Dallas Field Division

Caroline Navarro, Assistant Special Agent in Charge, Dallas Field Division

Mason Sherman, Special Agent, Dallas Field Division

Mink, member of Ann Arbor cell

The Quebecer, member of Ann Arbor cell

Ben Cahill, "former" ELF member who spoke at Holladay Park
Linda Oden, K2's significant other.
Katherine Delgado, AUSA Western District of Oklahoma
Jimmy Roy Holloway, Oden's lawyer
C. Robert Titus, CEO of Pittman Petroleum Company
Goat, member of New Orleans cell
Duane "Ocean" Larkin, leader of EMB
Dove, first martyr
FBI Special Agent Rowan Parks (alias, Kyra Jordan; alias, Aurora), the female undercover agent
Spider, leader of Boston cell
Storm, Boston University Associate Professor Kendall Wasley, member of Boston cell
Coyote, member of Minneapolis cell
Bison and Otter, members of Yellowstone cell
FBI Director Norman Boone
ATF Director Lucas Decker
Ant, the EMB member who 3-D prints the plastic gun and ammunition
Gordon Cline, President of the Green Earth Alliance
EMB's Governing Council: Ocean, Wolf, Spider, Oak, Jaguar, and The Electrician.
Frog, EMB member who does surveillance on NYSE
Cheetah, EMB member who does surveillance on Cos Cob substation
Panther, EMB member who smuggles first pieces of plastic gun into Dirksen Senate Office Building
Frank Quinn, FBI Special Agent at Logan International Airport
Rain, suicide bomber at the NYSE
Owl, the assassin
Secretary of the Interior Nolan Campbell
Officer Ray Amato, NYPD
Chad Herren, FBI SWAT Team leader at Trenton substation
Officer Devon Jacobs, Capitol Police

CHAPTER 1

9:28 p.m., Saturday, April 1, Al's Southside Tap, Missoula, Montana

"Eight ball, corner pocket." Special Agent David Ward tapped his cue on the intended target, lined up the shot and fired. There was a sharp *crack*, followed by a *thunk* that signaled the end of the game.

"Well, shit." Tommy Stafford shook his head. "Guess the next round is on me."

Ward grinned. "Guess so."

Stafford mumbled something about Ward's obviously misspent youth as he headed for the bar.

A few of the regulars chuckled at the exchange. Al's was a local bar, one rarely visited by the university crowd. Both men were frequent patrons, though Ward was known to be gone for long stretches at a time. It wasn't known why, just that his job often took him out of town. Nobody asked. It was that kind of place. No one had any real idea what it was that he did. That is, no one but Stafford. The retired cop had worked undercover. He could be trusted. He understood.

Ward studied the bar, his refuge. It was a dump by some standards. Those who entered couldn't be blamed for wondering if they had travelled back in time to the early sixties. Most of the odd assortment of memorabilia that adorned the worn walls dated to that era. A calendar from the Kennedy administration was still mounted behind the bar. The photo showed a smiling young president seated at his desk in the Oval Office. The month was November 1963. It had been left untouched ever since.

Al Hynes, the owner, was ninety-one years old and looked it. His weathered face had seen much. He still tended bar three or four days a week, dispensing wisdom whether requested or not. His presence added to the continuity. And that was the charm of the place. When you were there it felt as if things would never change. There was a comfort in that.

Stafford returned with the drinks.

"Rack 'em, Danno," Ward said.

"Oh, I get it. Funny."

One of the regulars snickered, almost spitting out a mouthful of beer. Ward chuckled, pleased with himself. He started to chalk his cue for the next game when his cell phone rang. Ward picked it up. The caller ID showed that it was his ex-wife, Maria. He hadn't heard from her in months. A glimmer of hope invaded. He knew that wasn't healthy and tried to suppress it, but it was there.

"Hi, Maria. How are you?" He did his best to sound pleasant, upbeat. But he heard *pathetic.*

"Hi, Dave. I'm good. How are you?"

"Great, doing great." It was a lie. He still thought about her every day, thought about all of the things he had done wrong, all of the things he would do differently.

There was a pause. "I'm in town."

Ward's pulse quickened. He could feel his heart pound. "Would you like to...?"

"I left something at the house," she interrupted, "a photo album of Mom's. I got it after she died. I'd like to pick it up."

His hope began to fade. He knew the photo album, knew exactly where it was. He had even planned to mail it to her, but never got around to it. Maybe a part of him had hoped that she would come back for it.

"Sure...of course," he said. "I could run home right now, meet you." Ward gathered his courage. "Maybe we could get some dinner or go for a drink."

There was silence on the other end. His heart sank.

"David, I don't think that's a good idea."

"Okay."

There was another pause. "Maybe you could just leave it on the deck."

"Yeah, okay," he said. "That's probably for the best." There were things he wanted to say, but there was no point. "I'll put it out tomorrow morning. I should be gone most of the day."

"Thanks."

Nothing was said for a moment. Then, she mercifully ended it. "Goodbye, David."

Ward took a deep breath, then another. "Goodbye, Maria."

The call ended. Ward stood there for a moment, staring down at his phone.

"You okay?" Stafford asked.

Ward looked up at his friend. "Not really."

CHAPTER 2

1:25 a.m., Sunday, April 9, along the outskirts of Park City, Utah

It was time for retribution. The thought that trees had been murdered to construct these edifices, that forest had been cleared to make way for these grotesque structures...these *vacation* homes. It made his heart ache, his blood burn. Yes, there would be retribution. These gluttonous rapists of the Earth would now pay for their crimes against her.

As the manual suggested, he had purchased the components for the timer and igniter far from the target, at various stores, using several false IDs or just paying cash. No one had asked a question. He appeared to be nothing more than a hobbyist. As for the accelerant, it was a mixture of fifty percent gasoline and fifty percent diesel, the diesel added to slow down the burn rate. The fuel had come from a dozen different stations within a thirty-mile radius. To avoid drawing attention, an approved gas can was always used. Transfer to the larger buckets that formed part of the incendiary device was done later.

The digital timer had been fairly simple to build. The manual was precise and well-thought-out regarding its construction. The same could be said for the instructions on the igniter. There were also helpful tips on where to place the completed incendiary device to assure maximum destruction. Clearly, the manual's author shared his righteous goals, even encouraged any means necessary to accomplish them. They were kindred spirits.

Reconnaissance had been accomplished with minimal difficulty. These were new log homes, almost complete, but still under construction. All three were located in a newly developed, unpopulated cul-de-sac that was surrounded by forest. The builders left each day no later than six o'clock. He had been able to slip in late at night with ease. While surveillance cameras were now common, it appeared that none were present at any of the sites. He chuckled. It was a foolish omission by the developer, one of Northern Utah's most prolific rapists of the environment.

He quickly moved toward one of the pre-selected locations and set the five-gallon bucket of accelerant in place. This one was in a recessed entryway, the perfect spot. As the heat rose it would be funneled directly into the building. Next, the timer and igniter were wired together and placed on the lid of the bucket. He knew that the flare, once ignited, would burn through the lid with ease, igniting the fuel mixture. When all was in place, he set the timer, moving quickly to the next location.

All three structures were repugnantly large. Each would require several of his delightful devices. He moved efficiently from spot to spot, setting up on porches, underneath low overhanging roofs on inside corners, anyplace that would effectively trap heat and prevent its loss to the atmosphere. The goal was to get fire to the rafters and collapse the roof. He was confident that his fiery mechanisms would accomplish their mission.

As soon as everything was in place, timers set to start the igniters at precisely the same moment, he slipped into the darkness. Stopping briefly to look back, he softly uttered the words, "For Mother."

The call had come in at quarter to two. Neighbors in a nearby cul-de-sac had reported flames coming from new construction on Meacham Court. Battalion Chief Reggie Turner raced to the scene, Engine Thirty-Seven right behind him. An additional fire engine was also en route. From the dispatcher's description, it might be needed.

Turner sped through one stoplight, then another, lights and siren blazing. The deafening horn of fire truck behind him could be heard as it passed through each intersection, warning any drivers out at this late hour to give way. At this time of night there was always the danger of a drunk driver blindly cruising out in front of an oncoming response vehicle, turning one tragedy into two.

At six blocks away Turner could easily see the orange glow. That was not good. The structure may already be engulfed. He pressed down on the gas. Turner knew the area. There were several very expensive homes being built on Meacham. They were fairly close to each other. The chances of the fire spreading from one house to the next were good. Turner grabbed the microphone from its bracket. "I'm gonna need another engine out at Meacham Court," he yelled into the mike.

"Roger that," Dispatch replied.

As he got closer, Turner could see the fire light up the night sky. A sinking feeling set in. Years of experience had given him a good read on such things. He could gauge the level of destruction from the height and intensity of that deadly glow. Fearing they were too late, he glanced in the rearview mirror. Engine Thirty-Seven was right on his ass. Turner was sure that the driver shared his concern.

As the vehicles turned onto Meacham the scene that greeted them was worse than imagined. All three homes on the cul-de-sac were in flames. "Son of a bitch," Turner said out loud. He'd been told that no one was in any of these homes yet. He prayed to God that his information on that was correct. Turner let the engine pass and parked out of the way at the lower edge of the circle. He jumped from his vehicle and ran toward the center of the cul-de-sac.

Firefighters quickly emptied Engine Thirty-Seven. As soon as their boots hit ground, another fire truck turned onto Meacham. Turner watched as the crews sprang into action. He barked instructions as hoses were uncoiled and water surged, blasting out toward the burning structures. The roofs had not yet collapsed on any of the homes, but there was little doubt they would all be a total loss.

As Turner contemplated the destruction, he saw it. Parked far back in a driveway that ran alongside one of the homes was a small pick-up truck. Did one of the workers leave it there, maybe ride with a buddy? Did it belong to the contractor or one of his subs? Was someone inside? Though he stood close to a raging inferno, Turner's blood ran cold.

"Captain Holmes!" Turner yelled at one of the firefighters. Holmes turned immediately. Turner gestured toward the truck. Holmes nodded his understanding. He signaled two members of his crew. Without hesitation, they headed toward the front door, pulling down their oxygen masks as they charged forward.

Turner felt his insides start to clench up as he watched the firefighters force entry into the structure. They were through the door within seconds, radioing their position as they began to search. One minute passed, two, three. At five minutes they had found no one. Turner nodded at Holmes. It was time for them to get out. Just as Holmes started to give the order an unearthly groan bellowed from the house. They all knew the sound.

"Out now!" Holmes screamed into his mike.

"Roger that," came the reply.

Every firefighter present watched the door. The seconds seemed eternal. Another groan, like the dying gasp of a mortally wounded bear, then a creak and the loud echoing snap as roof timbers began to crack.

"Shit, she's comin' down!" Holmes cried out. Several of his crew moved toward the door. He ordered them to hold.

Turner understood. Part of him ached to rush inside, but he knew the casualties could only mount if others went in now. Holmes had made the right call.

There was another loud creak. Then it happened. The timbers started to snap in succession. A thunderous roar echoed through the night sky as the enormous roof began to cave in. *God, please help them*, Turner silently prayed as he hung his head.

The cheer caused Turner to lift his eyes. Coming through the door as flames flared out around them were both men, one clearly injured, his arm draped over his colleague's shoulder. Turner let out a whoop as he threw a clenched fist into the air.

Turner saw the SUV out of the corner of his eye. It was the chief. An appearance by him at the scene was not unusual, but it was rare at this time of the night. Turner looked at his watch. It was after three o'clock. He assumed that his call to the Assistant Chief of Operations regarding his suspicions had resulted in a call to the boss. This kind of thing, in Park City, Utah, was unheard of.

Turner watched as Fire Chief Paul Ballard walked briskly toward him, his grim look clearly visible due to the glow from the still burning fire.

"What have we got?" Ballard asked, straight to the point.

Turner waved for Holmes to join them.

"As soon as we got here," Turner began, gesturing toward Holmes, "I think we were both struck by the fact that the fire in all three homes seemed to be at the same stage of development."

Ballard nodded. "And that could not have happened if one structure caught fire first and it then spread to the others."

"Exactly," Turner agreed. "Then, after we got things relatively under control, we found something pretty disturbing."

"Let's see it," Ballard said.

Turner led the way to the still smoldering section of one of the structures. It was an inside corner where two wings of the home came together under an overhanging roof, or soffit. He pointed to what appeared to be a melted puddle of plastic.

"Take a look," Turner said to Ballard.

The fire chief crouched down. He studied the object for a moment, then reached up and ran his hand through his graying hair.

"You can see the charred remains of a nine-volt battery there,"

Turner noted, "along with some wires, connectors, and what appears to be the remnants of a digital clock. In short, a timer."

"An incendiary device," Ballard said.

"The melted plastic was probably a five-gallon bucket," Turner added.

"So far, we think we've found five of these," Holmes said, "although this one is the easiest to make out. All of them are in strategic locations, in recessed entryways, on porches, anyplace that would channel heat into the building. We've located at least one at every house, but we'll find more."

"Accelerant?" Ballard asked.

"Probably kerosene, or some sort of gasoline and diesel mixture," Turner offered.

Holmes nodded his agreement. "Somebody really knew what they were doing."

Ballard stood. He placed his hands on his hips as he silently stared down at what was left of the device. Finally, he spoke. "Gentlemen, we need to call ATF."

CHAPTER 3

2:18 p.m., Monday, April 10, KSKI TV Studios, Salt Lake City, Utah

Brooke Talbot idly clicked through the emails received at KSKI TV's tipline. It was mind-numbing work. As usual, most of the messages started with something like *Why don't you do a story on…*Ninety percent were from the same bunch of crackpots that wrote in every day. She reminded herself that this was just part of the drill for all new reporters. Not exactly what she had envisioned when handed her degree in broadcast journalism two years earlier. Still, KSKI was a great place to launch a career. And she had to admit, sitting at her desk with a fresh cup of coffee beat the hell out of standing along some city street reporting on the latest traffic accident. It was certainly safer. Only last night she narrowly missed being picked off by two jerks in a pick-up who whizzed by while making lewd comments. She was pretty sure that it wasn't caught on camera when she flipped them off.

Brooke clicked on the next email. *Why is it that every time I see a cop in this city they're parked at a convenience store?* She shook her head. The one that followed was even worse. *Why do the mainstream media ignore the fact that the United Nations and the International Monetary Fund are taking over this country?*

"Oh my God," she groaned. Maybe traffic reporting was better. At least she was on camera.

Another click. The next email popped up. As Brooke began to

read she let out a small gasp. *Retribution has begun. The Park City fires were the first of many to come. Those who rape the Earth will pay for their crimes against her.* The email was unsigned.

What the hell? Brooke could feel her pulse quicken She didn't recall hearing anything about any fires in Park City. A quick internet search showed otherwise. An AP story from earlier that day popped up: *FIRE CLAIMS THREE HOMES IN PARK CITY.* Then she saw the subtitle: *Arson suspected.* She quickly scanned the story.

Holy shit, Brooke thought. She went back to the email and hit the print button. As her printer hummed to life, a surge of adrenaline pumped through her veins. She could feel her heart start to pound. Was this the big break that would get her off the traffic beat? Brooke snatched the email off the printer and headed for the station manager's office.

KSKI TV anchor Andrea Egan adjusted her jacket as she waited for the cue. The five o'clock broadcast was about to air. As the familiar theme music began to play, the countdown began. "Five, four, three, two, one, and we're on." She smiled into the camera and uttered her opening line. "Good evening, and welcome to the KSKI TV Evening News."

Co-anchor Ron Turley took the hand-off. "Tonight, in a KSKI TV exclusive, we report on a Park City arson and the shadowy claim of responsibility received right here at KSKI studios."

"That's right, Ron," Andrea continued. "For more details, we go now to our own Brooke Talbot who is live on the scene in Park City. Brooke, I understand that you first noticed an email claiming responsibility for the fires on our KSKI Tipline?"

"That's correct, Andrea," Brooke replied. She took a step to the side and swept her arm backwards to direct the viewer's attention to the destruction behind her. "As you can see, the three homes in this cul-de-sac are a total loss. Damages are estimated in the millions. Fortunately, this was new construction and the residences were, as yet, unoccupied."

"Absolutely horrible," Andrea said. "But tell us about this email."

"Right," Brooke replied. She pulled a piece of paper from her pocket and unfolded it. "Just after two o'clock this afternoon we received the following email on our KSKI TV Tipline." She began to read. "*Retribution has begun. The Park City fires were the first of many to come. Those who rape the Earth will pay for their crimes against her.*"

"Absolutely chilling," Andrea said. "Do we know anything about who authored this email?"

Brooke shook her head. "The email was unsigned. We have received no additional communication regarding the fires."

"What are authorities saying about this?" Andrea asked.

"Not much. At this point, official sources will neither confirm nor deny that arson is suspected. In fact, they seemed to be caught off guard when questioned about the email."

"What about unofficial sources?" Andrea asked, taking the cue.

Brooke nodded. "Unofficial sources tell me that arson is almost a certainty. And it appears that whoever is behind this has decided to communicate their intent through KSKI TV."

Andrea's brow furrowed. She shook her head slowly. "Fascinating," she said. "Fascinating, and disturbing."

"It is," Brooke agreed.

"We'll stay on top of this breaking story," Andrea promised the viewers. "Thank you, Brooke."

"You're welcome. This is Brooke Talbot, KSKI TV, reporting live from Park City, Utah.

CHAPTER 4

8:55 a.m., Tuesday, April 11, Bureau of Alcohol, Tobacco, Fire-arms and Explosives, Denver Field Division, Denver, Colorado

Special Agent in Charge Leroy Wheeler drummed his fingers on the desk. The news out of the Salt Lake City Field Office was not good, and the media attention did not make it any better. He looked at his watch. Where were they? He wanted to get the ball rolling on this before things got worse. Just then, there was a knock on the door.

"C'mon in," Wheeler said.

His administrative assistant, Beverly, stuck her head through the door. "Everybody's here," she whispered.

"Send 'em in."

Wheeler rose from his desk. Assistant Special Agent in Charge Mike McKenney was first through the door, followed closely by special agents Toby Combs and Ian Maness. All three were good hands, some of his best. Wheeler had a feeling this one would require all of their skills.

"Morning, Leroy," McKenney said. "You know Toby and Ian."

Wheeler nodded. "Good morning, fellas." He gestured toward the chairs facing his desk. "Have a seat."

Wheeler noticed that both Combs and Maness perched nerv-ously on the front edge of their chairs. It was a common posture for field agents called into the SAC's office. But Wheeler sensed that here it was something more. These men knew that this case could be a big one, and that Park City was the opening shot.

Wheeler turned to his ASAC. "Give me an update, Mike. What's goin' on out there?"

"No question it was arson," McKenney replied. "Toby has been over there already, talked to the Park City Fire Department people, and been out to the scene. I'll let him fill you in on what he found out."

Wheeler nodded, shifting his gaze toward Combs. "Toby, what've you got?"

Combs nervously cleared his throat. "There were three large homes. None of them were occupied. They were new construction. Not surprisingly, all three fires appear to have been set at the same time. They were all at the same stage of development when the fire department arrived." Combs referred to some notes. "So far, nine incendiary devices have been found. The evidence, as usual, is pretty burned up, but at least one of the devices tipped over and wasn't as badly damaged as the others. From what we can tell, it looks like they had fairly sophisticated timers, possibly SCR digital timers."

Wheeler looked at McKenney, who arched his eyebrows as if to say, *that's right.*

Combs continued. "It appears—based on the evidence and my hunch—that model rocket igniters, combined with matchbooks and road flares, were used to start the accelerant."

Wheeler started to get a sick feeling in the pit of his stomach. "What's our best guess on the accelerant?"

"Of course, we won't know for sure until we send some of the charred materials to the lab," Combs replied, "but my best guess would be a combination of gas and diesel." He looked at McKenney, and then added, "I'll tell you this, whoever placed these devices really knew what they were doing."

No one spoke for a moment. Finally, McKenney broke the silence. "We've seen this before, Leroy."

Wheeler nodded. "ELF," he said. The Earth Liberation Front,

or ELF, was an eco-terrorist organization known for a wave of arsons that began in the mid-nineties and continued for at least five years. Their most infamous attack caused a massive fire at a Vail ski resort that resulted in close to twelve million dollars in damages. A lengthy and difficult investigation by the FBI and ATF known as *Operation Backfire* resulted in the indictment of numerous members of the organization in 2006. Both he and McKenney had some involvement in the case. Many believed that *Operation Backfire* had effectively eliminated ELF as a threat. Wheeler had never been so sure. Now he was less sure.

"The type of incendiary devices, their placement, the targets," McKenney said, "combined with the communiqué received by the television station in Salt Lake City…"

"Pretty familiar," Wheeler agreed. McKenney had earlier provided him with a copy of the email sent to KSKI TV. "The message sounds like ELF."

"And the incendiary devices sound like they came straight out of the ELF Guide," McKenney added.

"And there's that," Wheeler acknowledged. He hated to think about it. The ELF Guide, officially known by the title *Setting Fires With Electrical Timers: An Earth Liberation Front Guide*, was a well-known arsonist's handbook, one hated by firefighters and law enforcement officers everywhere.

Wheeler stood up. "Gentlemen, let's get to work."

CHAPTER 5

10:17 a.m., Tuesday, April 11, The Office of Dr. Owen Caldwell, M.D., Missoula, Montana

Ward sat at the end of the examination table, clothed in nothing but his underwear. He felt vulnerable, and that was something he didn't like. It was once again time for his physical, a yearly job requirement that he had come to loathe. The nurse had already measured his blood pressure, which was high. He didn't anticipate better news on most other fronts. Life as an undercover operative was taking its toll. This just put an exclamation point on it.

There was a knock on the door. It opened before he could answer. Doctor Owen Caldwell stepped into the room, a knowing smile on his face. Ward knew that the expression was in anticipation of the good-natured ass-chewing that was about to be delivered.

"Hello, David. How are you doing?" Caldwell asked.

"You tell me, Doc."

Caldwell chuckled. "We'll discuss that."

"I'm sure we will." Ward had to admit that he liked the guy. It wasn't Caldwell's fault that he wasn't taking better care of himself.

"Blood pressure's a little high," Caldwell observed. He stuck a scope in Ward's ear.

"I suppose."

Caldwell checked the other ear, then grabbed a tongue depressor. "Say ahh," he ordered. His brow furrowed. "Hmm."

"Hmm, what?" Ward asked.

"It's nothing, just a little red. You quit smoking, right?"

Ward frowned. "Two years ago."

"Any relapses?"

"No." Ward paused. "Well, sometimes the job requires it." He knew that Caldwell was generally aware of his job description.

There was a skeptical look. "Requires it, huh?"

"Sometimes."

"Let's do an eye exam," Caldwell said. He pointed to a line on the floor. "Stand there, cover your right eye, and see if you can read the bottom line on the chart.

Ward started to read the line on the chart that signified twenty-ten vision. He missed a few. That had never happened before.

"Try the next line up," Caldwell said.

"Can I try the bottom line again?"

"No."

Ward sighed, then read the second line up without difficulty. A similar result occurred with his left eye.

"Hop back up on the table," Caldwell said. He placed a stethoscope on Ward's chest, moving it from spot to spot as he ordered his patient to take deep breaths. "When your blood tests come back how's your cholesterol going to look?" he asked.

Ward grimaced. They both knew the answer. "Probably not that great."

"Probably not that great isn't what we were going for, is it?"

"I know. I'll try to do better."

"Exercise?"

"Pretty regular," Ward lied. Truth was he had really slipped in that area.

"Drinking?"

"Social."

"Meaning?"

"Two or three." It was mostly accurate.

Caldwell stepped back and studied the patient.

"How are you doing emotionally, David?"

Ward had the sense that he wasn't going to be able to bullshit his way out of this one.

"I'm okay."

"Really?"

Ward knew that Caldwell was aware of the divorce, that it had caused some depression. Between that and the job, there were times that he just wasn't himself.

"I suppose I've been better."

"Caldwell nodded. "Do you want to talk to someone?

Ward didn't answer for a moment.

"No. I don't think that's necessary."

CHAPTER 6

11:05 a.m., Tuesday, April 11, Bobby's Hobby Shop, Reno, Nevada

The store was a small mom-and-pop, but well-stocked. Everything needed could be found here. He scanned the entrance, the corners, behind the counter, all the places a camera would normally be perched. There were no signs of surveillance equipment. Still, precautions were precautions. He wore a dark hoody and sunglasses. Not able to go completely clean-shaven, his ever-present beard had been trimmed back to a goatee. False identification had been procured, just in case, though the transactions would be in cash. The solder, 20-gauge wire and bullet connectors had been purchased at an electrical supply store. There, he had easily passed for an electrician. Here, if questioned, he was a model rocket enthusiast.

He noticed a convex security mirror mounted high in a far corner of the store. In it, his squat build appeared even thicker and lower to the ground than it actually was. That build, combined with his long, thick hair and wild beard, had earned him the nickname of the Troll. He didn't particularly care for it, but he had to admit that it fit. Besides, trolls lived in forests, in the mountains. They loved the earth. And that was why he was here. He loved Mother Earth and would do what was necessary to save her.

Word had quickly reached his group of the success in Park

City. They had been overjoyed. Images of the destruction there excited him. It must have been a glorious blaze. He had always enjoyed a good fire. After all, wasn't fire Mother Nature's way of clearing the overgrowth? The grotesque structures incinerated there had certainly been overgrowth, the worst kind.

Now, it was their turn to strike a blow. The target had been selected months earlier. It would pose a challenge, but its destruction would make a statement that could not be ignored. As Troll envisioned the inferno that would result he began to shake with anticipation. It would be magnificent. He had to remind himself, again, to be patient, careful.

Troll wandered the aisles, quickly zeroing in on the needed supplies. He located a silicone-controlled rectifier, or SCR. He took a half dozen. The 12-volt LEDs were nearby. Both items were commonly used by model rocket builders. They were critical components of the timer. One aisle over he found arguably the most important item of all, the model rocket igniter. It was the piece that really started the show. He selected one, carefully inspecting it, fondling it, almost lovingly. Smiling, he placed it in his basket. A handful more followed, but not too many. He was careful not to buy an excessive number of any one component in a single location. It would draw unneeded attention. A similar trip to another hobby store in a different town would occur later.

Satisfied with the items selected, Troll headed toward the checkout counter. He eyed the cashier, trying to determine if there would be any scrutiny. It seemed unlikely. The young man at the register was absorbed in his smartphone, texting furiously, seemingly oblivious to the world around him. Troll smiled at his luck. He placed his items on the counter. It took a moment for the cashier to look up.

"Find everything okay?" the young man asked unenthusiastically.

"Sure." Troll tossed his cash on the counter before there were any questions about method of payment.

The cashier began to scan the items. Troll noticed a spark of interest in him.

"Model rockets?" he asked.

Shit, Troll thought. He was prepared for this but could only carry a conversation on the subject about so far.

"Yeah," he said. "Just getting into it." Pleading novice might help fend off too many questions.

"I've been building them for years," the cashier said. He started to bag up the items. "Where do you launch?"

"I'm not from around here," Troll replied immediately. He glanced at his watch as if to say, *I'm in a hurry*.

"Where are you from?" the young man asked, not taking the clue.

You've gotta be kidding me. "San Jose," he said, using the first place that came to mind.

"Cool. I love it up there. Silicon Valley is where it's at. What do you do?"

Troll cursed himself. *What a stupid choice*. It should have occurred to him that this guy would be into all things high-tech. He needed to end this.

"Nothing too exciting," he said. "I'm an auto mechanic." *There's no way this guy works on cars*, he thought.

"Oh, that's cool." A blank expression came over the cashier's face. He was silent for a moment. "Anything else I can do for you?" he asked.

Troll could see he had found his way out. "No. That'll do it." He snatched his merchandise and quickly headed for the door.

CHAPTER 7

2:15 p.m., Wednesday, April 12, Tahoe Motor Lodge, just outside Truckee, California

It was DNA evidence that concerned him. It didn't take much: the tiniest amount of saliva, a single hair, even a skin flake would do. A clean room was needed to lessen the risk of leaving these samples, and a motel was a common option. The Tahoe Motor Lodge fit the bill. It was reasonably remote, cheap, and, due to its lackluster accommodations, almost empty. Troll had rented the room an hour earlier under an assumed name. He would not spend the night. No, by nightfall he would be long gone.

The long pants, long-sleeved shirt and knit cap had been purchased that morning. He changed into the clothes at a nearby convenience store. They would be discarded after the devices were built. Two layers of surgical gloves completed the outfit. He was ready to get to work. Troll stepped out of his car and entered the motel room.

As soon as he was through the door he donned the dust mask. Troll then began to lay out his tools: a soldering iron, digital voltmeter, wire strippers, scissors, a drill, testing bulb, and several other items. Various materials followed: SCRs, 12-volt LEDS, solder, 20-gauge wire, bullet connectors, 9-volt batteries, battery snaps, electrical tape, and Super Glue. These things would be used to construct the timers. Then there were the igniters. Troll unloaded the additional items needed to build them: matchbooks, road flares and model rocket igniters. Large plastic food containers would be used to transport the completed devices.

The work was delicate and time-consuming, but the manual, as always, carefully guided him through the process. As he worked, Troll thought of the members of his cell back in Spokane, their excitement over the impending attack. They had all played their roles, particularly with the selection of the target and surveillance over the last few weeks. It was agreed that the target must be significant, leaving no doubt that their group was now at war with the polluters. The blight of so-called development on the majesty of Lake Tahoe was a fitting recipient of their attention. If all went according to plan, that blight would come to an end. Fear would stop it. Investment would dry up. Insurers would refuse to provide coverage.

The Spokane group was one of many scattered about the country. He didn't know the location of the others, or any of their members. But he knew they were out there, all fighting the same sacred battle, all about to engage with all means and methods at their disposal. Their struggle had reached a new stage. They would take back the Earth from those who would destroy her.

Troll checked his watch. It was just past two o'clock in the morning, late enough he concluded. Activity never ceased at the nearby casinos of Stateline, Nevada, but his colleagues had scouted the location well. He knew exactly where to place the devices for maximum impact, and how to get to those locations without being noticed.

The Silver Trail Casino and Resort was close to completion. The grand opening was set for April 21. It would be the sixth such abomination located in this small Nevada border town. These monstrosities were a major cause of the deteriorating ecosystem of North America's largest alpine lake. Sediment in stormwater runoff from such developments had significantly decreased the famous clarity of the lake's blue waters. And then there was the environmental impact of the thousands of visitors who gambled at these casinos each year. It was time to stop the exploitation of this natural wonder.

Troll knew it was a long shot, the distance between the structures being significant, but his hope was the blaze would somehow travel from the Silver Trail to the neighboring casinos. Of course, gamblers were still present in those other establishments. In the event the fire did spread an orderly evacuation would be preferable, he supposed. But if lives were lost, so be it. It was a price worth paying. Their cause was paramount.

"For Mother," he said. The Troll then set to work.

Sam Powell finished the wiring on the bathroom fixture and then secured it in place. Only two left. He had promised the boss that the job would be done before he left for vacation. The Silver Trail was a big job for their union hall and he was happy to have the work. It had been a good year with an abundance of overtime, and that extra money was about to finance a long-awaited trip to Disney World. Sam smiled. Amy and the kids were so excited. With their departure time set for ten o'clock that morning, he was sure that none of the three were getting much sleep. As for him, he could always nap on the plane. That is, if the kids would let him. At six and eight years old, Connor and Hailey would probably squirm in their seats and jabber excitedly the whole way there. The thought made him chuckle.

Sam checked his watch. It was a quarter past two. Amy would not be happy. But then, he had promised the boss. Another half-hour and he should have it wrapped up. Sam sighed and set to work.

CHAPTER 8

2:47 a.m., Thursday, April 13, Tahoe Douglas Fire District Station 3, Zephyr Cove, Nevada

The alarm sounded jarring Andy Garner from a deep sleep. As always, adrenaline jolted through his system. Wide awake within seconds, he swung out of bed and jogged toward his gear.

The coats hung in a row, helmets on the rack above. Boots were on the floor with pants tucked into them and turned out in such a way that the firefighters could step right into both and quickly hoist the suspenders up and over their shoulders. Gloves and breathing apparatus completed the outfit. After five and a half years as a firefighter it took Garner no more than fifteen to twenty seconds to get dressed. As he grabbed his helmet, he paused for a second. Taped to the wall was a picture of his wife, Erin, and their young son, Jake. He put two fingers to his lips and then touched the photo, a kiss before whatever battle lay ahead.

The fire engine and ladder truck roared to life behind them. Garner turned to Ray Foster, his best friend in the department.

"What've we got?" he asked.

"It's a big one, that new casino over in Stateline," Foster yelled over the noise.

"The Silver Trail?"

"That's it."

With their gear on, the two did their traditional lucky fist bump. Both denied being superstitious, but neither was willing to stop. As they headed for the truck, Garner looked back over his shoulder at the photo of Erin and Jake. *I love you guys.*

Assistant Fire Chief Mark Shields slammed on the brakes. His SUV screeched to a halt two-thirds of the way into the parking lot surrounding the Silver Trail. Fire engines, ladder trucks and ambulances from multiple departments were on the scene. Half of the massive casino was already in flames. *Holy shit*, he thought. *This is a big one.* In his fifteen years with the Tahoe Douglas Fire District, Shields could not recall a structural fire anything close to what now burned before him.

As he stepped from his vehicle, the heat hit Shields in the face like a blast from a convection oven. Firefighters scrambled in all directions as even more trucks responded. Patrol units cordoned off the area as police kept spectators at bay. Blue, red and white lights banked off of the surrounding buildings completing the surreal atmosphere. Shields was momentarily dazed, but quickly snapped to his senses. Twenty yards off, C Shift Battalion Chief Jim Wu was headed his direction.

"All shifts have been called in," Wu announced, not wasting time with any pleasantries. "South Lake Tahoe and East Fork have responded, along with a few smaller departments."

"The chief is on his way," Shields said.

They both turned to look at the casino. Fire illuminated massive plumes of smoke that billowed up into the night sky.

"She's pretty well lost," Wu said. "We don't think there was anyone inside, not at this time of night. Place was still under construction. We've got a few guys in there checking the sections that aren't completely engulfed for any inhabitants."

Shields nodded. "Any evidence of the cause?"

"Not yet. Fire was well developed when we got here. I also heard some chatter about suspicious indications in a couple of the entryways."

"Such as?"

"What looked like a melted bucket, some wires."

"Son of a bitch," Shields said. He could feel a knot forming in his stomach. Just then, he spotted B Shift Battalion Chief Brett Hodges jogging toward them. Shields could tell from the look on Hodges face that it was bad.

"Just got a call from the electricians' local," Hodges yelled. "They think one of their guys is inside."

Andy Garner was closest to the area in which the electrician was thought to be working. The guy's name was Powell, Sam Powell. The information was that Powell was installing lighting fixtures in the hotel rooms. Nobody knew what room, or even what floor. The good news was that he was supposedly somewhere on the side of the casino that was not yet engulfed. The bad news was that the fire was moving at a rapid pace, and the smoke was getting thicker by the second. He would have to act quickly.

Garner raced from room to room. Radio communication told him the fire was spreading fast. Time was running out. He estimated that he had five minutes...ten minutes tops. *Damn it*, he thought as he finished the seventh floor of the east wing. The information they had said Powell was most likely working on the seventh or eighth floors but could be as high as the tenth. Garner knew that he would need at least five minutes to get out—maybe more if he was carrying a victim—and now he was headed the wrong direction...up.

Garner crashed through the stairwell and bounded up the steps to the eighth floor. His heart was pounding, his breathing heavy. Smoke was obscuring his vision. He could only give this a few more minutes. If he didn't find Powell soon there was nothing he could do. Chances were good it was already too late.

One room quickly searched, then another. Nothing. Garner's radio crackled to life.

"Andy! You need to get out now!" It was Battalion Chief Jim Wu.

"Just a couple more rooms," he radioed back.

"Out now! That's an order!"

"Roger that," Garner replied.

Just then, he saw it through the smoke. Abandoned in the hallway, some fifty feet ahead, was what looked like a tool belt. Garner ran toward it. As he got close he spotted the body. The description fit. It was Sam Powell. Garner checked for a pulse. It was there, but faint. Smoke inhalation had probably done its damage, but he would make damn sure the man got every chance to survive. Garner hooked his arms under Powell's armpits and pulled him to his knees, then to his feet. He then swung Powell's right arm behind his own neck, reached a hand between the man's legs and hoisted him onto his shoulders in a firefighter's carry. Powell was a big man, and they had a long way to go, but Garner was determined to make it. He pictured the photo back at the station, Erin and Jake. *I love you guys. I'll be home soon.*

It had been fifteen minutes since the last radio contact with Garner. Fire now raged throughout the casino. Jim Wu knew that the worst had happened. He felt hollow, shaky. His crew was devastated. Several wept openly. Wu had repeatedly been forced to order them not to attempt a rescue.

"Fuck it. I'm goin' in."

It was Ray Foster, Garner's best friend. Wu could see the tears streaming down the man's face, glistening in the firelight.

"Stand down, Foster! That's an order!" Wu barked. He understood all too well but had to be tough on this. One man lost was too many. They didn't need another.

"Stop me," Foster replied. He pulled on his breathing apparatus and charged toward the fire.

"Goddammit, Ray!" Wu yelled. "I said that's an order!"

Foster kept moving. Wu ran after him, signaling two nearby men to assist. They grabbed Foster, who started to fight, forcing them to take him to the ground. As they pinned him down,

Foster began to sob, his body shook. Between cries he repeated the same words over and over again. "I'm sorry, Andy. I'm sorry."

CHAPTER 9

9:27 a.m., Thursday, April 13, KTRT TV Studios, Reno, Nevada

Alan Hess grabbed a coffee before settling to do a little background research for a segment airing on the evening broadcast. Yet another biker rally was coming to Reno and word was a confrontation was likely between two rival gangs. The Reno and Sparks police departments, along with the Washoe County Sheriff's Office, were gearing up for possible trouble. It wasn't the first time. This was well-traveled turf given the city's history as a gathering spot for motorcycle gangs. Sometimes law enforcement was able to keep a lid on things, sometimes not. Either way, people loved a story about bikers. It was always a ratings boost.

Hess wandered down the hall toward his office. As one of the station's veteran reporters he was among the few who had what could legitimately be called an office. The younger reporters had cubicles, if that. Most didn't mind. They loved the job, fantasized about working for NBC or CNN. It was more than enough to sustain them. He remembered those days, back when he was young and hungry. But now, dreams of the big-time long gone, he settled for just doing a solid job and keeping the citizens of the Reno/Tahoe area informed.

"Hi, Al."

Hess turned toward the voice. It was Veronica Romano, the station's new meteorologist. She was seated in her cubicle, a colorful weather radar map splashed across her computer monitor.

Veronica gracefully spun her chair around to face him. He couldn't help but notice as she crossed her legs. *Damn, if I was only ten years younger*, he thought, *and single.*

"Good morning, Veronica." Hess gave her his best reporter's smile. *Nothing wrong with a little innocent flirtation.*

"Any big stories brewing?"

"Maybe, maybe not." He gave her the rundown on the biker rally. "I was just gonna call one of my connections at the PD, see what's up."

"I bet you have a lot of connections," she said, arching an eyebrow.

Hess chuckled. "Yeah. I guess." *Easy, boy.* He reminded himself that his third marriage was going well, and that he probably shouldn't screw it up. "You have a good day," he said. It was time to get out of there.

"You, too." Veronica smiled as she slowly uncrossed her legs and spun back toward her computer.

Whew, he thought. *Close one.* Hess took a deep breath, followed by a gulp of coffee. He moved quickly down the hall and into his office. As he took a seat he pulled out his phone and swiped through the contacts list. His finger tapped on the name, Sergeant Wally Townsend. After four rings Townsend's phone went to voicemail. Hess slipped the phone back in his jacket pocket. Townsend was always on the phone. He'd try back in a few minutes. To kill some time, he checked the station's tipline, known as uWitness. It allowed people to send in news tips, pictures, videos or whatever to an email address, uwitness@ktrt.com. Most of it was crap, but on rare occasion there was something useful. This morning there was only one new message. It was from an unusual email address: 14376asdfg@gmail.com. The subject line read *Stateline Fire*. On the drive in Hess had heard about a massive casino fire over in Stateline. Intrigued, he clicked on the email. The message was short: *First, Park City, and now Stateline. We will take back the Earth from those who would exploit her. More flames to come.*

Hess could feel his pulse quicken. A video was attached. He downloaded it and clicked play. The video showed the casino in what must have been the early stages of the blaze. Several distinct small fires could be seen, located at seemingly equal intervals. The fires grew rapidly, flames quickly spreading upward and then outward. Even without the accompanying message, it was obvious to an untrained eye that this was arson. Hess picked up his office phone and punched in the extension for his station manager.

KTRT anchor Terry Nash took his cue. Focusing on the teleprompter, he opened the broadcast. "Good evening. Welcome to the KTRT Evening News. Tonight, in a KTRT exclusive, we report on a devastating fire at the Silver Trail Casino in Stateline that claimed the life of one firefighter and the mysterious email claiming responsibility received through our own KTRT uWitness tipline."

"That's right, Terry." Co-anchor Abby Day turned from her colleague and faced the camera. "We go now to veteran reporter Alan Hess who is on the scene in Stateline, Nevada."

"Good evening, Abby." Hess turned to his right and pointed back toward what was left of the casino. "As you can see behind me the destruction here is total, with losses in the millions. But even more tragic, of course, is the loss of life. Authorities tell us that two men perished in the blaze: an electrician who was working late on the still-under-construction casino, and a six-year veteran Tahoe Douglas firefighter, Andy Garner. Reports are that Garner died a hero, trying to save the electrician whose name has not yet been released."

"An absolutely devastating situation there," Day added.

"It is," Hess agreed.

"And I understand that you actually discovered the email sent in to our uWitness tipline that seems to claim responsibility?"

"That's correct, Abby. Earlier this morning I noticed an email in the uWitness inbox that read as follows: *First, Park City, and now Stateline. We will take back the Earth from those who would exploit her. More flames to come.* Attached was a video that appeared to show the fire not long after it was set. Numerous individual fires were visible. They seemed to be set at equal intervals around the structure."

Terry Nash joined the exchange. "I take it authorities suspect arson?"

"There has been no official announcement to that effect," Hess said, "but unofficially we're being told that arson is likely. Obviously, the email and video we received factor into that."

"In fact, doesn't this incident bear striking similarity to one that occurred in Park City, Utah, earlier this week?" Nash asked.

"That's right, Terry. Early last Sunday morning a fire in Park City, Utah, destroyed three luxury homes that were in the final stages of construction. An email message similar to the one sent to us was received at a Salt Lake City television station shortly after that fire."

"Have authorities commented on a possible connection between the two fires?" Nash asked.

"I asked about that. At this point, they are being pretty tight-lipped about any potential connection."

"Were there any fatalities in the Park City fire?" Day asked.

"No, there were not. As both fires involved buildings that were still under construction there is speculation that whoever set these fires did not intend any fatalities."

"Nonetheless, two men lost their lives in this fire," Day added.

"That's right, Abby. And we should point out that Firefighter Andy Garner leaves behind a wife and young son."

"Absolutely tragic," Day said. "Alan, thank you for your excellent reporting on this important and developing story."

"You're welcome. This is Alan Hess, KTRT TV, reporting live from Stateline, Nevada."

CHAPTER 10

9:05 a.m., Friday, April 14, Bureau of Alcohol, Tobacco, Firearms and Explosives, San Francisco Field Division, Dublin, California

Special Agent Cesar Cruz paced back and forth outside the SAC's office. Everybody had heard about the arson at the Silver Trail Casino and the death of the young firefighter, Andy Garner. They all wanted this assignment. Garner was considered one of their own. The thought of his heroic death, the family he left behind, and then...the bastard that did this. Cruz prayed that he pulled the case. At fifteen years in, with half-a-dozen major arson investigations under his belt, he had to get the call. That had to be why he was summoned. He knew that there was a possibility it would go to an agent in one of the Nevada field offices, but this case was more likely to be worked directly out of field division headquarters.

The SAC, Special Agent in Charge Alex Burke, had called an unusual eight-thirty meeting for his management team. Cruz was most assuredly not management. He was simply told to make himself available, and wait until he was called in. The supervisors were all in there, probably discussing the political crap, the stuff that line agents weren't supposed to hear, even though they all knew it. Cruz didn't care about any of that bullshit. He just wanted to get to work.

"Nervous?"

It was Burke's administrative assistant, Iris. She was smiling but hadn't looked away from her computer monitor. Cruz loved her, as did all the agents. Iris had worked there forever and knew ATF's bureaucratic idiosyncrasies as well as anyone. More importantly, she handled her boss, who, if left to his own devices, could be a colossal dick. She also protected the agents like they were her own children.

"Me?" Cruz asked.

Iris looked up from her typing. "No, one of the five other agents pacing around here like an expectant father," she said.

Cruz laughed. As usual, she had depressurized the situation. He nodded toward the SAC's door. "I just never like going in there."

"Understood. It'll be okay."

Cruz studied her for a moment. These attempts usually failed, but he decided to give it a try. He sauntered over to her desk and leaned against the corner, folding his arms across his chest.

"So, um, hear anything about who's pulling lead on this one?"

"Nice try."

"Okay," Cruz chuckled. He retreated back to his pacing.

A few moments later, the door to the SAC's office swung open. Assistant Special Agent in Charge Bryce Warner walked out.

"Cesar, come on in." The ASAC's tone was solemn. There was no smile on his face. He shook Cruz's hand and then motioned for him to enter.

Cruz stepped through the door. The SAC was seated behind his desk, staring straight ahead as if lost in thought. Standing in front of the desk, his back to Cruz, was ASAC Wesley Birch. No one else was in the room.

Birch spoke first, without turning around. "I assume you've heard about the fire at the Silver Trail?"

"Sure, of course," Cruz replied. He was annoyed that Birch didn't bother to look at him, but it was just like the guy. Birch was arrogant, a ruthless climber known to use the bodies of anyone he perceived to be in his way as rungs on his ladder to success. He was not to be trusted.

"Are you familiar with the Earth Liberation Front?" Birch asked. He turned now, studying Cruz as he awaited his answer.

"Everybody in ATF is familiar with ELF," Cruz replied. He didn't feel like playing Birch's little game, but knew he had no choice. "Do we think they're behind this?" he asked.

"Not necessarily," Warner interjected, eyeing Birch. "The M.O. is similar, and the incendiary devices, best we can tell, seem to be straight out of the ELF Guide."

"You've heard of the ELF Guide?" Birch asked Cruz.

"Oh for Chrissakes," Warner muttered.

Cruz suppressed a smile. "Yeah, I've heard of the ELF Guide," he answered.

Birch pursed his lips. He stared at Warner. "The fact is," he said, "this fire, along with a similar event early last week in Park City, Utah, have the hallmarks of what we saw in Operation Backfire." Birch turned his gaze back to Cruz. "I assume you're familiar with…"

"Cruz has worked more arsons than you've ever heard of," Warner interrupted with a huff. "Of course he's heard of Operation Backfire." He turned to Cruz. "Cesar, there are some things here that raise the possibility of a resurgence of ELF, but we really don't know." Warner glanced at Birch and then turned his attention back to Cruz. "There were vague claims of responsibility sent to local TV stations after both fires," he said, "but in neither case did any specific group claim credit. The rhetoric is somewhat similar to what we heard from ELF." Warner read the two messages out loud.

"I found the television broadcasts regarding both fires online," Cruz said. "I've seen both."

Warner nodded. "You understand then that this case is drawing some considerable attention."

"I do," Cruz said.

The SAC finally spoke. "This one is being discussed at the top of the food chain," Burke emphasized. "We'll be under a microscope." He studied Cruz.

"It's a national investigation," Warner added, "and it's your case."

Cruz was elated. But the thrill wore off quickly as the magnitude of the responsibility settled in.

CHAPTER 11

9:55 a.m., Monday, April 17, Our Lady of Tahoe Catholic Church, Zephyr Cove, Nevada

From his vantage point at the front of the church, Assistant Fire Chief Mark Shields viewed the ritual with a heavy heart. He had always feared this day. Now it was real. They had lost one of their own. Bagpipes wailed outside as the pallbearers escorted the casket up the center aisle. Their class A uniforms, complete with white gloves, and their regal bearing, gave the funeral a military feel. Still, as they passed by, Shields could see moistness in their eyes as they blinked repeatedly in an effort to stave off tears. Two had completely failed. The most distraught was Andy Garner's good friend, Ray Foster. The sight of his tearstained cheeks caused Shields to well-up.

Firefighters entered, two-by-two, in a slow, solemn procession. Their dress uniforms were crisp, meticulous. Each carried a hat perched on an extended left arm. Black mourning bands stretched across their badges. All area fire departments were represented. After the firefighters came the police, then sheriff's deputies, state law enforcement. The list went on and on. Shields looked back through the mourners. Representatives from most of the federal law enforcement agencies were seated in the pews. Numerous local dignitaries were present. It was a tremendous show of respect.

Shields looked across the aisle at Garner's widow, Erin. Her expression was mostly one of shock. He could see that she was trying to stay strong for their son, Jake, who was seated next to her. The boy seemed bewildered. How do you explain this to a youngster, Shields wondered? As he contemplated the devastating impact on this young family his mind turned to thoughts of revenge on whoever was responsible. But, those were thoughts best left for later, he reminded himself. They were here to remember Andy Garner.

After everyone was seated the mass began. Shields was not a particularly religious man, yet he found the readings from the Scriptures comforting. The priest had a nice touch. He included a thoughtful prayer for Sam Powell, the man Andy Garner was trying to save. The sermon weaved together Bible passages of service to fellow men with those similar themes that guided firefighters everywhere. Shields studied his colleagues as the priest spoke. Honor, service, sacrifice: the words meant everything to these men and women. That was why this loss was felt so deeply. They had all lost a kindred spirit, a brother.

When Ray Foster rose to deliver the eulogy Shields braced himself. This was going to be rough. As Foster walked to the podium Shields glanced at Erin. The mere anticipation of Ray's words had already caused her composure to fail. Shields wished that he could go comfort her. He wondered if his longing to do so was, in part, also a desire to comfort himself.

Foster faced the mourners and unfolded some notes. Then, appearing to change his mind, he folded the notes and stuck them back in his pocket. There was a pause that seemed to last forever. He took a deep breath and began.

"Andy Garner never wanted to be anything other than a firefighter," Foster said. "He died doing what he loved." There was another deep breath. "He was my..." Foster's voice cracked. He looked down as he wiped away a tear. After a few seconds he raised his head and continued. "He was my best friend." Foster looked toward the casket. "He is my hero." Suddenly, Foster snapped to attention and raised his hand in a crisp salute. "Godspeed, my brother."

Shields was choked up to the point that he could barely breathe. Audible sobs from throughout the church were all that broke the silence.

At the conclusion of the church service law enforcement and fire service personnel filed out, two-by-two. Department personnel were followed by the Color Guard. At the funeral director's signal, the pallbearers moved toward the coffin and then escorted it back toward the church entrance. Once there, the officer-in-charge gave the command, "Present arms." The bagpipers began to play *Amazing Grace* as the pallbearers moved between the Honor Guard and toward the rear of the fire engine that would serve as caisson to carry the casket to the cemetery. Shields wondered how many times that same fire truck had carried Andy Garner on a call. Now it would carry him to his final resting place.

Once the coffin was loaded the pallbearers turned to face each other. "Detail, present arms," the officer-in-charge barked. White gloved hands rose in unison to salute a fallen comrade. The pallbearers then climbed aboard the caisson, two-by-two, four on each side of the casket, for the ride to the cemetery.

Shields estimated the funeral procession at close to a hundred vehicles, including two dozen from various fire and emergency service departments. He rode in the chief's vehicle, eighth in line. As they wound through the streets Shields saw dozens of citizens stop and place their hands over the hearts in a show of respect. Police cars blocked major intersections to allow the procession to pass through. As the line of vehicles approached them, officers would exit their patrol units, come to attention and salute. Shields was again moved to tears.

Two ladder trucks were positioned outside the entrance to the cemetery. Their giant ladders were extended and crossed to form an arch over the entry to the graveyard. They passed under and parked, then walked up a small hill to take their positions at the gravesite. As he stood there, Shields took note of the solitary bugler stationed seventy-five feet from the grave.

The caisson moved into place. When it stopped, the pallbearers exited and took their spots at the rear of the fire engine. They removed the coffin. The officer-in-charge called out, "Detail, attention." All fire department personnel immediately responded. The casket was then carried to the grave stand, with the family following immediately behind. As it was set in place, the officer-in-charge announced, "Parade rest." The coffin was then draped with an American flag.

Shields watched Erin and Jake as the priest came forward to conduct the committal service. He vowed to be there for them, especially the boy. He knew the department would step up. A college fund was already in place. They would do their best to take care of Andy's family.

After the final prayer the department chaplain stepped forward to conduct the last alarm ceremony. He explained that the ringing of a bell had always been associated with firefighting. The bell sounded the alarm that called firefighters to duty. When the fire was extinguished, three rings of the bell signaled the end of the fight. It would now ring three times to honor the life and service of Andy Garner. Three bells tolled in slow succession, the silence interrupted by no sound but the sobs and sniffles of the heartbroken.

"Detail, attention," the officer-in-charge commanded. "Present arms."

Shields came to attention. His right hand immediately rose in salute in almost perfect unison with the hundreds of firefighters and law enforcement personnel present. At almost that same instant the bugler began to play *Taps*.

Suddenly, Shields' attention was ripped from the flag-draped casket to Erin and Jake, The boy pulled away from his mother and raced toward the coffin, toward his father. Then, he stopped. His little body went rigid. Shields heard his own grief-stricken groan as Jake raised his hand in salute.

CHAPTER 12

8:32 p.m., Monday, April 17, Portland Cell Site of the Earth Martyrs Brigade, somewhere outside Portland, Oregon

The Silver Trail Casino arsonist was known to him only as Troll. That's how it was. No real names. The members of one cell did not know the names of the members of any other cell. In fact, they often knew only nicknames or first names for those in their own group. Also unknown to most was the precise location of the other cells. These were tactics borrowed from ELF and, in his opinion, improved upon. While it was true that a select few did have knowledge of the overall organizational structure, this was simply necessary to plan their missions, missions that were increasing in significance and sophistication. Besides, they were not ELF. No, the Earth Martyrs Brigade, also known as EMB, was something much more formidable. Wolf was sure of that.

ELF had essentially collapsed after Operation Backfire. Most of its members now denounced violence. Wolf considered them to be weak. They had deluded themselves into the belief that peaceful civil disobedience could accomplish their goals. In his opinion, it was beyond naïve to think that the tactics of Gandhi would rid the world of the corporate greed and exploitation of natural resources that now threatened the planet's very survival. More direct action was needed, and if that action involved violence, or even death, so be it. ELF had always prided itself on the fact that its attacks caused no injuries or fatalities. Such hesitance had doomed their mission. A few casualties should be expected in the battle to save Earth. This was something that Troll apparently understood. It was something that Wolf embraced.

As a former member of ELF, Wolf had learned much from Operation Backfire and its fallout. Chief among those lessons was the need to admit only the truest of believers. The filth that turned traitor and cooperated with the FBI in its investigation of ELF saved the government's case. Before that, the Feds had nothing. That was why the Earth Martyrs Brigade did not accept the weak. Its prospective members were thoroughly vetted, and it was well known among current members that a snitch would be dealt with in no uncertain terms. It had to be that way. The stakes were too high. Still, this was their first meeting since the casino fire, the first Brigade action to cause a death. And even though the Portland cell had played only a surveillance role in this arson, the fact that there had been two fatalities would likely expose those of insufficient resolve. If so, Wolf was prepared to deal with it.

Their meeting place on this occasion was an old barn off Oregon Highway 213, also known as the Cascade Highway. The owner was Ralph Holgate, an organic farmer sympathetic to what he believed was nothing more than a harmless group of young environmentalists who advocated for sustainable farming. In fact, two of the cell's members helped out on the farm. As a consequence, Ralph was happy to oblige when they asked to use the place. He never caused them any trouble. At age eighty-seven, Ralph was hard of hearing and suffering from cataracts, so even if he did somehow manage to wander in during one of their meetings he wouldn't learn much. All present knew to quickly change the subject to something such as the evils of pesticides should Ralph appear. That was, after all, an issue on which they could all agree.

Wolf looked out toward Ralph's farmhouse before he shut the barn door. The lights were off. It appeared that the old boy had already gone to bed. Not surprising given that he routinely got up at five in the morning and put in a twelve-hour day. Other than the hearing and vision problems, Ralph was a sturdy specimen for a man of his age. No doubt due to a lifetime of eating foods devoid of synthetic fertilizers and pesticides, Wolf thought.

As he slid the barn door shut, Wolf picked up the smell of marijuana. *Not again.* He had repeatedly warned them about this. It wasn't as if he was opposed to using pot, it was now legal in Oregon and he smoked it himself. But there was a time and a place, and this wasn't it. Why draw unneeded attention? What would happen if Ralph got wind of it? He spun around to see Sequoia pass the joint to Skye, who took a long toke and held it.

"Can we lose the joint?" Wolf asked.

Sequoia gave him a broad grin that said, *Chill, man.* He turned to Skye, who handed the ganja back to him. "No problem, bro," Sequoia said. He put the joint to his lips and inhaled deeply.

Wolf shook his head as he watched the last two inches burn off. It wouldn't surprise him if Sequoia could take out an entire joint with one toke. At six-foot-six and two hundred eighty pounds, Sequoia could take out a lot of things. The dreadlocks made him even more imposing. A former Division I linebacker, Sequoia was also a committed soldier, willing to do what was necessary to save *Mother*. That was what they liked to call Mother Earth.

Wolf did a head count. All nine members were present. They were a small cell in terms of numbers, but an important one. The operational know-how of the group was impressive. Any one of them could build a sophisticated incendiary device, place it and cover their tracks. All were familiar with the ELF Guide and a variety of monkeywrenching techniques. More importantly, they were all willing to employ these tools of sabotage to stop the corporate rape of the earth. The question now was how far they would be willing go. Wolf believed that he knew the answer...as far as it takes.

"I'm sure you're all aware of the successful action in Nevada," Wolf said, alluding to the casino fire. He knew the answer. One the cell's members, Fern, had been involved in surveillance of the site before Troll planted his devices. That was how it worked; surveillance was performed by members of cells other than the one that supplied the arsonist. "The destruction was total," Wolf continued. "A powerful message has been sent."

A small cheer went up. Wolf smiled as he watched his followers hug each other and high five. Several congratulated Fern on her role in the operation. Then he noticed Skye. She managed a smile. Was she squeamish about the loss of life? In Wolf's opinion, the firefighter and electrician were simply unavoidable collateral damage. He could press it with Skye but decided not to. Better, for now, to just keep an eye on her.

"And now, it's our turn," Wolf announced. "The next action will get national attention and will be discussed in high places. I can promise you that." He had their attention. "We will take down a power station in Omaha, Nebraska."

"Why Omaha?" Fern asked.

"It's the middle of the country. We show we can hit there, nobody will feel safe." Wolf provided some history. "An attack similar to what we have in mind occurred at the Metcalf substation outside San Jose, California, in 2013. Seventeen transformers were knocked out."

Sequoia appeared unimpressed. "What's so significant about that?"

"That substation feeds electricity to Silicon Valley," Wolf replied. "More importantly, experts suddenly realized that a coordinated series of similar attacks on substations around the country could crash the whole electrical grid. The electrical industry, when not spewing pollution, spends much of its time dealing with the threat from hackers. They are not prepared to deal with the type of low-tech attack that we have planned."

"Are you talking about using incendiary devices, explosives, what?" Sequoia asked.

"No." Wolf smiled. "AK-47s."

CHAPTER 13

9:34 a.m., Tuesday, April 18, Office of the Deputy Director, ATF Headquarters, 99 New York Avenue, NE, Washington, D.C.

Denver SAC Leroy Wheeler waited patiently outside the office of the deputy director. He had already been there for fifteen minutes, not wanting to be late for the nine-thirty meeting. During yesterday's conference of special agents in charge, Deputy Director Tyson Gifford had pulled him aside and asked him to come in the following morning to discuss the "eco-terrorist cases," as he put it. It was the first time that anyone had used the word *terrorist*, and Wheeler was a little surprised to hear that coming from the deputy director, especially this early in the investigation. It was a loaded term that got a lot of people's attention, and Wheeler wasn't sure that he wanted a lot of attention just yet.

Wheeler checked his watch again, nine forty-five. He picked up a magazine and started to flip through it. Just then, he heard the elevator doors open. Out walked Alex Burke, the SAC for the San Francisco Field Division. Gifford had mentioned that Burke would also be at the meeting. Wheeler knew that Burke was rumored to be arrogant. Still, showing up fifteen minutes late for a meeting with the deputy director was pretty dicey no matter how much self-esteem a person might possess. Wheeler stood up as Burke approached.

"Alex, good to see you," Wheeler said, extending his hand.

"Good morning, Leroy."

Burke's handshake was quick, non-committal. Wheeler

wondered if that might indicate trouble.

Burke straightened his jacket. "Understand there was a house fire in Park City that might be related to my eco-terrorism case."

And there it was, Wheeler thought. Burke took even less time to claim ownership of the case than he had imagined. Should he get into an argument with the pompous ass? Tempting as that was, it would be a waste of time. Wheeler knew that the casino fire had claimed two lives, including that of a firefighter. It would likely be run out of the San Francisco Field Division, at least for now.

"Yeah, that's right," Wheeler said with a smile. "We had a little house fire."

Burke smiled back at him, and then smoothed his lapel.

"Gentlemen, the deputy director will see you now."

Neither of them had seen the administrative assistant approach during their standoff. She opened the door to Gifford's office and held it for them. Wheeler stepped back and gestured toward the door.

"After you, Special Agent in Charge," Wheeler said.

Burke snorted, and then strode in. Wheeler was close behind.

"Director, good to see you again!" Burke said exuberantly, turning on the charm.

Wheeler noted the firm, sustained handshake the two exchanged.

"Have you met Leroy Wheeler, the Denver SAC?" Burke asked.

Wheeler shook his head. There was no end to this guy. Burke knew damn well that Gifford was acquainted with every SAC in the country. It was an obvious bit of condescension, one that could not possibly escape the attention of the deputy director. Wheeler saw Gifford give him a quizzical look. Wheeler gave a slight shrug.

"Of course," Gifford said. "We worked together in the Atlanta office for years. One of the best undercover agents there ever was." Gifford approached Wheeler and took his hand, then reached up and patted his shoulder. "How are you, Leroy?"

"I'm good, Ty."

Wheeler smiled at Burke. He continued smiling as the color drained from the San Francisco SAC's face.

"Sorry for the delay this morning," Gifford said, "but I was on the phone with the director."

"Not a problem," Burke said cheerily.

Not a problem when you're fifteen minutes late in the first place, Wheeler thought. He briefly considered alluding to Burke's arrival time but took the high road.

"I mentioned to the director that I'd be meeting with the two of you," Gifford continued. "He's aware of these fires, and the emails received at local TV stations after the fact." Gifford stepped toward a long conference table. "Please, have a seat," he said.

Wheeler noted that Gifford did not sit at the end of the table, instead taking one of the chairs along the side. It spoke well of him.

"Any luck tracing the emails?" Gifford asked.

Wheeler shook his head. "The email received at the Salt Lake City station came back to a local library. No identifiable information. No surveillance video. Nobody remembers anything unusual."

Burke's brow furrowed. "I'm afraid we've had the same result, only the email to the Reno TV station came from a library in Sacramento."

Wheeler nodded at Burke. Suddenly, he was reminded that they were both dealing with a serious problem. Personal animosities would have to be set aside. Something bad was happening. This was no time for a turf war.

"Is this a resurgence of ELF?" Gifford asked.

"Hard to say," Burke answered. "The incendiary devices and their placement in the Silver Trail fire seem straight out of the ELF Guide. Are you familiar with…?"

"*Setting Fires with Electrical Timers: An Earth Liberation*

Front Guide," Gifford interrupted as he plopped a copy of the document onto the table.

"Exactly," Burke noted, looking sheepish.

Wheeler bailed him out. "Same with the Park City fire," he interjected. Wheeler thought he caught a brief nod of appreciation from Burke. "That said, ELF always prided itself on avoiding casualties. If this is ELF, they have become far more radicalized."

Gifford nodded. He was silent for a moment, seemingly lost in thought. "Well," he finally said, "we need to figure who is responsible. If this is ELF, or some other eco-terrorist group, we need to figure out a way to infiltrate them, either through a confidential informant or an undercover agent."

Wheeler knew that Gifford had been an undercover operative himself at one point and was a strong supporter of that investigative technique as the best way to bring down an entire organization. Still, this would be beyond difficult.

"That's a tall order," Wheeler said. "We have nobody to flip and nobody to make an introduction to get our own guy in even if we did know what organization to infiltrate."

"I understand that," Gifford said. "ATF and FBI have a lot of intelligence from Operation Backfire and subsequent investigations, including several involving ELF's sister organization, ALF, the Animal Liberation Front. There are some cooperators who could at least introduce one of our people into the radical environmental and animal rights communities."

"It's a long shot," Burke noted. "But we have to start somewhere."

"Did you have somebody in mind, Ty?" Wheeler asked.

"Yeah, I do. Are either of you familiar with a guy by the name of David Ward?"

A smile crept onto Wheeler's face. Ward was an agent in his Field Division, technically assigned to the Missoula, Montana, satellite office, but sent where needed. "He's one of mine," Wheeler said. He turned to Burke. "Ward is the guy that brought down The Nation, that anti-immigrant vigilante group."

"That's him," Gifford said. "Sorry, Leroy. I should have been aware of the fact that he is one of your agents."

Wheeler waved off the apology. It wasn't a big deal. He was just glad that Gifford appreciated Ward's talents. Of course, it didn't hurt that the choice of an agent from his Field Division made Burke squirm in his chair a bit.

"Gentlemen, we need a win here," Gifford said. "This is shaping up as a major case." He paused. "I don't need to tell you, the Bureau is still trying to recover from Fast and Furious. We're under the congressional microscope and will be for a while."

Fast and Furious. Wheeler was surprised that Gifford had said the words out loud. The Operation Fast and Furious gunwalking debacle was not something that people at headquarters liked to talk about. But then, Gifford was clean, having had no role in the operation. He was appointed as deputy director after the whole mess had mostly played out. Wheeler was not sure why anyone had thought it was a good idea to let gun dealers sell firearms to known straw purchasers in hopes of tracking the weapons back to the Mexican cartels. It was bound to end badly and did. Of the many weapons sold and later used in violent crimes, one was a rifle used to murder Border Patrol Agent Brian Terry. All in all, a complete and utter catastrophe. The fallout included tighter control of undercover operations, generally.

"Another thing," Gifford added, "FBI is sniffing around this. This is our baby. We need to get out in front on it."

"Understood," Wheeler said.

Burke nodded. "Couldn't agree more."

Gifford stood, signaling that the meeting was over. "Good. Let's get to it."

CHAPTER 14

4:38 p.m., Wednesday, April 19, Lolo, Montana, just south of Missoula

From his back-deck Ward watched the Bitterroot River flow past. It reminded him of another river, the Rio Grande, and the countless immigrants who crossed it searching for a better life. Many had done little more than set foot in this country when confronted by the armed vigilantes of The Nation, a white supremacist hate group that had decided to combat illegal immigration their way.

Ward wondered how many poor souls had lost their lives to the murderers who formed The Nation's border assault teams. The debriefings that followed his infiltration of the group and their ultimate takedown indicated that the number was likely in the thousands. Most would never be found, their bodies left to decompose in the harsh terrain of the southern border, families back home left to wonder at the fate of their loved ones. At least it was over, for now. Every member of the organization's leadership was either dead or locked away in a maximum-security federal prison. The Nation had ceased to exist. The question was how long until a new group took its place.

Ward wondered what made people follow a man like Royce Lundgren, The Nation's leader. His charisma was undeniable, even though the message he delivered was evil. Lundgren was David Koresh, Jim Jones, Charles Manson...Hitler. Could it be that

the members of his flock were simply that desperate for something, anything, to give meaning to their hollow lives? Was their
need for identity and sense of belonging so strong that it required
the hatred, even eradication, of other races? Certainly, some were
simpleminded sheep, blindly following the herd. But others were
not. They were otherwise accomplished individuals, professionals, successful members of the business community, government
officials. Ward shook his head. It was beyond him. But then, le-
gions of historians, sociologists and medical professionals had
pondered such things for ages. Why should he be able to figure it
out?

Ward breathed in the crisp Montana air, then let it out slowly.
The infiltration of The Nation, known in the ATF community as
Operation Tex-Mex, was one that he had been lucky to escape
from with his life. The post-assignment depressurization had taken
a little longer than usual and had involved too much alcohol. He
looked down at the bottle of beer resting on the deck railing. Was
there an issue? He didn't think so. Still, it was probably good that
things at work had remained relatively calm in the ensuing
months.

"Dave! You comin' or not?"

Ward smiled. He welcomed the interruption of his dark
thoughts. It was Jim McNeal, a good friend and retired Missoula
cop. Along with Tommy Stafford, another retired member of the
Missoula PD, they had formed a so-called band. They lacked a
name and, thankfully, had still not played in public, despite Stafford's insistence that they were ready. Ward wasn't sure if they
were ready, but he was sure that the unknowing populous of
Greater Missoula was not.

"I'll be right in," Ward hollered back over his shoulder. He
sucked in another lungful of Montana air, took a swig of beer
and headed for the sliding glass door leading in from the deck.
Once inside, he locked the door, checked it twice, then slipped a
wooden dowel into the track to prevent the door from moving
should anyone be able to unlock it. This was a standard

precaution, one of many that accompanied the life he'd chosen, one of many that had driven away his ex-wife, Maria. He glanced at a picture of her as he walked through the living room on his way to the basement, and silently mouthed the words, *I'm sorry*.

"You guys ready to play or what?" Ward asked as entered the basement.

"There it is!" McNeal exclaimed. "Every fucking time."

Ward laughed. Truth was, he always left them waiting, and they never let him forget it.

"No shit," Stafford agreed, shaking his head. "Where's the commitment, man?"

Ward enjoyed the familiar refrain. These guys helped keep him sane, and they knew it. They had been there, on the streets, undercover. He slipped the guitar strap over his head and got ready to play.

"What's the genre this evening?" Ward asked.

McNeal looked at Stafford. With a jerk of his head he gestured to Ward. "Listen to him, *genre*."

Stafford rolled his eyes. "Seriously."

"Gee, I don't know," McNeal said. "Maybe classic rock?"

"I was thinking classic rock," Stafford added helpfully.

"Classic rock, then," Ward said, as if it were something out of the ordinary. He smiled at the exchange and was about to make a suggestion when his cell phone rang.

"Figures," Stafford said.

"Hang on a minute." Ward checked the caller ID on his phone. It was Denver, Field Division Headquarters. "Shit. I've gotta take this."

McNeal and Stafford exchanged a look that said they recognized this type of call.

Ward walked into an adjoining room. "This is Ward."

"Hello, Dave. Leroy Wheeler. How've you been?"

It was rare to get a call directly from the SAC. Something was up. Ward instinctively moved to the door and closed it. "Good, boss. How about you?"

"Fine. You somewhere you can talk?"

"Yes, sir."

"Have you heard anything about that casino fire at Lake Tahoe?"

"I heard it was arson, some sort of eco-terrorism thing. I know two people died, including a firefighter."

"That's right. Here's what else we know."

Wheeler briefed him on what ATF had learned so far, and the plan discussed at headquarters. He included a good bit about the firefighter, Andy Garner, who he was, how he died, and the family he left behind.

"I'm full in, boss," Ward said solemnly.

"I knew I could count on you, Dave. This is shaping up to be a big one. A lot of people will be watching."

"Understood."

"Good luck."

With that, Wheeler hung up. Ward knew that the call with the initial operational details would come tomorrow. Was he ready to get back in the game? He thought about Andy Garner, his family. Yeah, he was ready.

But before he left, there would be rock. Ward returned to the room where McNeal and Stafford waited patiently.

"Well, how long you gonna be gone this time?" McNeal asked.

Ward sighed. His thoughts went to Garner's now fatherless son. "As long as it takes," he said.

CHAPTER 15

6:35 p.m., Friday, April 21, private shooting range east of Oregon City, Oregon

It was safe to say that none of them could be called an accomplished marksman. Nonetheless, Wolf was confident that he would have them prepared for the mission that lay ahead. Though he now abhorred the practice as the slaughter of defenseless animals, he had grown up hunting and shooting rifles. Still, the AK-47 was something new for him, and it was totally foreign to the two cell members he had chosen to bring along.

Cobra, despite his name, gave no warning before he struck. Wolf picked him because of his proven stealth. Cobra could slip in unnoticed almost anywhere, and then slide away without a trace. Firefly was chosen more for his commitment to the cause. One of EMB's most accomplished arsonists, he had proven his dedication many times over. On this mission Firefly would function as the driver, while Wolf and Cobra would be the shooters.

The area was secluded. Their firing range was an open field approximately eighty yards in length that ended in a steep earthen mound designed to absorb the bullets and prevent stray shots. Forest surrounded the site. It was private land designed for just such a purpose by the owner, a militia-type who was happy to loan the land to those who wished to exercise their right to fire any weapon of their choosing. Wolf had little in common with the man besides a deep hatred of the government. Despite this common sentiment, nothing would be left to chance. Wolf told the man they were trying out new elk hunting rifles. He insisted that it was no problem for them to pick up all of the spent shell casings. In fact, they wanted to because they reloaded their own cartridges. This was met with a nod of approval. The truth was that the casings would be picked up so as to eliminate the evidence. But even if they missed one or two there would be no fingerprints. Latex gloves were worn when removing the bullets from their original box and loading them into the magazines.

Three AK-47s had been procured. As the most widely produced assault rifle in the world they were readily available, no questions asked. Here, they would be fired only in semi-automatic mode, both to reduce the chances of an accident and to lessen the possibility of detection. Avoiding detection was Wolf's specialty. Despite involvement in a half dozen attacks as a member of ELF, when the rats began to snitch no one could lay a finger on him. He had covered his traces, protected his identity. Even now, members of the Earth Martyrs Brigade knew little about him. He intended to keep it that way. There was little doubt that his present colleagues were more devoted and zealous, but the betrayal he had experienced with ELF left its mark.

Wolf handled his AK-47 with respect. It was a powerful weapon, and one needed for the job. The 7.62×39mm round fired by the assault rifle would easily penetrate the transformers, causing them to leak oil and eventually overheat. Large cardboard boxes had been assembled and marked on site to represent those transformers and the area on them they needed to hit. They were weighted down to limit movement on impact. The distance approximated Wolf's best estimate of the length of the actual shot based on internet satellite maps of the target substation. They would first shoot during daylight hours to familiarize themselves with the weapons. Later, they would fire under cover of darkness, using light-gathering scopes, to replicate the conditions during the actual attack.

Wolf took aim and fired. The bullet ripped into the target high and slightly to the left. He made a slight adjustment and fired again. This time he was low, but dead center. Unperturbed, Wolf took a deep breath, settled the sight on the spot he was aiming for and squeezed the trigger. This time he hit the mark. Satisfied for the moment, he turned to Cobra.

"Give her a shot," Wolf said.

Cobra aimed and fired. Dirt kicked up a foot in front of his target box and well to the right.

"Shit," Cobra muttered.

Wolf wasn't surprised. He expected this to take a while. They had all night.

Wolf looked at his watch. It was a quarter past nine. The last of the shell casings had been picked up. The weapons were loaded in the car. They were ready to leave. Cobra's accuracy had improved greatly over the course of the evening, to the point where he had consistently placed seven of ten shots in the target zone even in darkness. It was impressive and indicative of his determination, one of the characteristics that caused Wolf to select him for this mission in the first place. Firefly had also achieved reasonable competency. While he was to function as the driver, Wolf thought it best to also have him train with the weapon. Just in case.

In the morning they would pack for the trip and then head east. A location some distance from Omaha would be selected as the place they would meet the surveillance team from the Madison cell. They would receive an intelligence packet, complete with photographs and drawings of the target site, as well as the best escape route.

Wolf waited until Cobra and Firefly were in the car. There was a measure of trust with these two, but communication between cells was limited to senior leadership for good reason. It made any attempted infiltration of the EMB much more difficult, complicated the government's ability to build a criminal case and, in the event a member went snitch, limited the damage that individual could do.

Wolf walked approximately fifty yards from the vehicle. He pulled out the burner phone purchased for the occasion. It was one of several that would be used during the mission to provide anonymity and prevent tracking. After their use, all of them would be smashed and tossed into a lake or river. He punched in the number.

"Hello."

Wolf immediately recognized the voice of The Electrician, leader of the Madison cell. The Electrician was a virtuoso in the field of electrical timers. His were the most sophisticated and, as far as Wolf was aware, had never failed to work.

"It's Wolf."

"Good to hear from you, my brother. Are you prepared?"

"We're ready."

"Excellent. Work will be completed on our end this weekend, early Sunday morning."

"Do you have a proposed meeting place?"

"Yes, Lake Manawa State Park in Council Bluffs, Iowa, just east of Omaha."

"Very good."

"For Mother Earth."

"For Mother," Wolf replied.

CHAPTER 16

3:35 a.m., Sunday, April 23, electrical substation, Millard, Nebraska, southwest of Omaha

Taking out the electrical substation in Millard would have a significant impact. It served a large residential area in the southwest suburb of Omaha, as well as an industrial section and nearby big box retailers. As important as the target was the fact that after the attack the assault team could be on Interstate 80 and gone within a matter of minutes. The quickest escape route had already been plotted for them. They would transfer to a different vehicle hidden just over the Missouri River in Iowa in the event that they were observed leaving the area.

But the attack would come later, and by members of a different cell. Their job was surveillance, and they were good at it. Badger was dressed in black, head to toe, as was his counterpart, Greenhouse. They had come in on foot. There was a creek and tree line close to the substation that served as their immediate cover. A quick reconnaissance established the spot that would be the perfect vantage point from which the shooters could fire at the transformer's cooling systems. Walking in through the water would also eliminate footprints.

For days they had been observing the sight through high-powered binoculars, watching from various nearby parking lots, moving constantly so as not to draw attention, patiently noting the comings and goings of the workers who entered the facility, determining what security was in place. There was surprisingly little.

They had discussed whether to try to breach the perimeter fence and somehow mark the target. The attack on the substation outside San Jose had involved leaving piles of rocks to clearly identify where to shoot. That seemed an unnecessary risk. Badger was certain that the photographs and drawings of the site would precisely pinpoint where to hit. Light-gathering scopes would also be available.

Once the bullets punctured the cooling systems, oil would leak out causing the transformers to overheat and fail. The blackout would follow. He was certain that power would be rerouted quickly, limiting the power outage. Still, a powerful message would be sent. Those who understood such things would realize that a coordinated series of such attacks had the potential to disable the entire electrical grid. And that would certainly be the implication of the communiqué that would follow. The terror caused would be heightened by the professional nature of the job, no traces left behind. Even the shell casings found would offer nothing. There would be no fingerprints, the clips having been loaded by individuals wearing latex gloves. The AK-47s used in the assault would be tossed in the nearby Missouri River. Clothes and boots worn by the assailants would be discarded in some out-of-the-way dumpster.

Badger lowered his light-gathering binoculars. He turned to Greenhouse and smiled. This was the perfect mission for his comrade, a man who earned his nickname from both the hothouse in which he raised a variety of herbs and his relentless battle against global warming. Badger was convinced that Greenhouse would strap a bomb to himself and detonate it in a coal-fired power plant if he thought it would shut down operations. It was that intensity and commitment to the cause that had caused Badger to recruit his friend to the Earth Martyrs Brigade when they were both student radicals at the University of Wisconsin. Madison was a magnet for environmental activists, but most of them would only go so far. Greenhouse understood that they were in a battle for the planet's survival, and that personal sacrifice was necessary.

Badger signaled that it was time to go. They headed back along the creek toward the railroad tracks at the north end of the tree line. From there they worked their way back west through the trees and brush that lined the tracks until moving into the residential area and their waiting car. As they pulled away, Badger knew that they would never return to Omaha, but the country's attention would soon be focused there.

CHAPTER 17

1:48 p.m., Monday, April 24, Office of the Deputy Director, FBI Headquarters, 935 Pennsylvania Avenue, NW, Washington, D.C.

As a veteran agent and longtime SAC of the Las Vegas Field Office, Ramsey Kirkpatrick had seen a lot. Organized crime, high-level drug trafficking, kidnapping and political corruption were just a few of the things that routinely crossed his desk. This was something different. Eco-terrorism was not new to the FBI, but it was certainly new to him. That didn't matter. The Stateline, Nevada, casino fire had landed it squarely in his lap.

Kirkpatrick checked his watch as he entered the mammoth J. Edgar Hoover Building. He had roughly ten minutes to navigate his way upstairs. It wasn't his first visit to the deputy director's office, but that didn't make it any less nerve-wracking. Working any case that was being watched at this level could give a man an ulcer. That reminded him, he would need to pop an antacid after lunch at that Greek place. He loved gyros, but they always came back to haunt him.

Cruising quickly through security, Kirkpatrick boarded the elevator and rode up. As soon as he stepped off he recognized the SAC from Salt Lake City, Susan Ellison. Susan was a friend and classmate from Quantico. She was also one of the bureau's rising stars. He wouldn't be surprised if she ended up in the deputy director's office someday.

"Hi, Sue. "How've you been?"

"Ram, it's good to see you."

Kirkpatrick was never sure whether to give her a hug. She seemed unsure as well. An awkward handshake followed.

"Guess we all know why we're here," Ellison said. "I hear ATF is already on the case, but word came down from the DAG saying we should work it together.

Kirkpatrick nodded. He had heard the same thing. The Deputy Attorney General, or DAG, was the second-in-command at the Department of Justice. He was the one who actually ran day-to-day operations. If the DAG suggested that they work the case with ATF, they would work the case with ATF. "When the DAG speaks…"

"Deputy directors listen," Ellison said in a conspiratorial whisper. She looked around as if to check for anyone who might be paying attention.

Just then, a receptionist appeared. "They'll see you know," she said.

Kirkpatrick wondered who the "they" was. He had an idea.

The receptionist briskly escorted them to the deputy director's office, then knocked softly.

"Come in."

She opened the door and gestured for Ellison to go in. After Kirkpatrick entered she shut the door behind them. It closed with the solid *thunk* of a bank vault. At least it sounded that way to him.

The deputy director, Stuart Woods, rose to greet them. A broad smile appeared on his face as he approached Ellison.

"Sue, good to see you!" Woods said. He shook her hand, grasping it with both of his.

Kirkpatrick took note of the warm reception. He was aware that the two were acquainted but knew nothing beyond that. He wasn't proud of himself for the thought but wondered if whatever relationship they had might impact how assignments played out on this case.

"Nice to see you, too, Stuart," Ellison replied. "Los Angeles seems like an eternity ago."

Then Kirkpatrick remembered. Ellison once told him that her stint in L.A. briefly overlapped with that of Woods. He was suddenly a bit embarrassed that his cynical nature had once again got the better of him.

"Stuart, I believe you've met Special Agent in Charge Ramsey Kirkpatrick," Ellison said, stepping to one side.

Woods extended his hand. "Ramsey, nice to see you again."

Kirkpatrick questioned whether Woods had any actual recollection of his existence, but the man was polite. He'd give him that.

"It's my pleasure, Director."

Woods turned toward the conference table that ran along one wall of his office. It was walnut, highly polished, appearing almost unused. To Kirkpatrick, it had the look of a furniture showroom piece.

"Let me introduce a couple of folks I asked to join us," Woods said. "Robert Neville is our Executive Assistant Director for National Security."

Neville nodded once, as if no more acknowledgement should be expected from someone of his stature.

"And Maureen Tully is the Executive Assistant Director of the Criminal, Cyber, Response and Services Branch."

"It's a mouthful," Tully said with a smile.

Kirkpatrick studied the two. Neville looked the part, stern, trim, close-cropped hair, navy blue suit, white shirt. Tully, on the other hand, was matronly. She immediately reminded him of his sixth grade English teacher, Mrs. McGuffey. Nonetheless, he sensed that she was the far more capable of the two.

"Let's get started," Woods said, gesturing toward the chairs. When they were seated he began. "Obviously, we're all familiar with the Park City and Stateline fires. Robert has prepared a short summary of the bureau's efforts in the area of eco-terrorism." Woods turned to Neville. "Robert, go ahead."

Neville dimmed the lights and launched into a computer presentation on the FBI's longstanding investigation of animal rights and eco-terrorist organizations. This included Operation Backfire. Images on the screen showed the destruction caused by ALF or ELF at U.S. Forest Service ranger stations, U.S. Bureau of Land Management wild horse facilities, a Vail ski resort, a Chevrolet truck dealership, and various lumber and meat-packing companies. In all, Neville detailed seventeen arson attacks, as well as other acts of sabotage, causing millions in damages.

"The difficulty in infiltrating ELF," Neville said, "was mostly due to their use of semi-independent cells. The members in one cell rarely knew those in another cell, except on occasion by nickname. Ultimately, we were able to develop some confidential informants. It was difficult, but we got it done. ELF took a major blow in Operation Backfire. The indictment handed down in 2006 resulted in numerous convictions. But make no mistake, there are many organizations out there with similar goals whose members are willing to take what they call direct action. As you know, the incendiary devices used in the Park City and Stateline fires appear to be similar to those historically used by ELF. ALF and ELF, however, prided themselves on avoiding casualties. We don't know if this is some new, more radicalized version of ELF or if it's an entirely new organization. It seems unlikely that it is one individual actor."

"Do we know if any of these ELF people are still active?" Kirkpatrick asked.

"We believe so," Neville said. "For one thing, ALF and ELF are essentially sister organizations. ALF is still quite active. I would add that two of the individuals indicted in the Operation Backfire case, Josephine Sunshine Overaker and Joseph Mahmoud Dibee, are still on our domestic terrorism most wanted list."

"Any indication Overaker and Dibee are involved in this case?" Ellison asked.

"Not likely," Neville replied. "We believe both are abroad."

There were no further questions. Neville nodded toward

Woods, signaling that his presentation was done.

"The DAG has asked that we work this case with ATF," Woods said, "as we did in Operation Backfire. Obviously, they have considerable expertise in the areas of arson and explosives."

Kirkpatrick wondered how Woods really felt about that. The FBI usually wasn't too keen on sharing investigative responsibilities, or credit.

"Nonetheless, I consider this to be an FBI investigation," Woods said. "We have the expertise in eco-terrorism investigations."

There we go, Kirkpatrick thought.

Woods studied Kirkpatrick and Ellison for a moment, then spoke. "The case agent will be Bradley Royer, who is stationed here in D.C."

Kirkpatrick and Ellison exchanged a knowing look.

"Special Agent Royer has considerable experience with ELF and ALF," Woods said. "We believe that will be a considerable asset in this investigation."

Kirkpatrick sighed. So, headquarters would be running the show. Not good, he thought. Not good at all.

CHAPTER 18

3:27 p.m., Monday, April 24, Governor Tom McCall Waterfront Park, Portland, Oregon

Special Agent Bradley Royer checked his watch. It was almost three-thirty. By now the Deputy Director would have informed the Las Vegas and Salt Lake City SACs that headquarters was assigning one of its own as case agent. He could imagine how that went over. It would have been even worse if they had been informed that he was already in Oregon working the investigation.

Royer had checked in with FBI's Portland Field Office, as was protocol. He had not, however, contacted ATF's Seattle Field Division or their Portland Field Office. Given the directive to work the case with ATF, that could become an issue, but only if they found out about it. His goal was to keep this particular inquiry under the radar. Until he had a better handle on the ATF personnel involved, and the degree to which they could be trusted, he would keep his sources confidential...completely confidential.

It had been over ten years since his stint at the Denver Field Office. There, Royer had spent years investigating ELF and its sister organization, ALF. After moving to D.C. he had maintained his interest in the radical environmental and animal rights movements. He had also maintained his contacts, including this one, a confidential source by the name of Matthias Peavey. Still, it had been almost three years since his last contact with the man. The phone call insisting that a meeting take place had been met with something less than enthusiasm. In fact, Peavey was down-right rude. That was okay, Royer could deal with rudeness. What he needed was information, and this was the kind of information best collected face-to-face. He needed to look Peavey in the eye to gauge his reliability.

Governor Tom McCall Waterfront Park was the spot Royer had selected. It was a large park running along the west bank of the Willamette River. They would meet in front of an old paddle-wheeler that housed the Oregon Maritime Museum. From there, they would walk along the river until an isolated spot was located. That way, Royer could ensure enough space between the two of them and any other patrons who might be inclined to eavesdrop. As it was a public place, and in a city where Peavey had lived most of his life, Royer took the precaution of dropping the usual FBI attire in favor of a more Portland-esque look—flannel shirt, knit cap, jeans, trail boots. In a total breach of bureau protocol, he had even failed to shave for two days. Royer received exactly no second looks from anyone.

This inquiry was not without risk. Royer knew that. There was the possibility that Peavey would tip off the target, intentionally or not. And an unsuspecting target was almost always better. But Royer needed to know if ELF was behind these attacks. Peavey likely knew or could find out. His yes or no on the question was not a guarantee, but it could eliminate a lot of wasted effort.

Royer reached in his backpack and pulled out a tablet. After a few seconds he was able to pull up a photo of Peavey. It was dated, but adequate for purposes of recognizing him. The image that appeared on the device was straight out of the nineties' grunge scene—greasy hair, three-day stubble, ripped denim, flannel, beat up high-tops, a textbook example of the unkempt, thrift-store look.

Looking up from the tablet, Royer spotted a tall, reed-thin man approaching from the south. He was immediately recognizable as Peavey. Indeed, other than the addition of a few gray hairs, little in his appearance had changed. As he came closer, Royer could see that there wasn't a hint of recognition in his eyes. Peavey was clearly expecting someone sporting the G-man look. He walked past Royer, searching the area for the man he was supposed to meet.

"Looking for somebody?" Royer asked.

Peavey spun around. He studied Royer for a second. "Nice outfit," he said with a smirk.

"Good to see you, too, Matthias."

"Look, man. What's this about? I thought we were done. I got on with my life."

Looks like it, Royer thought. "Let's take a walk."

They headed north. Royer looked around to see if anyone was following them. "I need some information," he said.

"What kind of information? I don't know anything. I'm out of that scene."

Royer doubted that. ELF had been Peavey's whole world. Their ideology had been his religion. Royer was sure that Peavey was still tapped into that element. There was no reason for them to be suspicious of him. His name had never surfaced.

"I think you know plenty," Royer said.

"C'mon, man."

"You owe me. I kept you out of that shit."

Peavey's defiance seemed to fade. He suddenly appeared dejected.

"How long do I have to keep paying?" he asked.

Until I say you're done, Royer wanted to say. He kept the thought to himself. He needed to keep Peavey onboard.

"I just need to know if I'm headed in the right direction on something," Royer said.

Peavey sighed. "Okay."

"Did you hear about that casino fire down at Lake Tahoe?" Royer asked.

"Yeah, I heard about it."

"And there was another before that...Park City, Utah."

Peavey nodded. "And you want to know if ELF is responsible."

"Right on. And anything else you can find out."

Peavey stopped and turned to Royer. "The ELF I was a part of didn't kill people," he said.

"I know that," Royer said. He remembered how ELF had prided itself on avoiding casualties, though in his opinion that had been a matter of luck.

Peavey stared off across the river for a bit, then turned to meet Royer's gaze. "I'll see what I can find out."

The phone startled Royer, waking him from a dream about his father. The two of them were out driving, talking, just seeing what they could see, like they used to do when his dad was alive. The warm, nostalgic feeling was interrupted by another ring. Royer picked up his phone and looked at the display. He didn't recognize the number, but from the Portland area code guessed that it was Peavey. The time showed a quarter past one in the morning.

"Royer," he answered.

"Sorry for the late call, but I thought you'd want to hear from me as soon as possible."

Royer recognized the voice. It was Peavey. "Not a problem," he said, shaking his head to clear the grogginess. "What have you got?"

"I ran into a couple of people," Peavey said. "The subject of the fires came up. It's not ELF. In fact, that was said without me even asking. And these people would know."

"Okay. Did they have any thoughts on who might be responsible?"

"It wasn't discussed, but I got the impression they didn't have a clue."

Royer was silent for a moment, thinking. He was inclined to believe what Peavey was telling him. It confirmed his gut instinct. The fact that the incendiary devices used in the Stateline and Park City fires were similar to those used by ELF had never meant much to him. Hell, the ELF Guide was available on the internet, and was well known. Still, Royer wondered how Peavey could be so sure it wasn't ELF. It told him that Peavey still had his hand in the movement. It also pointed out the age-old quandary with confidential informants. As a law enforcement officer with many years of experience he knew that it was better for these people to separate themselves from their past lives, especially their criminal associates. It was really their only hope. At the same time, it was their continued involvement that yielded the best information. It all used to make Royer feel a bit dirty. Now, it was just part of the job. Besides, these people had made their own bed. They should be expected to lie in it for a while.

"So, we good?" Peavey asked, breaking the silence.

"For now," Royer replied.

"Right. I should've expected."

"Keep your ear to the ground," Royer said. "And stay out of trouble."

"Yeah. You, too."

Royer ended the call. He sat on the edge of the bed, staring out the hotel window. If this was not ELF, who was it? All at once, he had the sickening realization that the deaths in Stateline might not have been a complete accident. They could be facing a group that was truly capable of anything.

The lights of downtown Portland twinkled in the distance. Over the years this town had always been a hotbed of the radical environmental movement. Royer wondered if someone, somewhere in this city had the answers.

CHAPTER 19

3:24 a.m., Tuesday, April 25, electrical substation, Millard, Nebraska, southwest of Omaha

The car pulled over in a residential area north of the railroad tracks. Firefly would stay with the vehicle while Wolf and Cobra made their way to the electrical substation. The car would keep moving to avoid drawing suspicion. They would rendezvous back at this spot in exactly fifteen minutes.

Wolf and Cobra quickly scampered down the concrete bank of Hell Creek and moved southeast toward a culvert that ran under the tracks. They walked in shallow water as much as possible to avoid leaving footprints. When they came out on the south side of the culvert the creek bed and banks had returned to their natural state. There was ample tree cover along both sides, just as promised. They traveled half the length of a football field before coming to the spot identified in the drawings as the optimum location from which to fire. Wolf was pleased. The surveillance team had done its job well. They would be virtually invisible from this location even to any security cameras that might have been missed.

Wolf looked at his watch. Seven minutes had passed. They needed to act quickly. He and Cobra had already identified the transformers each would fire at from the photos that had been provided to them and from internet satellite maps. The exact spot to target was clearly marked on the surveillance team's drawings.

Wolf raised his AK-47 to look through the light-gathering scope. Cobra did likewise. The scope worked well. Wolf could easily see the area he needed to hit.

"For Mother Earth," Wolf said.

"For Mother," Cobra replied.

The sound was deafening as the two AK-47s opened fire. Nonetheless, Wolf could still hear the occasional loud ping as the 7.62×39mm rounds cracked into the transformers. After a minute that seemed like an eternity he raised his hand for the firing to stop. The silence was almost eerie after the explosion of gunfire. Wolf raised his scope again. He could see the oil spurting from the transformers as he quickly scanned the damage. They would overheat and rapidly begin to crash.

"Let's go!" he said to Cobra.

As they ran up the creek and through the culvert Wolf could see lights start to blink on in some of the houses. They needed to move fast. They scrambled up the concrete bank of the creek to the getaway car and a very anxious Firefly.

"That was loud as hell!" Firefly said as the two men tossed the AKs into the back seat and piled into the car. He hit the gas and they lurched forward. Within seconds the car was headed up 120th Street. By the time they hit Interstate 80 the blackout had begun. Wolf saw sections of the city start to shut down in waves. He smiled as he reached into the backseat to give Cobra a fist bump. This was a night that would send a message.

Ten miles to the east the clothes, boots, burner phones and AK-47s were tossed into the Missouri River. A few miles later they transferred to another vehicle, then headed north on Interstate 29. By sunrise they would be in South Dakota. After a short rest the three would head home on Interstate 90 through some of the country's most majestic scenery. Wolf was certain that he would enjoy that ride as much as any in his life.

CHAPTER 20

4:03 a.m., Tuesday, April 25, on the streets of Omaha, Nebraska

It was another sleepless night spent driving the streets, driving in search of something, or nothing. How many times had he done this, a hundred, a thousand? He just drove and drove...and drove. The thoughts kept coming, crazy thoughts in a furious, endless stream. He still had enough of a mind left to know they were crazy. But he couldn't fight them off. Even if could, there was the energy, it never died, until it did. Then he slept for days. But when he was stoked on the stuff it was like this. There was no rest, just movement, endless movement.

Tonight the itch was bad. Not just the itch under his skin, the bugs, those fucking bugs, but the itch for a high. It helped with the bugs. It made everything better. Maybe it made the bugs high, made them stop crawling. Yeah, that was it. Why hadn't he thought of that before? Cory Stevenson laughed, laughed at the bugs. The little fuckers were as addicted to meth as he was. He wondered if that first high was as good for them as it was for him. God, he shuddered just thinking about it. Like ten thousand orgasms, that's how he described it to someone. Someday he would get back to that. He just needed to find the right shit or make it himself. He was a good cook, when he had the right ingredients.

Cory glanced in the rearview mirror. It gave him a jolt. He looked pretty rough for twenty-nine years old. At one time he had been called handsome. Now, the skeletal, scab-covered face that stared back at him was anything but. He looked sick. But it wasn't enough to stop him. What did sometimes make him hesitate were the teeth—yellow, black, rotted, aching. Eight had fallen out, or was it nine? One thing was for certain, he wouldn't open his mouth to count. There were no smiles anymore, except maybe when the first waves of the high hit him. But when that happened he wasn't looking in a mirror. His eyes were rolled back in his head.

It wasn't just his appearance that he counted as a cost of his addiction. There were bigger costs, like his family. They were gone. When he met Emily she had the craving every bit as bad as he did. But she got the cure, and it took. Now, she didn't want to be around him, didn't want the kids around him. He got that. When he was on the stuff he was fucking scary, no question about it. But it was tough, especially not seeing the kids.

Then there were the jobs. They were all gone. He'd been fired from the last three because of attendance issues, whatever the fuck that means. Yeah, he didn't show once in a while, but when he was there he did the work of three men. He could outwork anybody. His last stint was as a roofer. Nobody on the crew could keep up with him. They were jealous. That's why those fucks would never cover for him. Shit, they all missed as much work as he did. The only friend he had there was Bruce, the ex-con who taught him how to cook. Bruce was a good man, and one helluva meth cook. His stuff was the best. The two of them could shingle a roof in half the time it took those other assholes when they were using Bruce's shit.

While Bruce had taught him well, supplies were getting harder to come by, especially the pseudoephedrine. Pseudo was the key ingredient and it was tightly controlled. The pharmacies kept logs to make sure nobody bought more than the amount allowed by law. He got around that by using suppliers, the pill gatherers who traded pseudo for the finished product. They were like a horde of hungry vampires, travelling all over hell to get their hands on as much product as possible. Problem was it was never enough. Cory thought back on the old days when there were ten-thousand-pill cooks. Now, five hundred was a typical batch.

Cory drove cautiously. It was easy to attract the attention of cops at four in the morning. It was the time of night when burglaries occurred. He knew that because he'd done more than his share. Sometimes he was looking for meth lab supplies so that he could cook up the shit himself, get it just the way he liked it. On other occasions he'd steal anything that he could sell or pawn to get the cash needed to buy the drug.

As he crossed into the suburb of Millard, Cory noticed the lights start to go out. What the fuck, he wondered? The blackout came in waves. Homes and businesses went dark. Streetlights went out. Then it occurred to him, no lights meant no electricity, and no electricity meant no burglar alarms. He carefully scanned the area, looking for just the right opportunity. Cory smiled as he spotted the store ahead, a Calder Pharmacy. He switched off his headlights and circled the block to come back around behind the store. Once the car was parked he opened the trunk to get his bag of burglar's tools, the most of important of which was the crowbar. He shut the trunk and headed for the back of the store. When he was about fifty feet from the vehicle he remembered something. Cory returned and reached under the driver's seat. His hand felt the cold steel of the Taurus 9mm handgun. Just to be safe, he thought.

"Shit!" Ryan Mercer cussed as he tripped over the small, handheld shopping basket. Somebody had left the damn thing in the middle of the aisle. Even with the flashlight he didn't notice it. The power outage had left the store almost totally dark. And the only battery-powered emergency light was in back in the *Employees Only* section. From the other side of the building it looked to be woefully underpowered. He headed that direction, hoping the backup light would last until the power came back on, or at least until he finished the three chapters left in the mystery novel he was reading.

The blackout couldn't dim his mood. It wouldn't be long now. Two weeks and he would have his criminal justice degree from the University of Nebraska Omaha. The security guard job at Calder Pharmacy had helped pay his way through college, but it was painfully boring. Now he would become a real cop, see some real action. He had interviews lined up with several area departments, and one solid offer from a sheriff's office out on the western side of the state. Ryan smiled. One thing was for sure, he wouldn't have any trouble handling night shift patrol. This job had prepared him for that, even if it did make him a little groggy during classes.

As he made his way toward the rear of the building, Ryan thought he heard something. It was a metallic creak. He stopped and listened. There, he heard it again. He reached to his side and unholstered his .40 caliber Glock. Switching off the flashlight, he crept along the aisle toward the sound. It was clearly coming from somewhere around the store's back entrance. The first thing that came to mind was a break-in, someone taking advantage of the power failure, someone not expecting to find a security guard on the premises. He thought about calling 911 but decided to do a quick check first.

When he reached the door to the *Employees Only* area Ryan carefully looked through the small window. From his vantage point he couldn't see the back door which was located at the end of a short hallway, down and to the right. The noise had stopped. Was the intruder inside? Did he give up? Or was it something else? Ryan slowly opened the door, careful not to make a sound. He slipped through and placed his back against the right wall of the hallway. Inching along the wall he looked for something that reflected the area around the rear entrance. There was nothing. He held the gun in both hands and moved to the end of the hallway. Ryan took a deep breath. *Stay calm.* He readied himself and swung out to the right, gun pointed toward the back door. The man that stared back was gaunt, fidgety. His eyes darted from side to side. There was a crowbar in his left hand.

"Put the crowbar on the ground, now!" Ryan commanded.

"Take it easy, bro," the man said nervously. "Take it easy."

It was then that Ryan noticed the scabs on the man's face. A tweaker, he concluded, probably trying to steal pseudo, maybe pain pills.

"Put the crowbar on the ground, now!" Ryan repeated. He took a step forward to show he meant business.

The man slowly crouched down as if to place the crowbar on the floor. At the same time his right hand moved toward his hip.

"Keep the right hand where I can see it!" Ryan ordered.

"Sure, bro. No problem," the man said.

It was then that the tweaker flung the crowbar at Ryan's head, causing him to jerk to the left. It was just enough of a distraction to allow the man to reach behind his back and pull out a gun. Ryan fired wildly, two, three times, as he felt himself get hit. He dropped to the ground, clutching his side. His hand came up bloody. Almost immediately his breathing became labored. Within seconds he started to feel lightheaded. Things grew blurry, dark. The last image he saw was that of the tweaker, motionless in a pool of his own blood.

CHAPTER 21

6:00 p.m., Tuesday, April 25, KONB-TV Studios, Omaha, Nebraska

Anchor Tyler Newcomb readied himself. Tonight's lead would be national news and needed to be delivered with appropriate gravity. He took his cue and turned to the camera. Words scrolled on the teleprompter as he began to read.

"Good evening, and welcome to the KONB Six O'clock News. Our top story is the blackout that affected large sections of the Omaha metro area and indications that it may have been caused by an act of domestic terrorism. We go now to our own Jacqueline Booker broadcasting live from Calder Pharmacy in Millard, the scene of an early morning burglary that ended in multiple fatalities. Jacqueline, what are authorities saying about what happened there?"

"Good evening, Tyler. Law enforcement sources tell us that there was a spike in burglaries during last night's blackout. Unfortunately, the one that occurred here ended with not only the death of the apparent burglar, but also with that of a young security guard working at the pharmacy. The guard, identified as Ryan Mercer, was a senior at the University of Nebraska Omaha. He was about to graduate with a degree in criminal justice and begin his career as a police officer."

"Absolutely tragic," Newcomb said

"It is," Booker agreed. "Authorities speculate that the reason for the break-in was a search for drugs, or possibly the raw materials to make drugs, such as pseudoephedrine, which is used in the manufacture of methamphetamine. The other individual involved, Cory Stevenson, was well known to law enforcement and had several prior drug-related convictions. It appears that Mercer and Stevenson shot each other during a confrontation near the rear entrance to the store."

"And as disturbing as this story is," Newcomb noted, "the possible cause of the blackout carries frightening implications. For more on that aspect of the story we go now to Lou Tesch who is at the Millard electrical substation where all of this appears to have started. Lou, what can you tell us?"

"Tyler, it's clear that what caused this blackout was no accident. Earlier today we received the following email at our studios by an unnamed group claiming responsibility. It read as follows: *What happened this morning can happen again, anytime, anywhere, and in a coordinated series of attacks. Those who understand the electrical grid understand the threat. We can bring down the nation's power supply. We hereby declare war on the power companies and all industries that contribute to climate change. As in any war, there will be casualties. If some must die in order for the Earth to be saved it is a small cost.*"

"Similar claims of responsibility followed a casino fire in Nevada and a blaze that destroyed several residences in Utah, both earlier this month," Tesch continued. "However, the rhetoric in this message is much more ominous."

"Just what caused the blackout?" Newcomb asked.

Tesch turned and pointed at the electrical substation behind him. "This attack involved assault rifles firing on transformers located at the substation. Bullets punctured the cooling systems causing oil to leak out. That caused the transformers to overheat. Once they failed the blackout occurred. Authorities have informed us that this was clearly a well-organized attack, not some random act."

"How was it determined that assault rifles were used?"

Newcomb asked.

Tesch gestured toward some tree cover that ran along a nearby creek. "It appears that the shots were fired from a vantage point along Hell Creek, which runs right by the substation. Dozens of shell casings were found there. An official who asked not to be named told us that they were consistent with the round fired by an AK-47. I should note that the AK-47 is a weapon that can operate in fully automatic mode."

"What about the claim in this email that this group—whoever they are—has the ability to take out the whole electrical grid?" Newcomb asked. "That's pretty scary stuff."

"It is. We spoke with an official at the Nebraska Power Association who reluctantly confirmed that a coordinated series of attacks like this could potentially disable the entire electrical grid."

"Have federal authorities been called in?" Newcomb asked.

"One would assume so," Tesch answered. "We called the local FBI office and were simply informed that they are aware of the situation. From my years of covering criminal investigations, I can tell you that the people involved in this case are deeply concerned."

"Lou, the previous incidents you mentioned were arsons, correct? Are authorities convinced that this attack is connected?"

"They can't say for sure and are being pretty tightlipped on that question. There was an almost identical assault on an electrical substation in San Jose, California, in 2013. They also can't, or won't, say whether this case is connected to that one."

"Wow. We'll be hearing a lot more about this story in the days to come," Newcomb said. "Thanks, Lou."

"This is Lou Tesch, KONB TV, reporting live from the Millard electrical substation.

CHAPTER 22

10:24 a.m., Wednesday, April 26, Office of the Press Secretary, The White House, Washington, D.C.

White House Press Secretary Elise "Ellie" Drake studied her notes. A few final touches and she would begin the short walk to the press briefing room and the daily give and take with the media. She was amazed that she had come to enjoy the banter. When she assumed the position at age thirty-five—it seemed like only yesterday—the encounters had terrorized her. For some reason, despite those early performances, the president saw promise in her and turned her temporary appointment into a permanent one. She remembered that trust every time she stepped foot into the press room. As much as anyone in the administration, she had the president's back.

A feverish scribbling in the margin of her printed remarks was interrupted by a knock. Drake looked up to see Chief of Staff Michael Cooper in the open doorway. A pre-briefing appearance by the chief was not uncommon. She and Cooper often exchanged thoughts beforehand. Failure to anticipate could cause the event to suddenly develop into a maelstrom.

"How's it coming?" Cooper asked.

Drake took note of the amiable smile on Cooper's face. He had always taken a rather easygoing approach with her, almost fatherly. With others he could be more, to put it politely, forceful. She had seen it. And while sometimes hard to watch, she knew it was born out of a fierce loyalty to the president.

"I'm getting there," Drake said. "Nothing too exciting. I'll lead with a fairly positive jobs report, note an improvement in the trade balance, and then segue into the president's upcoming trip to Asia."

"That will give you a chance to prod Congress to approve several long-stalled trade agreements," Cooper said.

Drake grinned as she picked up her notes and pointed to the handwritten comments in the margin. "Way ahead of you, as usual." She could get away with such comments to Cooper. Not everyone could.

Cooper chuckled. "If you were that far ahead of me those remarks would have been typed."

"Oh, fine," Drake said with mock disgust, tossing the notes onto her desk. She reminded herself that there was a reason this guy was running the White House staff. He was sharp as a box of tacks.

"There is something I want to discuss," Cooper said, suddenly turning serious.

Drake gestured toward a chair in front of her desk.

"Have you heard anything about the power outage in Omaha?" Cooper asked as he took a seat. "Happened early Tuesday morning."

"I did see something about that, yeah," Drake said.

"Some news outlets are referring to it as an act of domestic terrorism."

"That type of sensationalism is common. You know…"

"Problem is they're right," Cooper interrupted.

"Oh?" Drake sat up straight.

"AK-47s were used to shoot at a series of transformers at an electrical substation. When the oil in them leaked out it caused them to overheat and fail. Whoever did it knew exactly what they were doing."

"Oh my God."

"It gets a lot worse," Cooper said. "Some apparent eco-terrorist group has claimed responsibility. In an email to a local television station they claimed the ability to be able to crash the nation's entire electrical grid by coordinating a series of similar attacks around the country."

"Is that true?"

"I'm told that it's not out of the realm of possibility."

"Who is this group?"

"We don't know. They haven't given a name. FBI and ATF are looking into it. It may be a resurgence of the Earth Liberation Front, also known as ELF, a group that was very active in the late nineties. Earlier this month there were arsons in Park City, Utah, and Stateline, Nevada. There were claims of responsibility emailed to local TV stations following both fires that sound a lot like the one that followed the blackout in Omaha. The Nevada fire caused the destruction of a large casino that was under construction and close to completion. An electrician and a firefighter died in that fire."

"I remember hearing about the casino arson," Drake said.

"Problem is," Cooper continued, "from what I understand this doesn't entirely fit ELF's M.O. because they were known to avoid casualties. This group embraces them and said so in their last communiqué. Law enforcement is very concerned."

"You know the standard response we give in situations like this," Drake said.

"I do."

"If there are questions I'll just tell them that we are aware of the situation and that FBI and ATF are looking into it."

"And that it would be inappropriate to comment further concerning an ongoing investigation," Cooper added.

"Exactly," Drake agreed.

"And we're hoping that this trip will induce Congress to take action on several long-stalled trade agreements," Drake said, concluding her prepared remarks. "Now for the questions."

Drake looked over the group of reporters. "Teri," she said, pointing to the veteran journalist. Teri Garrison reported for one of the friendlier cable news channels and could usually be relied upon to get things off to a relatively good start. It wasn't that Garrison would lob a softball. There was no such thing in this room. It was just that, well, her network had a more favorable slant toward the administration. Most news groups had their constituency, and Teri's audience voted heavily for the president.

"What's the situation with the blackout in Omaha, Nebraska, yesterday?" Garrison asked. "Local media has reported that it was a well-planned armed assault on a series of electrical transformers that caused the outage."

Wow, that didn't take long, Drake thought. "We are aware of the situation," she said. "FBI and ATF are looking into it."

"News accounts are referring to it as an act of domestic terrorism," Garrison continued.

"That's a loaded phrase," Drake replied. "As I said, we're looking into it." She raised her hand to select another reporter, and a different line of questioning. "Maureen, did you…"

Garrison was undaunted. "In an email sent to KONB-TV in Omaha," she prodded, "an unnamed group claimed responsibility and stated that they could conduct a—I'm quoting here—*coordinated series of attacks* and *bring down the nation's power supply.* Is that true?"

Drake could feel the buzz in the room. Hands shot up. Notes were furiously scribbled. This was not good.

"Again, we're aware of the situation and looking into it," Drake said pointedly. "It would be inappropriate to comment further concerning an ongoing investigation." She knew that everyone in the room would understand this as a signal that questioning on the subject was over. But it was over only for the moment. To Ellie Drake it was clear that there would soon need to be a conversation in the Oval Office.

CHAPTER 23

1:10 p.m., Wednesday, April 26, Bureau of Alcohol, Tobacco, Firearms and Explosives, San Francisco Field Division, Dublin, California

The ATF San Francisco Field Division was housed in a contemporary office building in Dublin, California. The mostly glass exterior gave it a sleek, modern look. But it was far from San Francisco itself, and a long drive from the airport. Ward was glad they had finally arrived, and that the mission was about to begin in earnest.

Leroy Wheeler parked the car, saying little as he did so. Ward studied his supervisor. He was a big man, heavily muscled. Ward guessed him to be six-two, maybe taller. That size, combined with a jutting chin and crew cut, made him look more like an NFL linebacker. He was reputed to have been a gutsy agent. Ward didn't doubt it. Wheeler was also someone who had dealt with all of political bullshit involved with rising to the rank of Special Agent in Charge. Despite all of that, this situation clearly made him nervous. News of questions about the case at a White House press briefing earlier in the day certainly didn't help. The blackout in Omaha was clearly connected and was an ominous development. The pressure was on, and it showed in Wheeler's face. Nonetheless, Ward was glad that his SAC had come out to accompany him to this meeting. The San Francisco SAC, Alex Burke, was known to be difficult. And then there was the FBI.

"You okay, boss?" Ward asked.

Wheeler gave him a sideways glance. "Yeah, I'm fine." He shoved the door open. "Let's go get this shit over with."

As they walked up to the entrance Wheeler slowed. "Hang on a second, Dave." Wheeler looked around, as if to check for someone listening. "Look, let me do most of the talking in there," he said. "Burke is a prick. If anybody's gonna get into it with him it needs to be me."

"Understood."

"Same goes for the FBI. I don't anticipate a problem, but you know how those assholes can be."

"I've heard."

Wheeler huffed. "They sent up their SAC from Las Vegas, some guy named Kirkpatrick. He's supposedly a halfway decent guy, but his presence here tells me that FBI is planning to be very hands-on. If the deputy attorney general says we have to work with them then so be it, but I am not letting those glory hogs take over what should be an ATF operation."

"I'll speak when spoken to," Ward said, smiling. He was a little surprised by Wheeler's level of agitation and wondered if the SAC had some unpleasant history with the bureau.

"Good. Thanks." Wheeler stood for a moment with his hands on his hips, staring up at the building. "Okay," he said. "Let's go."

They walked in and flashed their credentials to get through security. Within a few minutes they were outside the office of Special Agent in Charge Alex Burke.

"Remember," Wheeler said, "let me…"

"Do the talking." Ward said. "I got it, boss."

"Sorry. It's just that…sorry."

They approached the SAC's administrative assistant.

"Good afternoon," Wheeler said. "We're here to see Special Agent in Charge Burke. I'm Leroy Wheeler, the SAC over in Denver. This is Special Agent David Ward."

"Hello. I'm Iris." She smiled at them. "We've been expecting you. You fellas hang on just a second and I'll see if they're ready for you."

She seemed pleasant enough, Ward thought.

"Okay," Iris said. She hung up. "Someone will be out to get you in just a moment."

Within seconds a man appeared in the doorway to Burke's office.

"Good afternoon, gentlemen. I'm Assistant Special Agent in Charge Bryce Warner. Welcome to California." Warner extended his hand to Wheeler and then Ward. "Come on in. Everyone else is here."

When they walked in Ward counted five more men in the room. The one who was obviously the SAC, Burke, remained seated at his desk.

"Hello, Leroy," Burke said. "I'll do the introductions." At that point, he rose from his chair. "This is Leroy Wheeler, the Special Agent in Charge in Denver." Burke gestured at other men one by one as he gave their names. "This is Special Agent in Charge Ramsey Kirkpatrick from FBI's Las Vegas field office. Special Agent Bradley Royer from FBI headquarters is their assigned case agent. Wesley Birch is one of my ASACs. You've met Bryce Warner. And finally, our case agent, Cesar Cruz."

Cruz sported a goatee, long hair and several prominent tattoos. Combined with a sinewy build, it gave him the look of an enforcer in some outlaw biker gang. Ward assumed that the man had done undercover work of that nature. His appearance contrasted sharply with that of the FBI men, especially Royer who looked like a bureau poster boy.

"And this is Special Agent David Ward," Wheeler said, completing the introductions.

There were handshakes all around. Cruz gave Ward a nod of acknowledgment that seemed to say, *I've heard good things.* Ward returned the gesture.

"Well, we've all been briefed on the background of this case," Burke said. "No need to rehash that." He sat down and motioned for the others to do likewise. "I assume you've all seen the reports out of Omaha."

There were nods of agreement.

"Regardless of that incident, the case will continue to be run out of this office," Burke announced.

Ward noticed a quick exchange of looks between Kirkpatrick and Royer.

"Excuse me," Kirkpatrick said. "This case is being run out of FBI headquarters."

"As far as FBI is concerned," Burke countered.

Wheeler leaned toward Ward. "Here we go," he whispered.

There was a stony silence as neither man yielded. Ward saw Wesley Birch start to squirm uncomfortably in his chair.

"Anyway," Burke continued, "we'll continue to develop Special Agent Ward's undercover persona. Work on that has already begun. Then we'll introduce him into the radical environmentalist community through one of the informants from Operation Backfire who is still under our thumb. That will allow us to initially focus on whether this is ELF or some..."

"It's not ELF," Royer interrupted.

"And just how do you know that?" Burke asked.

"I made inquiries through one of our informants in Portland."

"You made inquiries?"

Ward could see the color in Burke's face slowly go to crimson. The diminutive SAC looked as if he were ready to explode.

"That's right," Royer said.

From his smug expression and body language it was clear that Royer did not give a shit about aggravating the San Francisco SAC.

"Well, Special Agent Royer, did it occur to you that such an inquiry might tip off the target? Did it occur to you that your informant might have his own reasons for denying that ELF is behind this? Did it occur—"

"Of course it occurred to me," Royer said, his voice beginning to rise. "I investigated ELF for years. I know how they operate.

As far as this CI goes, I've got him in my pocket. He fully understands the consequences of feeding me bad intelligence on this."

"So you say," Burke shot back.

Royer sat forward. "Look, other than the nature of the incendiary devices, nothing about this says ELF. No casualties was part of their mantra. And as to these devices, anybody can get their hands on the ELF Guide."

Ward had to admit, Royer's comments made sense. Besides, in any undercover operation you eventually had to put some trust in your informants, particularly to make the introductions. Like it or not, that's just the way the game was played.

"You didn't inform us you were going to make this contact," Burke noted. "Did you talk to our Seattle field division, or at least the Portland field office?"

"Maybe I should have done that," Royer admitted.

"Damn right," Burke said.

To Ward's surprise, Wheeler intervened. "Alright, we all want the same thing here. The deputy attorney general says we're working together on this, so that's that."

Ward turned to Wheeler in amused disbelief. The look he got back could only be read one way, *shut up*.

CHAPTER 24

8:42 a.m., Friday, April 28, Bureau of Alcohol, Tobacco, Firearms and Explosives, San Francisco Field Division, Dublin, California

Ward drank another gulp of coffee. It was beginning to clear his head. Cesar Cruz had been determined to show him some San Francisco nightlife, and show him he did. Ward had stumbled into his hotel room sometime after three in the morning. The snooze button on the alarm clock was tagged at least three times before he rolled out of bed. It was not necessarily how he liked to start an operation, but Cruz was a hoot, and Ward had learned a long time ago the value of bonding with his case agent. It helped when the person tasked with keeping your ass safe actually liked you. That's why he was concerned by Royer's quick declination of the offer to come with. It could have been due to some residual hard feelings following the Wednesday meeting in Burke's office. Maybe Royer assumed that he and Cruz shared the SAC's opinions. That wasn't the case. In any event, Ward was determined to prevent the operation on the ground from becoming an FBI versus ATF thing. They could have that battle at the headquarters level, but not out in the field. If that bullshit impacted day-to-day operations it could cost him his life.

A conference room had been commandeered to serve as their command post. Ward wondered how many of these temporary war rooms he had been in over the years. At least a dozen, and that was only counting the major operations, the ones that warranted a name. This one definitely warranted a name. After a few drinks the less serious suggestions had included *Operation Scorched ELF* and *Operation ELF Crisp*. Both had merit, unless it wasn't ELF, and that was looking increasingly likely. They finally decided on *Operation Knock Down*. The name was a play on the firefighter's term for putting out a fire, knocking it down. It was a tribute to the young firefighter who lost his life battling the casino blaze. Like everything, the name would require supervisory approval. But Ward had learned that if you simply started using it in your reports the brass was stuck with it.

As part of his preparation Ward reviewed any case files he could get his hands on that involved investigations of organizations like the one he planned to infiltrate. Here, most of those came from *Operation Backfire*. He also had reports involving ELF's sister organization, ALF, the Animal Liberation Front, and materials concerning lesser known groups such as the Coalition to Save the Preserves and the Evan Mecham Eco-Terrorist International Conspiracy, or EMETIC. It all helped, but debriefings of cooperators usually provided the best information. There were several from *Operation Backfire* that were particularly useful. He read the reports of those debriefings and watched the interview videos. It helped him comprehend the mindset of these people, become one of them. Listening to their words was critical to understanding their thought process. In that vein, he viewed their websites, read their blogs. He also studied the history of the radical environmental and animal rights movements. As with all such causes, a thorough understanding required knowing how they came to be, and what they had done. It helped him walk the walk, talk the talk.

Playing the part also demanded mastering the monkeywrenching techniques used by these groups, including the ELF Guide and various other methods of sabotage and terrorism. Sadly, this was not exactly new territory for Ward. Many of the organizations he had infiltrated used similar tools of destruction. Anarchy and sedition were nothing new to him.

Ward stretched, then rubbed his hands over his face. He took another hit from his coffee. As he did, Cruz walked into the room.

"How you feelin'?" Cruz asked.

Ward eyed him. He wasn't sure he cared for the smile on Cruz's face. It seemed to say, *I've never felt better.*

"I'm alright," Ward lied.

"Yeah, you look like it." Cruz laughed. He placed two coffees and a box of pastries on the table. "From *Achermann's*. Best bakery in San Francisco."

Ward nodded his approval. He inspected the contents, eventually settling on an apple fritter.

Cruz dropped a thick packet on the table and slid it over to Ward.

"Your new identity," Cruz said.

Ward tore open the packet. He pulled out a driver's license, passport, birth certificate and the usual assortment of supporting documents. "*Joshua Thomas Young*," he said, reading the name on the license. "Yeah, I can work with that." He studied the picture. It was a photo from a few years ago when his undercover biker persona had necessitated long hair and a beard. "Good thing I let my hair grow out again."

"Better get to work on that beard," Cruz noted.

Ward rubbed the three-day growth on his chin. He was already off to a good start.

"We've got you set up in an apartment in Portland," Cruz said. "It's nothing fancy."

"What a shock."

Cruz chuckled. "Walking distance to some of the coffeehouses you'll want to frequent."

"Don't tell me I'll be working as a barista."

"Considered that, but you need to be in a better position to listen to the conversations around you and espouse your own radical views."

"Employment?"

Cruz grabbed a pastry from the box. "How are your computer

skills?" he asked.

"Pretty good, actually."

"That's what I was told. You'll be a software designer for a tech company located in San Francisco, Blue World Systems. Of course, it's an ATF front that will withstand scrutiny should anybody be inclined to investigate."

"By *pretty good* I meant compared to the average person," Ward said. He took a slug from the fresh coffee Cruz had brought in. "I don't know about pulling off software designer."

"From what I hear, you're being modest. Didn't you have a minor in computer science?"

"Yeah, but…"

"We've arranged for some additional training. Besides, the job will help explain your moderate hacking skills."

"Hacking skills? Wait a minute, I…"

"We won't have you pull off anything overly sophisticated. It would be too difficult for you to sustain the cover. Maybe a denial-of-service attack on the Department of Energy website or something like that."

"So you want me to do a DoS attack on DOE's website and shut it down?"

"It's just a thought," Cruz said. "We'll have it all set up ahead of time. You have to admit, it would get people's attention. We have to do something to make you interesting to whoever is doing this."

Ward nodded. That much was certainly true. "What's this additional training?" he asked.

"FBI has some talented white-hat hackers who will give you a crash course on the basics."

"That sounds interesting." Ward had to admit, he was impressed with the game plan Cruz had in place. "I just can't rely too heavily on this hacker persona," he said. "I can't keep it going if I'm scrutinized by someone with real skills."

"Sure," Cruz said. "You're an amateur at it. The point is you'll be an advocate for taking monkeywrenching into the twenty-first century. That will get their attention."

"I like it," Ward said. "So, does Blue World Systems have an office in Portland?"

"No. You telework."

Ward nodded. "So I can't be tailed to a fictitious workplace."

"Exactly. It also explains your presence in any coffeehouse, bookstore or wherever else you might be found. You can work anywhere. You can be where you need to be."

"And we're sure Portland is where I need to be?" Ward asked.

"It's as close to an epicenter as there is for this movement. Besides, we now have Royer's informant to make introductions. Sounds like his guy is better than anybody we've got."

"What do you know about this CI?"

"I talked to Royer about him yesterday. I think we're okay. He's a CI, you know? You ever met one that's perfect?"

Ward shook his head. "Not even close."

CHAPTER 25

7:36 p.m., Friday, April 28, Portland Cell Site of the Earth Martyrs Brigade, somewhere outside Portland, Oregon

Skye leaned against the open barn door, staring out over the farm. A cool Portland rain was falling, nourishing the crops, giving life. She had always felt that way about the rain, remembering how her dad had explained to his young daughter that rain was Mother Nature's way of giving the plants and trees a drink. She smiled at the memory, one that might have been the start of her lifelong commitment to environmental causes. She wondered if her father would be proud of her. Or would he consider this too much? She would never know. His death from cancer at the young age of fifty-seven still haunted her. Skye tried not to think of the gaunt, disease-ravaged specimen he had become at the end. Her memories were of a hearty athlete who loved the outdoors. No one in her father's family had died of cancer at such a young age. She remained convinced that the industrial chemicals he was exposed to as a factory worker took him from her decades too soon. Someone would pay for that. They would all pay for that.

She felt the big arms wrap around her as Sequoia came up from behind. His chin rested on the top of her head. At five-ten she was as tall as most models, but with him she felt petite. It was one of the things about their relationship that worked. Her height had always made her feel uncomfortable. Even though her friends now described her as beautiful, Skye still felt like the skinny, gangly girl she had been in high school.

"How are you, hon?" Sequoia asked.

Skye felt him press against her. It wasn't overtly sexual, but that was always barely below the surface.

"I'm good," she replied, resting her head against his shoulder. Skye thought back to when they first met. It was at a concert. The music was so loud that they could barely hear each other. But that didn't matter. The physical attraction needed no words. It was intense, and they were in bed before the night was over. The sex was great then, so great that it compensated for much else. It was still good, but no longer enough to hide the weaknesses in their relationship.

For her the attraction had started to wane. Sequoia—Dan was his real name, but they were not allowed to use those—was not complex. That wasn't a polite way of saying that he was stupid. He was not. It was just that his needs were...simple. There was little intellectual curiosity, at least beyond the issues that drove their cause. She needed more.

Skye had no doubt that he loved her. If anything, he was too emotionally involved. His behavior had become somewhat controlling. There were signs of jealousy. But even if she wanted to break it off, could she? Their membership in the Earth Martyrs Brigade complicated that. It created a kind of prison that bound them together. The group's recent activities compounded the situation. Maybe she was being silly. Maybe she expected too much. After all, she had an attractive man who loved her and shared her overarching mission in life. Shouldn't that be good enough?

"I have a few comments I'd like to share."

It was Wolf, fresh back from the attack on the Omaha substation. They had all seen the coverage in the news and were eager to hear the details. Skye gently slipped from Sequoia's arms. They made their way to the center of the barn were the group was assembled and sat down.

"The attack was a great success," Wolf said. "The surveillance team provided us with excellent intelligence regarding the site and the escape route."

Wolf paused. He smiled broadly. Skye was almost startled. Wolf rarely smiled. There was a joy in him she hadn't seen before.

"As we left the scene we could see the blackout begin to roll across the city," Wolf said. "The communiqué that followed has received attention at the highest levels. The entire nation is aware of our power…our cause."

Skye wondered at the choice of words.

"The gluttonous energy pigs of this country believe that we can bring down their precious electrical grid. Oh, they are scared. They are scared of what we can do."

"Right on!" Fern yelled.

"Righteous, brother!" Firefly exclaimed. "Righteous!"

The others joined in. Hugs and high fives were exchanged.

Wolf was visibly shaking, agitated. There was a gleam in his eye that Skye had not seen before. While she shared the thrill at the mission's success, there was something about Wolf's behavior that made her uneasy.

"Mother knows our love for her, our commitment. She knows that we would die for her!" Wolf proclaimed. "And those who would rape her will pay with their lives! We'll see to that!"

Skye looked around the room. No one seemed shocked by this pronouncement. There was something like a religious fervor in the room. She looked at Sequoia. He was as pumped as the rest of them. Skye forced a smile. Sequoia reached over and hugged her. While they embraced her thoughts went to the firefighter killed in the casino arson, the wife and little boy that he left behind. Wasn't he just doing his job? What crime against Mother had he committed? But she knew that Wolf was right about many things. Climate change threatened humanity. Habitat was vanishing at an alarming rate. Animal species were becoming extinct on a daily basis. The planet was in peril. And then there were those who had murdered her father. Skye felt her commitment return. He would be avenged.

As she separated from Sequoia, Skye looked up to find Wolf

watching her. He was oddly expressionless given his earlier state of excitement. Skye's blood ran cold. What did he suspect? Could he sense even the slightest doubt? They stared at each other for a moment before Wolf broke into a smile. She grinned, and then nodded approvingly. All was well.

CHAPTER 26

10:23 a.m., Saturday, April 29, an undisclosed location, San Jose, California

The short ride from San Francisco down to Silicon Valley had afforded Ward the opportunity to learn a little bit about Special Agent Bradley Royer. And a little bit was all he did learn. Royer, while pleasant enough, was not the type to share a lot about his personal life. He was all business. That was fine with Ward. He didn't need to be the man's new best friend. He just needed him to do his job. And on that point there was at least one possible issue. Ward studied his FBI handler. Royer was fit, clean-cut, and a bit rigid. Combined with the sunglasses, navy blue suit and crisp white shirt, he screamed Fed. That made Ward nervous. It would make any undercover operative nervous. He assumed that the FBI agent could blend in better on the street. If not, there would be a conversation.

The purpose for the trip, Ward was told, was for him to receive basic training in hacking techniques from two white hats working for the FBI. It made sense, of course, that they would be in San Jose, the capital of Silicon Valley. Both worked as part of an FBI red team that did penetration testing to help assure the security of the bureau's computer systems. Royer had warned him that the two were *a little different*. As far as Ward was concerned anything else would have been disappointing.

Royer parked his Dodge Charger in the lot of an unremarkable office building in the middle of downtown. As Ward stepped out and looked around he noticed the names adorning the much larger structures around them. Many of the technology giants were headquartered right here. What was the per capita income of this place, he wondered? What was the median IQ? Higher than his, he was afraid.

"So, these two genius hackers have names?" Ward asked.

"Need to know," Royer answered bluntly.

"Of course," Ward said. "Should I just call them Hacker One and Hacker Two?"

Royer snorted. "We refer to them—or I should say they refer to themselves—as Etherlord and Incubus."

"And these are the good guys?"

"I know, right?" Royer shook his head. "I don't get it."

"So how do these two end up on Team Fed?" Ward asked.

"Etherlord is one of the most talented hackers out there. I'd like to tell you that he helps us out of a sense of duty and all, but that would not be the case. His loyalty is assured by the United States Attorney keeping the indictment for unauthorized computer access and wire fraud in his back pocket."

"Got it."

"Wait until you meet him."

"If the name is any indication."

"Let's just say he suffers from a lack of social skills."

"What about the other one…Incubus?" Ward asked. "Isn't that some sort of evil spirit that has sex with women in their sleep?"

Royer looked at Ward. "Impressive. Yeah, that's right." He smiled. "I figure the kid chose the name because that was about the only way he would ever have a shot at sex with an actual woman."

Ward chuckled.

"Despite the name, he's actually not a bad guy," Royer said. "And smart as a whip. We recruited him at Defcon."

"The hacker convention?"

"Yeah. We've picked up some of our best computer people there. You should see NSA at that place. It's like the NBA draft."

They walked into the building and took an elevator to the third floor. Royer stepped out first and led the way to a plain white metal door. He held an ID card up to the keypad. Ward heard the click as the door unlocked. They stepped inside. The room was dimly lit, and a good ten to fifteen degrees cooler than the hallway. It housed a vast array of computer hardware, crammed in with little space to spare. A dozen large monitors scrolled data or displayed code, most of which might as well have been hieroglyphics as far as Ward was concerned.

Seated in front of one of the computer screens was a skinny kid who looked as if he were barely out of high school. The fast food wrappers and empty energy drink cans that surrounded him gave the impression that he hadn't moved in days.

"Incubus," Royer said.

There was no response.

"Incubus!"

The kid looked up, startled. "Oh! Hi!" He jumped up from his chair, brushing crumbs off of his pants as he stood. "Harold…" he started to say but caught himself. "I'm sorry. The name's Incubus," he said, extending his hand to Ward.

Ward suppressed a grin. "Nice to meet you." He didn't offer a name. The handshake that followed was exceedingly vigorous.

"Where's your partner?" Royer asked.

Incubus pushed his glasses up his nose then jerked his head to the right, a look of disgust on his face. Royer motioned for Ward to follow him. They made their way through a forest of cables and hardware to find the room's other occupant tucked back in a corner.

Staring straight ahead at his monitor, despite their obvious presence, was the hacker Ward assumed to be Etherlord. He was slightly overweight and, judging from the smell, hadn't bathed in days. Patchy stubble of approximately three days growth supported this assessment. A ketchup-stained T-shirt, sweatpants and flip-flops completed the look. There was no move to acknowledge them. Ward looked at Royer, who held up his index finger as if to say, *give it a minute.*

"Yes?" Etherlord asked, continuing to stare at his screen.

"The training we discussed," Royer said.

There was a long sigh. "If we must."

Etherlord spun around in his chair to face them. "And this is the trainee?" he asked, giving Ward the once-over.

Royer rolled his eyes. "Yes. This is the trainee."

Etherlord slowly rose from his chair as if some Herculean task awaited him. He walked between them without saying a word.

"Quite a charmer," Ward whispered.

"I did warn you," Royer reminded him.

"Glad to see the FBI finally relaxed Hoover's dress code," Ward muttered.

Royer chuckled.

Etherlord led the way to a long table where a trio of monitors and keyboards sat side-by-side. "You sit in the middle," he said, looking at Ward.

"Yes, sir," Ward replied.

Etherlord gave him a quizzical look, then took the seat to Ward's right. Incubus sat to his left.

"We'll try to keep this simple enough for you to understand," Etherlord announced.

Incubus shook his head. "Ignore him," he whispered to Ward. "He's like that to everybody."

"I'll start with the basics of a DoS attack," Etherlord said. "Try to keep up." He began clicking away on his keyboard at a furious clip.

"Let me start," Incubus said. "There are two basic types of denial of service attack, or DoS, attack. One method floods a particular service with so many communication requests that it becomes unresponsive. The other method involves crashing the service, often through the use of malware.

Ward nodded. "Understood," he said.

"Really?" Etherlord asked.

Ward briefly considered knocking the smirk off of his face.

Around six o'clock in the evening Ward and Royer emerged from the training session. Ward was drained, more from seven hours of Etherlord than from the amount of information that he had been expected to absorb. And this was only the first of several planned hacking seminars. He wasn't sure he could take it.

"I have to say, I'm impressed," Royer noted as they headed for the car.

"How's that?"

"It's quite an accomplishment for Etherlord to acknowledge that you show *some* capacity for hacking. And that after only one meeting."

Ward snorted. "Yeah, I was flattered."

CHAPTER 27

10:46 a.m., Monday, May 1, Paxton Ford, Oklahoma City, Oklahoma

It was a small gesture compared to some of those perpetrated by his comrades, but a necessary one. These gas-guzzling trucks and SUVs were destroying the Earth with their toxins, causing the climate to change, melting the ice pack, threatening the very existence of countless species. Something had to be done. Something would be done, and the Santa Fe cell would play its part. Lemur was sure of that.

The nickname, he was told, was due to his watchful eyes. That was fine. He was pleased to be associated with the ever-alert little primates from Madagascar. Their name was derived from *lemures*, ghosts of Roman mythology. All-in-all, it was a fitting moniker for someone whose mission was reconnaissance.

Their target was a deserving one. Paxton Ford advertised itself as the largest truck and SUV dealership in Oklahoma. And what better place to destroy these monstrosities than in an oil-producing state. Lemur reminded himself to contain his excitement. For now, he and Falcon were nothing more than a couple of customers looking for the best deal on a new vehicle. Lemur was in the market for a truck, Falcon an SUV. Between the two of them they should be able to get a thorough tour of the facility. That, along with their nighttime surveillance, would provide the information necessary for a map showing the arson team how to enter and complete their mission while avoiding security cameras and the rent-a-cop who patrolled the lot after hours.

The SUVs were in a different part of the lot, on the opposite side of the main showroom from the pickups. Falcon had already left with the salesman who was working on him. Lemur waited patiently for his sales representative, Mark, who was checking on some exciting new financing options. Despite a long night, Lemur had declined Mark's offer of coffee. The cups were made of Styrofoam.

As he stood waiting, Lemur stroked his freshly shaved chin. His face was without beard for the first time in seven years. But that didn't bother him. The beard would grow back quickly. It was the haircut. Falcon had done the honors, setting the clippers to the quarter-inch setting. It would take years to regrow, a sacrifice Lemur could only make for Mother. The end result, however, was convincing. Combined with the cowboy hat, plaid shirt, belt buckle, jeans and boots, his new look easily passed as native Oklahoman. Being a longtime resident of New Mexico he had encountered enough Texans and Okies over the years to pull off the accent. Falcon was equally convincing. Neither salesmen had looked the least bit doubtful when told that they had come in from Tulsa because their friend Jimmy Roy told 'em that this was the best place in Oklahoma to git 'em a truck.

"Mr. Thomas, are you ready to look at some trucks?"

Lemur turned to see Mark striding toward him.

"Yessir," Lemur said. "You bet I am. And call me Bobby Joe."

"Alright, Bobby Joe. Let's head out."

They walked out into the lot. "You lookin' for a two-wheel drive, four-wheel drive?" Mark asked.

"Probably a four-wheel drive. But I'd consider a two-wheel drive if the price was right," Lemur said with a laugh. The truth was he just wanted to cover as much of the lot as possible.

"I hear ya," Mark said. "We'll take care of ya."

No, I'll take care of you, Lemur thought.

They looked at a dozen or so trucks, mainly the less expensive models. Lemur assumed that the salesman had sized him up as a young guy without a lot of money to spend. He would take care of that, hint at family wealth.

"What'll ya be usin' it for?" Mark asked.

There it is, Lemur thought. "Daddy's got a small ranch, about eight hundred acres. I also need to pull my bass boat."

Lemur could see the salesman's eyes light up.

"Have you considered the King Ranch or Platinum models?" Mark asked.

"Let's take us a look at those," Lemur said.

There was an added bounce in the salesman's step as he ushered Bobby Joe Thomas around the lot. He chattered tirelessly about the features of the high-end models. Lemur heard little of it. All the while he was scouring the area for security cameras and hidden access points into the dealership.

"How big's that fishin' boat?" Mark asked.

"Twenty-one-foot Lund," Lemur replied.

"That's a nice boat," Mark said. His eyes gleamed.

Lemur wondered if the man would start to salivate.

"I do dome fishin' myself, ya know," Mark offered.

"That right?" Lemur did his best to look interested. The truth was the subject disgusted him. He was a vegan and believed that the fish, like all creatures, should be left in their natural habitat.

"Caught a six-pounder last Sunday," Mark announced proudly.

Lemur touched the brim of his cowboy hat. "That's a nice one."

"Let's take a look at this Platinum over here," Mark said, pointing at a truck three vehicles down the line. "This one has the 6.2-liter V8. Pull that boat with no problem."

"What's the mileage on somethin' like this?" Lemur asked.

"Oh, about fifteen city, twenty-one highway."

Lemur wanted to throw up. He regretted that he would not be there to watch this truck burn.

They spent another thirty minutes looking at various pickups.

Lemur could see that the salesman thought he had established a solid connection with Bobby Joe Thomas. It was time to gather the last bits of intelligence and get out of there.

"Security must be a real pain in the ass for a lot this big," Lemur said. "I mean, with all this inventory..."

Mark nodded. "You may have noticed, it's not the best neighborhood. We've had us a few break-ins."

"I'm sure y'all have."

"We have a security company that patrols the lot at night. But, truth is, the ol' boy they send over usually ends up fallin' asleep in his car over behind the service center."

Lemur shook his head. "Is that right?" *Good to know*, he thought.

CHAPTER 28

11:25 a.m., Monday, May 1, The Biscuit, Portland, Oregon

As they approached, Ward could make out a sign on the side of the building that had obviously been painted many decades earlier. Though badly weathered, he could still make out the name: *The Butler Biscuit Company.* It was a brick structure, late nineteenth century, located in an abandoned warehouse district far from the city center and hipster neighborhoods that Ward would frequent as Joshua Young, software designer and radical environmentalist. A loft on the top floor would serve as task force headquarters, their safe house. It was here that Ward would debrief, write reports, and download any digital recordings. This would be his home away from home away from home.

Cruz drove around back and pulled into an alley. "This is it," he said, "The Biscuit."

Ward liked the name. That wasn't the problem. "An apartment house?" he asked, dubious. "Won't there be too much traffic?" Neighbors sniffing around the unusual comings and goings surrounding their operations could pose a problem, a big problem.

"Not an issue," Cruz assured him. "The developer got out a little too far ahead of the curve in pioneering this area. No renters. No prospects for renters. He was happier than shit to have a customer. Gave us a bargain and didn't ask a thing. Hell, I probably could have told him we were setting up a meth lab and he wouldn't have blinked.

Ward looked up and down the alley, studied the neighboring buildings. There were no signs of life.

"I see what you mean," he said.

In fact, there had been few vehicles parked on the street as they travelled the last few blocks. It would be easy to spot a tail in this area, but it would also be difficult to lose one.

"Trust me. We're good," Cruz said as he retrieved a set of keys from his pocket. "Let's go take a look."

They got out of the car and walked toward what appeared to be a heavy steel door. Dumpsters were situated on either side. Cruz unlocked the door and shoved it open. They stepped inside. To the right was an industrial elevator. Cruz hit the up button. The doors rumbled open. As they ascended the old beast clanked and shuddered in a way that briefly gave Ward pause.

"You sure this thing's safe?"

"Not really," Cruz replied, grinning.

When they reached the top floor there was a jerk, after which they dropped a few inches.

"Like I said," Cruz noted, "the place was a bargain."

They exited the elevator, Ward going first, eager to extricate himself from the potential deathtrap.

Cruz unlocked a door that was just off the elevator. "This is it," he said.

Ward stepped inside. The loft was spacious, taking up most of the top floor. It was nicely done and would likely be in high demand in a better location. The contractor had installed ample windows, allowing a good view of the street below and surrounding buildings on all sides. Normally, too many windows would be a concern for a safe house, but Ward had noticed when they arrived that the tinting made it difficult to see in. Other than the standard kitchen appliances, the place was sparsely furnished, as in nonexistent. The only thing immediately visible was a long table and a half-dozen chairs. Two laptops were placed on either end.

"This will do," Ward said, nodding his head in approval. He turned toward Cruz. "I imagine my undercover crib is just as impressive."

"Incorrect," Cruz said. He smiled. "It is better furnished, though."

"I would hope."

"We'll get a bed in here for those times when you need to be, you know, *out of town.*"

"That would be helpful." Aside from debriefing and working on reports, Ward knew there would be times when he needed this place to depressurize, take a break from the role-playing. It helped him stay sane, especially during the longer operations. During this one his absence could easily be explained by the need to visit Blue World Systems' main office in San Francisco.

Overall, Ward was pleased. This was easily the nicest task force headquarters he had seen. He could recall several that were pretty rough: a decrepit, roach-infested motel room, an abandoned office building with no air conditioning, even a mobile home forfeited from a meth dealer. Yeah, this would do.

The door opened behind them. Ward's hand moved instinctively toward his weapon as he spun around. It dropped back to his side when he saw it was Royer.

"What do you think of the place?" Royer asked.

"Nice," Ward replied. "Who paid?" He thought he knew the answer.

"FBI," Royer announced, maybe a little too proudly.

Ward looked at Cruz, who rolled his eyes almost imperceptibly. It was another example of what they both knew—FBI got all the money. When the federal law enforcement dollars were doled out it was FBI first, with the remainder divided up among the also-rans. No wonder the place was so nice. Ward could remember a time when ATF agents had their cell phone minutes and mileage limited. He was sure that no FBI agent ever worked under similar restrictions. At least this time, he thought, the deep pockets might work to his benefit. The question was could the FBI play well with the other kids in the sandbox? That remained to be seen. Ward would do his part to make it work, not so much because of any great desire to enhance inter-agency cooperation, but for one vastly more important reason—his survival.

CHAPTER 29

9:24 a.m., Tuesday, May 2, Paxton Ford, Oklahoma City, Oklahoma

General Sales Manager Jerry Copeland sized up the young man seated on the other side of his desk. Ethan Cates was a good-looking kid, enthusiastic, with some charm. The potential was there, but the great salesmen were naturals. Sure, you could train them, get them to the point where they were better than most. He'd trained plenty. But the best of them had a gift. It remained to be seen if Ethan had that gift. For now, he was just another of the owner's special projects. Copeland had lost track of the young people from tough backgrounds that Fred Paxton had helped out. The guy had a heart of gold. Copeland just wished that every now and then they could hire a guy with some experience. Still, Paxton's approach certainly hadn't hurt business. One of the reasons the place was so successful was the dedication of its employees, and that was all due to the boss.

"How well you know Fred Paxton?" Copeland asked.

"Not well at all," Cates said. "I sold him a smartphone. We struck up a conversation and the next thing I know he was offering me a job."

Typical, Copeland thought. "What did you guys talk about?" he asked.

"Nothin' special. He asked me about myself. I told him that I was a graduate of Midwest City High School, played football there.”

“You were a Bomber?” Copeland asked. Midwest City’s football program was legendary.

“Yessir. Had a scholarship to play for the Sooners until I blew out my knee.”

“Sorry to hear that. They couldn’t repair it?”

“Tore my ACL, PCL, shredded the cartilage. Pretty much total devastation.”

“That’s tough.”

“Went from a full ride to trying to work my way through college. I’m just a few credits shy now, but it’s been difficult.” Cates looked down for a second. “My family doesn’t have much money.”

“You tell Fred that?”

“Yeah,” Cates said. “Didn’t mean to. Funny, you’re talking to the guy and next thing you know you’re telling him your life story.”

“That’s Fred.” Copeland couldn’t count the times he’d heard the same thing.

“You get all the new hire paperwork filled out?”

“Sure did.”

“Good.” Copeland stood up. “Let’s go around and introduce you to some of your new co-workers.”

“Sounds good.”

They made their way around the large main building, Copeland making one introduction after another. He was impressed with the kid’s demeanor, meeting each person as if it were a true pleasure. Yeah, Copeland thought, there was some potential in this one. He had to admit, the boss had a good eye for talent.

Just as they were finishing with the sales staff a voice boomed from the other side of the showroom floor.

“There he is!”

Copeland turned to see Fred Paxton striding toward them, hand outstretched, smile as wide as the Arkansas River spread across his face. His daughter, Molly, was right behind him.

“How’s my boy?” Paxton asked. He shook Cates’ hand and patted the kid on the back. “You takin’ care of him, Jerry?”

Yessir," Copeland said. "You know it."

"I think he's gonna be a good one," Paxton said. "In fact, I'm sure of it." He turned to his daughter. "This here's my little girl, Molly."

"Daddy!" Molly said in protest. "I'm twenty-four years old, with an MBA from the University of Oklahoma."

Paxton held up his hands in defeat. "I know, Sugar, I know."

Molly reached out to shake Cates' hand. "Molly Paxton. Nice to meet you."

"Ethan Cates. Pleasure's mine."

Copeland thought he saw a little spark, at least on Cates' part. He would have to talk to the lad about that, make sure he didn't get any ideas. Not that he could blame him. Molly was a beautiful girl, five-ten, honey-blond hair, with piercing green eyes. She was easy to look at. But, big-hearted as Paxton was, the last salesman who made a play for Molly was now selling used cars over in Elk City.

Molly was also in training to someday take over the dealership. She had worked there since she was old enough to wash cars and had done a stint in almost every facet of the business. Copeland knew that there was nothing Fred Paxton wanted more than to hand off the place to his little girl. When she once talked about moving out to the west coast to take a job it almost killed the ol' boy. Copeland could recall how the boss seemed to lose his spark. But Paxton was smart enough to play it cool and not stand in the way. Molly eventually changed her mind. She was an Oklahoma girl, and the car business was in her blood.

"Ethan, I'm havin' a little barbeque out at the ranch this weekend for the employees," Paxton said. "Hope to see you out there."

"I wouldn't miss it."

"Good!" Paxton gave Cates a quick pat on the back. "I'll let you boys get back to it." He and Molly walked toward the other side of the showroom where Paxton greeted someone who was clearly a longtime customer.

"Are you going to the barbeque?" Cates asked Copeland.

"You bet," Copeland said. "It's a good time. And wait'll you see the place. It's something else.

"Nice, huh?"

"You'd never know the guy grew up dirt poor."

"Is that right?" Cates eyes followed after Paxton.

"Yep. Sure nothin' for a kid to be embarrassed about, but he was. Fred was determined to make something of himself, have some real financial security."

Cates nodded. Copeland studied him for a moment, then went on.

"He's haunted by memories of his youth, not having enough to eat, always wearing the same ragged clothes to school. He gets emotional when he describes the indignities suffered by his father, who by all accounts was a decent, hardworking guy. The old man worked menial, backbreaking jobs his whole life, the kind of work that eventually destroys your body, and had little to show for it."

Cates shook his head.

"Fred built this place up from nothin', worked his ass off." Copeland looked over to where the boss stood, still engaged in conversation with one of his customers. "He's a real self-made man."

"That's impressive." Cates said.

"It is," Copeland agreed. "And I'll tell you somethin' else, that guy really remembers his early days in business, what it was like to live on the brink of failure. I can't tell you how many struggling entrepreneurs he's helped out with a loan or by throwing a little business their way."

"He's sure given me a chance," Cates said.

"You're far from the first. This place is full of people like you who got an opportunity to prove themselves."

"I won't let him down," Cates promised.

Copeland nodded. He was suddenly sure that the kid was going to work out.

CHAPTER 30

10:33 p.m., Tuesday, May 2, Ward's undercover apartment, The Hawthorne District, Portland, Oregon

Ward stared blankly at the television screen as he sipped a beer from one of Portland's many microbreweries. It was some variety of wheat beer. He was no expert, but it was good. It was the first of many that he would likely drink alone in yet another undercover apartment in yet another undercover operation.

The place was nothing special. There were two bedrooms, one of which would function as his office, a bathroom, living room and kitchen in an open configuration. Small, but more than adequate for his purposes. It was located in the Hawthorne district of southeast Portland, or "Hawthorne" as Portlanders referred to it. According to Cruz, this was the place to be, one of the true hipster hubs of the ultra-liberal city, with a good bit of hippie still left. From his initial survey of the neighborhood and its colorful residents, Ward was sure that Cruz was right. It was an area in which Joshua Young would fit right in.

Ward got up off the couch and went to the bathroom. The beer, his second, was working through him. As he finished, he turned and caught a glimpse of himself in the mirror above the sink. The beard was coming in nicely, full and, thankfully, still dark. His shoulder-length hair was pulled back in a ponytail. Ward went to the kitchen and grabbed his eyeglasses from the counter. He slipped them on and returned to the bathroom mirror. The black frames fashionable with the hipster subculture reminded him of something that his grandfather might have worn. Still, he liked the look.

Then there was the lingo. Learning to talk the talk was not always easy. He knew the rhetoric of the radical environmentalist crowd, at least as it pertained to their issues. But the day-to-day language of a subculture that was foreign to him was another matter. An internet search didn't get you very far. You had to hear it, practice it. He would wander the streets, hang out in the coffee houses, the local bars, the funkier shops, keep his ears open. As he had done many times in the past, he would bring that language back and practice it in front of the mirror, working on pronunciation, cadence, intonation, accent. Then, he would take it out to the public, try it out in locations away from the area where he was working, until it felt comfortable, until he was sure that he could pull it off. Only then would the mission truly begin. Fortunately, Ward had discovered that he had a real knack for this part of the job. An ear for music helped. But he had also learned to be careful not to overdo it. That could be the telltale sign of an imposter.

The clothes were also not simple. Wardrobe was critical. Years of experience had taught Ward not to overdress the part and keep it authentic. As with the language, he studied the people in Hawthorne and surrounding neighborhoods, focusing mostly on those from his own age bracket. He was a bit too old for pure hipster and needed to fit in with a wider set. The clothes he selected, mostly from thrift shops, were sort of a modified hippie-grunge look with a little hipster thrown in to keep it reasonably contemporary. Never remotely a slave to fashion, Ward was certain that he had not created any sort of marketable new look, but it was a look that would work. That was what mattered. Overall, Ward was confident that Joshua Young would easily pass as someone right at home in Hawthorne.

He walked to the window, grabbing his beer on the way. Ward studied the crowd below, an eclectic group that he soon would become a part of. As he observed their comings and goings a light rain began to fall, almost more of a mist. The first few drops caused those on the streets to look skyward. Accustomed to such weather, there was no rush for cover. Instead, umbrellas began to open. The variety of colors and designs created the effect of a blooming flower garden. Ward noticed, however, that many of the younger residents did nothing, simply going about their business, at most pulling up a hood or buttoning a coat. Apparently, it was considered uncool to stave off the elements with something as establishment as an umbrella. Ward smiled at youth.

As he stood in the window watching the rain, Ward's thoughts went to their frequent destination—Maria. He often thought of her when he was alone on assignment because that, more than anything else, was what had driven them apart. She had grown to hate the job that had taken the dream of a normal family life from her. Even though she was aware of what it involved when she signed on, Maria had underestimated the demands that undercover work placed on a spouse, on a marriage. At least he thought that was it. Maybe she had always known, but just hoped that he would come to value her more, that he would quit and find a normal job, or at least a less dangerous assignment that didn't take him from home as much. They were apart so often. He remembered discussions of children. She wanted them badly. But Maria finally realized that with him she would essentially be a single parent. She said it to him, and she was right. That conversation was still as fresh in his memory as if it had happened yesterday. He could vividly recall the hurt in her face as she finally acknowledged that it was over, realizing that the job would always mean more to him. Ward's eyes started to well up. Dammit, he promised himself that he wasn't going to do this. He rubbed the back of his hand across his eyes, then took the last swallow from his beer. Maybe he would have another.

CHAPTER 31

1:56 a.m., Wednesday, May 3, Paxton Ford, Oklahoma City, Oklahoma

There he was, just as advertised, asleep in his car behind the service center. The surveillance team was right about the security guard and, as far as Bud could tell, pretty much everything else. The photos, internet satellite maps and drawings, which included the location of security cameras, gave them a comprehensive overview of the place that would facilitate their mission, to rid the world, or at least this small part of Oklahoma, of these gas-guzzling enemies of the Earth. He was ready. The Boulder cell was about to make its mark.

It was time to make their entry. Bud turned to K2 and nodded. The spark in the other man's eyes was visible even through the narrow opening in the black ski mask. K2 had talked of little else over the course of the last month, his tone becoming ever more excitable, taking on an almost religious fervor. At times his rhetoric had made Bud uneasy. Commitment to the cause was admirable, but the job required a cool head.

They had trained extensively, including several mock attacks. Nothing was left to chance. Not only were the technical aspects practiced, they also endured rigorous physical training—running, weights, climbing, and, worst of all, the five-gallon buckets. One in each hand, filled close to the brim, they were carried as far as possible, as fast as possible. It was excruciating. But in the end a dozen trips of a hundred yards was no problem. Never an athlete, Bud was easily in the best shape of his life.

K2, on the other hand, was a natural athlete. He was also the electrician, masterful at constructing the intricate little timers that were so important to an effective attack. This particular task required many. Several days were spent in the garage of a sympathizer constructing the numerous triggering mechanisms. Keeping them intact during transport had been a major ordeal, particularly when combined with moving the quantity of accelerant needed for a job like this. But they had done it, driven by their will to strike a blow for Mother.

K2 went first. Bud followed closely behind, single file formation. Their route was carefully predetermined to avoid the security cameras. They moved quickly toward the main building. The large showroom portion of the structure had a two-story curved roof. It was adjoined by a one-story section that spread out behind and to one side of the showroom. This allowed them to place incendiary devices on top of the one-story section in such a way that the heat from the fire would be captured by the overhanging roof of the showroom. Bud was confident that this would speed fire to the rafters, causing the roof to fail and collapse onto the vehicles below. The thought made his adrenaline surge.

When they reached the building, K2 scaled the wall with little effort. As an expert mountaineer, most assumed that his nickname came from the Himalayan peak. Bud was aware that this was not the case. The name actually came from his fondness for the K2 that was a synthetic form of marijuana. Of course, Bud knew that it actually was something quite different, less predictable than the natural version. He knew all about both substances. After all, Bud was a reference to his avocation, purveyor of Colorado's newest legal product, marijuana. He sold the best pot in Boulder. Why not? It was one of Mother's most blessed creations. He was proud to be a supplier of this righteous herb.

K2 lowered a rope. They began the process of hoisting the

igniters, timers and accelerant onto the roof. This was the most difficult part of the job, but the training had prepared them well. They worked flawlessly, Bud travelling back and forth between the transport vehicle and the building, while K2 put the devices in place and set the timers.

The five-gallon buckets of accelerant became heavier with each trip. Despite the conditioning, Bud's arms and shoulders burned by the time he carried the last two. His hands started to cramp. *Suck it up*, he thought. There was more work to do, a lot more. The service center and body shop were housed in separate structures. They were next. Then there were the vehicles. Those would be last. Obviously, full-fledged incendiary devices could not be made for each. There was a simpler method involving plastic bottles and sponges. Those burned fast and had to be set immediately prior to departure, with only certain vehicles targeted. They were placed under the engine compartment. From what he had seen during training, they were surprisingly effective.

With the last device in place, K2 lowered himself over the edge and dropped down. They stayed close to the building and then ran the short distance between it and the service center. As they began to place their devices, Bud envisioned the glorious inferno that would result when the flammable substances inside ignited. It would be spectacular. Granted, the resulting pollution was unfortunate. But he comforted himself with the thought of the many trucks and SUVs that would be destroyed, the message that would be sent. How could anyone who cared about this planet fail to understand? And if they didn't, they were part of the problem.

The service center done, they moved on to the body shop. Only two of the big devices were left. Unfortunately, that meant less chance of total destruction. They were placed on either end of the building under the overhanging front roof. It was hoped that there was enough combustible material inside to fuel the fire and finish the job. It didn't really matter. They would have made their point.

As the last device was put in place at the body shop Bud

thought he heard a noise. It sounded like the scuffle of feet. Bud looked at K2 and put his index fingers to his lips. The sound stopped, and then started again. Bud pointed in the direction of the sound. K2 nodded. He had clearly heard it as well. They were out in the open, exposed. Bud looked around for cover. It was thirty yards to the nearest vehicle.

"What the hell?"

Bud turned in the direction of the voice. It was the security guard. The guard started to fumble for his gun, clearly surprised to encounter someone in his rounds. Bud cursed himself for not checking on him gain. The surveillance team had reported that the old man never moved from his car over the course of the several nights that they watched the place.

"Take it easy," Bud said. "Let's just…"

The gunshot cut him off in midsentence. At first, Bud wasn't sure what had happened. Had the guard fired? Then he saw the old man slump to the ground. Bud turned and saw the weapon in K2's hand.

"What the fuck?" Bud asked.

"It's called contingency planning," K2 said. The eyes visible through the slit in his mask were now emotionless. "You have a problem with that?"

Bud grew nervous, suddenly seeing himself as a possible casualty of the operation. *Say something*, he thought. "Not at all," he ad-libbed. "Mother demands it."

K2 nodded. Bud saw a bit of the spark return to his eyes.

"Let's get outta here," Bud said.

"Not until we torch a few trucks."

Bud thought he saw the gun come up a bit. There was no arguing the point, not if he wanted to live. "Let's do it," he said.

They ran from vehicle to vehicle, placing the bottles under the engine compartment of several dozen of the larger trucks and SUVs. Within minutes, most were in flames. Soon, the structures would ignite. Bud was terrified that they would be caught, they were certainly now in view of some of the security cameras, but

K2 seemed to be in some sort of martyrdom mode, and he was now the greater threat.

Finally, he couldn't take it anymore. "We've got to get out of here!" Bud yelled. If the crazy bastard shot him, so be it. They *had* to go.

K2 stood with his hands on his hips, surveying the damage. His eyes were wide with excitement. He finally seemed satisfied. Nodding his head, he held up a finger and pointed in the direction of their van. They had done enough.

Bud wondered if he would make it home to Boulder alive.

Fred Paxton was awake, again. He knew that at this point in his life he should sleep like a baby. He'd made it. At least that's what the balance sheet said. And he had solid, trusted employees that made the place run like a clock. But there was always that nagging doubt, the insecurity that came from a lifetime of struggle. He could never completely shake it. Every night he worried about the business, how to stay competitive, how to build a dealership that would last for Molly, and maybe for her children. There was always something to worry about, something to do next. Tonight his thoughts were mostly on his daughter. She sure didn't like it when he had introduced her to Ethan Cates as his *little girl*. He understood her point, but she was his little girl, always would be. He just wanted to protect her. Still, she was right. He had to allow her more independence, let her find her own way. He would always be there to guide her when she needed it...if she would let him.

Paxton's thoughts were interrupted by the sound of an email alert on his cell phone. He recognized the tone. It was the one that indicated the dealership's security cameras had picked up some activity. This was not unusual. Stray dogs, and even coyotes, sometimes activated the alert. Occasionally, it was the security guard. Most nights he turned off the phone before going to bed so he wouldn't be bothered by it. He debated whether to log into the camera app and take a look. Just a waste of time, he thought. Paxton rolled over and tried to go back to sleep. Then, the email alert went off again. "Shit. I suppose," he mumbled. Paxton sat up and swung his legs over the side of the bed. He grabbed the phone and logged into the security app. A selection of four available cameras appeared. The images were small, but there clearly appeared to be some activity on one of them. He tapped it to enlarge the view. It looked like…it was…fire! Several vehicles were ablaze! "What the hell?" Paxton asked loudly.

Susan Paxton stirred to life next to him. "What is it, Hon?" she asked.

Paxton showed her the image as he simultaneously grabbed the landline phone from the nightstand.

"Oh my God!" Susan cried.

Paxton punched in 9-1-1. An emergency dispatcher came on.

"There's a fire at Paxton Ford!"

"What's the address, sir?" the dispatcher asked.

As he gave the address Paxton glanced back at his smartphone. A figure clad entirely in black, including ski mask, appeared on the screen. Then, as suddenly as it had appeared, the figure vanished. Paxton's heart raced. He could barely breathe. Something was very wrong. He struggled to regain enough composure to tell the dispatcher what was happening. When he could finally begin to speak, the screens, one by one, began to go dead.

CHAPTER 32

6:02 a.m., Wednesday, May 3, WOKC TV Studios, Oklahoma City, Oklahoma

"Welcome to Your Morning Report." Anchor Melissa Dorrell dispensed with the usual news summary and went straight to the day's major developing story. "An overnight fire has destroyed much of Paxton Ford right here in Oklahoma City. We turn now to Morning Report correspondant Robin Rusk. Robin, what can you tell us about what's happened out there?"

Rusk gestured toward the scene of destruction behind her. "Melissa, as you can see this is a scene of utter devastation. Almost every major structure has been severely damaged. The showroom roof collapsed onto the vehicles inside. In addition, dozens more out on the dealership's lot appear to have been set ablaze. Most of those are damaged beyond repair."

"Robin, you said *set ablaze*," Dorrell noted. "My understanding is that WOKC received an email this morning from an unnamed group claiming responsibility."

"That's correct, Melissa." Rusk looked down at a sheet of paper in her hand. "The email that came to our tipline read as follows: *Global warming will be prevented only through direct action. Governments and corporations have demonstrated their utter inability to solve this problem despite the inescapable fact that the fate of all species hangs in the balance. Paxton Ford proudly advertises itself as the largest truck and SUV dealership in Oklahoma by sales volume. The carbon dioxide emissions of these vehicles are a major cause of this environmental catastrophe. Paxton's monstrous crime against our planet has now been addressed. The others have been warned."*

Dorrell shook her head. "Have authorities said anything about the note or who might be responsible?"

"No, they have not," Rusk said. "But as you are probably aware, Melissa, this appears to be the latest in a string of similar attacks that have occurred around the country over the course of the last month. All of them have been followed by emails to TV stations such as ours in which an unnamed individual or group has claimed responsibility."

"I understand that this incident may also involve a homicide?"

"That's correct," Rusk replied. "A security guard was found dead from an apparent gunshot wound to the chest. Officials have been even more tightlipped about that aspect of the case, but a source who asked to remain anonymous informs me that the guard may have discovered the arsonists and been shot as a result."

"How tragic."

"It is. And this is not the first fatality that has resulted from these seemingly related attacks. A fire that destroyed a casino under construction in Stateline, Nevada, resulted in the death of an electrician and a responding firefighter."

"Robin, have you talked to the owners? Do they plan to rebuild?"

Rusk nodded. "Moments go I spoke with the owner, Fred Paxton, who has graciously agreed to appear on camera this morning." The camera followed Rusk as she moved a few steps to her left. She placed her hand on the shoulder of her interview subject. "Mr. Paxton, thank you for being with us. First of all let me extend the sympathies of everyone in the WOKC family."

Fred Paxton took a deep breath, then wiped the back of his hand across his eyes. "Thank you, Robin."

Rusk looked into the camera. "Of course, we also want to extend our condolences to the family of the security guard who died," she said.

Paxton nodded vigorously. "Absolutely," he agreed.

"Officials have not yet released his name pending notification of family members," Rusk continued. She turned back to Paxton. "Tell us, do you plan to rebuild?"

Fred Paxton looked out over the destruction and what was left of his dealership. The struggles and sacrifices that had gone into the place swept over him. His eyes narrowed and his jaw set in a look of absolute deviance. "You bet!" he said. "This place is too important for too many people. We're sure as hell not gonna let a bunch of terrorists scare us off. We have to rebuild."

Rusk perked up. "You mentioned terrorists. Is there something more you can share with us?"

Paxton thought about the images he had seen on his cell phone, the figure in black. "Law enforcement has asked me not to discuss that."

Rusk instinctively knew that this cryptic comment was the dramatic point on which to end the report. She turned to the camera. "Melissa, there you have it. This is Robin Rusk, WOKC TV, reporting live from Paxton Ford right here in Oklahoma City, the scene of what appears to be a domestic terrorist attack."

White House Press Secretary Ellie Drake checked her watch as she hurried down the hall. It was a quarter after eight. Cooper would likely have been in for at least an hour already. There were many days he arrived at work as early six. As she approached his office she could hear him on the phone. Chief of staff or not, this couldn't wait. She barged in.

Michael Cooper was laughing at a comment made by whoever was on the other end of the call. When he looked up and saw the expression on Drake's face he cut it short.

"I gotta go," Cooper said. "Call you back later."

"Have you seen the news out of Oklahoma City?" Drake asked.

"No. What is it?"

"There was an attack on a Ford dealership down there," Drake said. "It destroyed the place. A security guard was shot and killed."

"Shit." Cooper rubbed his eyes. "I guess you're going to tell me that it's the same group that hit the casino and the electrical substation?"

"Looks that way." Drake pointed to his computer. "Do a quick search for WOKC TV in Oklahoma City. You can pull up the video clip of this morning's report and see for yourself."

Within a few seconds Cooper had pulled up the WOKC website and clicked on the link to the video. They watched in silence as the piece played, until the reporter referred to what she called "a domestic terrorist attack."

"Great," Cooper said. "That's just fucking great."

"Thought you'd like that."

Cooper pointed at a chair as he picked up the phone. "Have a seat." He punched in a number.

"What are you doing?" Drake asked.

Cooper looked her in the eye, his expression serious as death. "I'm calling the director of the FBI."

CHAPTER 33

10:06 a.m., Wednesday, May 3, on the streets of Portland, Oregon

Royer and Ward sat in the car watching the mid-morning Portland street life amble by. They had swapped the Dodge Charger for a Toyota Prius. The Charger was a little too well-known as a law enforcement vehicle. No point in advertising. Ward was dressed as Joshua Young, his undercover persona. Thankfully, even Royer had traded his standard FBI threads for more local attire. Ward looked him over. Royer was no threat to win undercover operative of the year, but at least he no longer stuck out like a sore thumb.

It was time to meet Royer's informant and start the process of entry into the radical environmentalist community. The plan was to do the introductions at a neutral location well away from the informant's normal stomping grounds and even further away from Ward's undercover apartment. It needed to be someplace that they would not encounter any of the people they planned to investigate. As a precaution, Royer would call his source shortly before the meeting to announce the location. Cruz and several local agents would then trail the informant to make certain that he had not been followed.

"You picked out a spot?" Ward asked.

"Yeah." Royer smiled, looking pleased with himself.

"Okay. What are you up to?"

"There's a Hoyberg's about ten blocks from here. Won't run

into any of his fellow tree huggers there."

Ward shook his head. Hoyberg's was a national burger chain, and a frequent target of environmentalists who accused the company of everything from destroying the Amazon to being single-handedly responsible for America's obesity problem. "You trying to piss this guy off?" he asked. "I need to keep him onboard."

"Oh, he'll stay onboard," Royer said. "Don't worry about that."

"I'm glad you're so confident."

"He knows damn well that if he were exposed his life would become pretty miserable."

Ward had heard that kind of vague assurance before. The problem was that keeping the cooperator in line was often necessary to his survival. Informants had a tendency to get nervous and stupid. Some even thought they could come clean and all would be forgiven, that those they had ratted on would understand their predicament. The truth was that the people who were targeted in federal investigations often weren't the forgiving type.

"What exactly is your hold on this guy?" Ward asked. "I'm sure you kept him from being indicted in the ELF case, but at this point he couldn't be charged in any of that if he went south on you. The statute's run."

Royer didn't say anything. Ward was starting to become uncomfortable.

"You wouldn't expose him just because he didn't play ball," Ward said, though he wasn't entirely sure it was true. "So, what's your hook?"

Royer sighed. He appeared impatient, almost as if explaining something to a child. "Aside from an obstruction charge if he gave you up or interfered with this investigation, this guy's whole world is the hardcore environmentalist movement. It's his identity. These are his friends. He wouldn't risk me outing him. Whether I'd actually do it if he simply refused to play along is another question. But he doesn't need to know that."

Even though he was irritated by the tone and cavalier

reasoning, Ward decided to let Royer cool off for a moment. He stared out the window, considering what he'd just heard. The obstruction thing was total bullshit, and Royer knew it. That would only come into play if his informant intentionally exposed the investigation. It was tough to prove and obviously did nothing to ensure cooperation in the first place. Ward knew that by the time an obstruction charge was filed the undercover operation was long blown, and he was quite possibly dead.

As for this guy's devotion to the movement, if he was so fucking devoted how'd they flip him in the first place? Royer's "hook" into the informant was dull, and on a frayed line. It wasn't much to base an operation on. Trouble was, they didn't have anything else to go with. The case was becoming more urgent each day. Just that morning they had been briefed on an arson down in Oklahoma that was clearly related to the other attacks. People at the top were getting nervous. Ward didn't like it when the brass was paying close attention. It had a tendency to force things before they were ready. Was this one of those times? Maybe. But they had to do something. People were dying. This group, whoever they were, appeared capable of anything.

Ward looked at his watch. "Isn't it about time to make the call?"

A hint of a smile appeared on Royer's face. He nodded. "Yeah, it's time."

"What's this guy's name?"

Royer hesitated. Ward recognized the instinct. All agents had a tendency to want to keep their sources to themselves.

"Peavey," Royer said. "Matthias Peavey."

Royer punched in the number, then he put the phone on speaker.

"Yeah."

It was clear that Peavey knew the call was from Royer despite the fact that the agent's number would not be displayed.

"You ready?" Royer asked.

"Ready as I'm gonna be."

"You familiar with a Hoyberg's on southeast Powell?"

There was silence on the other end. Finally, Peavey spoke.

"Hoyberg's? Are you fucking kidding me? You think that's funny. Those people are criminals. They're responsible for more environmental damage than..."

"Do you know where it's at or not?" Royer asked, cutting him off.

"Yeah." There was a pause. "I know where it's at."

Ward could hear the resignation in the man's voice, but it was the simmering anger that concerned him. They were not off to a good start. Royer's approach with cooperators was certainly not the method he would choose.

"Look, I'm not trying to agitate," Royer said. His tone was calm. "I just figure that it's a place where we won't run into... your kind."

Smooth, Ward thought.

"My kind?"

"You know what I mean."

"Yeah...I know what you mean."

Jesus, Ward thought. Didn't they train FBI agents in stuff like this?

"I just..." Royer paused. "Be there in ten minutes," he said, unable to come up with anything else. Royer ended the call.

Ward watched Royer, who didn't make eye contact.

"Don't say it," Royer warned.

"I'm not saying anything." Ward didn't think he needed to.

Royer punched in another number.

"Cruz."

"You got him?" Royer asked.

"Yeah, we're on him. He just came out the door." There was a pause. "He's getting into a white Chevy Volt."

"Of course he is," Royer said. "You know the location?"

"Hoyberg's on southeast Powell, right?"

"That's it."

"I'll let you know if we see any problems." Cruz terminated

the call.

Royer started the Prius and put it in gear. Ward was amazed by how quiet it was. The same was true between him and Royer. Little was said as they drove. Finally, Royer spoke.

"Look," he said, "sorry. Okay?"

Ward waved his hand as if to say, *don't worry about it.* "We're good."

"I really think this guy will be okay," Royer assured him. "He did good work for me before."

Ward nodded. History was the best indicator of how a cooperator would perform.

"I'm sure he'll be fine," Ward said. "A good track record tells the tale." He wondered if he was saying it as much to reassure himself as Royer.

When they were two blocks from Hoyberg's Royer again phoned Cruz."

"Any problems?" Royer asked.

"Nothing," Cruz replied. "He's by himself."

"Great. Thanks for your help."

Royer pulled into the Hoyberg's parking lot. The place was not overly busy. It appeared that they had hit the timeslot between breakfast and lunch when business cooled off. Maybe Royer had planned it that way. Ward wasn't yet willing to give him that much credit.

"There he is," Royer said.

The white Chevy Volt was parked at the end of the lot, well away from any other cars. The man standing next to it was tall and thin as a rail. He had the undernourished look of a vegan. The clothes were straight out of a Nirvana video. As they got closer, it appeared that Peavey might have skipped the shower that morning, and maybe the morning before. Ward had to admit, he wasn't overwhelmed with confidence.

Royer parked the Prius next to the Volt. "Here it goes," he said.

Ward gave him a single nod. "Here it goes."

Royer got out of the car, leaving the driver's door open. He approached Peavey. "Hello, Matthias," he said, extending his hand.

Peavey hesitated, but then accepted Royer's gesture. Ward noted the seeming change in the FBI agent's approach.

"You okay?" Royer asked.

"Like I have a choice?"

Royer smiled. "Let's go for a ride." He opened the rear passenger door and gestured for Peavey to get in.

Ward watched as Peavey climbed into the backseat. He appeared wary, but not nervous. That was good. Ward smiled at him. He'd wait for Royer to make the introduction.

Royer slid into the driver's seat, then turned back toward Peavey. "Matthias, I'd like you to meet Joshua Young."

"Nice to meet you, Matthias," Ward said. He reached back to offer his hand. "Please call me Josh."

Peavey shook hands. "Josh," he said, "I'm Matt."

"We really appreciate your help, Matt. Whoever is doing this is out of control. They don't care who they hurt."

Peavey nodded. "We never wanted to hurt anybody," he said.

"I know that," Ward assured him. "I know that."

Royer started the car and backed up. As he put it in drive and pulled away he made eye contact with Peavey in the rearview mirror.

"Now, here's the plan," Royer explained.

CHAPTER 34

12:18 p.m., Wednesday, May 3, Paxton Ford, Oklahoma City, Oklahoma

Special Agent Toby Combs had been on the first available flight after getting news of the fire early that morning. Fortunately, Denver being a hub, he was able to get out almost immediately. This was the Dallas field division's turf, but Leroy Wheeler had cleared it with the SAC in Dallas who was happy to have the help. Ian Maness had come with. That was fine with Combs. The more the merrier. And he suspected that there would be many more on this one. As Combs pulled into the Paxton Ford lot he could see that he had been right. The place was crawling with arson investigators and every other manner of law enforcement, federal, state and local.

"Holy shit!" Maness said.

Combs let out a low whistle. He had expected all hands-on deck, but what he saw before him was unprecedented. As he parked the rental Combs spotted two members of ATF's National Response Team. He wasn't surprised to see them. This case warranted sending the big dogs. He was sure that there were numerous ATF certified fire investigators on scene. If there was evidence to find, these guys would find it.

As they walked toward the dealership's showroom, or what was left of it, Combs saw something else, something not quite as welcome. Several individuals in navy blue windbreakers with the letters "FBI" across the back were interviewing what he assumed were employees of Paxton Ford. Arson scene or not, it was clear that the FBI was not going to let ATF control the scene.

"Look who's here," Combs said.

Maness snorted. "Big fucking surprise."

Combs consulted a local ATF agent. He pointed out the supervisor up from the Dallas field division who was in charge of the scene. It was damn rare to see a special agent in charge at the scene of an investigation.

"They sent the SAC?" Maness asked.

"Tells you a lot about how much attention this one is getting," Combs said.

They made their way over to where the SAC was standing. He was surrounded by half a dozen agents, but smiled when he saw them, almost as if they were long lost friends.

"You the fellas from Denver?" he asked, extending his hand.

"Yes, sir," Combs said. They introduced themselves and shook.

"I'm Jack Olin. Happy to have you here. We appreciate the help."

"Sir, isn't there an ASAC named Jack Olin in Houston?" Combs asked. "I talked to him on the phone a few years back. He got us some help on a lead down in San Antonio. Is he any relation?"

A few of the agents chuckled.

"Well, nice to finally meet you face-to-face," Olin said with a grin.

"Oh," Combs said, feeling a little sheepish.

"I took over in Dallas a few months ago," Olin added.

Combs nodded silently. He wasn't inclined to say much more at the moment.

"I know what you're thinking," Olin said. "Pretty rare to see a SAC onsite. Truth is, I miss being out in the field." He grinned. "I promise not to fuck it up too bad."

Combs immediately liked Olin. This guy sounded nothing like the politicians who usually inhabited the office. Combs was fortunate that his own boss, Wheeler, was much the same.

Olin grew serious. "One of the reasons I'm here is because this case is now being watched at the highest levels. You know what that means." He looked directly at Combs. "I'm not gonna hide down in Dallas with two levels of personnel between me and the action so that I can have some plausible deniability if things go to shit. We're in this together."

Combs studied the expressions of the others in the Dallas contingent. There was no hint of a smirk or a roll of the eyes. It appeared that they believed Olin and respected him.

"Sir!"

Combs turned to see an agent approaching. He had an older man in tow. The man appeared exhausted.

"Sir," the agent said, addressing Olin. "This is Fred Paxton, the owner."

"Mr. Paxton, I'm Jack Olin." Olin extended his hand. "I'm the special agent in charge of the Dallas field division."

"Pleasure to meet you," Paxton said. "Needless to say, I wish it was under different circumstances."

Olin nodded. "Understood, sir. I can assure you that ATF will do everything in its power to bring whoever is responsible to justice."

"I believe that," Paxton said.

The agent who had accompanied Paxton spoke up. "Sir, Mr. Paxton has some important information about the case. He has a security app on his cell phone that is linked to four of the surveillance cameras here at the dealership."

"Oh?" Olin appeared intrigued.

"Yes, sir," the agent said. He turned to Paxton. "Mr. Paxton, please tell us what you saw."

Paxton cleared his throat. "Well, like I was tellin' the agent here, the alert went off on my phone lettin' me know the camera had detected some kind of activity. It happens all the time. Usually, I ignore it. In fact, half the time I don't even have the thing turned on. But last night, I don't know, somethin' told me to check."

"What did you see?" Olin asked.

"At first all I saw was the fire, a few trucks burning. I called 9-1-1. As I was talkin' to the dispatcher, that's when I saw it."

"Saw what?" Olin leaned in, brow furrowed.

"Somebody dressed in black, head to toe, ski mask, the whole nine yards."

Combs looked at Maness who arched his eyebrow.

"It was only there for a second," Paxton continued, "then vanished."

"Is that camera footage stored someplace?" Olin asked.

Paxton and the agent both nodded.

"The cameras were destroyed in the fire," the agent said, "along with the footage stored on them. But, from what Mr. Paxton tells me, that information is stored on the cloud."

"Get a retention letter out to the app maker ASAP," Olin said. "Call them now so that they know it's coming. And make sure they appreciate the consequences of failing to comply."

"Yes, sir," the agent said.

Olin turned to one of the others in his entourage. "It's a long shot, but maybe we can use it for silhouette matching if we locate video of identified subjects to compare it to." He paused for a second. "Let's start canvassing the surrounding businesses, see if any of them have surveillance systems in place. Maybe one of them picked up something, a vehicle, maybe even a license plate number. Maybe a clerk at one of these all-night convenience stores around here saw something." Olin paused. "And start checking with local hobby shops, electronics and hardware stores. See if we can identify any suspicious purchases of the components for the incendiaries. They probably bought that stuff elsewhere and brought it in, but it's worth a shot."

Several members of the group moved off to follow-up on Olin's orders.

"How can we help?" Combs asked.

"Look around," Olin said. "FBI showed up in big numbers this morning. They have a lot of agents questioning employees. I want our people involved in those interviews. Butt in if you need to."

Combs smiled. "We can do that." He and Maness headed in different directions.

Combs headed back toward an area twenty yards or so in front of the burned-out showroom. Several folding tables and chairs had been set up there so that FBI agents could conduct interviews. He spotted a younger agent who was just starting an interview with a man Combs guessed to be a salesman. Combs walked up, made sure that the FBI agent saw his credentials, and pulled up a chair.

The agent shot him a look. "I got this," he said.

Combs checked his credentials. They identified him as Special Agent Dustin Wilkins.

"The SAC says we're involved in the interviews." Combs gestured with his thumb back toward where Olin was standing. "You wanna take it up with him?"

Wilkins sighed. "Fine." He turned his attention back to the interview subject.

"What's your name?" Wilkins asked, not looking up from his notepad.

"Mark Fuller."

"And what's your position here?"

"I'm a salesman."

Combs listened as Wilkins took Fuller through a series of questions designed to elicit his basic information: address, phone numbers, date of birth.

"How long have you worked here?"

Fuller shrugged. "I guess it's been about three years."

"You guess?" Wilkins asked.

For Chrissakes, Combs thought.

Fuller looked at Combs, then back to Wilkins. "Yeah...I'm pretty sure it's been just over three years."

"Any disputes with management over pay, promotions, anything like that?" Wilkins asked.

"You gotta be kidding me," Combs muttered.

Wilkins turned to Combs. "Excuse me?"

Combs ignored him. "Mr. Fuller, I'm Special Agent Toby Combs with the Bureau of Alcohol, Tobacco, Firearms and Explosives, otherwise known as ATF."

"Okay," Fuller said.

"I want you to know that you are not a suspect in this case or anything like that," Combs said. He shot a sideways glance at Wilkins. "We just want to ask you, and the other employees here, a few questions to see if we can develop any leads as to who might have done this. Okay?"

"Sure," Fuller said. "I want to help. Mr. Paxton has been good to me. I just don't think I know anything."

"Well, have you seen anything over the course of the last week or two that struck you as odd, anything out of the ordinary?"

"Can't say that I have."

Combs decided to ask it a different way. "Have you seen anyone who appeared to be nosing around where they shouldn't be, like they might casing the place?"

Fuller shook his head. "No."

Combs thought for a moment. "Has anybody said anything unusual or asked you anything out of the ordinary, maybe about security at the dealership, something like that?"

"Sorry," Fuller said. "Guess I'm not much help."

Combs looked at Wilkens, who had a smug look on his face.

"Okay," Combs said. "If you think of..."

"Wait a minute," Fuller interrupted. "There was that kid from Tulsa."

"What about him?" Combs asked.

"I remember. We covered half the lot looking at trucks. He made some comment about what a pain in the ass it must be providing security for the place. You don't think? He just seemed like a normal Oklahoma ranch kid." Fuller lowered his head. "Oh my God, I..."

Fuller looked sick. Combs felt sorry for him. "What did you

tell him?" he asked.

"I told him we have a security company that comes in at night...but that the guard usually falls asleep in his car parked behind the service center." Fuller buried his face in his hands.

Combs glanced at Wilkins, who failed to make eye contact.

"Okay, Mr. Fuller," Combs said. "Let's see if we can pin down some of the details."

CHAPTER 35

7:32 p.m., Wednesday, May 3, The Forest Glen Coffeehouse, Portland, Oregon

Ward had to admit that Matthias Peavey's first suggestion on where he might encounter members of Portland's hardcore environmentalist community seemed right on. The Forest Glen Coffeehouse screamed radical. From his perch at one of the corner tables, back to the wall, Ward could see posters and flyers promoting every sort of cause imaginable, and a few he couldn't have imagined. Some announced rallies to protest captive orcas or the exploitation of migrant workers. Others called for the release of this or that perceived political prisoner, at least one of the names recognizable to him as a cop killer. As for the patrons, the fact that he had no dreadlocks or piercings caused him to stand out. Ward glanced at his faint reflection in the coffeehouse window. The face that stared back was not one he would have thought might draw attention. Still, he wasn't quite prepared to sport dreads or get his lip pierced to sell it.

"And *you* had the latte, right?"

Ward turned to see the waitress set his drank on the table. She gave him a seductive smile. Or was that just wishful thinking? Normally a funky, nouveau grunge look would not appeal to him. But in this case it did nothing to hide a raw, ripe sexuality that could not be ignored.

"Yes I did," Ward said, smiling back at her.

The waitress did something like a half pirouette and looked back over her shoulder.

"Let me know if I can get you anything else," she said.

"I'll do that."

For a moment Ward forgot about the fact that Peavey was late. He suspected that the waitress made a lot of men forget about a lot of things. He also suspected that she made a lot in tips, including the substantial one that he would likely leave on the table.

Returning to reality, Ward checked his cell phone. Peavey had said a quarter after seven. Twenty minutes was not a big deal for a purely social engagement, but in this context it was a bad sign. Had Peavey lost his nerve, or worse? Ward told himself to relax and picked up his latte. It was then that he noticed the foam in the shape of a heart. He looked up to see the waitress behind the counter, preparing a drink. She was also one of the baristas. He looked back down at the foamy heart. No, couldn't be. It was probably just one of the easier shapes to make. He looked back up at her. She caught the glance, a sly smile appearing on her face. Ward started to seriously contemplate giving her something more than a tip. It was then that, out of the corner of his eye, he saw Peavey walk in.

Peavey scanned the room until his eyes found Ward. He nodded and headed toward the table. It was not the look of someone who had just spotted a friend. Ward would have to talk to him about that. The encounter had to appear normal, pleasant. Peavey would have to hone his acting skills. As he approached, Ward took the initiative.

"Hey, man. Good to see you," Ward said just loud enough as he stood to shake Peavey's hand. "Have a seat."

Peavey looked around as if to see if anyone was watching. *Jesus*, Ward thought. *This guy is going to take some work.*

"Take it easy," Ward said under his breath as they took their chairs. "Just be yourself."

"Got it," Peavey replied.

The same waitress as before appeared almost immediately.

"Can I get you something?" she asked Peavey.

"Espresso Macchiato," he said.

The waitress turned and leaned against the table. "How about you?" she asked Ward. "Can I get you anything else?"

"I'm good," Ward replied.

Ward thought he saw her nostrils flare ever so slightly as she gave him the once-over.

"I'm Naomi," she announced, lingering.

"My pleasure, Naomi. I'm Josh."

"Pleasure's all mine...Josh."

Ward struggled to remind himself why he was there. He nodded toward Peavey. "This is Matthias."

"Hello," Naomi said, barely taking her eyes off of Ward.

"Yeah, hi," Peavey said unenthusiastically.

Naomi turned to leave. She again glanced back over her shoulder, a move she had clearly perfected.

"Let me know if you need anything...Josh."

"Oh, I will," Ward replied.

Peavey watched the departing Naomi, then turned back to Ward. "Impressive," he said.

"Agreed." Ward hoped that their mutual appreciation of Naomi's form might help Peavey calm down. It would at least make the situation appear more natural.

"Anybody in here I should meet?" Ward asked.

Peavey took a quick look around. "Nobody too important," he said. "There's one guy over against the far wall. I've seen him at a few protests. Name's Jeb. Don't know his last name."

Ward wondered if that last part was true. In any event, they could use an introduction to Jeb as sort of a training run, iron out a few wrinkles before they encountered any of the major players.

"You know him well enough to make an intro?" Ward asked.

"Yeah, definitely," Peavey said. "I'll catch his eye, see if he comes over."

"Just remember what we talked about," Ward said. "Be yourself. Stick with comfortable subject matter. Once the intro is made, I'll take the lead and do most of the talking. I'll ask specific questions to keep you engaged. Above all, don't improvise."

"Yeah, I got it," Peavey said, sounding annoyed.

Ward doubted that, but, for now, Peavey was all he had to work with.

"Go ahead," Ward told him.

Peavey waited until Jeb looked his direction. When he did, Peavey gave him a smile and raised his hand in a casual wave. Ward saw Jeb excuse himself and rise from his chair to come over. *Here we go*, he thought.

"What's up, brah?" Jeb said as he approached.

Peavey stood. The two men exchanged a fist bump and then, to Ward's surprise, a brief hug combined with a couple quick pats on the back. The body language seemed to suggest that they were more than acquaintances. But Ward didn't yet have a thorough grasp of the culture. Maybe this was normal.

"How goes the cause?" Peavey asked.

"It's cool, man. It's cool."

"Hey, this is my man, Josh," Peavey said.

Ward knew them all but was a little unsure on what form of handshake to go with. Jeb solved the problem when he held up his fist, the bump apparently being his go-to.

"Josh Young," Ward said, fist up. "Good to meet you, man."

"Pleasure, Josh. It's Jeb Burke."

They took a seat. Ward listened as the two caught up. Jeb was between jobs but keeping himself busy with *the cause*. This apparently consisted primarily of protests and rallies. Ward heard no evidence of anything that hinted at actual monkeywrenching. Maybe Jeb just knew to keep quiet around a stranger, though Ward suspected that he was not really the hands-on type.

"Hey, there's a climate change protest on Saturday," Jeb said to Peavey. "You should come."

Peavey looked at Ward, seeming to ask for approval. Ward

gave an almost imperceptible shrug as if to say, *why not*. In fact, he was planning to invite himself, use it as an opportunity to work his way into their community.

"Where's it at?" Peavey asked.

"Holladay Park," Jeb said. "Starts at ten in the morning."

"I'll be there."

"That sounds like something I'd be interested in," Ward said. "Mind if I come with?"

Jeb smiled broadly. "Righteous, brah!" he said, raising his fist for another bump from Josh Young. "We'd love to have you there."

"Excellent," Ward said, seeing an opening. "If we can't break our addiction to fossil fuels and stop deforestation we'll destroy the planet and cause the extinction of almost every species on it, including our own. We've got to do something, even if it requires more direct action."

Jeb grew more somber. "I don't understand why everyone can't see that." He turned to Peavey. "I like the way your friend thinks."

"Yeah," Peavey said. "Me, too."

Ward noted Peavey's slightly sarcastic tone. He was fairly certain that Jeb had missed it, but it was one more thing that he would have to discuss with Peavey. For now, he had to focus on Jeb Burke.

"We've got to develop clean fuel sources and eliminate the use of coal and oil," Ward continued. In truth, he was concerned about global warming and the human activities that appeared to cause it. He just didn't share the belief that the solution required completely shutting down the world economy.

"Right on," Jeb said. "Right on."

It was a small first step in a difficult investigation, but Ward felt a spark of hope.

CHAPTER 36

8:37 a.m., Thursday, May 4, Southern Illinois University at Carbondale, Carbondale, Illinois

Ferret lowered his binoculars. It had been a long night, one of many. But now the day was close, the day when these murderers would pay for their actions. These so-called researchers who slaughtered Mother's creatures in the name of science would be made to suffer. This lab was the first of many that would be targeted by his new organization, the Earth Martyrs Brigade.

The early years as an activist with the Animal Liberation Front had been fulfilling, culminating for him with the masterful attack on the psychology laboratory at the University of Iowa. They had freed hundreds of animals, destroyed equipment, poured chemicals over data. Years of research were lost. They had even published the home addresses of the scum who worked there. The FBI was never able to successfully charge any of ALF's members. How it must have galled them to read the claims of responsibility on ALF's website and yet prove nothing. Once again he smiled at the memory.

Still, despite ALF's good works, he longed for more. The philosophy of the Earth Martyrs Brigade made sense to him. While ALF prided itself on never injuring humans, Ferret considered humans to be the enemy. Most could not be reformed. They were wasteful, indulgent, self-absorbed. Thus, to save Earth and its creatures, some humans would have to die. He understood that.

The Earth Martyrs Brigade understood that.

Surveillance over the course of several weeks by members of the Chicago cell had allowed them to establish the patterns of faculty, staff and interns working at the facility. They knew who arrived early, who stayed late. Campus security had also been monitored. They were beyond predictable. There were very clear windows of opportunity. Ferret was surprised and delighted by the lessons not learned here. There was no biometric entry system. It was as if these people were ignorant of the attacks of the past. He laughed. They were soon to learn a painful lesson.

Ferret watched and waited. These things took time. He could have followed some unsuspecting intern and stole their swipe card during a moment of inattention. He'd done it before, at bars, in the cafeteria, at the student fitness center. It wasn't terribly difficult but carried obvious risks. As good as he was, someone might see something, remember something. No, this was a better, safer method.

A young woman approached the entrance to the lab. Ferret raised his powerful binoculars. It was a distant view from this spot, but he couldn't risk getting closer, particularly given the long period of patient observation that was needed for this sort of thing. He could see her reach in her purse for the swipe card that would gain entrance. Ferret watched as she searched and searched. This could be it. He felt his pulse quicken. She couldn't find the card. He could see her frustration. Finally, she gave up, leaned down toward the keypad and punched in the code. His sight was unobstructed! Ferret repeated the numbers over and over as he reached for the small notepad and scribbled them down. Then, he picked up his phone and sent a one-word text: obtained.

Ferret dropped flat. He stayed low, crawling toward the industrial vent that had provided access to the roof. It was possibly the highest vantage point on university grounds. Still, one couldn't be too careful. It was a lesson learned through some close calls when he was younger, more excitable, and more careless. Since then he had perfected his skills. His small stature and slight build allowed him to gain entrance in ways that others could not. He had once even slipped into a lab through an air duct. That episode had earned him the nickname, one that Ferret cherished. He was proud to bear the moniker of those lovable, clever and stealthy little creatures. The fact that they were frequently used as test subjects made it even more appropriate.

This time it was mice and rabbits that would be liberated, provided with loving homes. The entry team was well-trained in quick extraction. If it became impossible to remove them all they would at least be freed so as to have a chance at survival. The alternative was certain death at the hands of their torturers. It was an easy choice. While that took place others in his group would search for whatever information they could find on lab personnel—names, addresses, birthdates, social security numbers, even the names of family members. All of this, along with a list of their crimes, would later be published for anyone to read and use as they saw fit. Suggestions as to that use would be made. And there were those who would make these peoples' lives hell, a hell they richly deserved, yet one that paled in comparison to the suffering they inflicted on Mother's beloved creatures.

Once all of the work onsite was accomplished, the lab would be destroyed. No small measures. It would be total destruction. They had promised him that. His only regret was that he could not directly participate in the annihilation of this hellish place. But that was how it had to be. He understood that. Another cell would perform that sacred task. It didn't matter. The message would be clear: the battle for liberation of Mother's creatures had risen to the level of total war.

CHAPTER 37

10:35 a.m., Friday, May 5, Bureau of Alcohol, Tobacco, Firearms and Explosives, Dallas Field Division, Dallas, Texas

Special Agent in Charge Jack Olin tossed the report on his desk. It was a quick summary of the findings to date on the Paxton Ford fire. Olin was generally pleased with the effort of his agents, but unhappy with the results. Even so, he couldn't claim to be surprised. These people knew what they were doing. In Olin's estimation they had taken the ELF playbook and improved upon it, if improved was the right word.

Olin turned to Assistant Special Agent in Charge Caroline Navarro who was in charge of the day-to-day operations in the case. She and Special Agent Mason Sherborn were the only others in the room. "Caroline, are we ready to proceed?"

"Yes, sir. Making the call."

Olin watched as Navarro punched in the numbers, first calling the SAC in Denver, Leroy Wheeler, then connecting Alex Burke in San Francisco. Wheeler was an old friend. Burke was not. Olin had experienced Burke's self-promoting behavior on more than one occasion. The man was not to be trusted and would be handled accordingly.

"Okay," Navarro said. "Everyone's on."

"Good morning, Leroy...Alex," Olin said. He could hear the disdain for Burke in his voice as he uttered the man's name and wondered if it was apparent over the phone.

"Morning, Jack. Thanks for arranging the call."

Olin recognized Wheeler's voice. "Not a problem, Leroy."

"Good morning, Alex," Wheeler added.

"Leroy, Jack."

And there was Burke. Olin waited to see if see if the San Francisco SAC added anything else. He did not. Olin looked at Navarro and rolled his eyes.

"I'm here with ASAC Caroline Navarro and Special Agent Mason Sherman," Olin announced. "Caroline is overseeing the case here, with my marginal assistance. Mason is our primary in the field. They'll provide most of the update."

"Hello, Caroline, Mason," Wheeler said. "I've known your boss for a long time. We'll talk."

Navarro laughed. "Can't wait," she said.

Olin smiled and shook his head. "Mutually assured destruction, Leroy."

"Fair enough," Wheeler said.

Olin paused to see if Burke added a greeting to the others. Nothing. Apparently he only spoke to subordinates to give orders.

"Alright then, let's get started." Olin turned to Sherborn. "Special Agent Sherborn will bring us up-to-date on what we've been able to find by canvassing the area surrounding the dealership."

"Wait a minute," Burke interrupted. "Shouldn't FBI be involved in this conference?"

"Oh, yeah," Olin said. "I guess I forgot to call them. He looked at Navarro, who covered her mouth. Olin could hear Wheeler's chuckle even over the phone.

"I just think…"

"Go ahead, Mason," Olin said, cutting off Burke.

"We've been interviewing staff at local hobby shops, electronics and hardware stores," Sherman said. "So far, nothing on that end of it."

"Not surprised," Wheeler interjected. "All of the components for the incendiary devices, other than the accelerant, were probably purchased somewhere else. I would guess out of state."

"Agreed," Olin said. "But you never know when somebody is going to get sloppy."

"True enough," Wheeler noted.

Sherman continued. "We've also talked to clerks at the convenience stores in the immediate area. None of them saw anything unusual, but the surveillance video from one of the stores may have provided something useful. It sits at an intersection about two blocks west of Paxton Ford. One of its surveillance cameras caught the image of a large white van at the stoplight. This was about twenty-five minutes before Fred Paxton saw the fire on his cell phone. Interesting thing is the van had Colorado plates."

"Could you get a number?" Wheeler asked.

"Only a partial," Sherman replied. "The angle, distance and a minor obstruction affected the view. We'll try to get the image enhanced, but I'm not hopeful on the plate number. Still, we might be able to pick up some other unique identifiers; dents, scratches, a dealership decal if we're lucky. It was a Chevrolet Express Cargo Van. They sell a lot of them. Even determining the model year is difficult because they don't change much."

"We're already running the plates...best we can," Navarro added.

"Hell, we'll run down the sale of every Chevy Express in the United States if we have to," Olin said.

"We can certainly do that," Navarro agreed. "We'll also request grand jury subpoenas for the phone records of known environmental radicals in this part of the country, see who they're talking to."

"I'm certain you gentlemen have done the same," Olin said. It would be fairly standard protocol for this type of investigation and he assumed that the other field divisions had taken those steps, but didn't want to risk offending his counterparts, at least Wheeler, by asking the question.

"We have," Wheeler noted. "Let's turn our records over to

ATF's analysts, see what they come up with."

"My thoughts exactly," Olin said. "Alex, is that agreeable?"

"That's acceptable," Burke said. "We are still waiting for records from a handful of phone companies who have been slow to respond, but we will make those available as soon as they are received."

"That's fine," Olin said. He suspected that Burke had not yet requested the subpoenas and that the slow response bit was just a cover story, but let it go.

"We should also get their text messages," Burke said, "subpoena their emails."

Olin looked at Navarro and Sherman. They appeared anxious. He knew why.

"As you're aware," Olin said, forcing himself to be as diplomatic as he could with Burke, "obtaining that type of content requires a search warrant, not to mention an identifiable suspect."

There was a brief pause, then Burke spoke. "Right," he said. "I just meant when we get to that point."

"Yeah," Olin said, "when we get to that point." Which had better be pretty damned soon, he thought.

CHAPTER 38

4:12 a.m., Saturday, May 6, Southern Illinois University at Carbondale, Carbondale, Illinois

There had been almost no movement around the lab for more than an hour. By now, most of the typical weekend student revelers had made their way back to their dorm rooms or apartments, or wherever it was they planned to spend the night. The last security check of the facility had occurred ten minutes earlier. If the surveillance team was right, no guard would be back through the area until sunrise. Now was the time. Mink raised her right hand and gestured them forward.

A half-dozen members of the Ann Arbor cell emerged from their hiding places and moved swiftly toward the entrance. Mink entered the code on the keypad and they were quickly inside. Surveillance cameras were identified, exactly where the drawings showed them to be. Within seconds the lenses had been covered by black spray paint, totally obscuring their view. Mink looked at the rabbits and mice penned in their small cages. They were agitated. Did they sense that freedom was at hand, that the torture would soon end? "It won't be long now," Mink promised.

They had brought in as many animal crates and carriers as could safely be transported without raising suspicion. It was not as many as Mink would have liked, but most such facilities had a large number of these on location. What had once been vehicles of death would now be vessels of freedom. Still, with only a half-dozen members of her crew present, it would be necessary to place several rabbits in each. Only so many trips to the transport vehicles would be possible. As for the mice, plastic containers had been brought in. Each of them could hold a large number of the animals. A hinged lid allowed for a mouse to be quickly placed inside without the risk of others escaping. The animals, once safely removed, would be placed with sympathizers throughout the network, caregivers who would treat them as equals, not as property. If there were too many to transport they would at least be given their freedom. Anything was preferable to the inhumane treatment received in this wretched place.

They set to work. One by one the rabbits were extracted from their cages and placed in the carriers. Some were difficult to catch, undoubtedly associating abduction by humans with pain and suffering. Mink held one white rabbit for a moment, attempting to comfort it as it struggled to get away. "We're here to free you, my love," she cooed. "The suffering is over." The rabbit became frantic and Mink lost her grip. She tried in vain to capture it but could not. The small creature escaped through an open door as one member of her team left with a loaded crate. Better free than imprisoned here, Mink thought. At least now the animal would have a chance. She grabbed another rabbit from a cage and quickly forced it into a carrier.

"We've found personal information!"

Mink turned to see the Quebecer standing beside her. His eyes gleamed with excitement.

"Names, addresses, even phone numbers," he said in his thick French accent. "An actual printed list."

Mink touched his arm. She loved seeing him like this. His passion for saving Mother's creatures matched her own. A veteran of the animal rights movement, he had helped hide members of ALF and ELF in Canada during the fallout from Operation Backfire. Most of them were still in the wind.

"How many?" she asked.

"The entire staff it would seem, including student interns."

Mink could feel her heart pound with excitement. How could

they be so stupid? Most facilities had learned to protect this information after the ALF attacks. Such a discovery was now rare. Oh how these monsters would pay. Everything about them would be posted on the internet, along with a list of their crimes. Appropriate retribution would be suggested, for them and their families, but only in the vaguest of terms. There were those who knew what to do.

Mink stroked her hand along the portion of the ski mask that covered the Quebecer's cheek. She wanted to kiss him but there was no time. They would make love later, still under the excitement of the moment, but far away from this place.

Mink returned to work. There were more animals than they had anticipated. Some would have to be freed instead of transported. She gave the order. Crates were carried outside and opened, the rabbits shooed into an adjacent woods. Most went that way, some did not. The mice scattered in all directions.

"Be free," Mink said as she placed one small rabbit under a tree. "Be free, my love." The rabbit sat motionless, seemingly unsure of what to do next. "Go now," Mink said. "Go!" The rabbit hopped off.

When the last of the animals had been removed Mink gave the order to destroy the lab. Acid was poured into the computers. Equipment was smashed. Papers and disks were gathered and piled together on the floor. Mink then ceremoniously dosed them with a mixture of gasoline and diesel fuel. That done, she nodded to the Quebecer. Moving components next to the pile, he quickly combined accelerant, timer and igniter into an incendiary device. Once the timer was armed he placed three more devices at strategic locations around the facility.

Time was short. Mink directed everyone except the Quebecer to leave. When they were gone she took him by the hand and turned to face him. The temptation was too strong.

"For Mother and her creatures," she said.

Mink raised that part of the ski mask covering the Quebecers mouth, at the same time uncovering her own. They embraced and shared a passionate kiss, then ran for the door.

Professor Leonard Whitmire surveyed the charred remains of his lab, of his life's work. He felt dizzy. The scene was surreal. He had already been told of the email in which some unnamed animal rights group claimed responsibility. The anger was there, and he knew would emerge in full force later. For now, it was overwhelmed by shock, by loss.

"Professor! Oh my God! Why?"

Whitmire turned to see Alicia Holstrom approaching. She was one of his most promising graduate assistants, a brilliant student with a bright future. She was crying. He was certain that she saw this as an insurmountable setback in the research for her dissertation. He put his arm around her as she wept on his shoulder.

"Why don't they understand?" she sobbed. "Don't they understand that what we do helps people, helps children?"

Whitmire was at a loss. He started to speak but was interrupted by a young reporter. He recognized the call sign on her microphone. She was with a St. Louis television station.

"Professor Whitmire?" the reporter inquired.

"Yes."

"I'm Natasha Colfax with KMSL TV in St. Louis. Do I understand that you're the chairperson of the Psychology Department here at SIU?"

"That's correct."

"Would you be willing to answer a few questions on air?"

Whitmire looked over the destruction, then studied the anguish in the face of his young student. "Yes, I would," he said.

Colfax signaled her cameraman. "We should be live in about thirty seconds," she said. "Is it Leonard Whitmire? Have I got that right?"

"That's correct."

Whitmire gently pried Alicia Holstrom loose and gathered his thoughts. There were some things he wanted to say, needed to say. He wanted viewers to understand what had really happened here, that this was terrorism, not the noble act of some animal welfare society. He watched as the reporter took her cue, briefly summarizing for the audience what was known so far, including the email.

"We're live with Professor Leonard Whitmire, Chair of the Psychology Department here at SIU. Professor, this must be a devastating loss for you and your staff."

"We've lost many years' worth of research," Whitmire said. "In particular, several members of our staff had made ground-breaking advances in understanding the causes of autism. I'd like to hear these so-called activists, whoever they are, explain their actions to the parents of a child suffering from that disorder."

"You mentioned so-called activists. Have the authorities told you anything about who they think is responsible?"

Whitmire shook his head. "No. Law enforcement has provided me with no specifics. My understanding is that the email did not name an individual or group."

Colfax held up a piece of paper. "I have the email here. It refers to you and your staff as torturers and sadists. Do you want to respond to that?"

Whitmire bristled. "I can assure you and your audience that we observe the strictest protocols governing animal testing so as to ensure the most humane treatment possible. People need to remember that without this testing science would not be able to discover the causes and cures for the most horrible afflictions facing humanity. Every drug is tested on animals before being tested on humans. How do you tell a mother that her dying child could not be saved because we couldn't test a potentially lifesaving drug?" Whitmire felt the anger start to take over. "And there's something else your viewers need to know. The people who did this simply released many of these animals on campus. I'm told that two of our white rabbits were hit by cars. Those are the ones we know about. I can promise you that many more will be killed by predators, as will the mice."

Colfax spun to face the camera. "And there you have it. This is Natasha Colfax, KMSL TV, reporting live from Carbondale, Illinois."

Whitmire decided that Colfax must have sensed she was about to completely lose control of the interview. She was correct. Maybe he should be glad that she had cut him short, stopped the impending tirade. But he wasn't. He was mad and wanted the world to know.

CHAPTER 39

10:25 a.m., Saturday, May 6, Holladay Park, Portland, Oregon

It was a small park, one city block, and thick with trees. Nonetheless, turnout for the climate change protest was good. Ward estimated the crowd at around three hundred. It was a fairly diverse group. Many resembled the crowd at the coffeehouse: dreads, piercings, tattoos. Others were more mainstream in appearance. Then there were the sketchy sorts, those who regularly prowled the area, less concerned with climate change than with their next target.

Signs and placards decried fossil fuels and deforestation, condemned Big Oil and its political lackeys, extolled the use of clean energy sources such as wind and solar. Much of it Ward could agree with. Some of it, however, was unrealistic and naïve. There was no question that climate change was a serious problem, but it was one that he thought should be resolved through peaceful, democratic and economically sound means. He was concerned that the activities of extremists made it vastly more difficult for legitimate environmentalists to accomplish their objectives.

Ward strolled through the crowd, occasionally exchanging a nod or greeting with those who met his gaze. As he waited for Peavey he tried to identify the individuals likely to fall in the radical camp. He knew better than to make judgments based on appearance. Any veteran of law enforcement knew that many of the most dangerous perpetrators looked like your next-door neighbor. Ward studied the signs, listened to the rhetoric, tried to spot those advocating a more hands-on approach. After several minutes of this he thought that he caught reference to the term *monkeywrenching*. It was a term synonymous with sabotage for those in the movement. Ward couldn't hear what else was said in conjunction with its use. He scanned the crowd immediately around him. One young man was gesturing wildly, making animated comments as the crowd around him nodded its approval. There was a fiery gleam in his eye, a look that Ward had seen before. He moved closer.

"They're not gonna stop on their own," the young man said, "not while there's money to be made! They let us fight and die in Iraq to protect their oil profits!"

Several in the crown murmured their agreement.

"We've got to stop them!" the protestor continued. "No more drilling! No more fracking! And no more pipelines!"

Ward listened for a few minutes. He doubted that a true saboteur would draw this much attention to himself in an open forum. And the comments, while provocative, were not exactly a direct incitement to violence. Ward suspected that the people he was looking for watched and listened at events like this, and sometimes, only sometimes, recruited. That's what he wanted: to be recruited.

As he stood there, Ward saw Peavey's friend, Jeb Burke, approach.

"Hey, Josh!" Jeb said. "Glad you could make it, brah." He followed with the obligatory fist bump. Jeb nodded toward the speaker. "That guy's full of shit, man. No chance he'd ever chain himself to the gate of a nuke plant. He comes to these things to hook up."

Ward laughed. "Is that right?"

"Just watch him. Makes a big speech, gets some young thing entranced, and then it's back to his place to smoke and have at it." Jeb chuckled. "Not that there's anything wrong with that. Am I right, brah?"

"Not at all," Ward agreed. He hoped that Jeb wasn't now going to invite him to smoke pot. If it was a matter of life and death he'd do it but use of controlled substances by an undercover was frowned upon. His usual way out was to claim to be a recovering addict. That usually worked.

"Look, there he goes now," Jeb said.

Ward saw a young girl scribble something on a piece of paper, presumably her phone number, and hand it to the speaker. She appeared to be no more than seventeen or eighteen, a high school kid. He desperately wanted to go over and warn her or rip the phone number from the guy's hand. It was one of those moments, like so many before, where a small wrong could not be righted. He had to focus on the greater mission.

"There's Matthias," Jeb said, waving at Peavey.

About fucking time, Ward thought. He could see that his comments to Peavey on tardiness had accomplished nothing.

"What's up?" Peavey asked unenthusiastically.

"Not much," Jeb answered. He studied Peavey. "You look rough, brah. Long night?"

"You could say that," Peavey replied.

"Righteous," Jeb said, holding up his fist.

Peavey did look rough. What the hell was that about, Ward wondered? He needed this guy to be sharp.

"Yeah, righteous," Ward said. Peavey looked at him, then quickly looked away.

"Give us the blow-by-blow, man," Jeb said.

Ward arched his eyebrows and waited.

"Later," Peavey said.

"Uncool, brah." Jeb shook his head. "Uncool."

In the middle of the park was a fountain. Water shot from the ground in small dancing bursts, forming arches through which children ran and played. A small stage had been set up nearby. Ward noticed that a man was preparing to speak. Most of the crowd had gravitated toward him. It was apparent that this was someone more respected than the speaker they had been listening to.

"Who's this guy?" Ward asked.

"Ben Cahill," Peavey said. "You'll want to hear him."

They walked toward the stage. Jeb excused himself to go speak with someone. Peavey looked around, then leaned toward Ward.

"Cahill is former ELF," Peavey said softly.

Ward nodded.

"He's unrepentant," Peavey continued. "But you'll hear no specific call for direct action. He knows how far to take it. He also knows that the message is understood."

Cahill began. He used no microphone, and no notes. He railed against Big Oil, coal-fired power plants, the automobile industry, deforestation, both major political parties and half a dozen other things. The crowd was more than receptive, true believers. While Ward agreed with some of Cahill's views, it appeared that the man wanted to return the world to an eighteenth-century agrarian lifestyle. The comments were devoid of economic realism or any understanding of geopolitics. Nonetheless, Ward had a role to play and he would play it. When Cahill asked for questions or comments from the crowd, Ward let a few others take their turn and then jumped in.

"We need more clean sources of energy: wind, solar, geothermal," Ward said. "The science is there. The oil companies, their lobbyists and the politicians they own are simply preventing full implementation of these technologies so that they can maximize their dirty profits."

"Amen to that, brother," Cahill said.

Ward continued. "My belief is that there will be no change without direct action by us, the citizens." He looked around, gesturing with both arms at the people who surrounded him. "Our planet is under assault. All species are threatened. Are we not entitled to defend ourselves?"

The crowd expressed its agreement. Ward could hear the chatter calling for more hands-on measures. He could see Cahill studying the group and its response to his provocations.

"If you ask me," Ward said, "we should shut down the power plants, stop the assembly lines that churn out the gas-guzzlers, prevent the lumber companies from raping our forests, and throw out the politicians who lack the will to stop the desecration of Mother Earth."

The crowd grew louder in its approval. Many of those assembled touched the man who spoke the truth. Some became agitated, ready to march to wherever they were needed to do whatever was necessary. Ward could see that Cahill was now studying him, avoiding direct incitement himself, but nodding his head in clear agreement with what was said.

Ward watched Cahill closely as he spoke his final words to the crowd. "We should do these things using all means at our disposal!"

Ward saw Cahill smile. Joshua Young would soon introduce himself to the former member of ELF.

CHAPTER 40

9:53 a.m., Monday, May 8, Oden's Flower Basket, Boulder, Colorado

Toby Combs pulled up in front of the small flower shop and parked. Over the course of the last few days he and Maness had interviewed the owners of thirty-two Chevy Express Cargo Vans. With a partial plate number the Colorado Division of Motor Vehicles had come up with eighty-three possible matches to the van seen on the convenience store surveillance video. And those were only the white ones. God help them if it had been painted since the attack. Fortunately, almost half of them served as delivery or service vehicles for some business and had the company name or logo painted on the side. While it was possible that a savvy criminal might simply have added a logo sometime in the intervening days, Combs knew that was unlikely given the established nature of most of the businesses. For now they were focusing on the unadorned white vans, their most likely match.

Combs turned to his partner. "Remind me of the name on the registration."

"Oden," Maness replied. "Linda Oden."

Combs turned off the ignition. "How old?"

"Twenty-nine."

"Okay. Let's go talk to Linda Oden."

They approached the flower store. It was small, occupying the middle space in a one-story commercial structure that also contained a bike shop and a coffeehouse. As they entered, a small bell above the door announced their arrival. There were no customers. A young woman appeared from the back of the store. She was rather plain and wore no discernible makeup but was not unattractive. Her long brown hair was tied back in a ponytail. She wore a flannel shirt tied off at the waist, hiking shorts and boots. A variety of simple braided necklaces and bracelets completed the look. It was what Combs referred to as the "nature girl" look.

"Hi. May I help you?" the young woman asked cheerily. A radiant smile changed her from plain to pretty.

"I hope so," Combs said. He flashed his badge. "I'm Special Agent Toby Combs, Bureau of Alcohol, Tobacco and Firearms. This is Special Agent Ian Maness."

Maness nodded.

"Okay," the young woman said. Her smile started to fade.

"We're looking for a Linda Oden," Combs said.

"I'm Linda." The smile had now completely vanished.

Combs found himself disappointed. He preferred it when his suspects looked the part. But then, with this case, maybe this did constitute looking the part.

"We'd like to ask you a few questions." Combs said.

Oden's brow furrowed. "About what?"

"Your van, among other things."

Oden crossed her arms over her chest. Combs read it as more of a defensive gesture than one of defiance. He was sure of it when she put one foot in front of the other and began to rock, almost imperceptibly, back and forth.

"What about my van?"

Maness spoke up. "Is there someplace we could sit down?"

Oden hesitated for a moment, then nodded. "Follow me."

She escorted them to the back of the store and to a table that she clearly used to prepare arrangements. Two dozen or so loose flowers were spread out next to an empty vase.

"Let me clear these away," Oden said. She quickly moved the

items and pulled up some chairs. "Please, sit."

When they were seated, Combs pulled out a notepad and began. "So you do own a white Chevy Express Cargo Van, correct?"

Combs studied Oden. She adopted a quizzical look as she glanced back and forth between he and Maness.

"What's this all about?" she asked.

Combs didn't want to make this antagonistic, at least not yet, but he knew better than to let a subject direct the interview. "I'm sorry. I'm going to need you to just answer the question."

Oden sat back in her chair, again crossing her arms. "Yeah…I have a van like that."

"Where is it?" Combs asked.

"It's parked out back. Why?"

Combs placed his pen on the table and took a breath. "Ms. Oden, this will go faster if I ask the questions and you answer them. Okay?"

Oden was silent for a moment, staring at the table. Combs knew what that could mean. She was thinking about whether any further answers might implicate her, and whether she should ask for a lawyer. He was surprised it seemed to be happening this quickly. It was one reason why agents usually didn't read the Miranda rights to an interview subject unless they had to. They didn't want to plant the seed. She was not in custody, so no Miranda rights were read to her. Combs wondered if her hesitation meant that someone had prepped her for this, the possibility that the feds could come knocking. She looked up at him, her eyes narrowing slightly, lips pressed together in a thin line.

"Go ahead," she said.

"What's the van used for?" Combs asked.

"Uh, deliveries," Oden said, her tone sarcastic. She gestured at her surroundings. "You may have noticed that I run a flower shop."

Combs sighed. He glanced over at Maness, who rolled his eyes.

"Where were you last Tuesday night and during the early morning hours of the following Wednesday?"

"At home."

"Can someone verify that?"

"You mean like a roommate or something? No. I live alone." Oden paused for a second, then spoke. "Wait a minute. I downloaded a movie through my Amazon account. I assume you have the capacity to check that, right? Isn't that what you people do, look at citizen's phone records, see what they've searched on the internet?"

Combs was developing an intense dislike for Linda Oden. But he'd been here before. *Keep it professional*, he reminded himself. *It's a big case.*

"Would you be willing to give us your password to verify that?"

"If it makes you go away."

Combs chuckled. He did that sometimes when he wanted to strangle somebody. "Okay. What is it?"

Oden gestured with her hand as if to say, *give it*. Combs tore a sheet from his notepad and slid it over to her, along with his pen. She scribbled something on the paper and passed it back to him. Combs read it. He smiled. Her password was flowergirl@420. Instinctively, he looked around the room for any indicators of cannabis cultivation. Seeing none, he passed the note to Manass, who laughed.

Oden smirked. "Glad you two are amused."

"Moving on," Combs said. "Have you loaned the van to anyone, or has it been on loan to anyone, at any point during the last two weeks?" He phrased the question carefully, knowing how interview subjects would become super literal when in a pinch.

Oden hesitated, looked away. Combs antennae went up. It was beginning to seem that whoever had prepped her had forgotten a few things.

"I think I'd like to call a lawyer," Oden said.

Combs glanced over at Maness. They exchanged an almost

imperceptible nod.

"Ms. Oden," Combs said, "thank you for your time. We'll show ourselves out."

Linda Oden did not look up.

As soon as they were outside and in the car Combs dialed the Denver field division. He was quickly connected to the SAC's office.

"What's up, Toby?" Wheeler asked.

"Boss, I think we've got something here," Combs said. "I thought I should pass it on to you directly."

"Shoot."

Combs described his interview of Linda Oden, sparing few details.

Wheeler grunted. "I'll call Jack Olin. Then I'll talk with the U.S. Attorney myself. Tell him we've got one they might want to put in front of the grand jury."

CHAPTER 41

6:21 p.m., Monday, May 8, Green Glow Cafe, Portland, Oregon

To his relief it was Cahill who suggested they meet. Ward knew that if he had been forced to make the invitation it might have raised suspicion. There was little doubt that a guy like Cahill had stayed mostly under the radar by being wary of those who approached him. Intelligence had confirmed what Peavey said at the rally, Cahill was former ELF, unrepentant. There had not been enough to build a case on him. ATF believed that he was possibly still active. His careful comments and body language when they spoke on Saturday told Ward that this conclusion was likely accurate. There was nothing overt, of course. Cahill was far too cautious for that.

Joshua Young would be thoroughly vetted before Cahill even considered bringing him into the fold. Tonight, it would likely be Cahill asking most of the questions, and Josh Young had better have the right answers. The wild card was Peavey. He would not be present tonight. Ward could not discount the possibility that Peavey might have tipped off Cahill, either out of a misguided sense of loyalty or a miscalculated attempt at self-preservation. It was a constant risk with informants and, as always, had Ward on edge.

They were to meet at six-thirty. Ward came early to assess the surroundings. From what he could see and hear, Green Glow Café made The Forest Glen Coffeehouse look like a den of conservative thought. Given the pungent smell, and the number of lighters he had seen flick to life, Ward suspected that the vast majority of the café's patrons were quite high. That could be useful if lowered inhibitions led to increased chattiness. He wondered if Cahill would partake. He also wondered if Cahill would expect him to do the same. That could be problematic. His recollection was that public use was still prohibited. Even though apparently not enforced here, he could hang his hat on that prohibition or the time-honored recovering addict routine.

Ward looked at his watch. It was six-thirty on the nose. He looked up to see Cahill walking through the door. He was surprised. Some preconceived notion had caused him to expect the man to be late. Ward reminded himself to be careful about that. As tempting as it sometimes might be, any susceptibility to thinking in stereotypes was dangerous for an undercover agent. Expect the unexpected was a worthy mantra in his profession.

Cahill spotted Ward and started in his direction. On the way he exchanged greetings with several people. The man appeared to be well known at Green Glow Café.

"Josh, how are you?" Cahill said as he extended his hand.

Ward rose from his chair. Cahill's traditional handshake was another surprise. But then, the man was in his late forties.

"I'm good," Ward said. "Thanks again for the invitation."

They sat.

"Well, I thought we should get to know each other," Cahill said, settling in. "Your comments at the protest impressed me. It's always good to meet someone of the same...philosophy."

Ward read this last word as a signal that things might go in the direction he had hoped. *Take it slow*, he thought. *Don't appear too eager*. "There are few issues more important," he said.

Cahill leaned forward. "I would suggest that there is no issue more important than survival of the planet."

"Fair enough." Ward looked around. "Interesting place. Are you a regular?"

Cahill smiled. "I come here for the food and the lively debate, not the marijuana. Gave it up years ago. Found it was dulling the senses, stealing my drive." He paused and leaned back in his chair. "Besides, now that it's legal…it loses some of the thrill."

Ward chuckled. "Understood." Again, stereotypes, he thought.

"Feel free," Cahill said. "Don't let me stop you."

"I quit two years ago," Ward lied. "It was becoming more lifestyle than recreation."

"Exactly."

A waiter arrived to take their order. Ward ordered one of the vegan sandwiches and a beer, an ale from one of the local breweries. Cahill did likewise.

"So, what do you do for a living?" Ward asked.

"Organic farming," Cahill said. "Got in on it early. I've got a place southeast of the city. Business has been good."

Ward nodded. "Glad to hear it. A changeover to sustainable farming practices is absolutely necessary for our survival. Of course, I don't have to tell you that."

"Corporate farms are poisoning the earth with their fertilizers and pesticides," Cahill agreed. "Look at the dead zone in the Gulf of Mexico caused by the runoff."

Ward shook his head. "Why can't people see it? We should all eat nothing but organically produced foods."

"No argument from me."

Cahill nodded at an acquaintance on the other side of the room and then turned back to Ward.

"What do you do, Josh?" he asked.

This was a critical moment. Ward knew that he had to be convincing yet provide only that information necessary to answer Cahill's questions. *Stick to the cover story*, he thought. *No ad libbing.* "I'm a software designer for Blue World Systems," he said. "It's a tech company located in San Francisco."

"What brings you to Portland?"

"I live here. I've got a place in Hawthorne, not far from the Bagdad Theatre. They let us telework."

"Wave of the future," Cahill said, "and better for the environment. No commuting means no emissions."

"Absolutely right," Ward agreed. "It was one of the things that sold me on the company."

"Where did you grow up?"

"Boston." A fictional history had been established in Massachusetts that would withstand all but the most intense scrutiny. Still, Ward knew all too well that no cover was perfect, not if those who wanted to know checked deep enough. A recent case had proved that point.

"Long way from home," Cahill noted.

Ward nodded.

"Significant other?" Cahill asked, continuing the inquiry.

"Not anymore," Ward said. "But that's how I ended up in Portland. I'll just leave it at that." It was a good answer, one that Cahill was unlikely to pursue, and one that could be used to explain many loose ends.

Cahill nodded. "Enough said."

"In any event, I like it here. My kind of people."

Cahill looked around the room. "Couldn't agree more." He paused for a moment. "So, where did you go to college?"

"Boston University," Ward replied. It seemed that the questioning was going beyond mere conversation. Or was it? Suspicion was a friend, but paranoia was a foe. It was a fine line, one that was hard to walk. Maybe he was simply failing to hold up his end of the conversation.

"Good school," Cahill noted.

"Loved it there," Ward said. "Best four years of my life." Again, arrangements had been made in case of inquiry. There were even transcripts, with a very respectable grade point average.

The waiter brought their food and drinks.

Cahill raised his beer in a toast. "To sustainable living."

Ward clinked his glass against Cahill's. "To sustainable living." He took a drink. The beer was excellent.

They ate and chatted amiably for the next fifteen minutes. Ward managed to turn the conversation away from the history of Joshua Young and toward that of Ben Cahill. Cahill, like most people, was quite happy to talk about himself, and Young was a good listener. It ended when Cahill spotted someone he knew and flagged her over. A slender brunette approached. Her movements were catlike as she slid between the tables on her way toward them. As she drew close, Ward could see the eyes: dark, intense, serious. The woman and Cahill embraced, kissed each other's cheeks. To Ward's eye it was not a gesture of love or sexual desire, but one of respect, and perhaps a camaraderie born of a shared cause. When the two separated, Cahill turned to Ward.

"Fern, I'd like you to meet a new friend, Joshua Young."

The way Cahill said it seemed to constitute some sort of signal, an approval. Still, Ward was surprised when Fern leaned in to hug him. When she let go he spoke.

"Nice to meet you, Fern." Along with Cahill, she would be mentioned in the report he would write later. "I'm sorry. I didn't catch your last name."

She smiled. "It's just Fern."

Ward felt the hairs on the back of his neck stand up.

CHAPTER 42

9:48 a.m., Wednesday, May 10, United States District Court for the Western District of Oklahoma, Oklahoma City, Oklahoma

"You're up."

Assistant United States Attorney Katherine Delgado turned to see her colleague exit the grand jury room. It was her turn. She was about to present the first witness in what could turn out to be one of the biggest cases of her career. What would happen next was anybody's guess.

The grand jury was six months into their one-year term. As was typical by this point in their tenure, they had now heard about enough murder and mayhem in their little corner of the world to be thoroughly disgusted and ready to indict. Most members eventually came to see themselves as an arm of law enforcement. They were part of the team. This group was no different. Delgado had seen it many times. When a new grand jury came in they had exaggerated notions of governmental overreach, media-driven ideas that the innocent were often falsely accused and railroaded. They were quickly dissuaded by what they heard in the room she was about to enter. What they actually saw, in almost all instances, was the professionalism and thoroughness of the officers, agents and prosecutors who appeared before them. Delgado wished that all Americans could experience service on a grand jury.

Delgado walked to the small witness room to fetch Linda

Oden. From what she had read in the reports Oden's cooperation was anything but certain. The woman had attitude. Toby Combs had described her using the technical law enforcement term, *a piece of work*. Still, Delgado knew that there was something different about being under oath in front of the grand jury. The candor displayed by the previously recalcitrant often amazed her. Delgado opened the door.

"Okay, Linda. Are you ready?"

"Ready as I'm gonna be," Oden said, her arms crossed defiantly. "You subpoenaed me. What choice do I have?"

Delgado ignored the question. "Let me remind you of a few things before we go in there. I'll ask most of the questions. The grand jurors can also ask questions, but most don't. Still, it is their right. If they delve into something personal that has nothing to do with why we're here I'll try to rein them in a bit. Okay?"

"Sure. Thanks so much."

Delgado was developing an intense dislike for Oden. *Keep it professional*, she thought. "I'll also read you your rights," she continued. "We call it an 'advice of rights.' We do this with every civilian witness that goes in front of the grand jury. I don't want you to feel like I'm singling you out."

"Oh, no. I don't feel like you're singling me out at all. I'm sure everybody gets to do this at one point or another."

Delgado could feel the smirk on her face. She'd had enough of Oden's shit. It was go time. "Alright," she said. "Let's get in there." Delgado pointed to the door.

They walked down the hall to the entrance to the grand jury room. Delgado unlocked the door and ushered Oden inside. She pointed to the witness stand and to a man standing alongside it.

"Go up there," she said curtly. "The foreperson will swear you in."

Oden was hesitant as she approached the witness stand, now fully out of her element. The foreperson asked her to raise her right hand. She affirmed that she would tell "the truth, the whole truth, and nothing but the truth."

We'll see about that, Delgado thought. She spread her notes on the podium that faced the witness stand and began.

"Please state your full name for the record and spell it," Delgado said, her tone purposely stern. The friendly approach had already failed.

"Linda Marie Oden." She spelled it.

"And how old are you?"

"Twenty-nine."

"At this point I'm going to read you your rights," Delgado said. "Please listen carefully." She read through the advice of rights given to civilian witnesses.

"Do you understand those rights?" Delgado asked.

"Yeah, I suppose," Oden said.

"Well, do you understand them or not?"

"Yeah."

Delgado saw several grand jurors roll their eyes. They already had this woman figured out. She started in with the questions. "Where do you live?"

"Boulder, Colorado."

"And what is your occupation?"

"I own a flower shop."

Delgado looked at the grand jury. She could see that they were a bit puzzled as to why this young woman was appearing before them. It would become clear soon enough.

"Do you own a Chevy Express Cargo Van?" Might as well get right to it, Delgado thought.

Oden hesitated, and then answered. "Yes, I own a van like that."

"I'm not asking if you own a van like that. I'm asking if you own a Chevy Express Cargo Van. Do you?" Delgado had learned the importance of a getting an exact answer on the record, particularly with an evasive witness.

Oden appeared agitated. "Yes. I own a Chevy Express Cargo Van." She looked at the grand jurors. "I use it for the business: to haul supplies, make deliveries, that sort of thing."

"Is it white?"

"Excuse me?"

"The van, is it white?"

Oden sighed. "Yes. It's white."

"Did you loan the van to anyone at any point during the period from, let's say, the last week in April of this year through Monday, May eighth?" It was the money question, the one that could open the door.

Oden stared straight at Delgado. There was an odd look of contentment about her, a sort of peacefulness. It was if she had just come to terms with her place in the world. "I refuse to answer on the grounds that I may incriminate myself."

Delgado heard one of the jurors gasp. She, on the other hand, was not completely surprised. "So, you're invoking your Fifth Amendment right?" she asked.

"I am."

Oden's look of contentment was gone. To Delgado, she now appeared smug.

"So be it," Delagado said. She turned to the foreperson. "May the witness be excused?"

"She may," the foreperson replied.

Delgado escorted Oden from the witness stand to the door. When they were outside the grand jury room Delgado stepped in front of the uncooperative witness. She kept it short and to the point. "We'll be in touch. You can count on it."

As Oden stepped back, Delgado could see it in her eyes, the flicker of doubt.

Delgado stomped down the hall of the U.S. Attorney's Office, getting more pissed off with each step. She couldn't shake the image of Oden, so smug and self-satisfied, her cause so righteous. What a load of shit. She was a criminal, a terrorist, just like the rest of them.

Delgado zeroed in on the criminal chief's office. She could

hear that he had someone in there. She didn't give a shit. She forged right in.

"Oden pled the Fifth," Delgado announced, interrupting the conversation in progress.

Criminal Chief Lester Madden raised his hands, palms up, as if to ask, *what the hell?*

"Sorry," Delgado said. "I'm just so fucking…"

"Calm down, Kate," Madden said. "Take a breath."

Delgado did just that. It helped, a little.

"How far into it did you get?" It was Delgado's friend and colleague, Emily Vaughn. "Did she admit anything?"

"Yeah, she admitted that she owned a white van, the right make and model. It was when I asked her if she had loaned it to anybody from late April through last Monday."

"So she definitely knows something," Madden said. "Question is, how much?"

"Yep." Delgado knew the route she wanted to go. "I say we get her immunity, force her to testify. Then she can either answer the questions or be found in contempt and sit in jail until she gets her shit together."

Madden nodded. "I'll talk to the U.S. Attorney."

Oden waited until she was several blocks from the courthouse and then retrieved the cell phone from her purse. She punched in the number and pressed call. They were throwaway phones, safe. That's what he'd told her. He answered almost immediately.

"How did it go?" he asked.

"I did it," Oden answered, "just like you said." She could hear the excitement in her own voice. She loved to please him.

"I'm proud of you," he said. There was a pause. Then, he spoke again. "For Mother."

Oden closed her eyes. "For Mother," she said softly.

CHAPTER 43

1:36 p.m., Wednesday, May 10, The Biscuit, Portland, Oregon

Ward glanced in the rearview mirror. Nothing seemed unusual. His circuitous route had exposed no tail. But that didn't mean no one was there. On this occasion additional precautions had been taken. The Prius that he was using as an undercover vehicle had been swapped for another car, one that was left for him in the parking lot of a large home improvement retailer a half mile back. If anyone noticed his vehicle at the store its presence was easily explained; he was planning some renovations to his apartment. If they saw the swap, well, that was another matter. Ward knew that it was probably too early for his activities to have raised any serious suspicions, but you could never be too careful, not when an informant like Peavey was involved. What seemed like overkill could keep you from getting killed.

The building was straight ahead. He could see the sign, *The Butler Biscuit Company*. It was time to visit the safe house, debrief, write some reports, talk to Cruz and Royer about their next steps, and take a break from being in character. Over the years he had found that the reprieves from playing his role were essential to his mental well-being. Besides, it would just be nice to have a conversation with normal people, to the extent that Cruz and Royer could be considered normal. Ward laughed. Maybe he didn't even know what normal was anymore.

Ward turned left, then left again and pulled into the alley

behind the building. He parked and sat for a moment, watching, listening. There was no movement in the alley. No cars passed by its entrance. Satisfied that no one had followed him, Ward quickly exited the car and strode toward the heavy steel door that served as the back entrance. He unlocked it and shoved it open with his shoulder. Inside, he could see the industrial elevator to his right. Ward remembered his last ride on the old relic, not sure he would get out with his life. He briefly eyed the stairs. Then, with considerable hesitation, he pushed the up button. When the doors opened he took a deep breath and stepped inside.

Somewhat claustrophobic anyway, Ward had a particular fear of being trapped in an elevator. He was trying to confront it, and this contraption was a real test. The modern versions were bad enough, but at least people could be summoned, there was a way out. This thing, however, didn't appear to be up to anybody's code. He clutched the handrail as the rumbling, shuddering ascent seemed to last an eternity. When the elevator finally reached his floor Ward prepared to jump out, forgetting what had happened last time. Again, there was a sudden jerk, after which the car dropped several inches, causing Ward to lose his balance. When the doors did clank open he scrambled out, cussing the old beast as if it were personal.

Regaining his composure, Ward unlocked the door to the loft and stepped inside. Royer was sitting at the table, clicking away at one of the laptops. Apparently lost in thought, he gave a half-assed wave. Cruz was in the kitchen making coffee.

"Have you had lunch?" Cruz asked.

"Actually, no," Ward answered. In fact, he was feeling hungry.

"Good." Cruz tossed him a sandwich, still in its wrapper.

"What is it?"

"I don't know. Some deli combo thing," Cruz said. "It's good. Just eat it."

Ward obliged. It was good. "What have you got to drink?" he asked.

Cruz looked in the fridge. "Not much. Too early for a beer?"

"A little early and I'm on duty…sort of." He jerked his head toward Royer. "Besides, the FBI is here."

Royer looked up from his laptop. "What the fuck?"

Cruz feigned shock. "I didn't think FBI agents were allowed to swear."

"Hoover was known to prefer *what the copulate*," Ward quipped.

Royer shook his head. "Funny," he said, and went back to whatever he was typing.

"I'll take some of that coffee when it's done," Ward said. He took his sandwich over to the table where Royer was seated and pulled out a chair.

Royer glanced up. "Sorry. Just want to get this email sent."

"Take your time," Ward said. He took another bite of his sandwich.

"There," Royer said. "Done and sent." He looked up at Ward. "So, what's been happening?"

"I'm meeting the right people. I've got good feeling about it. It's just gonna take time."

"Yeah," Royer said, "about that. The pressure is really ramping up. Did you hear about the attack on the lab at Southern Illinois?"

Ward nodded. "Sounds like ALF. Not so?"

Royer shook his head. "We don't think so. ALF was always quick to claim credit. That didn't happen. This looks a little bit more like what we've been dealing with. Might be former ALF members who want to be part of a more radical organization."

Cruz joined them, placing three mugs of coffee on the table.

"Thanks," Ward said. He took a sip. "Let me tell you what I've been up to." He briefed them on his encounter with Jeb Burke at The Forest Glen Coffeehouse, the climate change rally, and his meeting with Ben Cahill and Fern at the Green Glow Café.

"Sounds promising, but Brad's right," Cruz said, nodding toward Royer. "The pressure's on. My ASAC is calling every day. Burke is breathing down his neck. The director is being briefed on a daily basis. Worst of all, as I'm sure you could guess, the White House is calling the director."

"Ditto with us," Royer added. "They're expecting miracles."

Ward took a deep breath. None of this surprised him, but that didn't make it any easier. The expectations and consequences for this one were off the charts. "What else is happening with the case?" he asked. "Any leads?"

"Looks like they may have a woman who loaned her van to the Paxton Ford arsonists," Cruz said.

Ward perked up. "That's great. How did they find her?"

Cruz explained. "Problem is, she just pled the Fifth in front of the grand jury. I got a call a couple of hours ago."

"Are they gonna give her immunity, force her to testify?" Ward asked

"That's the plan," Cruz said.

"I don't know," Royer said. "Some of these people are hard-core. She may refuse anyway and take the contempt time. They see themselves as martyrs." He told them about a grand jury standoff that arose during the investigation of an ALF attack on a lab at the University of Iowa and the resulting protest by ALF supporters at the federal courthouse. "They came from all over the country," he said.

"So, what's the next step?" Cruz asked.

"I think it's time to do something to really pique their interest," Ward said. "You had mentioned the possibility of a staged DoS attack on the Department of Energy website. You think we can set that up?"

"With the interest in this case, I'm sure we can," Cruz said.

"You can arrange a denial-of-service attack on the DOE website?" Royer asked.

Cruz nodded.

Royer appeared impressed. "They'll really let you shut down their website as part of our undercover op?"

"It's more like appear to shut it down," Cruz said. "And we've done this kind of thing before."

Royer's eyebrows raised. "Cool."

Cruz turned to Ward. "As we discussed, the real point of this is to set up a situation in which you can convincingly advocate for taking monkeywrenching into the twenty-first century. I think that that will really get their attention."

Ward nodded. "I agree. I've been giving this some thought. My conversation with Cahill and Fern leaves me confident that they would be receptive to that. Let me work on cementing those relationships. Then I'll set up a date, get them together and execute the attack."

"Sounds good," Cruz said.

"What's your sales pitch on the cyber monkeywrenching?" Royer asked.

"I'll suggest hacking into the computer systems of power plants, oil companies, lumber businesses, et cetera, and sabotaging their systems," Ward explained. "I'll make it clear that I'm not capable of the sophisticated hacking that I'm advocating. Recruiting talented black hat hackers to the cause is the key."

"Sounds scary," Royer said. "Is this an idea we really want to plant in their heads?"

"Can't believe some of them haven't already thought of it," Ward observed. "Besides, I need a way in, and this is a way in."

CHAPTER 44

9:03 a.m., Thursday, May 11, United States District Court for the Western District of Oklahoma, Oklahoma City, Oklahoma

"Are they all here?" Delgado asked. There were always a few members of the grand jury who straggled in late.

Witness Coordinator Becky Turner looked up from her paperwork. "Believe it or not, everybody was here bright and early. You're good to go."

"Fantastic!" Delgado was eager to get to it. Today, she would be up first. Things had moved quickly after Oden's refusal to answer questions the day before. The grant of immunity had come through as quickly as she had ever seen. It was testimony to the attention this case was getting in the highest quarters, a fact that made her a little anxious, and a lot fired-up. An attorney had also been appointed for Oden. Jimmy Roy Holloway was a well-known Oklahoma City criminal defense lawyer, and a real character. He would not have been Delgado's first choice, or her fifteenth, but she had no say in the matter. That was left to the *sound* discretion of the court. Hopefully, Holloway had given his client some decent advice and they could end this little episode.

Delgado walked the short distance to the witness room and rapped on the door.

"Come on in," came the voice from inside.

Delgado recognized the exaggerated southern drawl of Jimmy Roy Holloway. She took a deep breath and entered.

"Hello, Jimmy Roy," Delgado said, her voice flat.

"Kate!" Holloway said, as if he were surprised and delighted to see her. "How are you this fine mornin'?"

"We'll see in a few minutes," she shot back, not inclined to entertain Hank's phony banter. His feigned obsequiousness hid a cunning mind, one always contemplating the next strategic move. "May I address your client?" she asked, straight to the point.

"Of course," Holloway said. He made a theatrical step to the side as he swept his arm toward Oden. "We're all ears."

"Ms. Oden, I won't repeat what I told you yesterday. Obviously, the situation has changed. Suffice it to say, and as I'm sure Mr. Holloway has explained, now that you have been given a grant of immunity you cannot refuse to answer questions on the grounds that the answers may incriminate you. The Fifth Amendment right against self-incrimination is out the window. Do you understand that?"

"Ms. Oden has a complete understanding of the situation," Holloway said, answering for his client.

Delgado remained focused on Oden. "Do you understand that a refusal to answer could result in a finding of contempt and jail time?" Delgado asked her.

Again, Holloway spoke. "I have explained the consequences to..."

"Yeah, I get it," Oden said, interrupting her attorney. "I answer your questions or you people lock me up." She crossed her arms. "I think it's bullshit."

"What Ms. Oden means is that she questions the legitimacy of coercing testimony in this fashion," Holloway said. "She takes the government's threat seriously."

Delgado looked Oden in the eye as she responded to Holloway's comment. "It's not a threat," she said. "I promise you that."

Delgado turned toward the door. "Let's go."

As they started toward the grand jury room Delgado maneuvered herself so that Oden was out front. She then quietly gestured for Holloway to drop back.

"So, is she going to talk?" Delgado asked, her voice a whisper.

Holloway smiled. "Your guess is as good as mine."

Delgado studied him for a moment. It was bullshit. He knew.

They came to the door. Delgado and Oden entered. Holloway waited outside. Oden did not have the right to have counsel present in the grand jury room. Delgado directed Oden to the foreperson, who again administered the oath. When Oden was seated at the witness stand, Delgado began.

"Please state your full name for the record and spell it," Delgado said.

"Linda Marie Oden." She spelled it.

"Ms. Oden, have you been appointed counsel?"

"I have."

"And what is his name?"

"Jimmy Roy Holloway."

"Is Mr. Holloway aware that you are here today?"

"He is."

"In fact, is he present at the courthouse and available to consult with you?"

"That's my understanding."

"Okay. Now, yesterday we were here and you asserted your Fifth Amendment right against self-incrimination. Is that correct?"

"Yeah."

"And since then have you been granted immunity?"

"I suppose."

Delgado sighed. "Well, have you or not?"

"Yeah."

Delgado approached the witness stand. "I'm handing you what's been marked Government's Exhibit Number One. Do you recognize it?"

Oden looked it over. "Yeah," she answered.

"What is it?"

"It's a letter that says what I say can't be used against me. Basically, it says that I won't be prosecuted."

Delgado retrieved the letter and handed it to the court reporter. "I'm offering Government's Exhibit Number One." As she walked back to the podium she studied the grand jurors. They were at full attention, sensing the magnitude of the moment.

"Okay," Delgado said, "let's pick up where we left off yesterday."

"If you say so...counselor."

Delgado stared at her. Several of the grand jurors shook their heads.

"I do say so," Delgado shot back. *Keep your cool*, she reminded herself. *You hold the cards.*

Oden smirked.

Delgado took a deep breath and started again. "Do you own a white Chevy Express Cargo Van?" she asked.

"I already answered that question."

"Do you own a white Chevy Express Cargo Van?" Delgado repeated immediately.

Oden adjusted herself in the witness chair. She looked away for a moment, her jaw clenched, and then glared at Delgado. "Yes. I own a white Chevy Express Cargo Van. Is that a crime?"

"I'll ask the questions," Delgado said sternly. Linda Oden was wearing thin. It was time to find out what the woman intended to do. "Did you loan that van, the white Chevy Express Cargo Van, to *anyone* at *any point* during the period from the last week in April of this year through Monday, May eighth?"

Silence.

"Do I need to repeat the question?" Delgado asked.

"No," Oden replied. "I have no intention of answering any more of your questions."

Delgado shook her head. "Let me get this straight, so that we're clear on the record. Despite the grant of immunity, you are refusing to answer any more questions. Have I got that right?"

"Yeah...you've got that right."

Delgado nodded, and then smiled, menacingly. *Game on, sweetie.* She turned to the foreperson. "May the witness be excused?"

"She may."

United States District Court Judge Harlan Shadle wasted little time in finding Linda Oden in contempt following her refusal to testify after being granted immunity. Delgado knew what was next.

"You will be held in custody for the remaining term of the grand jury," Shadle announced. "You may purge your contempt by agreeing to testify before that same grand jury."

Oden appeared stunned, as if she did not believe that this could actually happen. *Welcome to the big leagues*, Delgado thought.

"Your Honor," Holloway began, "Ms. Oden is a young woman with no significant criminal history. She is a respected businesswoman in her community. Surely, the court could allow her some time to get her affairs in order before reporting for custody. A week should be sufficient."

"I'm sure you explained to Ms. Oden the potential ramifications of her conduct should she refuse to testify," Shadle said to Holloway. "Am I mistaken, Counselor?"

"No, Your Honor. You are not mistaken."

"Your client knows what she needs to do to get out," Shadle said.

Holloway slumped back onto his chair, defeated.

"Mittimus shall issue immediately," Shadle announced. He turned to the deputy United States marshals stationed in the courtroom. "Take her into custody."

A burly deputy assisted Oden to her feet and placed her in handcuffs. She appeared unstable, on the verge of fainting.

"Counsel, is there anything else we need to address?" Shadle asked.

"No, Your Honor," Delgado said cheerily as she sprang up from her chair.

"No, Judge," Holloway said.
"Court is in recess," Shadle announced.

CHAPTER 45

8:52 p.m., Friday, May 12, Green-Glow Cafe, Portland, Oregon

This time it was Joshua Young who suggested they meet, and Cahill had accepted immediately. Naturally, Josh was agreeable when the idea of inviting Fern was mentioned. *She liked you*, Cahill had said. And that was the idea, Ward thought. Fern was almost certainly tapped into the more radical elements of the environmental movement.

As Ward entered the café the aroma of marijuana wafted over him. He didn't hate the smell, but he didn't like it either, and the thought of smoking the stuff held no appeal. Aside from issues of legality and addiction, he just wasn't interested in becoming that mellow. He needed to maintain his edge, maintain control, particularly when those around him did not.

Ward scanned the room. He spotted Cahill at a table along the north wall. Fern was with him, as was another young woman. It was an unexpected complication. She was an unknown quantity. Ward had planned to broach the subject of hacking as the monkeywrenching of the twenty-first century, not necessarily suggesting that they do it, but simply that it might be a noble pursuit for those so inclined. The reaction would dictate his next steps. He was fairly certain that Fern and Cahill would be receptive to the idea, but now he had to gauge this woman's ideology, and her commitment.

As he drew closer to the table, Ward could see that the woman with them was quite beautiful. It was that natural, vibrant, sort of beauty: youthful, fresh, unspoiled. He found it difficult not to stare.

Cahill spotted him and stood. "Hello, Josh. Good to see you, man." They shook hands.

"Joshua." Fern smiled as she rose from her chair to hug him. "I prefer Joshua," she said as she slowly broke away. "It means savior, deliverer. And it reminds me of the Joshua tree, a sturdy, resilient survivor."

"Well, then," Ward said, "Joshua it is."

Fern seemed pleased with herself. An arched eyebrow and a hungry smile told Ward that he needed to move carefully, that she may want more than a friend. After a moment she remembered the woman beside her.

"I'm sorry," Fern said. "This is my friend, Skye."

"My pleasure," Ward said. She made no move to embrace. Apparently, that was Fern's thing. He extended his hand. She took it, her long, slender fingers wrapping warmly around his. She held his hand there for a moment as she spoke.

"I've heard good things about you," Skye said. "You seem to share our cause."

Ward stared into her eyes, momentarily lost. Their color may have been the source of her name, an endless blue. He gathered himself. "I guess I do," he said, looking at Cahill. Her comment was a good sign. The night might go according to plan after all.

Ward suddenly realized that he was still holding Skye's hand. He quickly let go. Fern had noticed as well, and her smile had withered. She looked at Skye, assessing her from head to toe. Something like resignation appeared on her face. Or maybe it was closer to contempt. Ward knew that he would have to play this carefully. He could not afford to alienate either of these women.

They sat.

"Ben was telling us about your comments at the climate change protest," Skye said.

"A kindred spirit," Cahill noted.

"I am," Ward agreed. "I just hope we're not too late."

Fern nodded. She leaned in, her eyes showing the same intensity Ward had seen the other night. "That's why we need to act now," she said, jabbing her finger for emphasis. She looked up and stopped. A waiter was approaching. The apparent concern at being overheard was not lost on Ward.

"Can I take your order?" the waiter asked.

Fern and Skye both ordered a glass of pinot noir from one of Oregon's certified organic vineyards. Ward followed suit. Cahill ordered a wheat beer produced by a local microbrewery.

When the waiter was gone, Fern resumed. "As I was saying, we need to take action. The government is feckless, corrupt, owned by corporations. I say we…"

"Fern," Cahill interrupted. "Tonight, why don't we all just get to know each other?" His look told her to cool it.

Fern sat back, chastened. But she nodded her agreement. Ward suspected that it was not the first time she had been similarly restrained. More importantly, the exchange told him that he was exactly where he needed to be. He decided to take the initiative.

"Well," Ward said, "I'd have to agree with Fern. The government is incompetent and corrupt. Corporations won't do anything on their own. If the citizens don't act no one will. What are we supposed to do, just sit by and watch the Earth bake?"

"Absolutely not," Cahill said.

Ward noticed the three exchange glances. He couldn't read it. Were they indicating that he had passed some initial test, or reaffirming that they needed to take it slow? He pressed on, sensing that this could be the moment.

"You know who could make themselves useful on the environmental front," Ward said, "the hackers."

"What do you mean," Skye asked.

"Groups like Anonymous," Ward said, "or any of the so-called black hat hackers. If they want to do something really useful instead of just protest gestures or their usual mischief they could hack into the computer networks of oil companies, power plants, government agencies, maybe real estate developers, and sabotage their systems."

Ward saw Cahill give Skye a quick glance.

"I may not have mentioned that Josh works for a San Francisco-based tech company," Cahill said. "He's a software designer. What was the name of the company, Josh?"

"Blue World Systems," Ward said. He paused for a moment, considering his next move. "Are any of you familiar with the term monkeywrenching?" he asked. He knew that he was taking a chance here.

"I've heard of it," Fern said.

Ward could see that she was suppressing a smile. The three again exchanged looks.

"I guess I'm suggesting that a little cyber monkeywrenching might be a good thing," Ward said.

There were nods of approval all around. Ward sensed that he had struck a chord. Just then, the waiter brought their drinks. When he was gone Cahill raised his glass in a toast.

"To Mother Earth," Cahill said.

"To Mother," Fern added.

They clinked glasses and drank.

The night was going well, Ward thought. But was it going too well? When things seemed too easy it could be a sign that he had been compromised. His thoughts went back to the informant, Peavey.

"So, have you ever done any hacking?" Fern asked, straight to the point.

"Me?" Ward asked. A sly smile crept onto his face. "I have no idea what you're talking about."

CHAPTER 46

1:14 p.m., Monday, May 15, Pittman Petroleum Company, Tyler, Texas

It was hard to believe their good fortune. C. Robert Titus, the CEO of Pittman Petroleum, was a smoker, and he took a break to light up at the same time and place every day. Over the course of a week of surveillance he had consistently appeared through a nondescript side door at corporate headquarters at almost exactly a quarter after one, Sunday being the only exception. Goat chuckled. It had long been said that smoking can kill you, but he was sure the surgeon general never meant it like this.

The purpose and method of the attack had not been disclosed to him. This was unusual. Goat was a trusted member of the New Orleans cell and a veteran of the movement. He had to admit, he was a bit insulted, but he understood the need for secrecy. He had only been told that access to Titus was the key to the operation's success. He assumed a kidnapping, with the ransom being the cessation of certain controversial activities by Pittman Petroleum. Goat had read that Titus recently appeared before Congress to defend the practice of fracking as a method to extract oil and natural gas. He assumed that this had vaulted Titus to the top of someone's target list. That was fine with him. He was more than happy to help send a message to Big Oil, especially on this issue.

Goat looked at his watch. It was a quarter after. He trained his binoculars on the side door through which Titus had regularly appeared. He watched for a minute or two as nothing happened. Goat checked the time again. It was now eighteen minutes after. Maybe it had just been a late lunch. He watched for several more minutes. Had Titus left town? Was he out sick? The man had always appeared like clockwork. Goat was about to lower the binoculars when he saw the door handle start to turn. Titus emerged. He quickly extracted a pack of cigarettes, tapped one out and placed it in his mouth, but then fumbled with the lighter as he struggled to get his fix. There was a look of something like desperation until the cigarette was finally lit. A long drag followed. Titus held the smoke for a moment, and then slowly let it out, as if releasing all the worries and stress of the day.

Despite Pittman Petroleum's considerable security measures, there was no one with him. Goat wondered if the guards were aware of the chief's little afternoon break. They had to be, didn't they? Security cameras were everywhere. Pittman Petroleum was a big target. Every inch of the place was under surveillance. At least it appeared that way. If the operation took place here the assault team would have to move quickly, very quickly, with no mistakes. From experience, Goat knew that the cigarette break would last no more than five to ten minutes. But there were no other real options. Goat had watched the residence. If anything, it was more impenetrable than corporate headquarters. Titus had invested in a truly state-of-the-art security system for his home, likely due in large measure to the fact that the three young children from his second marriage lived there. In addition, an armed detail drove him to and from work, always varying the route. They were pros, all former military or law enforcement. Pittman contracted with one of the leading corporate security firms. It was not a crew that EMB wanted to, or needed to, encounter. If an abduction happened at all, this is where it needed to take place. This is where Titus was most vulnerable.

Still, Goat was concerned. If it was a kidnapping there was no room for error. He had plotted the quickest routes in and out, noting the limited options due to the city's confusing street system. He was told that the assault team would handle all other aspects of the transportation arrangements. This was also unusual. Goat desperately hoped that the others knew what they were doing. The stakes were high and being captured was not an option.

"Dove, you are the chosen one. The message you will carry is one of salvation for our planet." Ocean held her shoulders as he looked deep into her eyes. "Mother sends you as her messenger, as her disciple. You alone can destroy this evil that imperils our Earth."

"Our cause is just," Dove chanted, as if in a trance.

"No cause is more just," Ocean assured her. "Your selfless act will inspire generations. It will alter the perilous course of our planet. You will save the oceans, the mountains, the forests. All of Mother's creatures will owe their continued existence to you."

Ocean stroked her cheek. She was beautiful, angelic. He knew that her beauty would dispel suspicion. No one would question her. It was man's nature.

"I am humbled," Dove said, lowering her eyes.

"Be not humbled," Ocean said. He raised his arms in triumph. "Be uplifted!"

Dove smiled. An expression of utter peace swept over her youthful face. Ocean knew that she would not falter.

CHAPTER 47

7:58 p.m., Monday, May 15, The Forest Glen Coffeehouse, Portland, Oregon

Ward stood a block down the street, partially hidden by a utility van. The spot afforded him a good view of the entrance to the coffeehouse. Fern, Skye and Cahill had been invited. He told them eight o'clock, said there was something he wanted to show them. The women had readily agreed. Cahill was noncommittal. Ward wondered what to think of that. Did Cahill suspect something? Simply have other things to do? Or was he just keeping a safe distance? From what Peavey had said Cahill knew how to walk right up to the line but not cross it. He was a motivator, even a recruiter, but not an activist, not in the truest sense of the term.

Ward wanted them to arrive first, see if anyone else was with them, if anyone else was watching. It was unlikely, but unfortunate surprises were avoided by taking precautions. He checked the time. It was just past eight. Were they spooked? Again, he thought of Peavey. There was that nagging doubt, always present. Could their informant really be kept in line?

Then they appeared, Fern and Skye, out of nowhere. There was no Cahill. It wasn't a surprise, or a particular disappointment. Perhaps he had already served his purpose. The introductions had been made. These two women were far more likely to be a direct link in. If Cahill arrived later, that was fine. If not at all, so be it. It was time to go. Ward retrieved his phone and punched in the number for Cruz.

"They there?" Cruz asked.

"Fern and Skye. Negative on Cahill."

"Does that matter?"

"No. I've got who I need."

"We're good on this end."

"Roger that." Ward looked at his watch. "I'm at five after. I'll be set up and working in fifteen minutes."

"DOE will shut down in twenty. They'll only stay down for ten minutes. That was all I could get. They initially offered five. Remember, timing is everything, brother."

"Twenty-five after," Ward confirmed. "Got it." He ended the call.

Ward strode across the street, laptop case slung over his shoulder. It was time to cast the bait and see if he got a bite.

As he entered Ward could see that the place was not busy. He had hoped that might be the case on a Monday night. If there were too many people around someone might get nervous, or he might be viewed as careless. That was not the impression he wanted to make. These two had to be convinced that he understood the need for complete secrecy.

He spotted Fern and Skye at a table against the west wall. They both smiled. He smiled back and headed their direction. An open chair on the far side of the table would allow him to sit with his back against the wall. He preferred that for security reasons, but also, in this case, because the computer screen would be visible only to those he chose to share it with.

"Hello, Joshua," Fern said. She stood and hugged him, lingering just the slightest bit too long.

"Joshua." Skye rose from her chair. This time there was no handshake. Her arms slipped around him for a quick embrace, coupled with a kiss on the cheek.

"Well, nice to see both of you," Ward said. He removed the laptop case from his shoulder and hung it on the back of the chair. Fern took note.

"I take it the something you wanted to show us is on the computer," Fern said, nodding toward his laptop. "A bit of a disappointment," she said playfully, "but that's okay."

Ward was caught off guard. He could hear a hint of nervousness in his own laugh. Skye giggled.

"I think you'll find what I have to show you…stimulating," he said, recovering a bit.

"We'll see about that," Skye said, clearly not wanting to be left out of the banter.

Ward could see that they were both really enjoying this. He would play along, within limits. He hoped that he wouldn't be forced to fend off Fern. That could create problems. As for Skye, he doubted that she was serious. If she was, it would be a test to fend her off. But that was one of the rules. No fraternization. He knew agents who had ignored that, at great cost.

A waiter came to take their order. Skye asked for a cappuccino. Fern ordered a latte, as did Ward. After he was gone, Ward unpacked his laptop, turned it on and logged in.

"Look at him," Fern said, "absolutely no foreplay."

Ward smiled but said nothing. He typed for a moment, then spun the screen around so that they could both get a look. It was black, except for a few lines of what looked like code at the top.

"I was thinking about our conversation the other night," he said, "on cyber monkeywrenching. Given everyone's interest, I thought that a quick demonstration might be in order." He studied their reactions.

Fern's brow furrowed. She leaned in, clearly eager to hear more. Skye's raised eyebrows, on the other hand, made him wonder if he had misread her.

Ward looked directly at Skye. "If you prefer I not?"

"I'm sorry," Skye said. She quickly looked about the room. "I am interested, but are you sure it's…safe?"

Ward spun the laptop back around so that the screen was facing him. "I promise you, no one here will have the slightest idea what we're doing."

Fern nodded. Ward could see she was ready to get on with it.

"Okay," Skye said. She placed her elbow on the table and rested her chin in the palm of her hand. "Let's see what you've got."

Ward smiled. He began to type. "I sense that you two can keep a secret, and that you will appreciate what I am about to do." He knew that by allowing them to witness what would appear to be a major federal offense he would demonstrate his willingness to put his trust in them. He hoped, and believed, that by doing so they would reciprocate and welcome him into the fold.

"Are you familiar with the term DoS attack?" Ward asked.

"Sure, a denial-of-service attack," Fern responded.

"That's right," Ward said. "There is also what is called a distributed denial-of-service, or DDoS, attack. A DoS attack is sent by one person, whereas a DDoS attack comes from more than one person or a botnet."

"I've heard the term," Skye said. "I know it's some array of compromised computers."

"Exactly," Ward agreed. "In basic terms, it's an army of compromised, interconnected computers that can be controlled by a third party." He continued to type, keeping an eye on the time. It was twenty after. He had five minutes.

"There are numerous methods of attack," Ward said. "One of the most common is to flood a site with outside communications requests through a botnet. This overwhelms the site with traffic, causing it to freeze up. Another method, in very general terms, is to crash the system through the use of malware. Obviously, there are many ways to accomplish this." He looked up from his laptop. "I prefer the latter approach." Ward could see that he had their attention.

"So what's the target?" Skye asked.

Ward looked at her and smiled. "The Department of Energy."

"No way!" Fern blurted.

"I have things in place," Ward said. "All I need to do is execute." He spun the computer around so that they could see the screen. The DOE's website, energy.gov, was on display. He clicked on several internal links to show them that the site was fully operational. Just then, the waiter approached. Ward turned the laptop back around to hide it from his view. He checked his watch. It was twenty-three after. He had two minutes.

The waiter dawdled, eyeing Skye as he slowly served their drinks.

"Thanks," Ward said to him. "We're good for now." It was brusque, but he had to get him out of there.

"Oh. Okay," the waiter said sheepishly. "Let me know if you need anything else."

"We'll do that," Ward said, not making eye contact. He didn't want to be rude to the kid, but there was no choice.

Ward started to type as the waiter wandered off. "DOE is too cozy with Big Oil," he said. "They pay lip service to renewable energy sources. In reality, they are part of the problem. Let's send them a message."

"Sounds fun," Fern agreed.

"Just a few more things," Ward added. "There." He turned the laptop so that they could all watch. The screen was filled with code. He looked at Fern, and then Skye. "Ready?"

"Do it," Fern said.

Skye nodded.

Ward pushed the *enter* key. Code began to scroll down the screen. After thirty seconds or so it began to slow down, and then stopped. He glanced at the time. Twenty-seven minutes after eight. He briefly considered turning the laptop so that only he could see it when he tried to access the Department of Energy website but decided to put his faith in Cruz. With one hand he typed the URL for the DOE website into the address bar so that the women could see it, and then hit *enter*. A symbol on the screen indicated that the computer was thinking. It continued for approximately thirty seconds and then a message appeared: *website is currently unavailable.*

Ward smiled. The bait was cast.

CHAPTER 48

1:07 p.m., Tuesday, May 16, Pittman Petroleum Company, Tyler, Texas

Dove stopped her car on the frontage road that ran past the entrance to Pittman Petroleum's global headquarters. The building was approximately one hundred yards from her location. The grounds were expertly landscaped, better maintained than most city parks. To her eye, though, the look was artificial, not remotely comparable to the beauty of nature in its pristine state. No, these grounds were Big Oil's idea of nature; carefully controlled, used to serve their own ends. It confirmed her purpose.

Dove raised the hood and activated her hazard lights, completing the appearance of a vehicle in distress. Moving back behind the driver's side of the car she checked her clothes, making sure that everything was in place. Almost as an afterthought, she stole a quick peek at her reflection in the side view mirror. Lipstick was retrieved from her purse and applied. She pressed her lips together and then puckered. A quick fluff of her golden blonde hair followed. Satisfied, she checked her watch. It was twelve minutes after one. She took a deep breath and began to walk.

His words played over and over in her mind. *Mother sends you as her messenger, as her disciple. You alone can destroy this evil that imperils our Earth.* Her adrenaline surged. The magnificence of their cause drove her forward. She strode toward the building, an eye on the door where she was told he would appear. Dove looked at her watch. It was one-fifteen.

She saw him emerge. Her heart raced. She watched as he withdrew the pack of cigarettes, removed one, and lit it. She was close now, thirty yards away. *Your selfless act will inspire generations. It will alter the perilous course of our planet.* She began to breathe hard. Stay calm, she thought. Remember your instructions. Be friendly, do nothing to alarm him. Move quickly, but not aggressively. Give him no time to react.

At twenty yards he spotted her.

"Hello. Can I help you?" he asked, wary, but not alarmed.

Dove brushed a golden lock aside and smiled. It had the desired effect. He suddenly seemed calm, completely unaware. She was at fifteen yards. She needed to be closer.

"I'm so sorry," she said, pointing back at her vehicle with the hood raised, flashers blinking. "My car broke down on the road over there and the battery is dead on my cell phone."

He smiled and reached in his jacket. "Not a problem. Use mine."

He held out his cell phone. She moved toward him. Her breathing was deep, but rapid, impossible to control. She could feel the vest squeezing against her every time she inhaled. *You will save the oceans, the mountains, the forests.*

She took his phone and stepped back a few feet, out of his reach. "Thank you...Mr. Titus."

A look of alarm spread across his face at the mention of his name. Her hand slipped to the pocket trigger that would detonate the explosives. She envisioned Ocean's face, reveling in the pride he would feel.

"C. Robert Titus, Mother Earth now demands her justice."

Titus stumbled backwards, his expression now one of terror.

Dove smiled. *All of Mother's creatures will owe their continued existence to you.* She closed her eyes and pressed the trigger.

CHAPTER 49

6:30 p.m., Tuesday, May 16, CBC News, New York, New York

The recorded introduction began: From New York, this is the CBC Evening News, with Bryson Daley.

Daley focused on the teleprompter and began. "Good evening. Our lead story tonight focuses on the rise in eco-terrorism, which today escalated to a new level. A suicide bomber approached the headquarters of Pittman Petroleum in Tyler, Texas, encountered the company's CEO, C. Robert Titus, and detonated an explosive vest strapped to her body, killing them both instantly. It is being called one of the most alarming acts of domestic terrorism in this country's history, drawing worried reactions from across the globe. We turn now to CBC correspondent Paige Gable who is in Tyler."

"Good evening, Bryson. Authorities are describing this suicide attack as a disturbing new development in the tactics being used by domestic terrorists, in this case radical environmentalists who appear to have taken a page straight from the jihadists' playbook. At just after one o'clock this afternoon a young woman approached Pittman CEO C. Robert Titus as he took a smoke break just outside the company's headquarters building visible behind me. When she was within a few feet of Titus she detonated the suicide vest that was strapped to her body. How do we know this? The entire episode was caught on Pittman's security cameras. Law enforcement has not released that video because of the ongoing investigation. We are told it is extremely graphic. Of course, all of this raises the question of how does an attack on one of the country's top executives take place at what is, by all accounts, an extremely secure corporate location. Pittman contracts with one of the leading private security firms in the country, Blackstone Logistics. A source tells CBC News that for this attack to have succeeded in this manner the building must have been under surveillance for at least several days. Blackstone has refused our requests for comment, citing their own ongoing internal investigation."

"Paige, are there any clues as to who is responsible for this attack or the reasons behind it?" Daley asked.

"Yes. An email was received at a local Tyler television station, KETK. In it, a group identifying itself as the Earth Martyrs Brigade claimed responsibility." Gable looked at a piece of paper in her hand. "The message, in part, reads as follows: *Big Oil has paid a price for its exploitation of our planet. It will continue to pay. Mother Earth has secured only partial justice.* Bryson, it should be noted that Titus recently appeared before the House Natural Resources Committee where he defended the controversial practice of fracking as a method for extracting oil and natural gas. There has been some speculation that this might have elevated him as a potential target."

"What about this Earth Martyrs Brigade?" Daley asked. "Is this a group that was on anybody's radar?"

"Not as far as we know," Gable said. "But this attack does fit a pattern of similar incidents that have occurred across the country over the course of the last several weeks. Those include an arson involving the Silver Trail Casino in Stateline, Nevada, which cost the life of one young firefighter, an attack on an electrical substation in a suburb of Omaha, another arson of a Ford dealership in Oklahoma City, and the destruction of a research lab at Southern Illinois University in Carbondale, Illinois. After each of those attacks a local television station received an email similar to the one received by KETK here in Tyler. They all claimed some sort of retribution for crimes against the environment. But none of those earlier messages identified the responsible group. Authorities are now speculating that this Earth Martyrs Brigade may have been behind all of the previous attacks. One thing we do know, this frightening attack has cost C. Robert Titus his life. He leaves behind a wife and three young children."

"Just a terrible story out of Texas today," Daley said. "Our thanks to Paige Gable for her report from Tyler. Now, for more on the national implications of this story we go to Washington, D.C. and our Justice Department correspondent, Aaron Raines. Aaron, what are officials there saying about the Earth Martyrs Brigade and this tactic of suicide bombings now being employed by eco-terrorists?"

"Well, Bryson, they're not saying much. We have been able to confirm that the FBI and the Bureau of Alcohol, Tobacco, Firearms and Explosives, better known as ATF, are conducting a joint investigation into the possibly related attacks mentioned earlier in our story. Beyond that, we've been told very little. ATF, of course, is still struggling with the fallout from the Fast and Furious debacle of a few years ago. They are under tremendous pressure to produce a big win. But there is the distinct impression that the Earth Martyrs Brigade is a completely unknown entity. The group's name, along with the nature of this attack, demonstrates their willingness to employ tactics previously unseen in the world of eco-terrorism. That has federal authorities very worried. Today's attack, along with the frequent, successful use of suicide bombers by various terrorist groups around the world, amply demonstrates the tremendous difficulty in stopping this type of assault."

"Has there been any comment from the White House?" Daley asked.

"No. In fact, the White House has been conspicuously silent." Raines referred to a note he was holding. "At a press briefing earlier today White House Press Secretary Ellie Drake, in response to questioning on this matter, simply stated: *As you know, we never comment on anything that is the subject of an ongoing federal investigation. Rest assured, the president has been in contact with officials at the Justice Department and is receiving regular briefings on this situation. He has full confidence in federal law enforcement and their ability to bring this case to a successful conclusion."* A hint of a smile appeared on Raines' face. "Bryson, as you and those of us in this business know quite well, the White House often comments on matters under investigation. The response today seemed an attempt to dodge further questioning and is indicative of a case that has no solid leads. Clearly, the White House is struggling with how to respond. This is Aaron Raines, CBC News, the Justice Department."

"A disturbing scenario for sure," Daley said, "and a story we'll continue to follow. Thank you, Aaron."

CHAPTER 50

9:07 a.m., Wednesday, May 17, the White House, Washington

President Samuel T. Buckley wanted some answers. What was this Earth Martyrs Brigade? Who was their leader? How many members did they have? What the hell did they hope to accomplish, a return to some sort of eighteenth-century agrarian society? And, most importantly, how could they be brought to justice? *Domestic terrorism* was a term he did not want to hear, and he was hearing it a lot, on news broadcasts, in the papers, everywhere. Emails and letters were pouring into the White House by the thousands and were demanding action. People were scared. They needed reassurance. They wanted to believe that their government still had the capacity to get this situation under control. He wanted to believe it as well, and he was about to ask the hard questions that would give him the answer.

Buckley studied the assembled group, some of the best people in his administration. The usual affable banter that preceded many of these meetings was absent. Heads were bowed. Expressions were serious, grim. It was the Oval Office as war room.

"Bob Titus was a friend of mine," Buckley said, referring to the assassinated CEO of Pittman Petroleum. "What do I tell his widow when I call her this morning?"

There was silence. Buckley realized he would be forced to call on someone. It was a problem with the presidency. People didn't want to tell him what he didn't want to hear, even when he desperately needed to hear it. It was as if having the words come out of your mouth somehow made you responsible. But then, the concept of killing the messenger went back to Shakespeare, even Plutarch. He couldn't blame them. This time, though, even the usually outspoken remained quiet. His chief of staff and good friend, Mike Cooper, remained mum. Buckley turned to his attorney general, William Bradford, one of his most trusted advisors.

"Bill, what is the FBI telling you?" Buckley asked. "This Earth Martyrs Brigade, who are they?"

Bradford was seated on one of the couches. He straightened when addressed by the commander-in-chief. "To be perfectly honest, Mr. President, we don't know. As you're aware, there have been a number of seemingly related attacks, all with some supposed environmental motive, all involving claims of responsibility sent to local TV stations." He summarized the attacks and the messages received for everyone in the room. "Until now, however, the group never identified itself by name. We initially thought that this might be a resurgence of ELF, the Earth Liberation Front, in a more radicalized form. The incendiary devices used in some of these attacks, for example, were very similar to those developed and employed by ELF. While there may be some former ELF members involved, it now appears that we are dealing with a totally new, and much more violent, organization."

"So, we know nothing," Buckley said. "Great. What are we doing about it?"

"We have some leads," Bradford said. "We've identified the van used in the Ford dealership arson in Oklahoma City."

"Has that led to anything?" Buckley asked.

"I'm afraid not," Bradford replied. "ATF interviewed the owner. They don't think she was directly involved, but believe she loaned the van to someone who was. She won't give up the name. The U.S. Attorney's Office down there put here in front of the grand jury, but she pled the Fifth. They gave her immunity which eliminates her ability to refuse to answer on Fifth Amendment grounds, but she still refused to talk."

"What happens at that point?" The question came from National Security Advisor Brent Dixon.

"If the individual still refuses to answer they are found in contempt and locked up," Bradford answered. "That's what happened here. Judge Harlan Shadle put her in jail for the remainder of the grand jury term. He told her she could purge her contempt, and get out, by testifying before the grand jury."

"So, unless she talks we've got nothing there," Buckley said. "Anything else?"

"We have footage of the arsonists at the dealership," Bradford offered, shaking his head.

"But?" Buckley asked.

"But they are dressed in black, head-to-toe, wearing ski masks. There is no way to identify them from that." Bradford leaned forward, elbows on knees, resting his forehead on his hands as if praying.

Buckley studied his attorney general. Bradford, the venerable Beltway insider, had seen a lot during his decades of service. He had dispensed sage advice to many administrations and weathered innumerable storms. But today he seemed at a loss. It told Buckley just how serious the situation was. He softened his tone.

"What else are we doing, Bill?"

Bradford didn't look up as he answered. "We've subpoenaed internet and phone records, scoured surveillance video from any location where cameras might have caught a glimpse of anything useful, talked to store owners and checked records at any location where components of the incendiary devices might have been purchased, talked to everyone we can find who might have seen something." He looked at the president. "Sir, we are doing everything possible. I promise you that."

Buckley nodded. He knew it was true. He just didn't like the truth.

"Don, do your folks have anything?" Buckley asked his Secretary of Homeland Security, knowing the answer.

Donald Gage shook his head. "I'm sorry, Mr. President. I wish

I had better news."

Buckley turned to his EPA Administrator, Elizabeth Keefer. "Liz, you are my point person on environmental policy. That makes you a target." He paused. "You need to be careful."

"I agree," Bradford said.

There were nods all around the room.

"Understood, Mr. President," Keefer said.

The former governor of North Carolina had seemed, to some, an odd choice as administrator of the Environmental Protection Agency. But Buckley saw her as a rising star and one of the most capable people in his administration. He also knew that she had served two tours in Afghanistan during the early years of the war. Until now, no one would have thought that to be directly related to the duties of her office.

Buckley turned from the group. He walked over to the windows that looked out over the Rose Garden. "I need to say something to the American people," he announced. "They need reassurance." He turned back. "I just wish that I felt more reassured."

Ellie Drake nervously clenched the podium in the James S. Brady Press Briefing Room. The daily give and take was about to begin. What the assembled collection of correspondents did not know was that the president was about to make a surprise appearance. She was informed that he felt compelled to make a statement to reassure the public that everything possible was being done to identify and apprehend these terrorists. That was understandable, but she had mixed feelings about her boss appearing in front of this group of veteran reporters without any good answers. It could get ugly. She had advised him to make his statement without taking questions and prayed that he would follow that advice. Drake looked at her watch. It was time.

"Ladies and gentlemen, the president of the United States," Drake announced. She backed away from the podium. Otherwise relaxed journalists snapped to attention. Cell phones lit up. Texts went out. Keyboards clicked. The word spread that something was up.

President Samuel T. Buckley strode into the room. He gave every appearance of confidence and command of the situation. The bullet that ripped into his chest during the attempted assassination in El Paso had caused more damage than most knew, leaving lasting effects on his health. But to the general public and the majority of political observers he appeared as strong as ever, even stronger. The incident seemed to have steeled his resolve. And it had sent his popularity ratings through the roof. Drake knew that this would be one of those times when he would have to draw on that bank of goodwill.

"Good afternoon, everyone," Buckley said. "I'd like to make a few comments about this recent spate of attacks by so-called eco-terrorists, including the assassination yesterday of Robert Titus, CEO of Pittman Petroleum. First of all, our thoughts and prayers are with Bob's family. Bob was a friend. The horrific and completely unjustifiable events that occurred in Tyler, Texas, leave us all shocked and saddened. Similarly, our thoughts and prayers go out to all of the victims of these heinous acts." Buckley paused for a second, and then stared straight into the camera. "I want to assure the American people that we are doing everything possible to hunt down and apprehend those responsible. I promise you, they will be brought to justice."

There was a flurry of activity in the room. Hands went up. Buckley ignored them and continued with his remarks. "I referred to the perpetrators as so-called eco-terrorists, so-called because they deserve no special moniker. They are, in fact, simply terrorists. Using any other term risks tainting the good name of legitimate conservationists, environmentalists and animal rights activists who do good work that helps better our society. The acts of a handful of criminals should not and cannot have that effect."

More hands went up. "We will keep you advised as the investigation develops," Buckley said. He exited quickly, ignoring the barrage of questions that exploded behind him.

CHAPTER 51

7:12 p.m., Thursday, May 18, Green Glow Cafe, Portland, Oregon

Fern had reached out to him through Cahill. There were more people to meet. Ward knew it was more vetting. He was making inroads, but progress was slow. It was the nature of the game. These things took time. But as with every undercover operation, there came the point when management wanted results, demanded them. After the suicide attack on the CEO of Pittman Petroleum the pressure would be intense. Still, he couldn't force it. To do so was death.

Ward entered to the familiar aroma of marijuana and the mellow laughter of the stoned. He scanned the room. Fern and Skye were seated at a table away from the other patrons. They spotted him and waved. There was no Cahill, but two men were seated with them, one of them was the size of an ox. Ward started toward the group. As he drew near he became Joshua Young.

Everyone at the table stood. "Joshua," Fern said as she rose to embrace him. She lingered. A hand slid down his arm as she let go.

"Hello, Josh," Skye said. She gave him a quick, almost perfunctory hug, glancing sideways at the man mountain next to her as she did so. To Ward, it was obvious that this was the boyfriend. The open flirtatiousness she had exhibited the other night was gone.

"Josh, I'd like you to meet Sequoia," Skye said. "My significant other," she added, almost as an afterthought. Sequoia did not seem to notice.

"Nice to meet you, Josh," he said, smiling pleasantly. Sequoia reached out his hand. Ward took it. Despite the man's size, the handshake was relatively gentle. Ward assumed that he had the kind of confidence that eliminated the need for any of that grip strength as a contest of manhood bullshit. It certainly appeared that Sequoia did not view him as a threat.

"And this is Wolf," Fern announced. The way she said it indicated that she was presenting their leader.

"Joshua Young," Ward said, taking the initiative. He held out his hand.

"Joshua," Wolf said, accepting the offered hand. There was no smile. The tone was noncommittal. "Please, have a seat." He gestured for the others to do likewise.

This was clearly the man in charge, Ward thought, the one who would decide whether he was to be brought into the fold, at least this fold.

"Would you like something to drink?" Wolf asked.

"Sure," Ward replied.

Wolf summoned the waitress. She came over immediately and took Ward's order. When she was safely out of range Wolf began.

"Fern shared with me your hacking exploits," he said, wasting no time. "Impressive."

"Thank you," Ward said, glancing at Fern, who smiled at him.

"Your thoughts on cyber monkeywrenching are…intriguing," Wolf noted, obviously choosing his words carefully.

"I think the potential impact is enormous," Ward said. "Of course, it would take the involvement of people with skills far greater than mine."

"Perhaps," Wolf said. He paused. "What sort of involvement would you like to have?"

Ward leaned forward. "The sort that makes things happen. I'm not concerned about crossing lines, if that's what you mean. This is too important."

Wolf smiled. It was a signal to the others. There were nods of approval around the table. Whatever they were as a group, he was clearly their leader. Ward could see it in the way they looked at him, wanting his approval, always seeming to wait for his lead. There was a respect, maybe even a little fear. Ward's instinct told him that Wolf was hands-on, involved in an operational sense. What's more, he seemed the type that could be part of the command structure, at least to the extent that there was one. Ward just hoped that it was the command structure of the group that claimed responsibility for the suicide attack on Titus, the so-called Earth Martyrs Brigade.

Wolf rested his arms on the table, leaning close as he stared into the eyes of Joshua Young. "We'll see what we can do to get you more...involved."

Ward nodded. "I'd like that."

The conversation stopped as the waitress approached with Ward's drink. She seemed to sense that she had interrupted something and left quickly.

When she was gone Wolf raised his glass. "To Mother Earth," he said.

"To Mother," the others added in unison.

To Ward it had the ring of cultish chants he had heard in the past. It gave him a chill. "To Mother," he said, and then took a drink of his beer.

Ward decided to take a chance. "So, why all the nicknames?" he asked.

Everyone looked to Wolf.

"It's just better that way," he said humorlessly, ending the inquiry.

"Understood." So much for that, Ward thought, afraid he had overstepped. Maybe he could lighten the mood. He looked at Sequoia. "Yours I get."

Skye giggled. Sequoia noticed. The most the big man could manage was a smirk, not seeming to care for the fact that Joshua Young had made his girlfriend laugh. There was some jealousy there, Ward concluded. Perhaps his earlier assessment of Sequoia's confidence was mistaken. Ward had noticed that Skye seemed to be stealing guilty glances at him, looking away whenever they made eye contact. That could turn into a problem, a big one, roughly the size of a redwood tree. Ward could handle himself pretty well. He had proved it on more than one occasion. But Sequoia was the kind of specimen who could easily crush most men. Ward knew that he would have to be careful in his interactions with Skye.

The anonymity they sought with the nicknames spoke volumes. It was a trick borrowed from ELF. Ward wondered if any of them knew the true identities of any others in their cell, which is what this little group had to be. He wondered how they acquired the nicknames. Did they choose their own, or were they named by the cell leader? As he knew when he first met her, Skye's name had to come from the hypnotic, endless blue of her eyes. The reason for Fern's name was not apparent at all. She seemed more panther than plant. But Ward could easily understand why Wolf was Wolf. The cunning and intensity were palpable. He was a dangerous character, and this was his pack. Despite Sequoia's size, Wolf was clearly the alpha male. Ward concluded that Wolf had named himself.

Over the course of the evening their discussion centered on environmental issues, but there was no mention of any specific attacks, or even any further reference to monkeywrenching, cyber or otherwise. It was clear that Wolf had told the rest of them to keep quiet on those issues. Joshua Young was still being vetted. Ward was sure that tonight was just the first of many steps in that process. Wolf had subtly quizzed him about his background. He got exactly the same story that had been told to Cahill: from Boston, went to Boston University, software designer for Blue World Systems, moved to Portland for a woman who was no longer in the picture. Fern had perked up on the last point. Between Fern and Skye, particularly Fern, Ward wondered if he might have to rekindle that fictitious relationship. One thing he did know was that Wolf would check out every aspect of his story. His cover was good, but none was perfect. It often simply depended on how far somebody wanted to dig.

"Hey, wait up."

Ward turned to see Fern approaching quickly. She had caught up with him halfway to his car. Normally, he would be wary of an ambush in this type of situation. But this was likely an ambush of a different kind. He'd had the sense all night that she wanted to get him alone.

"Hi," Ward said pleasantly.

"Mind if I walk with you?" she asked.

"Not at all."

Ward looked at her and smiled. Her interest was earnest and flattering. Despite the context, he had to admit that he found her attractive. She didn't have Skye's classic beauty, but her animalism made up for it. Ward was curious, but that's all it could be, curiosity.

"I enjoyed tonight," Fern said, "getting to know you a little better." She was close to him, their shoulders touching as they walked.

"Thanks. I enjoyed it, too."

"Wolf is impressed with you," she said.

"He's quite intense," Ward noted.

"It comes from his commitment to the cause, and his fear of traitors."

"Oh?"

Fern didn't immediately respond. "I shouldn't say anything else," she finally replied.

"Understood," Ward said. And it was true, he understood the situation perfectly. Wolf is former ELF, he thought. The traitors referred to were the cooperators in Operation Backfire. It only made sense. Peavey had told him that Cahill was former ELF. Ward wondered if Wolf had helped lead the more radical elements of ELF to something new, something more violent, the Earth Martyrs Brigade.

"This is me," Ward said as they approached his Prius. "Are you parked nearby?" he asked, intending to escort her to her vehicle.

"Right over there," Fern said, pointing to a small black car a half block away.

"Can I walk you?" he asked.

Fern turned to face him and moved close. "I was kind of hoping we could..." She reached up to kiss him.

Ward backed away. "I'm sorry," he said. "I..."

Fern looked down. All of a sudden she seemed more hurt schoolgirl than radical environmentalist. Ward felt a pang of guilt. He reminded himself why he was there.

"It's just that there's someone else," he lied.

"Who?" Fern asked. "Sorry. That's none of my business."

"No. It's okay. It's the woman I moved here for."

"I thought she was out of the picture?"

"We've been talking," Ward said. Now he had a problem. Eventually, he would have to supply a name for this fictitious girlfriend. Wolf would have her checked out.

"I understand," Fern said, looking dejected.

Ward sensed that she didn't believe him. He wanted to give her a face-saving way out.

"I don't know what will happen," Ward said. "Maybe, if it doesn't work out with her..."

"Thanks," Fern said, interrupting him. She kissed his cheek and headed toward her car.

Wolf entered the number on the burner phone—a Boston area code—and hit the call button.

"Hello?"

The tone of the voice was cautious, as expected. This pleased him. "It's Wolf," he said.

"Hello, my friend. What can I do for you?

"A possible new recruit," Wolf replied, "someone who seems potentially quite useful."

"And you would like to have this person checked out." It wasn't a question.

Wolf enjoyed interacting with a professional, and Spider, leader of the Boston cell, was every bit that. "His name is Joshua Young," Wolf said. "He claims to be from Boston and to be a graduate of BU."

"Employment?"

"Software designer for Blue World Systems, a company allegedly based in San Francisco."

"But he works in Portland?"

"Teleworks out of his apartment."

"Plausible."

Wolf shared what little additional information Fern, Skye and Cahill had been able to draw out of Joshua Young. Despite their expertise and experience in such matters, it wasn't much. That's what concerned him.

Spider was silent for a moment, as if waiting for more. "Not a lot to go on," he finally said.

"I know," Wolf said. "I know."

CHAPTER 52

9:12 a.m., Friday, May 19, The Biscuit, Portland, Oregon

Ward checked his rearview again. Nobody was there. Even though he had not given his address to Wolf or any of the others, he had to go on the assumption that they knew it. A member of the cell unknown to him could have followed him back to the apartment after one of the meetings. They might have been waiting outside or disguised as a patron. Ward recalled that Cahill had exchanged greetings with several people at the Green Glow. With others there had been only a subtle acknowledgment. Could it have been one of them? Had Wolf signaled someone last night? Did he miss it? He could feel the beginnings of a familiar anxiety.

Once they knew where he lived it would be easy to set up surveillance from one of the many nearby shops or restaurants, wait for him to move. Spotting a tail was not as easy as it seemed in the movies. Again, he had taken a circuitous route, switched cars halfway, made a series of unpredictable turns, sped through traffic lights just as they changed from yellow to red, all the tricks designed to expose the careless follower. So far, there were no signs that he had company, at least not this time. But someday soon they would be there. And it was Wolf that had him on high alert.

Ward entered the alley and parked, constantly monitoring his surroundings. Satisfied that he was alone, he slipped from the car and moved quickly to the back entrance of The Biscuit. He unlocked the steel door and shoved it open. There, waiting for him, was his nemesis, the elevator. Ward took a deep breath, then another. He reached out for the up button, hesitated, and then pushed it. The stairs beckoned as the doors rumbled open. *God-dammit*, he thought, *just get on the fucking thing*. Ward stepped inside before he could change his mind. He pushed the button for the top floor. As the old beast ascended, he could feel the sweat start to form on his brow and upper lip. His heart raced faster with each clank and shudder. *This is good for me*, he kept telling himself. Finally, it reached his floor, shook violently, and then dropped a few inches. *Fuck this*, Ward thought as he jumped out. He took a few seconds to calm down before unlocking the door to the loft.

As expected, he was the first one there. Cruz and Royer wouldn't arrive until closer to ten o'clock. That was good. It would give him time to get started on his reports. Management would want to see evidence of progress, on paper. He would be sure to color things in such a way that it would buy as much time as possible. It wasn't dishonesty, more a matter of emphasis. There were always those in the chain of command who disfavored un-dercover operations, who lacked the patience to let things play out. It was true in every case he had worked and would be even more so in this one. The pressure for results, something for the po-litical types to show an anxious public, would be mounting by the hour. He could only imagine what Cruz and Royer were feel-ing. Their supervisors would be monitoring every development, micromanaging every move, breathing down their necks. It was times like this, cases like this, when he relished the relative insu-lation provided by being deep undercover. The pressure was still there, but he didn't have to constantly hear about it.

Ward went to the kitchen and started a pot of coffee. A cup of java always helped with the writing process. In fact, he had a hard time working without it. Once the coffee was brewing he fired up one of the laptops, pulled up a report template, and started to type. The words came easy, he just wished there were more to write. After thirty minutes or so he sat back and read what he had written. When he looked at it on paper he could see how much of it was arguably conjecture. He could see the progress, but he knew that the minders would want more, much more. While he was close to infiltrating this group, he didn't even know if it was the right group, and he might not know for some time. Cruz and Royer would face a barrage of questions about the viability of the operation, why the resources involved wouldn't be better utilized elsewhere. Even worse, their bosses would be interrogated at the deputy director level, or higher. Ward decided that some editing was in order.

A few minutes later Ward heard a key in the lock. Instinctively, he reached for his gun. The door swung open. It was Cruz, smiling, again carrying food. Ward had noticed that the man ate constantly and thought about food in the rare moments when he wasn't eating. Still, Cruz appeared fit.

"Let me guess," Ward said, "donuts."

"I prefer the term pastries. Less negative connotation."

Ward chuckled and went back to his typing. Cruz poured himself a cup of coffee and carried the box of pastries to the table. He helped himself to one and then shoved the box over to Ward.

"Reports?" Cruz asked, nodding at the laptop.

"Yeah."

Cruz put his feet up on the table. "How'd it go last night?"

"Made some good progress."

"Glad to hear it. The SAC is on my ass. Make it a good read. I need to show him something."

"Way ahead of you," Ward said. "I'm writing it up real nice. Even Burke might be impressed, or at least moderately encouraged."

"Doubt it. He still thinks it should be somebody from his field division doing the undercover bit."

There was a rap on the door. "It's Royer." The FBI agent walked in.

"What's with the announcement?" Cruz asked.

"I didn't want one of you two shooting me," Royer said.

"Fair enough," Cruz agreed. "Donut?" he asked, pointing toward the box.

Ward looked at him. "I thought they were pastries?"

"That's only for ATF," Cruz whispered, loud enough for Royer to hear him.

"Funny," Royer said. He took a donut, then went to get a cup of coffee.

After Royer came back to the table Ward detailed the events of the previous evening, including his impressions of Wolf, the situation with Skye and Sequoia, and Fern's failed attempt to connect.

"Well, aren't we mister irresistible," Cruz quipped, causing Royer to chuckle.

"Yeah, yeah," Ward said. He knew this was coming. "Trouble is I don't need Fern thinking I blew her off. I had to tell her I might be getting back with my ex. Now I've got a problem."

"You mean we've got a problem," Royer corrected him. "Now we have to make your girlfriend appear."

Cruz feigned a suspicious look. "Maybe that was his plan all along."

Royer ran with it. "Pretty lame way to meet women if you ask me."

"Fuck you two," Ward said. Then he relented. "Yeah, it's true. I'll meet 'em any way I can."

The three of them shared a laugh.

"Seriously, though," Royer said, "we need to come up with somebody."

Cruz nodded.

"I agree," Ward said. "If they never actually see her it will raise suspicion."

There was silence as they pondered the next move. Finally, Royer spoke. "I might have just the person," he said.

Not another FBI Agent, Ward thought. He and Cruz exchanged a look.

Royer noticed. "Trust me," he said. "You'll like her." He stood and pulled his cell phone from his jacket. "I need to make a call."

CHAPTER 53

10:22 a.m., Friday, May 19, The FBI Academy, Quantico, Virginia

Five shots rang out in quick succession. All hit their mark. Both terrorists dropped where they stood...dead.

Special Agent Rowan Parks smiled and holstered her weapon, a paintball gun that looked like the real thing. It was another successful training exercise at Hogan's Alley, the mock town constructed by Hollywood set designers on the grounds of the FBI Academy. With all the businesses one might find in any urban area, Hogan's Alley provided a realistic setting in which new agents and old could enhance their abilities in everything from firearms skills to processing crime scenes. This time it was small group of terrorists who stormed the local hotel and took hostages.

"Nice shot," one of the terrorists said as he jumped up from the ground.

"Thanks," Parks said. "Always a pleasure to take out you ISIS scum." The *terrorist* was one of the many local actors hired by the FBI to portray an assortment of bad guys at the training facility. The stressful scenarios they helped to create were essential to the training needed to minimize reaction time and make the right decision. You heard it said time and time again from agents in the field who successfully handled a dangerous situation, *my training took over*. It had to become almost instinctive.

The actor approached her. Parks looked him over. He was

good-looking, despite the jihadist attire.

"My name's Colton," the actor said. "You know, I was thinking that as you shot me and all you might make it up to a guy by going for a drink."

Parks smiled. "Nice try, but I don't date terrorists."

Colton grinned. "Can't blame a guy for trying," he said. "I have a thing for ladies with guns...and handcuffs."

"Glad to hear you support law enforcement. The answer is still no." She looked him over one more time, thought about it for a second, but decided her initial decision was the right one.

Colton started to say something when Parks' cell phone rang, saving her from any further interaction with the actor. "I need to get this," she said.

"Parks," she answered.

"Rowan, it's Bradley Royer."

"Hey, Royer. It's been awhile. What's up?"

"Been busy. Have you been following these eco-terrorist attacks, the Earth Martyrs Brigade?"

"Who hasn't? Hell, it's all over the news."

"Right. Well, I'm involved in an undercover operation out in Portland, Oregon. We have an agent here who appears poised to infiltrate a cell that might be involved."

Parks had to admit that she was a little envious. Royer was involved in the biggest case going on anywhere right now.

"The agent," Parks asked, "is he one of our guys?"

"No, ATF."

"I heard they were involved. Is he any good?"

"Yeah, he's good," Royer said. "You remember The Nation, that white supremacist group that tried to assassinate President Buckley?"

"Sure."

"He's the one that took 'em down. If he hadn't infiltrated and discovered their plan Buckley would be dead."

"Impressive. So, you say this cell might be involved?"

"They are definitely hands-on radical environmentalists. We're just not sure yet if they are part of the Earth Martyrs Brigade, EMB."

"So, I take it you think this Earth Martyrs Brigade is behind all of the attacks?"

"It's a strong possibility, but we're not sure yet. At first we thought it might be some resurgence of a more violent version of ELF, but now it doesn't look that way."

"Exciting stuff."

"I'm glad you think so."

Parks felt a little jolt of electricity. "You got something for me?" she asked, hopeful.

Royer described to her where they were at in the investigation, the recruitment and vetting of Joshua Young. Parks had been involved in her share of undercover work. She understood what it was like to lay the groundwork, and how much time it took to safely work your way in.

"So, why do you need me?" Parks asked.

"Part of the cover story is that Joshua Young moved to Portland for a woman, but they broke up. One of the cell's members, Fern, has shown a strong interest in Young. She followed him out of a café where they'd all met one night and made a move on him. Young fended her off with a story about possibly getting back together with the ex, said they'd been talking. He's afraid that if it looks like he just blew her off it could compromise his chances of infiltrating the cell. I agree with him. A hostile member will just serve to enhance any suspicion."

"So my big role is to be the girlfriend. Have I got that right?"

She could hear Royer chuckle.

"Something like that," he said. "I also wouldn't mind having one of our people directly involved in the undercover aspect, and you're one of the best."

"I'm flattered."

"It's not flattery."

"I'll have to talk to my supervisor," Parks said, "see if I can get it approved."

"I don't think that will be a problem," Royer assured her. "This one is getting all the resources requested and then some. I can call headquarters and make it happen."

"Do it," Parks said. "I'm in."

"Outstanding."

"By the way, this agent, what's his name?"

There was silence on the other end.

"I know the protocol," Parks said, "but you already told me that you can make this happen."

"Ward," Royer said. "David Ward."

"Good guy?" Parks asked.

"Yeah, seems to be."

"What's he look like?" Parks asked. She knew this would fluster Royer, who was a little uptight.

"I don't know," Royer said. "He's okay, I guess."

Parks laughed. She enjoyed prodding Royer like this. She didn't really care what Ward looked like.

"What do you mean *he's okay*?" she asked.

"I guess he's good-looking," Royer said, his voice rising ever so slightly. "What difference does it make?"

Parks could almost see Royer squirming. She decided to give him a break. "It doesn't," she admitted. "Just having a little fun."

"Hilarious," Royer said.

"Seriously, though. Do you like the guy?"

"Yeah, I do," Royer said. "He's down-to-earth, a straight shooter."

"Good. It's a lot easier to fake a relationship if I like him," Parks noted. "And making it seem real can be the difference between success and failure."

"True enough," Royer said.

It can also be the difference between life and death, Parks thought.

CHAPTER 54

1:03 p.m., Friday, May 19, Boston University, Boston, Massachusetts

Spider climbed the steps to the Stone Science Building and the Department of Earth and Environment. There were numerous sympathizers at BU, but Associate Professor Kendall Wasley was much more. Known by the moniker Storm, she was a fierce proponent of direct action. Her compelling lectures on climate change had inspired many followers. Of course, this advocacy occurred only in Spider's circles. Were the university to learn of it she would be terminated. If her other activities were discovered it would result in much more than a mere firing. She would most certainly be arrested. Storm's scientific skills had proved useful to the Earth Martyrs Brigade on many occasions, and in many ways.

Today, the request that Spider would make was much simpler. There were many potentially useful recruits, many who voiced their support, who talked a good game. But there were few who could really carry through, and fewer still who could be trusted. ELF had learned that lesson the hard way. As a former member who was betrayed by someone he once considered a friend, Spider understood the need for proper vetting better than most. The Earth Martyrs Brigade could not afford any weak links. Evidence of devotion to the cause and a willingness to endure whatever consequences came with it had to be apparent, and unquestionable. *Martyr* was the operative word. If there was ever any doubt of that the killing of Robert Titus through the sacrifice of their beloved Dove had proven otherwise.

Spider entered the building and made his way to the small office where Storm lived the other half of her double life. He had offered to meet elsewhere, but she said that she felt safest here, that it was easier for them to be followed, watched, and overheard in a more public setting. Here, they could close the door. No one would pay any attention. It would seem to be just one more meeting with one more graduate student, the references to environmental issues easily explained by the context. Though somewhat counterintuitive, Spider concluded that she was probably right. She usually was.

He stopped in front of her office and knocked. "Professor Wasley?"

The door creaked open. Storm appeared. When she saw it was him she grabbed his hand and pulled him inside. They embraced, kissing on each cheek. He stepped back and looked at her. The dark, disheveled hair and wild brown eyes reminded him of the other reason for her nickname, one he had provided. Her passion was for more than the environment, something she had demonstrated to him on numerous occasions. They were not a couple in any usual sense of the word. She was too unconventional for that, as was he. There were no expectations. Perhaps it was that spontaneity that excited them. When it happened it was a torrid encounter. Looking at her now he felt the stimulation.

Storm closed the door and locked it. Spider allowed himself a brief fantasy, even though he knew it couldn't happen here. Previous experience told him that anything physical with her would unquestionably draw attention.

"You were vague on the phone," she said, indicating that they should sit. "What can I do to serve the cause?"

Spider could see her excitement. He knew that the relatively mundane task he was about to present would disappoint. Still, she would understand the need.

"There's a new recruit...in Portland," he said.

Storm appeared confused. "Does he need instruction in more sophisticated bomb-making techniques?" she asked. "We have many good people on the west coast who are quite capable of..."

"It's nothing like that," Spider interrupted. "He claims to have been a student here."

"In the Department of Earth and Environment?"

"No, he just said that he was a student at BU."

"And what do you need me to do?"

"Confirm that. See if he engaged in any protests or other civil disobedience. Check to see if he was ever expelled. Things like that."

"You want me to conduct a background check?"

Her disappointment was palpable. "Sorry," Spider said. "You're here. You have access to school records. It needs to be done."

"Not very exciting," she said, almost pouting.

"You know why I'm asking. You know the risk we face."

Storm nodded. "I do. It's not a problem. We can't be too safe."

"Thank you."

"Is there any particular reason that you're questioning this person's commitment?" she asked.

"No. Simply being careful."

"What's the name?"

"Joshua Young."

"Do you have his year of graduation, major?"

"No, though he claims to be a software designer for a company by the name of Blue World Systems. So, possibly some sort of computer science-related degree. He is an advocate of cyber monkeywrenching. In fact, he demonstrated its usefulness with a denial-of-service attack on the Department of Energy website."

"Impressive," Storm conceded. "I can understand the interest." She appeared lost in thought for a moment, as if contemplating the possibilities, then spoke. "How about a middle name or date of birth?"

"Not yet." Spider provided what little else he knew of Young's background.

"Not much to go on."

"I realize that. We do have people checking other aspects of his story."

"Good. I'll see what I can find out here."

Their business concluded, Spider's mind drifted back to the thoughts he had on arrival. "Since I'm here," he began, "any classes to teach this afternoon?"

One eyebrow arched seductively. "Why?" she asked. "What did you have in mind?"

Bicycling home that evening Spider could think of little more than the afternoon with Storm. He sometimes regretted that there was no commitment. But it was what it was. He could live with it. Yeah, he thought, he could definitely live with it.

Spider felt his phone vibrate. He stopped in a small city park and retrieved his phone. It was her.

"Miss me already?" he asked.

"Funny," she said. "I've got something."

"That was fast."

"I aim to please."

"And you do."

She laughed. "Anyway, there have been three students with the name Joshua Young at BU in the last twenty years. One didn't graduate. Another was a history major. The third graduated with a BS in computer science in 2002."

"Okay. Good."

Spider listened as Storm relayed what additional information she was able to glean from the accessible online student records. It wasn't much, but there was nothing that raised any red flags. There were also no indications of any previous activism.

"I'll keep looking," she promised, "but it appears from this that he's legit."

Spider thought for a minute. "Do the records show a current address?"

"Nothing in this database," Storm said. "Let me see if there is anything in the alumni records."

Spider waited as she checked. He could hear the clicking of the keyboard in the background. After several minutes she spoke. "Glad you asked. It shows an address...in Portland, Oregon."

"Just a second," Spider said. "Let me grab a pen."

CHAPTER 55

1:18 p.m., Tuesday, May 23, Portland International Airport, Portland, Oregon

Ward looked at his watch. Special Agent Rowan Parks was due to arrive any minute. It was a mere four days since Royer had made the request. Ward could not recall an instance when approval for adding an additional undercover operative had gone through so quickly, not to mention over the weekend. It was a testimony to the attention this case was receiving in the corridors of power, and to the pressure building for something, anything, which could be called success. That was an ever-increasing cause for a concern. And it wasn't the only thing. The speed with which this new agent had been brought in bothered him. How could they put together an undercover persona that would withstand scrutiny in that short amount of time? They had supposedly coordinated the details with Cruz, but other than that ATF's people had not been involved. It was no way to run an operation.

Ward finished his coffee and headed for Concourse E, Parks was on a connecting flight from Chicago. As he walked along he carefully monitored for any signs that he was being followed. An airport terminal was the perfect place to tail someone, the hustle and bustle, hundreds of people naturally heading for the same concourse, many for the same gate. Otherwise suspicious behavior was easily explained by the normal flow of foot traffic. It was beyond difficult. Because of that the performance of each operative was critical.

Despite his concerns about her preparation, Royer's description of Parks had him intrigued. She was described as an almost singular talent, a chameleon who could meld into any undercover scenario. He had also seen the pictures. She was attractive, even beautiful, and would be easy to spot. It was extremely important that they immediately recognized each other when she exited the ramp into the concourse. Reunited lovers was the impression they had to leave with anyone who might be watching. She had, of course, seen pictures of him as well. This initial interaction would be a critical test, one that would let him know much about the chances of success or failure, and maybe even survival.

As he approached Concourse E Ward heard the announcement that the flight from Chicago had arrived. He waited patiently as the passengers began to disembark. One dozen, then another exited the plane. He didn't see her. A dozen more entered the airport. No Parks. He checked the piece of paper on which he had jotted down the flight number. It was the correct flight. Had she missed her connection? Had they pulled the authorization at the last minute? Surely, somebody would have called him. Ward began to pace, concerned.

Then, she appeared. The pictures did not do her justice. She was tall, maybe five-ten, her build athletic, but womanly. To Ward she had the appearance of a model for fitness apparel. But it was the face that captured his attention. Her hazel eyes were lively, intelligent. There was a sparkle in them that spoke of a life lived with passion. They were framed by high cheekbones and dark eyebrows. Her lips were full, sensuous, the kind that induced carnal thoughts. The long, brunette hair was pulled back in a ponytail that was flipped up on one shoulder. Ward momentarily forgot why he was there and why she had arrived.

"Josh!" she said, running toward him.

Dammit, Ward thought. *What is her name?* He had been so caught up in the moment that her undercover name had vanished from his mind. *Think.* Panic started to set in. Then, he had it;

Kyra...Kyra Jordan.

"Kyra!" he said.

They embraced. She pulled back slightly and looked him in the eyes, stroked his cheek, and then kissed him, passionately, or at least it seemed that way to Ward. The kiss lingered, soft, supple, and then repeated. Her mouth moved on his. Ward's head started to swim. His body began to respond. People around them stepped back and watched. All told, it was a convincing performance on her part. Ward wasn't so sure that any part of it was a performance for him.

Parks hugged him again and whispered in his ear. "Thought you were gonna draw a blank on my name."

Ward crashed back to reality.

"Not likely," he said. "Nice kiss," he added, struggling mightily for some witty response.

"Don't get any ideas," she whispered. "All part of the act."

Ward felt a twinge of disappointment.

Parks reached down and took his hand. "Let's go get my luggage," she said. "I can't wait to get you back to the apartment."

Ward saw an older woman raise her eyebrow at the comment. The gentleman with her, presumably her husband, looked longingly at Parks. He gave Ward a knowing smile and a nod of congratulations. His wife caught the exchange. She spun the old man around and marched him off without comment.

They walked along, hand-in-hand, toward baggage claim, to all outward appearances a couple in love. The casual conversation fit the role. There was no operational talk. They were strictly in character. As they strolled along, Ward saw many an appreciative look follow Parks, most by men, but plenty by women. Of the latter, the majority seemed jealous, a few desirous. But the natural attention Parks drew made any unnatural attention more difficult to spot. Ward briefly wondered if she were too good-looking, if someone more common in appearance would allow them to blend in better. Was he simply being sexist? Maybe so. In any event, it was becoming clear to him that this mission would have its own unique challenges.

They retrieved Parks' luggage from the baggage carousel. There was less than Ward had anticipated given the amount of time that she might have to be there. Parks hoisted one smaller bag over her shoulder and pulled up the handles on two pieces of rolling luggage. "You can take that one," she said, nodding toward the bag that was left. "Where are you parked?"

Ward looked around, self-conscious and concerned at appearing so unchivalrous. It seemed out of character. "Please let me help you with those," he insisted. Parks seemed to get the point. "Thanks, sweetie" she said, relinquishing the handle on one of the rollers.

They walked to short-term parking and loaded the luggage into Ward's Prius. Once they were inside the vehicle Parks turned to him and extended her hand. "Special Agent Rowan Parks," she said. "Nice to meet you."

CHAPTER 56

9:12 p.m., Tuesday, May 23, Baker, Montana, near the route of the Keystone XL Pipeline

Coyote steered his truck into the parking lot of the Transcontinental Bar and Grill. The old man working at the motel desk had told him that the name came from the construction of Baker along the rail line of the now defunct Milwaukee Road. Whatever. He didn't give a shit about any of that. The more important information was that the place served as a hangout for the workers building the Keystone Pipeline, one of the greatest threats to the environment ever perpetrated by the human race. Those workers would soon pay a price for their role in creating this scar across the land.

The Minneapolis cell had formed by tapping into a rich vein of activism that flowed through the Twin Cities. Those dissatisfied with the half measures of groups like ELF and ALF had eagerly embraced the more militant philosophy of the Earth Martyrs Brigade. He was one of them. Little time remained to alter the course of the Earth's decline. Direct action was needed. Bloodshed was required and was soon to occur. He was saddened by the fact that his role was merely that of reconnaissance.

Coyote parked the truck. He checked himself in the rearview mirror. The beard had come in nicely, dark and full. A welder's cap, worn Carhartt jacket, flannel shirt and work boots completed the look. He was a welder from South Dakota who had come in looking for work on the pipeline. He was told that this was the place to go, that someone here could steer him in the right direction. They would steer him in the right direction alright, just not one that they could have possibly anticipated. Coyote smiled at the thought as he exited the truck.

As he walked in, Coyote barely drew a glance. He was just one more working man in a place that was full of them. It was exactly the reaction he had hoped for. He headed toward the bar where only one open seat remained.

"Anybody sitting here?" he asked the man to his right, a grizzled, leathery specimen in a welder's cap.

The man eyed him as if measuring an opponent. "Nope," he answered, and went back to his beer.

Coyote took a seat. He nodded to the man on his left, another rough-looking customer, his face reminiscent of a parched lakebed in some drought-stricken corner of the globe. The man nodded back. Coyote ordered a beer and attempted to start a conversation.

"You on the pipeline?' he asked.

The man looked at him for a moment, considering whether to engage. Finally, one corner of his mouth curled into something that was cross between a snarl and a smile. He spoke through yellow, tobacco-stained teeth in a voice that sounded like a cement mixer.

"Yeah, I'm on the pipeline," he said. "You?"

"Looking for work," Coyote answered. "Guy at the motel told me this might be a good place to get a tip on who to talk to."

The man nodded. "I suppose he's right." He eyed Coyote's cap. "Welder, I take it?"

"Yep."

The man's eyes narrowed. "Union?" he asked.

Coyote was fairly certain that he knew the right answer. "Yes, sir," he lied. Having anticipated this, he had a forged union card ready to display if pressed.

The man smiled and held out a huge, gnarled hand. "Name's Walt," he said.

Coyote shook quickly, hoping Walt wouldn't notice the relative absence of scars and calluses on his own hands. There were some things that you just couldn't fake.

"Carl," Coyote said. "Carl Thompson." It was a safe, relatively common name.

"Where you in from, Carl?"

"South Dakota, Rapid City to be precise."

Walt grinned. "Been to Sturgis twenty-eight years straight," he said proudly.

Coyote knew that he was referring to the Sturgis Motorcycle Rally which was held in the small town of Sturgis about twenty miles northwest of Rapid City. Walt looked like he would fit right in.

"Been there many times," Coyote lied. He knew enough about the event to talk in generalities but didn't want to get pinned down on any specifics. He needed to change the subject.

"How 'bout you, Walt? Where you from?"

"Billings…born and raised. Been there all my life, other than a short diversion into the Marines Corps."

Coyote feigned a respectful nod in acknowledgement of the man's service. Just then, the bartender brought his beer. Walt's was getting low. "Get my friend another," Coyote announced.

"Appreciate it," Walt said, tipping his bottle as a gesture of gratitude. "Now, let's talk about getting you some work." He waved over the bartender and asked for some paper. A piece was torn from a small notepad by the cash register and placed in front of him.

Walt pulled a pen from his jacket pocket and began to write. Coyote noticed how the pen seemed out of place in the welder's thick, rough fingers.

"Here are the names and numbers for two of the job site supervisors," Walt said. "Both have hiring authority. Neither one is too much of an asshole." He flipped over the sheet of paper. "And this is a map out to the trailer that serves as the office for this stretch of the project." When he was done he slid the paper over to his new friend. "Tell them I sent you."

"Will that get it done?" Coyote asked with a smile.

"Fuck no," Walt said with a gravelly laugh. "But it's a start."

Coyote chuckled. He almost hoped that Walt wasn't hit in the attack that would follow. But if he was, fuck it. Walt looked like a guy with a pretty big carbon footprint.

Walt's directions were dead on. Coyote drove past the trailer that served as the job site office. The lights were still on and there appeared to be considerable activity both inside and out. As he had been told, work was ongoing, twenty-four seven. He could see the arc of a welder's torch in the distance.

Coyote checked his watch. It was a quarter past one. He drove another mile and turned onto a gravel road. Another half mile and he pulled into the entrance to a farm field and turned off the truck. There were no lights to be seen other than the faint glow from the work site well off in the distance. Coyote exited the truck. Now dressed in black, he began the hike back toward the pipeline.

Fifteen minutes later he approached the site. Light-gathering binoculars hung from his neck, but a normal set would have likely sufficed. The work site was well lit, so well-lit that his primary concern was to avoid being seen. He used the natural cover to work his way around the job location as he carefully mapped the area: the available routes in and out, the best vantage points, the location of the workers. When he returned to the motel he would complete the packet that would be provided to the assault team. How he wished he could be with them. Their efforts would change everything. Afterwards, no amount of money would entice the workers needed to complete this abomination.

CHAPTER 57

7:16 p.m., Wednesday, May 24, Ward's undercover apartment, The Hawthorne District, Portland, Oregon

Wolf had asked to meet at the Green Glow later that night. Ward was surprised that when he mentioned the arrival of Kyra it was insisted that she come along. There was little choice but to agree. It was risky to throw Parks into the fire this soon. There had been limited time to prep her. But opportunities arose when they did. You had to be ready to take advantage of them. Still, something told him that Wolf had ulterior motives.

Ward heard the shower turn off. Parks was cleaning up after going for a run. He had to admit the sight of her in her tights had been hard to ignore. He reminded himself to keep it professional. An involvement could compromise judgment, with lethal consequences. He heard a hairdryer start up. It was impossible not to imagine her standing at the mirror, the warm air blowing through her dark hair. His mind drifted to places it shouldn't go.

Moments later the door to a steamy bathroom opened. Parks emerged, wrapped in nothing but a towel. Her skin was flushed... healthy. The aroma of lotion on warm flesh followed her. Ward envisioned the application.

"Sorry," she said casually. "Forgot my robe."

"Not a problem," Ward replied. He meant it.

Parks headed toward the refrigerator. "I need a drink. What've we got?" She bent over, checking the contents.

Ward briefly considered averting his eyes but chose otherwise. "There's some pretty good beer in there," he said. "It's from a local brewery. Sorry, I don't have much else."

"Beer works." Parks opened the bottle and took a long swig. "Whew, that hit the spot." She leaned over the kitchen counter, fingers caressing the bottle. "So, why do you think Wolf asked to meet?"

Her question caused Ward to snap out of his beer commercial fantasy. "Don't know," he said. "Maybe he was planning to involve me in something. That's sort of how he left it last time. Now that you're coming along he won't discuss anything operational. He'll want to check you out."

"I'm ready." Parks took another swig from her beer. She looked down at herself and then, smiling, back up at Ward. "Or at least I will be in a few minutes."

Somehow he was sure that she would be more than ready.

"That's it," Ward said, nodding toward the Green Glow Café as they passed by. "You'll find it...interesting."

"I'm sure," Parks replied.

They found a spot a block away and parked the Prius.

"Prepare for a secondhand buzz," Ward said as they approached the door. He went to open it, but Parks beat him to it.

"Whoa," Parks said as they walked in. "You weren't kidding. I thought you couldn't use marijuana in public?"

He gestured across the room. "As you can see, the rules are not strictly enforced."

Parks nodded. "Inevitable that this is where it would end up," she said.

Ward spotted Wolf. He was at the same table they had used the week before. Was it considered to be his table? Last time Ward had been left with the distinct impression that management catered to Wolf. That was a situation worth keeping in mind. More importantly, Fern was with him. Wolf knew that Joshua

Young was bringing his girlfriend. Was Fern tasked with vetting her? He had to assume that Wolf had no idea what had transpired between he and Fern. She wouldn't tell him that, would she? Then it hit him, what if she had been put up to it? No, it couldn't be, could it?

"She's here," Ward said.

"Who?"

"Fern, the one who made a move on me, the reason you're here."

"Interesting," Parks said. A mischievous smile appeared on her face. "Game on, Fern. Nobody messes with my man." She reached down and took Ward's hand. "Let's go, Josh."

Ward felt a thrill as her fingers intertwined with his. Convincingly playing the role of Kyra Jordan's boyfriend was going to be the easy part of this operation.

As they approached the table Ward saw the expression on Fern's face go from serious to a strained sort of pleasant. She eyed Kyra Jordan up and down, adopting an expression similar to the one he had seen when she introduced him to the beautiful Skye. It was a little sad. No, she had not been put up to it. When she made her play for him it had been the real thing.

Ward thought about how these human moments always found their way into investigations, vulnerable, sometimes even kind incidents involving otherwise bad people. He always wondered how they ended up where they were. It was nature and nurture, but the nature wasn't always evil. In fact, it was often something else. There were those who were weak and impressionable, many with a desperate need for a sense of belonging. Others combined a sense of entitlement and a desire for immediate gratification with a lack of appreciation for long-term consequences. What, he wondered, had brought Fern to this point? Was it simply what it seemed, a badly misguided idealism? If so, it made her no less dangerous. That much he knew for sure.

"Joshua," Wolf said, extending his hand.

"Hi, Josh," Fern added. She made no move to embrace him as

she had on previous occasions.

"And this must be…" Wolf started to say.

"Kyra Jordan," Parks said, taking the initiative. She took his hand in both of hers. "Wolf, is it?"

"It's what I go by," Wolf said, almost apologetically.

Ward was surprised. He sensed that some dynamic had already changed.

"And this is Fern," Ward said, gesturing.

"Pleased to meet you," Parks said, nodding at her.

"You, too," Fern replied through a forced smile.

"Please, sit," Wolf said. As they did, the questioning began. "So, Kyra, what do you do for a living?"

Parks went smoothly into her cover story. "I do website design," she said. "I mostly work from home."

"How did you and Josh meet?" Fern asked.

Ward noticed that Wolf shot her a look. Either the questioning was to be left to him or Fern had come in before her cue.

"Yes, tell us," Wolf said. "How did you and Josh meet?"

"We met in college." Parks lovingly placed her hand on Ward's shoulder. "Seems like such a long time ago."

"You've been together quite a while," Fern observed, ignoring Wolf's glare.

Parks laughed. "Not really. We were both with other people back then. There was some interest, but…you know how it goes," she said to Fern. "We actually ran into each other several years later at a wedding reception, one thing led to another…"

"I see," Fern said, eyeing Ward.

Wolf gestured to a waiter, who came immediately. Ward wondered if he did it to stop Fern. If so, it had no effect. She started back in almost immediately after they ordered their drinks.

"I understand the two of you just got back together?" she asked.

Parks gave him a stern look as if to say, *you told them that*. It was beautifully played.

"That's right," she said, keeping her eyes on Ward. "We had

a rough patch, but we're through that." She reached down and gave his hand a squeeze. "In fact, I moved in with him this past weekend. He had to sign a one-year lease. I was renting on a month-to-month basis. It made more sense."

"Sure," Fern said, looking disappointed.

Ward could see that she appeared to be reluctantly coming to terms with the fact that the relationship between Josh and Kyra was real. If she only knew, he thought.

"Where was it that you lived before?" Wolf asked.

"I was on northeast Shaver," she answered.

Ward felt a surge of panic. Had Parks thought this through? What if Wolf pushed for a specific address? Parks patted his hand to tell him, *I got this.*

"It's a long street," Wolf said, smiling. "Where at?"

"Right where it intersects with Martin Luther King Junior Boulevard. It's a big apartment complex. We didn't really know any better when we first moved out here. Right, Josh?"

"That's right," Ward said. Did the FBI have a safe house down there, he wondered?

"The nice thing was," Parks continued, "it had a LEED Gold rating. Very environmentally friendly."

Wolf nodded. He seemed satisfied with the answer. It was then that the waiter brought their drinks and took their dinner order. A welcome reprieve, Ward thought.

After some small talk, Wolf started back in with the questions.

"Joshua here seems to be quite the ardent environmentalist," he said. "Do you share his views, Kyra?"

"I do," Parks said. "If anything, I make him look pretty tame."

"Is that so?" Wolf asked.

"It is," Ward said.

"It's one of the things that drew us together," Parks said. "It's also what drew us to Portland. We wanted to be in a city that had a strong environmental ethic. In that regard, we couldn't think of a better place."

"No question about that," Fern interjected. She looked at

Wolf. Ward saw him shake his head.

"My fear is that the damage to our planet is quickly approaching the point at which it will become irreversible," Parks said, "if we're not already there."

"I'm afraid we are," Wolf said.

"Our government lacks the will to change course," Parks added. "It's up to the citizens."

Wolf raised his glass in a toast. "To Mother Earth, and to those who would protect her," he said. "May their mission be successful."

As he took a drink, Ward wondered at Wolf's last comment. It almost seemed to refer to something specific. He grew concerned.

Wolf looked back over his shoulder as he approached his car. No one was around. He punched in the Boston number and pressed the call button as he entered the vehicle.

"Hello?"

"It's Wolf. I have another request."

"Of course."

"The name is Kyra Jordan." Wolf provided what additional specifics he had been able to obtain throughout the evening. There weren't many.

"I'll do my best."

"You always do."

CHAPTER 58

10:32 p.m., Wednesday, May 24, the Keystone XL Pipeline, just outside Baker, Montana

Lightning crackled across the horizon, an electric purple hue illuminating the storm clouds from within. Seconds later, the thunder rolled. To Bison's ears it was the manifestation of Mother's rage as she looked down upon the Keystone Pipeline and the horrid scar it cut across her land. It was announcement that her warriors were coming, and that they would stop this abomination, even if those who would build it must die.

Even in the dark Bison could see that the gravel road was seldom used and poorly maintained. There was little chance that any traffic would pass by. He parked the black sedan in the entrance to a cornfield, the one noted on the map. They exited and locked the vehicle, not that it would matter if it were searched. There was nothing inside to tie it to them or the Yellowstone cell—no indicia of lease or ownership, no DNA, no anything. The plates would come back to a California vehicle, having been removed before it was junked.

No farmhouses were within view. The only light that could be seen was the faint glow from the work site a mile distant. Bison and Otter adjusted their weapons and began the hike. It was difficult terrain. At a good clip it would take them almost fifteen minutes to get within range and sight in. Still, they would be in place well before the shift change, thus providing the opportunity for maximum impact.

They drew near. As had been reported, the site was well-lit. That, along with the high-grade, light-gathering scopes on their rifles, made it unnecessary to get too close. They were both excellent shots, having honed their skills over weeks of practice. Bison was confident that they could hit their mark. Of course, they also wanted to keep their distance to maximize their chances at escape. There were other battles to fight. Even so, for Bison the prospect of martyrdom was not unacceptable. Indeed, he sometimes fantasized about it. It would show Erin that he was capable of greatness, worthy of the love she had not given him in life. Though he loved her, he wanted her to taste that remorse. His pace quickened.

When they were at an appropriate distance from the site Bison signaled for Otter to halt. Dropping to one knee, he used a small penlight to consult the map that had been prepared by the surveillance team. Bison had no idea who or how many had done the reconnaissance, or how their materials had come to him, he only knew that they were excellent. The perfect vantage points for a sniper were expertly mapped. Within minutes they had identified the best spots. He would take the more northern position, while Otter would set up almost one hundred yards to his south. The crossfire effect would cause confusion and add to the chaos, immeasurably increasing the terror. It was an attack that would figure prominently in the annals of the cause, one that would inspire their warriors for generations. And as for the Keystone Pipeline, no one would work on it or any other such artery of filth again. The pipeline industry would be dead and this insult to Mother would be eradicated for all time.

They activated the chronograph function on their watches. The firing would start in five minutes, just before the shift change at eleven o'clock. It would continue for one minute. At that point they would head for their vehicle. No further shots would be fired unless needed to cover their retreat. The escape route was a series of little used country roads that eventually led to Interstate 94 and escape. A vehicle swap had been arranged at a rest area, just to be safe. The key was to be out of the area before law enforcement had anything in the air. The sound of chopper blades cutting through the night was something he did not want to hear.

Bison nodded at Otter and mouthed the word, *go*. As his comrade vanished into the darkness Bison unfolded the bipod stand on the Remington 700. He settled in, flat on his belly, and peered through the sight. There was considerable activity around the pipeline as workers began to come and go. He cursed them, greedy scum who would irreparably damage the planet for nothing more than money. It had to stop. He looked at his watch. Thirty seconds to go time. Bison began to count down in his mind. He pressed his eye to the scope and selected a target, his first of many. Five, four, three, two...

The first shot hit its mark. Bison saw the welder collapse into a heap. Those around him seemed confused, unsure of what was happening. Another went down just after Bison heard the crack of Otter's rifle. Then the workers knew that they were under fire. Men ran, dove for cover, heads swiveling as they tried to figure out where it was coming from, where to hide. Bison pulled the trigger. Another dropped. There were screams of terror. They pointed in every direction, except his. It was utter chaos, just as he had hoped.

They dropped one by one, the shots coming in rapid succession. Some of the workers tried to pull their wounded colleagues out of harm's way. Bison focused on the weathered face of a man in a welder's cap who was attempting to drag another to nearby cover. The wounded man was large, going maybe three hundred pounds. The welder's yellow, tobacco-stained teeth were clinched together with effort as he struggled to move the big man. Bison watched for a moment as the welder made slow progress, a foot at a time, the strain so real that Bison could almost feel it himself. They were close, so close, a large generator just a few feet away. Three, maybe four surges forward and they would be there, safe. Bison placed the crosshairs on the welder's cap. One surge, two…he squeezed the trigger. The cap exploded into blood and brain mater. Bison felt his heart thud in his chest, felt himself going erect. He was told that could happen. He liked it.

Bison looked at his watch. He had been firing for one minute and five seconds. *Dammit*, he thought. It had gone so fast. But it was time to move. He rose to his feet and slung the rifle over his shoulder. There was no time to collect casings. It didn't matter. Both weapons would be at the bottom of the nearby Yellowstone River in short order. Even if found, they would have no finger-prints or any DNA trace to tie them to either he or Otter.

Despite his size, Bison moved quickly, catching up to Otter in a few minutes. He could hear the shouts and screams behind him as the chaotic scene at the worksite continued to unfold. They charged ahead at a dead run, struggling to maintain their footing in the dark. When they were halfway across the field it began to rain, hard. Twenty yards from the car Bison went down in the mud, losing his grip on the rifle. He jumped up and went down again. Crawling toward the rifle he clutched it and then moved carefully toward the waiting Otter.

"C'mon, man!" Otter yelled. "Let's go!"

Bison scowled at him as he threw the rifle in the trunk. Seconds later they were loaded in the black sedan, flying down gravel roads at a wild pace, tires spinning as they occasionally lost trac-tion. The wind howled, sweeping the rain sideways, dousing the windshield and making it difficult to see. But even through the storm they could soon see the faint flicker of emergency lights in the distance and hear the far-off wail of sirens as first responders raced to the massacre they had left in their wake.

CHAPTER 59

8:43 a.m., Thursday, May 25, Office of the Chief of Staff, The White House, Washington, D.C.

The phone hadn't stopped ringing since he walked in the door at six-thirty that morning. White House Chief of Staff Michael Cooper had been besieged with calls about what was already being referred to as the Keystone Massacre. The so-called Earth Martyrs Brigade had claimed responsibility. Everybody wanted to know why the Buckley administration seemed incapable of containing the threat posed by a bunch of eco-terrorists. He wanted a better answer to that question himself, and none was being provided. Just as Cooper thought about making another call to the director of the FBI, the phone rang again. He grabbed the receiver off the hook.

"Yeah, Sally," he said to his longtime receptionist. "Who is it this time?"

"You got time to talk to Senator Hutchins?" she asked. "He seems pretty adamant."

Cooper rubbed his head and groaned. It was a call he had expected, and there was no way to duck it. Thad Hutchins was the senior senator from Montana. The attack had occurred in his state. These were his constituents. Plus, he had been a strong Buckley supporter during the last election.

"Yeah," Cooper moaned, "put him through."

As soon as he heard the click indicating that the connection was made, Cooper spoke. "Senator, my condolences to the victims of—"

"Mike, what the hell is going on with this investigation? This is the country that defeated Hitler, won the goddamn Cold War! We can't stop a bunch of eco-terrorist hippies? My constituents want some answers! Goddammit, I want some answers!"

Cooper closed his eyes and rubbed his temples as he contemplated how to respond. The placid assurances of the White House press room would do little to placate a United States senator, particularly one who had once served as U.S. attorney. Hutchins knew the drill. There was no way to bullshit him. Cooper decided that he was forced to go with the truth. His prior relationship with Hutchins afforded him the luxury of being blunt.

"Shit, Thad!" Cooper exclaimed. "Don't you think I would like to have some answers? We're doing everything we can to stop this. Everything! These bastards are sophisticated, disciplined and dedicated. It's a bad fucking combination. You know I can't get into the particulars of the investigation—to the extent I'm even aware of them—but I can promise you that we are leaving no stone unturned. We are following up on every lead, no matter how remote or seemingly insignificant."

"I understand that," Hutchins said, his tone calming, "but folks are scared by this. Nobody knows where these crazies are gonna strike next."

"I can assure you, the president is very sensitive to that. He wants this group stopped more than anybody. We are getting daily briefings on the case, and he has had numerous conversations with the relevant law enforcement officials."

"Maybe he needs to apply a little more pressure," Hutchins said, "let people know that their jobs could be at stake."

"I think that a phone call direct from the president of the United States is quite a bit of pressure, Thad. That fact alone likely suggests to the recipient that their job could be in danger, don't you think?"

Hutchins grunted. "I suppose. It's not a call I would have

wanted when I was U.S. Attorney."

"Exactly," Cooper said. "Look, I'll make sure the president is aware of how important this is to you. You've been a good friend to this administration and he will want to know." Cooper was sure that this little stroke would mollify Hutchins and let him get off the phone.

"Well, I've done whatever I can to help out my good friend Sam Buckley," Hutchins said, "and I'll continue to do so in the future."

Hutchins' attitude had done a one-eighty. He was now back on board, at least for the time being. Cooper felt that he had done his job.

"Much appreciated, Senator," he said. "You're one of our country's real leaders on Capitol Hill. The president always speaks highly of you." Cooper thought he felt a bit of his breakfast coming up in his throat.

"And I of him," Hutchins said cheerily. "If there's anything I can do to help on this end of Pennsylvania Avenue don't hesitate to call."

"I'll do that," Cooper said. "My best to your family."

"The same to yours," Hutchins replied. "And please give the president my best."

"I'll do that."

Cooper hung up the phone. He let out a long sigh. *They don't pay me enough*, he thought. He stared at the stack of newspapers on his desk. The Keystone story was the lead article in every one. It led all the morning news broadcasts. This was a story that had legs, long legs. And it was a problem that threatened to overwhelm the President's agenda. He picked up the phone.

"Sally get Director Boone on the line, and conference in Lucas Decker over at ATF. Tell them it's urgent."

"On it, Chief," Sally replied.

FBI Director Norman Boone had been nominated by the last administration but was a good man who had done a solid job with the bureau, implementing needed changes. The president had faith in him. Decker was one of their own picks, having been selected to head the beleaguered Bureau of Alcohol, Tobacco, Firearms and Explosives only a year earlier. A tough former U.S. Attorney, he had been brought in from the outside to help rebuild and reinvigorate an agency damaged by scandal and low morale. His first year on the job had been cause for optimism. Now he was faced with this. Cooper could only imagine the pressure the man must be feeling. It would be almost as bad for Boone. He only hoped that the two of them could give him something, anything that the president could use to reassure a worried nation.

CHAPTER 60

8:14 p.m., Thursday, May 25, on the Cascade Highway, some-where outside Portland, Oregon

Ward sat on an aftermarket bench seat that had been installed in the rear of the cargo van in which he was now riding. The space in front of him was open. There were no other seats, other than those of the driver and passenger. It was an odd configuration, one that raised disturbing possibilities, including kidnapping and execution. It was not hot inside the vehicle, yet he was sweating. Did they notice? Had this been a mistake? Maybe, but he had to do something, particularly after the attack on the Keystone Pipeline. Pressure was mounting. Cruz and Royer had not come right out and said it, but they were desperate for results, feeling the heat, as was everyone involved in this investigation. It was time to get aggressive, and this was an opportunity that he could not ignore, if opportunity was the right word.

It was Wolf who had invited him to *go for a ride*. Normally, this was not the kind of thing that an undercover agent wanted to hear. While Ward was confident in his cover story, doubt came from the fact that Kyra Jordan had not been invited to join them. Maybe it was nothing more than they were not yet done vetting her. That was likely. But Ward could not shake the thought that they had discovered a hole in Parks' background. A flaw in her story could become a flaw in his, leading to a ride to a remote location. The Earth Martyrs Brigade, if that's who he was now with, had certainly shown themselves capable of killing anyone who stood in their way. He had to assume this would include law enforcement. Ward's mind went back to the firefighter, Andy Garner, and his family. He could not let them down.

Cruz and Royer were behind them somewhere in a follow vehicle. The thought offered limited comfort. It was critical that they stay far enough behind to avoid being spotted. Ward knew that he could be dead and dumped in a field before they could do a damn thing. It wasn't the first time he had been in this type of situation, but that sure as hell didn't make it any easier.

He had no idea where they were headed. Wolf had said little during the ride. Were they going to some sort of meeting place, to the scene of a potential attack, or to the place of Joshua Young's intended demise? Ward also didn't know what to make of the fact that he hadn't been blindfolded. That could mean a couple of things: they believed there was no need because he would not be coming back, or they trusted him. Concentrating on his own survival, Ward focused his sight out the front windshield, noting markers along the way, all the time carefully watching for Wolf's eyes in the rearview mirror to see if they might divulge something of his intent.

Ward felt the heft of the pistol strapped to his ankle. It gave him comfort, though he wondered how he would explain it if they frisked him. More and more people now carried, but it still might seem odd to some that a software designer and environmental activist was packing. Well, he would cross that bridge if he came to it. The old standby of having once been the victim of a mugging sufficed for most.

The van began to slow. Wolf hit the turn signal. Fern, who was in the passenger seat, turned to Ward.

"We're here," she said, smiling.

Ward nodded. The smile from Fern was a good sign. He didn't see her being so cheery if this was a hit. Then he had second thoughts about that.

"Where is here?" Ward asked.

"You'll see in a minute," Wolf replied, though the question had clearly not been directed to him.

They had been on the road for thirty minutes and in a mainly rural area for at least ten. Ward knew that they were due south of Portland. He had seen signs showing they were on Oregon Highway 213 and indicating that they had passed West Linn and Oregon City. Beyond that he knew little. The place they were turning into appeared to be some sort of farm. He could see crops, though they were too distant to make out the type. A tractor sat unattended next to one of the fields, and chickens ran free, scattering as the van came down the gravel drive. As they curved to the right an old farmhouse appeared. The lights were off, but a pickup was parked in front. Just beyond the house was a barn. It was there that Wolf stopped. Fern looked back at Ward.

"This is where it happens," she said.

There was nothing particularly ominous in the pronouncement. Still, Ward saw Wolf shoot her a look, as if to say, *not yet.*

Fern stepped out and opened the sliding door on the side of the van. When she did, Ward could see that there were already several vehicles present. This was it, some sort of meeting place. He felt a jolt of adrenaline. He was in. Stay calm, he reminded himself. Ward stepped out as Wolf came around the side of the van, a guarded smile on his face.

"Welcome to our fellowship," he said. "We believe you will find it to be a group of…likeminded individuals." Then Wolf's smile vanished. "What is said here stays here. It is a rule strictly enforced. Do you understand?"

"Of course," Ward replied. The threat was scarcely veiled.

"Good. We believe you can do much to help our cause." Wolf held out his hand. As Ward shook it the hint of a smile returned to Wolf's face. Ward hoped that it was truly one of camaraderie, and not simply in anticipation of some sadistic pleasure. He turned to Fern. There was nothing about her that indicated anything bad was about to happen. Despite their failed connection, she seemed pleased to have him there. He started to relax, as much as the situation would allow.

Wolf gestured toward the barn. Fern led the way. She slid open the large door to expose a small group already present inside. Ward spotted Skye and Sequoia, along with five others. He wondered if the nine comprised the entire cell.

Skye smiled and came toward them. Sequoia did not.

"Hello, Josh," she said. "Welcome."

"I'm happy to be here," Ward said. It was true, but not for reasons anyone there understood.

"In this place you will be known as Lightning," Wolf said. "As you know by now, we discourage the use of real names for reasons of security. Lightning seemed an appropriate moniker for one who can strike quickly through the internet."

"I like it," Ward said. Something along the lines of Eagle or Hawk would have been better, he thought.

One by one Wolf introduced those members of the cell that Ward had not previously met: Cobra, Firefly, Mouse, Rabbit, and River. Each seemed pleased to have him there, to welcome a new environmental warrior. Ward spent the evening visiting with them, discussing environmental issues, espousing direct action. All the time, Wolf watched him closely. None of the members discussed operational details. Ward was certain that there were such details but concluded that Wolf had instructed them to avoid those topics, presumably until Lightning, as he was now known, was fully accepted. That meant that there was some further test. The question became whether it would be a test mandated by Wolf, or one that Ward was able to offer himself and then pass to prove his credibility. He would need to talk with Cruz and Royer about another staged cyber-attack.

Toward the end of the evening Ward found himself in a conversation with the aptly named Mouse, a diminutive man who, based on his claimed training as an electrical engineer, was likely an adept creator of sophisticated timers. As he and Mouse discussed the relative merits of hybrid vehicles, Ward started to overhear an exchange between Cobra and Wolf.

"Last night was an incredible success," Cobra said. "Keystone has come to a halt and won't start up again anytime soon."

Ward went rigid. He saw Wolf quickly glance his direction, then take Cobra by the elbow and move him off to a different section of the barn. Ward could not hear the subsequent exchange between them but could clearly sense their elation. There was no question now. He was someplace that he needed to be.

CHAPTER 61

9:27 a.m., Friday, May 26, at a deserted shooting range outside Austin, Texas

The 3D printer had cost a mere six hundred dollars. A sufficient quantity of thermoplastic had been obtained without difficulty. The design software was easily found and downloaded from the internet. The entire production had occurred in the spare bedroom that he now used as an office, with his neighboring tenants having no inkling that a weapons manufacturer lived next door. Ant was astonished at how simple it had been to build a plastic gun, one that would be utterly invisible to metal detectors. The firing pin, which consisted of nothing more than a roofing nail, could be slipped through security with minimal effort. And now, finally, there was the capability of producing plastic ammunition. Ant quivered at the thought. This would change everything, he thought...everything.

Federal law required that a plastic gun contain a metal part so that it could be picked up by a standard metal detector. The requirement was a joke. Even if the manufacturer chose to comply, the part was not necessary for the gun to fire and could be easily removed before the shooter attempted to gain entry to the relevant facility. Ant wondered at the political compromise that yielded such a foolish result. Whatever forces caused it, he thanked them. They had secured the means by which an epic blow would be struck in defense of Mother.

Ant pulled into the lot and parked. The range was deserted this early in the morning. Even if it weren't, few in Texas would question his right to produce and fire such a weapon. Indeed, the novelty had begun to wear off. Still, there was no need to attract undue attention, particularly given this gun's eventual mission. He didn't know the particulars. He didn't need to know. It was enough that he had been assured of the importance of his contribution. His ignorance as to the ultimate use provided protection for him and the group. It also allowed him to speculate, in an enjoyable fashion, as to the many ways in which his weapon might be utilized to further the cause.

Now it was time to test-fire his baby. He had read that earlier models occasionally exploded, injuring the shooter, particularly when firing regular ammunition and multiple rounds. Those bugs had been mostly worked out. Still, there was some apprehension. He had never attempted anything like this. And despite the cause, Ant had no desire to lose a few digits, or worse.

Ant retrieved the case from the back seat. He unlocked it and removed the gun. The sixteen separate pieces had already been assembled into the final product. It was an odd-looking contraption for sure. Made of white plastic, bulky, and with a short, thick barrel, it certainly was nothing that would win any design awards. He weighed the weapon in his hand. It was light compared to a standard firearm, but every bit as lethal.

Moving to the range, Ant took one of the silhouette targets obtained for the test and set it up in front of an earthen mound at the end that captured the fired rounds. He stepped back, studying the target, smiling at the possibilities as to who it could represent. Perhaps it would be a member of Congress, maybe a cabinet secretary, or even another oil company executive. For him, the target mattered less than the means. The use of an undetectable firearm, particularly in a location that was believed to be secure, would strike terror in the hearts of those who would exploit Mother's treasures. None of them would feel safe. How could they not change their ways to appease Mother's defenders?

Ant paced off the distance that he assumed would exist between the shooter and the target. He had no way to know. It was just a guess. Twenty feet seemed reasonable for the first shot. He would also try at thirty and forty feet. He would shoot quickly, knowing that the actual scenario would allow little time to aim. Satisfied with the spot, he loaded the weapon. Then, he took a deep breath, lifted the gun and fired.

The good news was that the weapon did not explode. The bad news was that the bullet hit the paper target, but outside the human silhouette. Perhaps he had fired too quickly. Ant replayed the shot in his mind. He then reloaded the gun, raised it and fired again. This time he hit his mark, a tear opening in the center of the chest. Ant smiled. He envisioned a certain conservative senator, one indebted to Big Oil's campaign dollars, sprawled out on the floor of the Capitol rotunda, a pool of blood spreading around him like the oil slicks that seemed to cause him little concern. It was a beautiful image.

The next shots came from thirty, forty and even fifty feet. Ant was surprised at the weapon's accuracy. There was little doubt that the assassin, if even a fair shot, could accomplish the mission. It seemed more than he could believe. But it was true. He had just seen it with his own eyes. The full magnitude of what was possible began to hit him. He stared at the funny-looking gun in his hand, contemplating its place in history, his place in history.

Returning to reality, Ant quickly retrieved the target and cleaned up all evidence of his presence. He walked briskly toward the car where he locked the gun in its case, placing it and the other items in the trunk.

As he pulled out of the lot, Ant tapped the button on his steering wheel that activated the hands-free phone system. When prompted, he stated the name of the person he wished to call, at least the name he knew him by.

"Hello." The voice was calm, soothing, otherworldly. "You have results."

"It works!" Ant could not contain his excitement. "And even

better than I could have hoped!"

"Excellent. You have done well."

"Thank you." Ant savored the approval. It was of enormous importance to him, even more so than the approval of his father, which never came.

"Be it all for Mother's glory," the man said.

"For Mother," Ant intoned, "for Mother."

CHAPTER 62

10:05 a.m., Friday, May 26, The Biscuit, Portland, Oregon

"This is it, the Biscuit," Ward said as he parked the car.

"Interesting," Parks noted, looking up at the building.

"We're the only tenants," he added.

"Huh." Parks rolled her eyes.

"Don't judge until we get up there. I was pleasantly surprised."

"If you say so."

They got out and walked to the heavy steel backdoor. Ward unlocked it and shoved it open.

"After you," he said.

They walked in. The elevator was there, waiting for him, like death. Ward briefly considered suggesting the stairs, then thought better of it.

"We're on the top floor," he said, making no move to activate the metal beast.

They stood there for a moment. Parks gave him a quizzical look and pushed the up button. The door clanked open. She stepped inside. Ward hesitated.

"You coming?" she asked.

"Yeah, I'm coming."

Ward walked in and braced himself. The doors rumbled shut. The old tank began to ascend, shuddering and groaning the whole way up. He glanced at Parks to see if she was watching him. She was.

"You okay?" Parks asked.

"I'm fine," Ward lied. He took a deep breath, then another.

The elevator shuddered to a halt at their floor, and then promptly dropped a few inches. Ward was pretty sure that he didn't gasp out loud. He snuck a look at Parks, who was eyeing him suspiciously. He quickly stepped off, doing his best to act as if nothing were wrong.

"This is it," he said, unlocking the door. They stepped inside.

Parks looked around. "Not bad."

Cruz was in the kitchen making coffee and tending to yet another box of pastries. He grinned and nodded hello, his eyes brightening at the sight of Parks. Royer was seated at the table. He looked up from his laptop, rising to his feet when he saw who was with Ward. Smiling broadly, he came over to her.

"Rowan, it's good to see you." He shook her hand, the grip lingering just a second or two beyond the norm. Ward sensed that Royer might have attempted a hug, were it not such a breach of FBI decorum.

Cruz came over carrying the box of pastries. "Cesar Cruz," he said, offering his hand.

"Rowan Parks," she said. They shook. Cruz shot Ward a look that said, *you lucky son of a bitch*.

"Donut?" Cruz offered, holding the box out to her.

"Sure," Parks said, picking one. "The only thing I had for breakfast was this guy's questionable coffee," she added, jerking her thumb at Ward.

Cruz grinned.

"Okay if I help myself to some of yours?" Parks asked, nodding in the direction of the brewing pot.

"Oh, I'll get it," Cruz said.

They sat at the table as Cruz went for the coffee.

"You need to write up what happened last night," Royer said, straight to the point. "We need to show management some progress. I made some calls this morning, gave the nutshell version, but they'll want to see some paperwork. Everybody is on our ass."

"That's no shit," Cruz added as he brought over four steaming mugs of coffee. "Burke won't leave me alone. Calls me ten times a day."

"Your SAC?" Parks asked.

"Unfortunately."

"I'll write it up this morning," Ward promised. He had briefed them the night before as soon as he was back at the apartment. The response was relief that they were on the right group combined with the sobering sense of responsibility that came with that realization. "I'll make it a good read," Ward assured them.

"Include your new nickname," Parks said.

"Nickname?" Cruz asked.

Ward shook his head. "Thanks," he said to Parks.

"Tell it," she insisted.

Ward sighed. "Lightning."

Cruz grinned. "Nice. Sort of suggests quick performance."

"That's disappointing," Parks noted.

"Here we go," Ward said. He eyed Cruz. "It's related to my supposed ability to strike quickly on the internet."

Cruz nodded solemnly. "Sure it is. "I'm sure that you strike very quickly, and then get out."

Parks laughed out loud, and then covered her mouth.

"Fuck you," Ward said with a chuckle.

"I hate to break this up," Royer said, "but I just got an email straight from the deputy director asking for a status update."

Ward saw all levity in the room vanish in an instant.

"What was the exchange between Wolf and this Cobra on the Keystone attack?" Royer asked. His fingers were poised over the keyboard.

Ward thought for a moment. "Cobra said *Last night was an incredible success*. Then he added something along the lines of *Keystone has come to a halt and won't start up again anytime soon*."

Royer typed, repeating the words back to himself as he did so.

"What do you think it meant?" he asked. "Do you think they were somehow involved in the planning, or just aware of it?"

Ward rubbed his chin. "My guess is they were just aware it was going to happen. But who knows? I could easily see Wolf as part of some overall command structure. And there obviously has to be some coordination among the cells. I remember his toast from the other night at the cafe. Referring to the protectors of Mother Earth, he said *May their mission be successful*. Even at the time I had the sense that he was referring to something specific. Now I think it might have been Keystone. I wouldn't have guessed Cobra to be any sort of leader. He seems more the foot soldier type. It's possible that Wolf may have simply confided in him. But again, who knows? I haven't been around Cobra other than last night."

Royer continued to type, which made Ward nervous. "Why don't you let me write all of this up, look it over before we send anything out," he suggested.

Royer stopped typing. He stared at the laptop, saying nothing. Ward could understand his reluctance to agree. The man was under enormous pressure to produce. And an email from the deputy director was not something that could go unanswered for long.

Royer turned to Ward. "How long will it take?"

Ward picked up his coffee, moved to one of the other laptops and fired it up. "Give me fifteen minutes," he said.

CHAPTER 63

1:17 p.m., Friday, May 26, on the streets of Boulder, Colorado

The analysis of Linda Oden's phone records, emails and social media activity had yielded several persons of interest, or so it had seemed. She was in frequent contact with a number of individuals who could be described as having significant involvement in the radical environmental community. Toby Combs had initially been hopeful, but as he and Ian Maness worked their way through the list it became clear that most of Oden's associates were more talk than action. More problematic, they all had alibis. There were only a few names left, and none of them seemed particularly promising, their contact with Oden being sporadic and seemingly benign. But, as he and Maness both knew, in a case like this one no lead could go ignored.

"What's this guy's name again?" Combs asked.

"Eric Harper." Maness checked the master list. "Let's see. Thirty-one years old. Been a resident of Boulder for thirteen years."

"So, he came for college and stayed."

"That'd be my guess."

Maness looked off to his right. "That's it, over there." He pointed to an active apparel store, Boulder Outfitters.

Combs pulled into the lot and parked.

"Can I see the picture again?" he asked.

Maness handed it to him. "He recently renewed his license.

Picture's pretty current."

Combs studied it. Harper's hair was close-cropped, his eyes dark and penetrating. When combined with a thick black beard, they gave him an intense, almost angry look.

"Okay," Combs said, "let's do it."

They walked inside. Maness spotted him first. "Over there," he said, pointing toward a section filled with climbing gear. Harper was talking to a customer, explaining the relative merits of a particular harness.

They moved toward him.

"Eric Harper," Combs said. It was not a question.

Harper looked up quickly. Combs saw something that looked like flight instinct in his eyes. Not waiting for a response, Combs identified himself.

"Special Agent Toby Combs, Bureau of Alcohol, Tobacco and Firearms." He held up his credentials.

There it was again, that look, as if Harper was assessing his odds. Combs saw him glance over his shoulder in the direction of an exit. Maness seemed to notice as well, moving off to Harper's side to cut off that potential avenue of escape.

"This is Special Agent Ian Maness," Combs added, gesturing toward his partner.

Maness nodded.

"We'd like to ask you a few questions," Combs said.

Harper looked at his customer. "Please excuse me," he said, as if nothing were wrong. The customer moved off, looking confused.

"Is there someplace more private?" Combs asked.

Harper sighed. "Let's go in the supply room," he said.

They went in back. As soon as they were out of earshot of any staff or customers Harper developed an attitude.

"What's this about?" he asked.

"Do you know a Linda Oden?" Combs asked.

Harper looked at Combs and then Maness, then back to Combs.

"Yeah, I know Linda."

In Combs estimation it took Harper slightly too long to answer. He was assessing what they already knew, whether he could get away with a lie.

"How do you know her?" Combs asked.

"She's a friend. Why?"

"Has she ever loaned you her van?"

"She has a van?"

Harper's look was vaguely smug. And there was a squint in the eyes that Combs didn't like. Something about it seemed to mock them. Combined with his reaction when they initially approached, it caused Combs to get that familiar feeling, the sense that there was something here. He pulled out a small notepad and pen.

"A Chevy Express Cargo Van, white," Combs said. "Has she ever loaned it to you?"

"I don't know anything about any van," Harper said, smiling.

Combs decided to float some bullshit, see if it got a reaction. "What if she told us otherwise?" he asked.

"I don't know why she would say that," Harper answered.

"Okay," Combs said. He smiled back, then pretended to make some notes. Looking up, he studied Harper for a moment. The smug smile persisted, defiant. Combs could see that this guy was unlikely to break. He decided to ask the money question, see if it resulted in any sort of tell.

"Where were you in the early morning hours of May 8th?" he asked.

"At home, in bed," Harper answered, with little hesitation.

"You seem fairly certain of that?"

Harper hesitated. "That was a weekday, right? I would have had work the next day."

"Sure," Combs said, scribbling in his notepad. When finished, he slipped it in his pocket, and then looked Harper in the eye. "Thank you. You've been very...cooperative."

A look of puzzlement flashed across Harper's face. "Uh... you're welcome," he said, almost as if it were a question. Then he recovered a bit. Smiling again, he added, "Please don't hesitate to contact me if I can be of further assistance."

Maness grunted at the amateurish comment.

"We'll do that," Combs noted.

Combs and Maness had moved to an adjoining parking lot to avoid detection. It was almost three o'clock by the time Harper came outside. From their vantage point they could see that he was on the phone, and in an animated discussion. He was unaware that he was being watched. Maness raised the camera and focused the telephoto lens on Harper. He began to film, the camera set to video mode. Harper was gesturing, pacing back and forth. It was exactly what they had hoped for. After three or four minutes he ended the call and went back inside.

"You get it?" Combs asked.

Maness checked the playback. He grinned. "Every second of it."

"Outstanding," Combs said. "We'll get a copy to the FBI lab. They can run it through their silhouette matching program, compare it to the video of the arsonist from the security app on Paxton's cell phone. It's a long shot, but they've had some success with it in bank robbery cases."

"I've read about it," Maness said, "but never used it in a case."

"Usually, they'll have a bank surveillance video of an otherwise unidentifiable suspect. You know, ski mask, ninja outfit, that sort of thing. They'll compare that to a video of a known suspect, matching the silhouette, movement pattern, etcetera. It's not DNA, but it's not bad."

"Beats the shit out of anything else we've got," Maness said.

"True statement," Combs agreed. "But match or not, we're gonna keep a close eye on Mr. Eric Harper."

CHAPTER 64

8:25 p.m., Friday, May 26, Ward's undercover apartment, The Hawthorne District, Portland, Oregon

Parks was in the kitchen area preparing dinner. Ward's offer of assistance had been met with a skeptical glance, in response to which he had agreed that she was probably right. Instead, he settled in at the kitchen counter with a beer and a copy of *The Oregonian*. After quickly looking through the paper, and finding little of interest, he turned his attention to her.

"Where did you learn to cook?" Ward asked.

"I didn't," Parks replied. "I've got a few standbys, and you're getting one of them, lasagna."

"Sounds good to me," Ward replied. It did sound good. He was famished.

"I'll do a Caesar salad to go with it," she added. "And I picked up some bread from that bakery down the street. Sorry, there's no dessert."

"I don't need any." Ward rarely had dessert, other than ice cream. He did like his ice cream.

They were silent for a moment as she worked. "So, why did you join the FBI?" Ward asked. It was an easy conversation starter.

Parks paused for a moment, then resumed putting the lasagna together. "My dad was a cop."

"How did he feel about his little girl going into law enforcement?"

"He hated the idea," Parks said. "But after he was killed in the line of duty there was little chance I would do anything else."

"I'm sorry," Ward said, now regretting that he had asked. Part of him wanted to know how it happened, but he would leave to her on whether to take it any further.

Parks sprinkled the last bit of cheese on top of her creation and carried it to the oven. Then, she washed her hands and poured herself a glass of wine.

"You've heard of El Rukn?" she asked.

Ward nodded. Most in law enforcement were familiar with the notorious Chicago-based gang.

"It was a drug bust," she said. "There was enough to arrest a half-dozen of their senior leadership. An early morning raid was planned. Unfortunately, El Rukn had somebody on the inside. They knew it was coming. My dad and one other officer were killed. Several more were badly injured. Two of the shooters fled the country. One of them, the one who killed my father, has never been found."

Ward shook his head, unsure of what to say. Everyone who carried a badge understood the risk and knew that they might not come home to their family on any given day. It was a risk that Maria had understood all too well, one that had driven her away.

"It was a Sunday," Parks said. "He had promised my mom that he would be home in time for Sunday dinner. The food was on the table when Dad's partner showed up at the door, tears running down his face. Mom let out an unearthly wail, and then dropped to the floor in a heap. I was twelve at the time. Of course, I knew instantly what had happened." Parks stood silent for a moment, then took a sip of her drink. "He was my hero. He meant everything to me. It was then that I vowed to become a cop."

Ward knew that she had been with the Chicago PD for five years before moving to the FBI. He guessed now that the switch was motivated in part by some notion of pursuing her father's killer as a fed. Ward saw Parks look up from her glass. She was studying him.

"I know what you're thinking," she said. "That I joined the bureau to track down Dad's killer."

Ward didn't want to lie to her. "I would totally get it…if that's what you did." He saw the hint of a melancholy smile appear on her face.

"I can't deny it was part of the reason," she admitted. "When I was on the PD I spent every spare moment working my dad's case. The brass never called me on it. They left me alone. Besides, by then, nobody else was really working it anyway."

"And by then you could see who really had the resources to pursue an international fugitive," Ward added.

"Exactly. Silly, huh?"

"Not at all."

"What about you?" she asked.

Ward thought for a moment. The reasons were many, but out of respect for her story he chose to save them for another time. Besides, for him, maybe the better question was why he stuck with it. "Let's just say that I felt the calling," he said. "There are bad people in the world that need to be brought to justice."

"Hear, hear," Parks said, raising her glass.

After a sip she put down her drink and went to work on the salad. Ward found himself viewing her in a new light. While he had already developed some respect for Parks as a professional, he now viewed her as even more of a colleague. The trouble was, she was no less an object of desire. If anything, he found her more appealing. He reminded himself again of the dangers that could arise from becoming involved with a fellow agent, especially one working the same assignment. It probably didn't matter, anyway. Even if she was interested, she likely had better judgment than to get involved with him.

Dinner was eaten at the kitchen counter. There were no dimmed lights, no candles, nothing that suggested anything like a date. They knew better. At least Ward hoped that he knew better. Their conversation consisted of a relatively modest exchange of war stories and shared observances on the merit of those who rose to the level of management in federal bureaucracy. Eventually, though, the discussion turned to relationships, and how the demands of the job made them difficult.

"My ex-wife, Maria, finally concluded that the job was more important to me than she was," Ward said. He wasn't sure that he wanted to share this with Parks, but here they were, and she had been open and candid about so much.

"Was she right?" Parks asked.

For some reason the question surprised him. And though he wasn't sure why, Ward felt that Parks had the right to ask it.

"Yeah, maybe," he said, "at least at the time."

"But not now?"

She was staring at him intently, as if the answer were important to her. Or was he imaging that?

"I don't know," he said. It wasn't much of an answer. But it was honest.

Parks nodded. The faraway look in her eye told him that she understood. Ward could feel it then more than ever, the sense of duty that they shared.

Parks looked at the clock. "I didn't realize it was that late," she said. "I'll clean this up."

"Let me help," Ward said, jumping to his feet.

They cleared the table and loaded the dishwasher, saying little as they cleaned up. Ward felt comfortable in the relative silence, knowing that they had made a connection. Over the course of the evening he had come to know Rowan Parks better, and he liked her.

"I think I'll turn in," Parks said when they were done. "I may go for a run in the morning." A few seconds later she added, "You're welcome to join me."

"I may do that," Ward said, though he wondered if he were in good enough shape to keep up with her.

Not quite ready for bed, Ward moved to the couch and picked up the remote. He turned on the television and began to surf through the channels.

Parks walked toward her bedroom. She paused in the doorway and turned back toward him. "Good night, David," she said.

Ward looked up. The vision of her there, smiling sweetly, was one that he knew would stay with him forever. "Good night, Rowan," he said.

CHAPTER 65

9:28 p.m., Saturday, May 27, fundraiser for the Green Earth Alliance, Manhattan's Upper East Side

It was the third fundraiser of the year and another spectacular turnout, this time taking place in the penthouse apartment of one of New York's wealthiest real estate moguls. The irony was not lost on Gordon Cline as he sipped his drink and studied the glittering collection of celebrities, politicians and moneyed upper crust that had collected to support the organization he had founded a dozen years earlier.

The Green Earth Alliance had grown into one the largest environmental organizations in the United States thanks to his exposure of a bogus organic certification racket and one movie producer's decision to turn the story into what became an award-winning documentary. The movie garnered an Oscar nomination, and Cline and the Green Earth Alliance were off and running. Endorsements and contributions began to flow in at a rate he could not have imagined.

It was an improbable story of success and one with which Cline was not entirely comfortable. He doubted the commitment of these people, knowing most used their support of the cause to further their own interests, be it increased ticket sales, more votes, or simply bragging rights in their competitive social circles. In truth, they all disgusted him. But their money was necessary to perform good works. It was an economic reality from which he could not escape.

"Gordon!"

Cline turned to see the actor Ryan Landry approaching, arms outstretched to embrace him. Landry considered himself to be one of Hollywood's greenest celebs, an impression no doubt cultivated by his public relations people. Cline knew the reality. Landry owned a fleet of sports cars and lived alone in an eighteen-room mansion. The few solar panels on his roof provided a small percentage of his personal energy demands. Landry was a hypocrite with an enormous carbon footprint.

"So good to see you," Landry said, coming on for the hug. A kiss to each cheek followed.

Cline struggled not to recoil.

"An amazing turnout," Landry noted, surveying the room. "I count three Oscar nominees, five Golden Globe winners, three Grammy recipients. It's simply astonishing, a testament to you and your important work, Gordon."

"Thank you, Ryan." Cline took note of the fact that Landry had only identified entertainers, even limiting that observation to only those bestowed with one of their industry's self-congrat-ula-tory awards. Of course, he probably wouldn't recognize the members of Congress, CEOs, or Nobel laureate also present in the room.

"I think we will do well tonight," Landry observed as he put his arm around Cline's shoulder.

We, Cline thought, disgusted. Someone snapped a photo. Probably a photographer hired by one of Landry's PR people. The photo op complete, the actor started to move away.

"We'll chat later," Landry said, eyeing a young model. "Congratulations on a super night."

"Thanks," Cline said to Landry's back. The actor was already moving, zeroed in on his next conquest.

Cline downed what was left of his drink and sat the glass on the bar. He desperately wanted to leave.

"Another?" the bartender asked.

"God yes," Cline said, turning to face him. "Make it a double."

"Mr. Cline?"

It was Senator Amelia Trudel, one of the most ardent environmentalists in Congress. Cline considered her to be chief among the handful of politicians who could legitimately call themselves green.

"Hello, Senator. I'm happy you could make it tonight."

"Wouldn't miss it." She leaned closer to Cline. "I am about to introduce legislation that would significantly expand the streams and wetlands covered by the Clean Water Act. Relying on regulations issued by the Environmental Protection Agency has proven difficult. As you know, this Supreme Court is unlikely to support a broad reading of EPA's authority in this area. We need to solidify the gains we've made with legislation that leaves little doubt as to the agency's reach on this issue."

"Agreed," Cline said. "But you know a bill like that is unlikely to pass the Senate. The House certainly won't approve it. And even it did, the president would veto it. What's the point?" Cline thought he knew the answer but asked anyway.

"Let them go on record as opposing it," Trudel said. "I have to try. Eventually, people will come to understand the dire environmental threats facing our planet and the life-altering consequences that will ensue if we do nothing."

"When is that going to happen?" Cline asked. "Look at the huge percentage of the population who are climate change deniers despite all scientific evidence to the contrary." The thought depressed him.

"You can't be that hopeless," Trudel said. "Certainly you believe there is some chance of success? Why else would you do all of this?"

Cline smiled. "Of course there is a chance of success," he said, "thanks to good people like you." In fact, he did think that there was a chance of success, a good chance. But it wasn't due to the efforts of any of the pretend environmentalists who surrounded him here, at least not directly. It was true that their money helped, and in ways that none of them could imagine. He turned to Trudel.

"Senator," he said, "Let me buy a drink for one of the good guys."

Cline watched the people of New York flash by as the cab returned him to his hotel. He wondered if any one of them understood what life on Earth was supposed to be. If it were up to him all of this would be returned to its natural state, and those who remained would live an agrarian lifestyle, one even more sustainable than that which existed centuries before. He had read earlier that New York City was founded in 1624. It was almost four hundred years since this land had been used in the way that Mother intended it. Maybe someday, he thought.

The disposable cell phone had been purchased that morning. Cline retrieved it from his jacket. He eyed the cab driver, concluding that the man was paying little attention and likely understood limited English. He punched in the number and pressed the call button.

"How was your evening?" asked the voice on the other end.

"It went well," Cline said. "Our cause continues to be well-funded. You should expect a contribution soon...through the usual channels."

"For Mother," the voice said.

"For Mother," Cline repeated.

CHAPTER 66

6:58 p.m., Sunday, May 28, The Forest Glen Coffeehouse, Port-land, Oregon

Ward and Parks waited a block from the entrance to the coffee-house. Wolf and Fern had been invited to meet them at seven o'clock. This time there had been no mystery. They were told that another cyber-attack was planned, and that it would get people's attention. Both had promised to be there, but it was almost seven and neither had arrived. Were they suspicious? Maybe they were somewhere nearby, watching, waiting to see if Joshua Young, now known as Lightning, would come alone. He had not. Kyra Jordan was with him. Ward had purposely failed to disclose this ahead of time, not wanting to risk their failure to appear because of Kyra's presence. She was still an unknown commodity to them. But Ward knew that if Kyra witnessed the cyber-attack in front of the others and voiced her approval it could ease her acceptance into the group. At least that was the hope. If they didn't show it was all for nothing.

The attack this time was something quite different. The target was Pittman Petroleum, the very company whose CEO, Robert Titus, had been killed by an EMB suicide bomber just two weeks earlier. The thought was that the audacity of the attack would greatly impress the terrorists. FBI had taken the lead in setting it up. The approach to garner Pittman's cooperation had to be handled with great delicacy. It was hoped that their traumatic experience would motivate them to take extraordinary measures in attempting to bring down the Earth Martyrs Brigade.

The initial contact was made by FBI Deputy Director Stuart Woods. He personally visited the acting CEO of Pittman, Preston Dawes, and asked for the company's cooperation, sharing only those details absolutely necessary to secure the company's assistance. Dawes immediately agreed. It was a brave step. The attack, designed to take Pittman's website offline for several hours, would result in a flood of questions from shareholders and concerns on Wall Street. Only Dawes and his chief systems administrator would be in the know, although Woods had agreed to let Dawes clear it with his board of directors so that he had some coverage when the shit hit the fan.

It was also agreed that after EMB was brought to justice that enough of the details could be shared publicly to assuage Wall Street's concerns and calm the company's shareholders. Even with that, everyone understood that what Pittman had agreed to was extraordinary. Dawes had told Deputy Director Woods that they had to help so that Bob Titus would not have died in vain. Ward vowed that he would not squander this opportunity.

Ward looked at his watch. It was five after. The pre-arranged blackout of Pittman's website would occur at precisely seven-twenty. He still needed time to set up, lay the groundwork. If Wolf and Fern didn't get there soon they would have to abort.

"Where the hell are they?" Parks asked.

"I wish I knew," Ward said. His thoughts went back to the informant, Peavey, and his doubts about the guy. If Peavey went south it could blow up everything. The thought constantly nagged at Ward and had even given him nightmares. There was one helluva lot riding on the staying power of a single informant.

Ward checked his watch again. He saw Parks do the same. It was now eight after.

"If they aren't here in the next two minutes I'll need to make some calls," Parks said.

"I know," Ward agreed. He thought for a second. "Let's go

in. I need to get everything in place. Maybe they're watching, maybe not. We'll have to take our chances on their reaction to your presence."

Parks nodded. "Agreed," she said.

They moved from their hiding place and toward the coffee-house, chatting amicably for the benefit of any observers. Once inside they quickly found a table, the place being near empty. Ward removed his laptop from its case and powered it up. He checked his watch once more. It was now fifteen after.

"They're here," Parks whispered. "And they have company."

Ward looked up. Wolf and Fern were walking toward the table. To his surprise, Cobra was with them. From their expressions he concluded that they were just as surprised to see Kyra.

"Thank you for coming," Ward said, extending his hand to Wolf. "Hi, Fern," he added. Ward acknowledged Cobra with a nod and shook his hand as well.

"I invited Cobra," Wolf said. "He is interested in…what's the term?" Wolf asked, turning to his accomplice.

"Hacktivism," Cobra replied, looking around as if to see if anyone was listening.

"Yes. Hacktivism," Wolf said. "I assume that's not a problem."

"Not at all," Ward lied. He was extremely concerned. What if Cobra actually possessed some expertise? What if he asked questions that Ward couldn't answer? Fortunately, the code that had been provided was legit. The hack, in a sense, was real. It was a DoS attack similar to the one launched against the Department of Energy website, only this one would be more disruptive. At least it would seem that way. Those on the receiving end at Pittman already knew how to deal with it, but would play their parts, letting the attack run its course for a day or so before eradicating the malware. Ward thought back on his training from Etherlord and Incubus. It was time to channel the white hat duo.

"Kyra has a similar interest," Ward noted. "Do you have much…experience?" he asked Cobra.

"Some," the terrorist replied. A sly smile crept onto his face.

Ward wondered if it indicated understatement or bluff.

Wolf sat down, not waiting for an invitation. The others followed suit. Ward adjusted his laptop and began to work. He checked the time in the lower right-hand corner—eighteen after.

"It's almost ready to go," Ward announced.

Wolf's brow furrowed. "Is there some rush?" he asked. "You've told us nothing about the target."

Ward had wondered if this degree of freelancing would be accepted now that he had been welcomed into the group. He suspected not. Wolf was clearly one to maintain total control. But this was an essential part of the plan to gain their confidence and secure the acceptance of Kyra Jordan into the group. He had to make this happen, and the clock was ticking.

"The target is Pittman Petroleum," Ward announced, still typing. He glanced up from his laptop. The looks around the table ranged from surprise to shock. The expression on Wolf's face slowly changed from one of concern to something approaching bemusement. Ward was disgusted, but the reaction made him decide to take a chance.

"Is that a problem?" he asked, looking to Wolf for the approval that he prayed would come.

"It is not," Wolf said. "Just be certain that you don't leave a trace."

"There will be no trace," Parks interjected. "Joshua is the best."

Ward spun the laptop so that the others could see the screen. The Pittman Petroleum website was displayed. He clicked on several links to demonstrate that the site was operational.

"There is no greater enemy than Big Oil," Ward said. "Sending a message to Pittman now will demonstrate that they are not beyond reach, regardless of any precautions put in place following the death of Robert Titus. It will have a major impact." He contemplated a verbal ploy that might get an admission from Wolf, and then went with it.

"If the Earth Martyrs Brigade wants to claim credit, so be it."

There was no comment from Wolf. Ward turned the computer back around and started to type. Cobra rose from his chair and came around behind Ward, leaning in to watch him work. Ward felt his pulse quicken, wondering if Cobra might spot some flaw, some strand of code that might expose the whole thing as staged.

"A DoS attack by malware," Cobra said. "Impressive…if it works. Pittman undoubtedly has a fairly sophisticated security system in place."

"It'll work," Ward said confidently. He looked at the time display. It was twenty after. Ward once again spun the computer around so that the others at the table could watch. Code filled the screen. He hit the *enter* key. The code scrolled quickly at first, but then began to slow, finally coming to a stop. Ward leaned over the table and typed in the URL for Pittman's website, then hit *enter*. A spinning symbol appeared on the screen. It seemed to sit there forever, taunting him as he prayed the attack would work. Finally, a message appeared on the screen: *website is currently unavailable*. Ward struggled not to emit an audible sigh of relief. He looked around the table. Fern nodded her head in approval. Parks smiled and rubbed her hand on Ward's shoulder. Wolf chuckled softly.

"Any idea on how long the site will stay down?" Cobra asked.

"Hard to say," Ward replied. "It's a sophisticated piece of malware, but I would think Pittman has the resources to resolve it in a day or so. Still, the fact that they would appear susceptible to attack at all will get Wall Street's attention and frighten investors. Word will get out." Ward smiled. "I would imagine that Pittman's stock will continue its recent decline."

"Fine work," Wolf said.

Ward knew that a further bridge had been crossed. He wondered if Parks had crossed it with him.

Wolf leaned forward, his hands clasped together, elbows resting on the table. "A question," he said. "What type of ability is needed to disrupt the power grid?"

"More ability than I have," Ward replied.

"Too bad," Wolf said. "Our more rudimentary methods, while effective, lack the broad, lasting effect we desire."

Ward felt his blood pressure surge. He was sure that Wolf had essentially just admitted to involvement in the attack on the electrical substation in Omaha. *Show nothing*, he reminded himself. He glanced at Parks who remained impassive.

"I'm sure that many of your methods will have lasting effect," Ward observed.

Wolf smiled. "One hopes," he said.

As soon as they were alone and a safe distance from the coffeehouse Parks spoke up. "You know we're going to have to report this up the food chain right away," she said.

"I know," Ward agreed.

"And you know that they will order us to work on getting enough for an arrest as soon as possible so they can show some results to the public. That's the way those assholes always think. And it's especially true on this one."

"I know." It was almost as if Parks were reading his mind.

"We need to stay in, get enough to bring down the whole organization," Parks said. "Taking out one cell won't accomplish shit. The rest of them will just double down on secrecy and become that much harder to infiltrate. Besides, I think this Wolf guy has some broader role. I think he is part of management at a national level."

Ward stopped and turned to her. He was really starting to like Parks. "I know," he repeated. "I have a plan."

"Oh? And what's that?"

"I have a couple of guys who I think can explain things in terms they will understand."

CHAPTER 67

8:56 a.m., Tuesday, May 30, Office of Deputy Director Tyson Gifford, ATF Headquarters, 99 New York Avenue, NE, Washington, D.C.

Leroy Wheeler wondered if a deputy director of the FBI had ever set foot in ATF headquarters. He doubted it. But it would happen today. Stuart Woods was set to arrive at nine o'clock. It was a testimony to the importance of ATF's role in *Operation Knock Down*. Alex Burke, special agent in charge of the San Francisco field division, was already present, as was the Dallas SAC, Jack Olin. Several other SACs and ASACs would be conferenced in on a secure line. Special Agent Bradley Royer had been flown in from Portland. Wheeler knew that this meeting would chart the course of the investigation going forward.

The big question was whether Ward and Parks would stay in and try to get enough to bring down the entire Earth Martyrs Brigade, or simply gather sufficient evidence to support a quick arrest of the Portland cell members and then shut down the operation. Wheeler knew where he stood. It remained to be seen who else had the guts to see it through. The politics of this one were at the nosebleed level, and that almost always resulted in bad investigative strategy.

Tyson Gifford nervously tapped a pen on his desk. Wheeler studied him closely. He had known Ty for years and had never seen him like this. The man looked haggard. It was obvious that the case was taking a toll on him. Hell, it was taking a toll on all of them. Waco hadn't caused this much stress. Fast and Furious wasn't even close. The pressure was enormous. Wheeler hoped that Gifford could stand up to it and resist the push for quick results. If he could, the director would likely do the same. Gifford had Lucas Decker's ear.

It was well known that Decker relied heavily on his second-in-command. That was a situation common to federal law enforcement agencies. The boss had the political resume, with the deputy supposedly selected on the basis of demonstrated know-how. It was the latter who actually ran the day-to-day operations of the organization. ATF was no exception. Fortunately, with Gifford the know-how was legit. He had earned the respect of the rank and file.

The phone rang. Gifford grabbed it. "Okay," he said, then hung up. The deputy director of the Bureau of Alcohol, Tobacco, Firearms and Explosives rose to his feet and strode to the door, his face grim. As he swung the door open a plainly forced smile appeared on his face.

"Stuart," Gifford said. "Good to see you."

Stuart Woods entered the room like a battlefield commander, erect, in charge, focused, surrounded by his lieutenants. His navy-blue suit, starched white shirt and red tie looked like Wheeler's image of the FBI uniform. Woods quickly shook hands with Gifford and then turned to introduce the three individuals with him: Robert Neville, FBI Executive Assistant Director for National Security; Maureen Tully, FBI Executive Assistant Director for Criminal, Cyber, Response and Services Branch; and Ramsey Kirkpatrick, SAC of the Las Vegas Field Office. Gifford then introduced the ATF personnel. He left out Royer. But it quickly became apparent that Woods knew his subordinate. They exchanged pleasantries in a way that suggested familiarity and mutual respect. Wheeler tried to take some comfort in that.

"Let's get started," Woods said.

Wheeler looked at Olin who arched his eyebrows in response. This was a major breach of protocol. It was Gifford's house. He should have the lead. Wheeler wondered if this was how the whole thing would go. Typical FBI, he thought. But then Woods seemed to catch himself.

"If you're ready, Ty," Woods said to Gifford.

"Let's get to it," Gifford replied. He turned to Burke. "Alex, why don't you summarize where we're at so far."

Wheeler listened as Burke brought everyone up to date, including the details of Ward's staged cyber-attack on Pittman Petroleum and Wolf's subsequent comments, the comments that had resulted in their meeting.

"What exactly did this Wolf say?" Woods asked.

Burke consulted Ward's report. "Wolf had asked about the type of hacking ability necessary to disrupt the power grid. Ward replied that it was more than he possessed. It was then that Wolf said, *our more rudimentary methods, while effective, lack the broad, lasting effect we desire.* Ward took this to be a reference to the attack on the electrical substation in Omaha. That clearly seems correct. And all of this was, of course, after Ward had heard Wolf and another member of the cell discussing the attack on the Keystone XL Pipeline as an incredible success. He did not believe that the two of them had been involved in that incident but did have the impression that they knew about it ahead of time."

Woods nodded. "Not enough for an indictment, but he has clearly tapped into some major players. What's your recommendation?"

Burke didn't hesitate. "We leave Ward and Parks in long enough to secure concrete evidence of the Portland cell's involvement in the Omaha event and then make the arrests. We can then continue the investigation into the other incidents, hopefully securing cooperation from the Portland members by ratcheting up the pressure on them. I'm sure we would be able to get cooperation plea agreements from several of them. We have an uneasy public that needs to see some success here. People are nervous. The stock market is roiling due to the uncertainty of where the next attack might occur. Work on the pipeline has shut down. I don't have to tell any of you about the pressure that has been coming from Congress."

Wheeler snorted. This was exactly what he had expected from Burke. The San Francisco SAC just wanted to show success on an undercover op being run out of his division, make himself the hero. Wheeler could envision Burke's smiling face at the press conference announcing the arrest of the Portland cell members. The truth was that Burke didn't give a shit about the long-term effects on the investigation that would come from acting too quickly. His primary and perhaps only concern was career enhancement. Wheeler looked at Olin, who was shaking his head. Gifford was watching them both.

"Leroy, I take it you have a different perspective," Gifford said. "Go ahead."

"If we just take down the Portland cell it will do nothing to stop the Earth Martyrs Brigade," Wheeler explained. "In fact, it's likely to have the opposite effect. EMB appears to operate in semi-independent cells, much the same way ELF did, with the critical difference that EMB is far more radical. If we just take out Portland the other cells will double down on secrecy and became that much harder to stop. There is certainly no guarantee that any of the Portland members will cooperate. I'd say there's a damn good chance that none of them will. They're zealots. You will recall that one of them blew herself up to take out Robert Titus." Wheeler realized that he was getting too worked up. He took a breath and continued. "Even if some of them did cooperate there is a real question as to whether they would know anything about the activities or membership of the other cells. The only possible exception to that is Wolf. According to Ward's report, both he and Parks think that Wolf might be someone with an overview of EMB and its operations, some sort of senior management. Ward wants to stay in and go deeper. He says that Parks feels the same way. That's likely the only way to learn what Wolf knows, or to bring down EMB as an organization." Wheeler looked around the room, making eye contact with everyone present. "I've known David Ward for a long time. He's the best. I trust his instincts on this. We need to let him do his job and let Parks do hers."

"I completely agree," Olin said, adding his support. "We don't know what else these people have in mind, and we won't find out by arresting the members of one cell. What if they pull off something big and it comes out later that we blew an opportunity to stop it by acting too quickly for what will look like political reasons?"

Wheeler surveyed the room, watching the reactions. Olin was playing hardball now, speaking a language that management could understand, essentially telling them that they did not want to go down in history as those who wasted the opportunity to prevent the next 9/11. It was tough stuff, and it hit the mark. Wheeler could see Burke start to open his mouth to respond and then stop.

Gifford spoke up. "I'm inclined to agree with Leroy and Jack," he said. "I say we leave our UCs in place, let them see where it goes."

Wheeler was pleased that his boss stepped up, putting his vote out there first instead of playing it safe and waiting for Woods to voice an opinion. Gifford knew the value of a good undercover operative, having done the work himself. And he certainly knew that David Ward was one of the best UCs in the business. Gifford was the one who suggested him for the mission in the first place.

All eyes were on Woods. He nodded solemnly, saying nothing for what seemed an eternity. Finally, he spoke. "I appreciate the point of view expressed by Special Agent in Charge Burke," he said, "but I have to concur with the opinions that support leaving Ward and Parks in place for the long haul. History will not judge us kindly if we squander our chance to eliminate what is possibly the most significant domestic terrorist organization of our generation." Woods rose from his seat and reached across the desk to shake Gifford's hand. "Let's see it through. I'll talk to the director.”

Wheeler was hopeful but knew that the political winds could be fickle.

CHAPTER 68

11:47 a.m., Tuesday, May 30, in United States Marshals Service custody, Oklahoma County Jail, Oklahoma City, Oklahoma

Linda Oden sat at a table, staring at the same view that she had stared at for nineteen days and counting. Her pod was a small common area of bolted down tables and benches surrounded by jail cells. Dozens of inmates, all dressed in orange, milled about. Some talked to themselves, their conversations animated. Others just sat with a glazed look in their eyes, pondering their predicament, or haunted by their past. A few started fights and were quickly dealt with.

Then there were the predators, studying the others, looking for the weak. Many of the people she was housed with were little more than animals. No, that was wrong. They were something less than animals. Mother's creatures had nobility. Most of these specimens were deceitful, manipulative, self-absorbed, violent. It was a bad place full of bad people. This was not a place she was supposed to be. Oden desperately wanted out, but there was only one way to accomplish that, and she wasn't ready to go there.

There was nothing to do, nothing to occupy her mind except her own thoughts, and her growing doubt. There was no one she could talk to. In a place full of individuals who could blather on endlessly about their own problems, how they were wronged by the system, set up by some supposed friend, or whatever other excuse explained their current circumstances, there was no one who would truly listen and understand.

Oden was lonely, lonelier than she had ever been. Even though he was partly the reason she was here, it was Eric she missed the most, even more than her parents. She understood why he couldn't contact her, but it hurt. She loved him, even more than the cause. She loved him more than Mother. That was why she had loaned him the van. It was for Eric, to make him happy. She wondered what the others would say about that. Would any of them understand? She thought not. Their zealotry was total, with all things to be sacrificed for Mother.

None of them had done so much as put a dollar on her jail account. None of them had visited her. No one had spoken publicly to support her sacrifice. She recalled that ALF had very publicly supported their own in a situation similar to this in Iowa, even staging a large protest outside a federal courthouse there. Members had come in from around the country to show their support for two of their own who had refused to testify. She hadn't expected that, but something. There would be nothing of the sort from these people. Why did she ever get mixed up with them?

She knew the answer, of course. Again, it was Eric. She wanted to share his interests, share his passion. Now she wondered if he even loved her, had ever loved her, or was just using her. She didn't know that answer.

Her parents didn't understand. They wanted her to talk, to purge the contempt and be released. Of course, they didn't know what was involved. Oden had told them as little as possible. She didn't want them to know. It would put them at risk, and not just from the authorities. Her parents were ardent environmentalists, but this would be too much for them. Even though somewhat radical in their views, they were not anarchists. Neither had ever been arrested. Her father had visited once, early on. It had not gone well. Her mother came almost every day, always pleading with her to come clean and help herself. Each visit ended in tears.

But the cause was just, wasn't it? Earth was in peril. If they didn't act, who would? Still, she had to question some of the methods. Why so much damage? Why did the security guard at the Ford dealership have to die? Would he really have been able to identify them? It seemed unlikely. Why didn't they just tie him up? He didn't tell her, but she knew who pulled the trigger. It had to be him. She had seen the intensity, the near religious fervor. It was part of what attracted her to him, but it was also what frightened her the most.

Linda wondered about the flower shop. Her mother and sister were trying to keep it afloat in her absence. But they had their own lives, their own responsibilities. Both had jobs and had used up most of their paid days off to staff the shop. What would happen after their vacation leave was exhausted. The business operated on a narrow margin. She knew that if she wasn't out soon it would fail. That possibility made her physically ill. She had put so much of herself into that place.

"Lunchtime, ladies!"

Oden was startled from her thoughts. It was the matron with her slop cart. Perfect timing, she thought. Most of the inmates put on weight while in custody. For many of them mealtime was the only thing to look forward to. She, on the other hand, had lost several pounds.

"Here you go," the matron said as she slid the tray toward Oden.

Already with no appetite, the sight of the unappealing gruel almost made Oden vomit. It didn't help that the entire place and most of those in it stank. "No thanks," she said.

"Suit yourself," the matron said, "But I have to serve you. It's in the regulations."

Oden sighed and took the tray. An inmate seated nearby offered her assistance.

"If you ain't gonna eat that I will," the woman said.

Oden estimated her weight at somewhere north of three hundred pounds, well north. One tray of food would scarcely amount to a snack for this behemoth.

"Go for it," Oden said. She shoved the tray to the other woman who grunted her thanks while continuing to shovel food into her mouth. There was something about it that pushed Oden past her breaking point. She lowered her head to the table and began to cry.

CHAPTER 69

8:11 p.m., Tuesday, May 30, Portland Cell Site of the Earth Martyrs Brigade, somewhere outside Portland, Oregon

Wolf was driving the same cargo van that had transported them before. Cobra sat in the front passenger seat. Neither said much during the trip. Parks sat next to Ward on the bench seat in back. He wondered if she had the same concerns that plagued him. She must, but there were no tells with Parks, even to a trained eye like his. She was as cool as they come, a pro's pro. He studied her. The pleasant smile never left her face as she casually watched for markers along the route. He knew that's what she was doing, making a mental note of road signs, homes, businesses, anything that could be used to retrace the route later. It wasn't necessary because Cruz and Royer were behind them in the follow car and knew the location of the cell headquarters. Parks was aware of that, but training and habit took over. Ward was doing the same thing.

They were almost there. Ward took Parks' hand. It was the signal they had agreed on. He looked down at their intertwined fingers, wondering if she could sense his tension. The paranoia present on his first ride to the farm had returned. The fact that Wolf had invited Kyra Jordan did not mean that they were safe. His operatives were likely done checking her cover story. They either found nothing amiss, which made inviting her safe, or there had been a problem. Ward knew that an undercover identity could only go so far. If a savvy investigator dug far enough it would be exposed as such. It was simply impossible to create a fake persona as comprehensive as a real life. The secret was to have a story with more layers than the number through which the other side was willing to dig. They had to be convinced of the lie before they got through to the truth.

How many layers were there in Kyra Jordan's story? Ward could always assess the strength of his own cover before going in. He didn't like the fact that he was now relying on a false identity that he never had a chance to review.

He looked at Parks. She gave every appearance of someone enjoying an evening drive through the country. Her calm demeanor provided some reassurance. The weight of the handgun strapped to his ankle provided more. Ward was confident that they would have a good chance if things went south, unless it was an ambush. He would have to be extra vigilant. They could not let Wolf and his people get the drop on them. But would Wolf really bring them here to kill them? Did that make any sense? Why not some more remote location with fewer witnesses? Then it occurred to him, what better way to ensure that the others stayed in line than to execute two interlopers right in front of them? It seemed exactly the kind of thing that Wolf would enjoy. Ward swallowed hard.

They turned in at the farm. The gravel crunched under the van's tires as they traveled down the drive and toward the old farmhouse. Wolf parked and turned to the woman he knew as Kyra Jordan.

"This is it, Kyra," he said. "This is where we make a difference."

Ward could see that Wolf wanted to impress her. He couldn't blame him. It was something they would work to their advantage. Parks picked up on it.

"I can't wait to see it," she said.

Wolf exited and came around to passenger side of the van. He opened the sliding door and held out his hand to help her out. Parks took it. Ward followed. As with the last visit, several vehicles were already present.

"Welcome to our fellowship," Wolf said.

Ward recalled it as the same greeting he had received.

"We are a group of likeminded individuals who believe that direct action is the only way to save our planet," Wolf continued. "As I told Lightning, what is seen and heard here must stay here. The consequences for violating this rule are…unpleasant. Do you understand?"

"I do," Parks replied.

Wolf opened his arms to embrace her. Ward could see that he was earnest in welcoming Parks. She was in. they were in. A wave of relief washed through his body. He tried not to show it.

Wolf led them to the barn. He slid open the large door to expose a group of seven already assembled. It was the entire cell, at least as far as Ward knew. Skye smiled and came toward them. This time Sequoia came with her, clearly relieved at seeing Joshua Young with his significant other.

"Hello, I'm Skye," she said. "And this is Sequoia."

"Nice to meet you," Parks replied. She gave Sequoia an appraising look. Ward could see that Parks wanted to make some quip about the appropriateness of the nickname. She held back.

Fern also came over to greet them.

"Hello, Kyra," Fern said. There was a resignation in her voice. She looked at Ward and smiled meekly. Ward found himself feeling bad for her. He had to remind himself what she was. Wolf pulled the woman he knew as Kyra Jordan to his side. "Here, you will be known as Aurora, for the Aurora Borealis," he whispered.

"I like it," Parks said, placing her hand on Wolf's arm.

They turned to face the group. "I'd like to present our newest colleague," Wolf announced. "She will be known here as Aurora."

Ward stood back and observed as Wolf introduced Aurora to the other members. Parks seemed at ease as she engaged each of them, flowing seamlessly from one conversation to the next. Ward was impressed by how flawlessly she played her role, and at how expertly she played Wolf. He seemed to hang on her every word. It was understandable.

As Ward watched Parks work the room it dawned on him that he had barely thought of Maria since meeting her. It caused a twinge of guilt. He still had feelings for Maria. But the attraction to Parks was undeniable. *It's a bad idea*, he reminded himself once again. How could it even work? They were both devoted to their jobs, maybe too devoted. They worked for different agencies, lived in different parts of the country. *Just cool it*, Ward thought. But as he watched her he started to care less and less about the reasons it was wrong.

Eventually, Wolf and Parks were off by themselves. Ward debated whether to rejoin them. Wolf might be inclined to share more if left alone to impress Parks. He decided to wait for a signal from her. She would let him know when it was a good time. After a few minutes it came. Parks smiled and waved him over. As he approached, Ward could hear that Parks had already managed to engage Wolf in a useful conversation.

"So, I assume that the group is self-funded," Parks said matter-of-factly.

It was a subtle invitation for Wolf to counter her assumption, to brag.

"Oh, you'd be surprised to hear where some of our funding comes from," he replied.

"Surprise me," Parks said.

Wolf hesitated. Ward could see that he wanted to tell her, to impress her.

"Have you heard of the Green Earth Alliance?" Wolf asked.

Ward's heart almost stopped. The Green Earth Alliance was one of the most respected environmental organizations in the world. He had even made a few donations over the years. If there were truly a connection between the Alliance and the Earth Martyrs Brigade it would be a bombshell and a lot of prominent people would be greatly embarrassed. Ward recalled reading in his briefing materials about the connection between Earth First and ELF. But this was something far different. Earth First was no

Green Earth Alliance.

"Of course I've heard of it," Parks said. "You mean to tell me they are funding direct action?"

A wicked smile crept onto Wolf's face. He didn't answer the question. It was then that Ward noticed Cobra watching them intently.

CHAPTER 70

10:43 a.m., Wednesday, May 31, Bureau of Alcohol, Tobacco, Firearms and Explosives, Denver Field Division, Denver, Colorado

Special Agent Toby Combs was putting the finishing touches on a report for his latest felon in possession case. It involved yet another gangbanger who couldn't abide by the prohibition on having a weapon that came with the status of felon. The charge was a great mechanism for taking out proven thugs and predators before they found their next victim. Combs understood that after a conviction most gang members would not return to the streets unarmed. He got that. But that was the point. They shouldn't return to the streets at all. The only chance at breaking the cycle was to move elsewhere and get new friends. If they went back to the same lifestyle, then they had to be prepared to pay the consequences.

As Combs was typing the last few sentences his cell phone rang. "Combs."

"Special Agent, this is Constance Leaton from the FBI Lab. I'm calling about the videos you submitted for silhouette matching. Have you got a minute?"

Combs sat up straight. "Yeah, sure." He waved his hand at Maness, whose desk was nearby, gesturing for him to come over. "Can I put you on speaker?" Combs asked. "Special Agent Maness is working the case with me. I want him to hear this."

"Not a problem. Tell me when you're ready."

Maness hustled over. "What's up?" he asked.

"It's the FBI lab about the videos," Combs whispered, his hands covering the phone's receiver.

Maness grabbed a chair.

Combs activated the speaker function. "Go ahead," he said.

"Well," Leaton said, "I've had an opportunity to compare the known video of Eric Harper to the video of the arsonist obtained from the security app's cloud storage system."

Combs didn't like the tone in her voice. He glanced at Maness. Judging from the look of resignation on his face they shared the same bad feeling.

"While the latter video was very short," Leaton continued, "it did provide enough for silhouette matching analysis."

Combs perked up. He looked at Maness who was leaning forward in his chair, elbows on knees, listening intently.

"And?" Combs asked. It seemed to him that these lab people always dragged it out, giving maximum dramatic effect to their role in the investigative process.

"I'll send out the final report today and email you a copy," Leaton added, "but I wanted to call and give you a heads-up on my findings."

There was a pause, as if she were waiting for some sort of acknowledgement. Combs looked at Maness, who rolled his eyes.

"We very much appreciate that," Combs said. "What've you got?"

"Based on my analysis of height, build, movement patterns and the various other criteria that we typically consider, I have concluded that Eric Harper cannot be excluded as the arsonist in the security app video. Simply put, the results are inconclusive."

Combs ran his hand over his face. He looked at Maness and shook his head. It was mostly frustration over the results, but also some annoyance at the long buildup to what could have been said in a couple of sentences. He reminded himself that Leaton was on their side and probably didn't like disappointing them.

"We appreciate the heads-up," Combs said, trying to sound

sincere. He thought for a moment. Most of the better lab people he had ever worked with had their formal opinion, but also their informal take, something akin to the cop's hunch. He decided to give it a shot.

"Between us, Constance, what do you think? Have we got the right guy?"

There was a pause on the other end of the phone. Then Leaton spoke. "I couldn't testify to it in court, but yeah, I think you've got the right guy."

Combs looked at Maness and nodded. "Thanks, Constance," he said. "Much appreciated."

"My pleasure."

Combs ended the call as he rose from his chair. He turned to Maness and smiled. "What do you say we go out and do a little surveillance?"

CHAPTER 71

11:43 a.m., Wednesday, May 31, Ward's undercover apartment, The Hawthorne District, Portland, Oregon

Parks rummaged through the refrigerator, looking for something to make for lunch. The pickings were slim, little more than leftovers from the few meals that she had prepared and an assortment of condiments. Time to stock the kitchen with some healthier items, she thought. It was hard enough to watch your diet on these missions, and they had eaten too many restaurant meals since she'd arrived. Plus, there was no way to tell how long they might be here.

Ward was seated on the couch, reading the sports section. "I'm gonna go out and pick up some groceries," Parks said. "Anything you want me to get?"

"How are we fixed for beer and coffee?" Ward asked.

"Really? That's it?"

"I have my priorities."

She laughed. "I'm gonna walk down to that place just east of here on the other side of Hawthorne. They have a pretty good selection."

"Want some help?" Ward asked. "You might have a lot to carry."

"How much beer do you think I'm gonna get?"

Ward smiled.

"No, thanks," she said. "I'll be fine. Besides, I want to nose around the neighborhood a bit, see what I can see." The truth was Parks also wanted a little alone time. She had grown rather fond of Ward, but it was hard to be around anybody all day, every day.

Parks slipped her weapon into her ankle holster, then grabbed her purse. "See you later," she said over her shoulder as she walked out the door.

"Be careful," Ward said after her.

Parks strolled down Southeast Hawthorne, peering in the windows of shops and restaurants as she went, making mental note of the places where she and Ward could pretend to be a real couple. Part of her wanted it to be more than pretend. The handsome agent was funny, intelligent, yet down-to-earth and without conceit. Their jobs allowed them to relate to each other in a way that was impossible with civilians. The work had put an unbearable strain on the two serious relationships in her life. The same had apparently been true for Ward and his ex-wife. She wondered if, maybe? Could it really be possible for the two of them? There was so much that would get in the way. And that would always be the case, unless she found a way around it. She put the notion out of her head. They had work to do, and she had groceries to buy.

When she arrived at the store Parks grabbed a shopping cart and began wandering up and down the aisles. The place handled far more than groceries. There were appliances, electronics, clothing, furniture, and more. She briefly fantasized about making their little apartment more of home, then came to her senses. *Cut it out*, Parks thought. *Not the time, and not the place.* She grabbed some butter and yogurt, then headed for the liquor section where she found some local beers that she thought Ward might like. After that, Parks rolled her cart over to the produce department where she selected lettuce, cucumbers and onions.

As she began to look through the tomatoes Parks observed an individual at the far end of the aisle. It was a man wearing a stocking cap and sunglasses. Something about him seemed familiar.

She avoided eye contact and acted as if she hadn't noticed him. Parks picked a few tomatoes, then moved to the fruit. She chose a container of blueberries, some apples and bunch of bananas, all the while keeping an eye on the man in the stocking cap. He seemed to be watching. Was it her imagination? Was it the always present paranoia of the undercover agent? Maybe the guy was simply interested in her. She had been the subject of a few attempted grocery store pickups over the years. Who was it that put that notion in the minds of men anyway?

Parks left the produce area. She already had about as much as she could comfortably carry back to the apartment and wanted to see if the man followed her through the store. Bread and cereal were the only other items on her list. She took her time in the bread aisle. He didn't appear. Maybe it was nothing after all. It was then on to the cereal aisle where Parks found her brand of oatmeal. As she turned to put the box in her cart, the man passed by the opening at the end of the aisle. He shot a glance her direction and then quickly looked away, too quickly.

There was one checkout counter without a line. Parks went to it and began to unload her items. She was almost done when she noticed the man in the stocking cap at the far checkout. There was a customer in front of him. He seemed impatient as the other patron struggled with her payment, the device apparently not picking up the data from her debit card. Parks took her time, making sure to allow her follower the chance to keep up. When it appeared that he had successfully paid for his conspicuously small number of items Parks moved toward the exit. Once outside, she walked a block west. The man in the stocking cap had exited the store and was approximately thirty yards behind her. Parks stopped and retrieved the cell phone from her purse. Not looking back at the man behind her, she called Ward.

"Hello," Ward answered.

"Hi, honey," Parks said, loud enough to be overheard. "Could you meet me at the door and help me with the groceries?"

"Hi, honey?" Ward asked. "I assume there's a problem. I'll be right down."

"I'll be there in a few minutes," Parks said cheerily. "Thanks. Love you."

Parks resumed walking, occasionally slowing to window shop as she went. This forced her pursuer to catch up and pass behind her. He kept his head down as he quickly moved by. She caught his reflection in the glass. This time she got a good look. It was Cobra. When he was well ahead of her, Parks started toward the apartment. As she approached the front entrance she saw Ward. He came out to meet her.

"Hi," she said, and then leaned in to kiss him. Ward played along smoothly, returning the kiss, then picking up most of the bags to carry up to the apartment. As they went inside Parks looked back to see if she could spot Cobra. He was nowhere to be seen.

Once they were in the apartment Parks began to explain.

"There was a guy tailing me in the store," Parks said, "stocking cap, sunglasses, etcetera. He started to follow me back to the apartment."

"And that's when you called."

"Right. After that I slowed to do a little window shopping, forced him to either catch up or turn off in another direction. He passed right behind me. When I caught his reflection in the store window I recognized him. It was Cobra."

Ward's brow furrowed. "So he was watching the apartment beforehand."

"I'm sure."

"But why follow you to a grocery store?" Ward asked. "Seems like a good place to get noticed, and that's exactly what happened."

"Maybe he's trying to find out if we're an actual couple, you know, really living together. He may have wanted to see if I bought groceries for two."

"That's possible. In any event, something made him suspicious." He paused. "There is also the possibility that he wanted you to see him."

"I thought about that. Last night, I noticed that he seemed jealous of the attention I was getting from Wolf, or if not jealous then at least concerned about it."

"I noticed that, too. From what I can tell he seems to be the second-in-command. It might be that he sees a threat to his status, or he may have his own agenda."

"Or they found a flaw in one of our cover stories," Parks said. "There's never been one that was perfect."

"A fact I've learned the hard way," Ward said. "Do you think we should pull out?"

"Hell no!" Parks said.

Ward smiled. "Good. Me, neither."

Parks was relieved. This was the case of a lifetime, and the two of them might be the only hope for stopping these terrorists and whatever they had planned next. She also wasn't quite ready to say goodbye to Special Agent David Ward.

CHAPTER 72

11:14 p.m., Thursday, June 1, on the streets of Boulder, Colorado

Combs and Maness had followed Eric Harper almost continuously since getting the call from the FBI lab. So far, there wasn't much to show for it. He had done little more than go from home to work and back again. That was until around eight o'clock that evening when they followed him to a local bar. The entrance was a half-block from where their car was parked. Harper had gone in alone. Another ATF agent, Carrie Duncan, who was unfamiliar to Harper, had done a walk-through shortly after his arrival. She observed nothing unusual. It was reported that Harper was alone, sitting at the bar.

Combs knew that they could follow the guy for days, maybe weeks, and turn up nothing. Harper was probably being extra careful after the encounter at his workplace the week before. His phone records had so far provided little that was useful. Immediately after the first interview they had subpoenaed subscriber information and call logs for the only phone number they could identify to him. The records covered a period going back six months. It would take time to do a thorough analysis of the logs and follow up on any leads developed there. Combs doubted they would yield much. The Earth Martyrs Brigade seemed too savvy to conduct any business on normal cell accounts. Combs was sure that most of their planning was done on throwaway phones, face to face, maybe even through encrypted communications. High quality encryption was now easy to obtain, and a source of great frustration to law enforcement. A search warrant for the content of Harper's emails and text messages might yield more, but they were a long way from having enough for a warrant. Combs knew that no judge would approve one based on the mere fact that Harper and Linda Oden were acquainted combined with an inconclusive silhouette match. The truth was they had little more than that.

"Maybe it's time for another walk-through," Maness suggested.

"Yeah, I agree," Combs said. Duncan was stationed behind the bar, watching the rear exit. Combs called her cell. She answered before the second ring.

"Duncan."

"Can you do another walk-through?" Combs asked.

"Not a problem. You want me to get close if he's talking to anybody?"

"Sure. Text me if anything is happening."

"Will do."

Minutes later Combs received a text. *He's sitting at bar with woman. They seem friendly.* Seconds later, another appeared. *Hand on her back. She touched his leg. More than friends.* Combs smiled. He showed the messages to Maness.

"Looks like Harper has moved on from his flower girl," Maness said.

"Sure does." Combs had an idea. He replied to Duncan's text. *Can you get photos of lovebirds without being noticed?*

The reply was instantaneous. *Yes.*

Almost immediately photos began to appear on Combs phone. They captured various displays of affection between Harper and the woman. He shared them with Maness as they came in. In the last shot they were kissing. Combs sent another text to Duncan. *Great pics. Text us when they leave.*

Twenty minutes went by before Combs' phone signaled another incoming text. He grabbed his cell. *On the move.*

"Get your camera ready," Combs said. "They're on the way

out."

"I'll set it to video," Maness said. He focused the telephoto lens on the entrance. "We can print stills off of it if we need to."

"Good idea."

The couple emerged from the bar. Harper had his arm around the woman's shoulders. She was smiling, nuzzled in close to him. They travelled west. After a few seconds her arm slipped around his waist. This did not appear to be their first time together. They gave every impression of exactly what they appeared to be— young lovers.

"You getting this?" Combs asked.

"Every second of it. This is great stuff."

Combs started his car and put it in gear, waiting for them to get far enough ahead. When they were a block-and-a-half distant he began to pull away from the curb. The couple moved slowly, seemingly content to enjoy their stroll on a pleasant June evening. Combs struggled to stay far enough behind and avoid detection. When they had gone three blocks they started to slow, stopping in front of an apartment building. They turned to face each other. There was some discussion. They kissed. More discussion followed. The woman retrieved something from her purse. It appeared to be her keys. She took Harper by the hand and led him to the door. They went inside.

"This is gonna be helpful," Combs said.

Maness nodded. "Oh yeah."

They waited, just to be sure. By three o'clock in the morning they were sure enough. Combs turned to Maness, who was now struggling to stay awake.

"Let's call that AUSA down in Oklahoma City, Delgado, tell her what we've got. Maybe she can talk to Oden's lawyer and arrange for us to take another run at her."

"Sounds good," Maness said. "If I were her, I sure wouldn't sit in jail for this asshole."

CHAPTER 73

10:37 a.m., Friday, June 2, The Cabin, Yellowstone Cell Site of the Earth Martyrs Brigade, somewhere outside Yellowstone National Park

He had parked three miles back and hiked in, as was expected of all who visited this place. Now, in a small clearing, it sat before him. Wolf smiled at the sight, the spiritual center of their movement. It was no compound. That sort of thing was reserved for cults, militias, white supremacists. They were none of that. His people were freedom fighters, battling those who would yoke the Earth to their own selfish, capitalistic pursuits. No, this was definitely no compound, not in its nature or in its size. In fact, it was modest by any standards, a cabin with two small bedrooms, a living room, and a kitchen of sorts. There was no electricity, no running water, and no carbon footprint to speak of, except that which came with the occasional fire in the old stone fireplace. It sat on a mere half-acre of land. A hiker who stumbled across it would hardly suspect that it housed a cell of the Earth Martyrs Brigade, let alone the most important cell. But to Wolf, it was the perfect spot, centered in one of Mother's most splendid creations, a constant reminder of what they were fighting for.

Wolf relished these meetings, though there was a small part of him that dreaded them. Ocean was an inspiration but was also unnerving. Perhaps it was the intensity in his dark brown eyes. They seemed to measure you, at once assessing your strength and uncovering every weakness. Or maybe it was the ever-present smile. It was calm, almost gentle, yet exuded a powerful confidence, and something more, something like omniscience.

Wolf had seen Ocean work his magic, had witnessed his persuasive powers. The man's capacity to bend others to his will was something like one might have seen in a Rasputin, Manson, or Hitler. But, unlike them, Ocean's goals were admirable, indisputable, necessary. Wolf saw him as more Christlike, leading his flock, and then all humanity, away from their sins against Mother and toward the righteousness of sustainable living and the preservation of Earth. There was one difference, of course. In their struggle if a few Romans need die, then so be it.

As Wolf approached, the cabin door opened. It was Spider, the leader of the Boston cell. He was one of the six, the group that made up their governing council. There were no titles, no specifically defined responsibilities. Communication between the cells was accomplished through them. They were representatives of various regions of the country: Spider from the northeast, three others from the midwest, southeast and southwest, and then himself. Wolf represented the northwest, including the west coast.

The group met infrequently. Meetings were dangerous. They left traces, at least for those who knew where to look. To further minimize risk they knew little about each other, no real identities, no addresses, only necessary contact information. This did not lessen their bond but increased it. They were united in their sacred purpose. They were the chosen who implemented policy and directives, his directives. Input was offered and received, but the ultimate decision always rested with him. Ocean was their oracle. All core philosophy and significant strategic decisions emanated from him.

"Wolf, my friend, how are you?" Spider extended his hand.

"I'm good," Wolf said. "This place, it energizes me. He energizes me."

Spider nodded. "Mother's spirit is strong here. And she speaks through him."

"Indeed she does."

"These are momentous times."

"The world has taken notice."

Spider nodded. "It has, and it will. Let's go in." He led the way.

Once inside, Wolf first looked for Ocean. Not seeing him, he acknowledged the others, nodding his greetings to Jaguar, who represented the southwest, and Oak, the southeast envoy. The Electrician, leader of the Madison cell, was present for the midwest. His people had been of great assistance in the attack on the substation in Omaha. Wolf went to him.

"Good to see you, my brother. Thank you once again for your help."

"Our pleasure," The Electrician said. "You did magnificent work in Omaha."

The others voiced their agreement.

Wolf looked around. "Where is he?"

"In there," Jaguar whispered, indicating toward one of the bedrooms. "He's meditating."

Wolf nodded. It wasn't unusual behavior for Ocean. He was known to engage in meditation and cleansing rituals before their meetings.

"Any idea yet what this is about?" Wolf asked. There had been little said in advance regarding their agenda. Again, this was not unusual. For reasons of security no operational information was shared until absolutely necessary. It was a policy that had served them well.

Jaguar shook her head. "He hasn't said much since we arrived."

"Then I guess we wait," Wolf observed. He found a seat and settled in, resting his legs from the long hike to the cabin.

They talked for some time, rejoicing in their accomplishments and the public alarm. It was seen as an awakening, the first steps in humanity's true education as to the dire state of the planet. But it was also a call to arms, one that they believed many would ultimately embrace as they watched the Earth Martyrs Brigade lead the way. Then, as if their positive energy drew him forward, Ocean emerged.

"Welcome, comrades!" he said, arms outstretched toward them as he entered the room. "My warriors!" Ocean touched each of them, a shoulder, a hand, even stroking Jaguar's cheek as he gazed into her eyes. "Your battle to defend Mother, to avenge her, inspires me." He paced around the group. "There have been great victories. The world has taken note. Some shake with fear, as well they should. But most should find hope in what we've accomplished. It will take time, but they will come to understand and to follow our courageous example. How could they not?" He stopped and faced them. "Those who don't, those who would despoil Mother, use her gifts for their own greedy, filthy purposes...they and their precious possessions will perish."

There were murmurs of approval.

Wolf leaned forward. "What's next?" he asked.

"My friend Wolf, always ready to prowl, to seek his moment and attack." Ocean smiled, then closed his eyes. His pressed his hands together, as if in prayer, and then raised them to his lips. "The time has come to demonstrate our reach, to prove that we will never go away, never be stopped. Mother's enemies will be cowed, or they will be removed. We will teach humanity what it can live with, and what it must live without."

Wolf listened in awe as Ocean described his plan.

CHAPTER 74

8:37 p.m., Saturday, June 3, Portland Cell Site of the Earth Martyrs Brigade, somewhere outside Portland, Oregon

This time Fern had been their ride to the meeting. There was no effort to disguise the route. It was one good sign to counterbalance the tail by Cobra earlier in the week. Maybe he was simply acting on his own, Ward thought, trying to protect his position of influence with Wolf. It seemed plausible. There was nothing to indicate that Wolf was suspicious. In fact, it was quite the contrary. He was once again entertaining the beguiling Kyra Jordan, now known as Aurora, and sharing more than he should. Cobra hovered near the two of them, watching every move, listening to every word. Ward wondered if Parks should make an effort to pull Cobra in so as to seem less of a threat. On the other hand, that might create more problems than it would solve. For one thing, it could inhibit Wolf's inclination to share.

Ward once again found himself talking with Mouse, this time discussing the relative merits of various plant-based biofuels as an alternative to ethanol, a substance that Mouse seemed to consider a scourge on humanity. Ward wondered what energy sources would be acceptable to these people. They had complaints about everything. Wind turbines were a blight on the landscape that killed too many birds. Solar used too much water and caused loss of habitat. Hazardous materials were used to manufacture the panels. And on and on it went. They were long on complaints.

The one thing they didn't offer was solutions. Anarchy was not a solution. Ward did his best to appear interested, all the while keeping an eye on Cobra.

"A huge percentage of the nation's corn crop is now used for ethanol," Mouse lamented. "This has reduced food production. And then there's the carbon dioxide caused by the production process."

Ward nodded solemnly. He glanced at Parks. Thankfully, she gestured for him to join her and Wolf. Ward was relieved, but also concerned by the expression on her face. The brightness and laughter were replaced by a look of worry.

"Excuse me," Ward said to Mouse. "I see I'm being summoned. We should continue this discussion later," he lied.

"Absolutely," Mouse said. He moved off to converse with the other members, seemingly eager to share his views with as many of them as possible.

Ward moved toward Parks and Wolf. As he did, he could see that the conversation between the two had become more intense. They were huddled together. Cobra had edged closer. But it appeared by his body English that Wolf might not want Cobra to overhear whatever it was that he was sharing with Parks.

As Ward joined them, Wolf turned and spoke. "I was telling Aurora that I just returned from a meeting. It was there that we discussed our next...gesture." A wicked smile appeared on his face.

"I take it there is some group that decides these things?" Ward asked. He noticed that Parks gave him an almost imperceptible shake of the head as if to say, *already tried that.*

Wolf ignored the inquiry. "This gesture will be significant," he said.

"How so?" Ward asked.

Wolf looked about, taking particular note of Cobra's location. He lowered his voice. "Suffice it to say that it will be multi-pronged and coordinated."

"Interesting," Ward said. "Is there anything we can do to help?"

Wolf stared at him for a moment, studying him. Ward began to wonder if he had somehow miscalculated by offering assistance. The pause grew awkward, then uncomfortable. Ward felt a twinge of panic. Finally, Wolf spoke.

"I'm glad you asked," he said.

Ward tried not to show his relief, or excitement. But his muscles quivered. His skin felt electric. Did it show? He quickly glanced at Parks, who displayed nothing.

"Our impact would be enhanced if a series of denial of service attacks occurred at the same time," Wolf explained.

"DoS attacks are no problem," Ward said. He looked at Parks, who nodded her agreement. *Yeah, no fucking problem at all*, he thought. He was talking out of his ass, but there was no choice other than go for it. This was their big break. "When and where?" he asked.

Wolf smiled and put his hand on Ward's shoulder. "There will be plenty of time for that later," he said.

Ward considered pushing him, explaining that he needed the details in advance so that he could do the prep work. But Wolf's demeanor, and Parks' body English, said back off.

"Fair enough," Ward said. He put his arm around Parks' waist. "We're just happy to have the opportunity to help the cause."

Ward saw Wolf focus on the arm now encircling Parks. Had he made a mistake? Keeping the sexual tension between Wolf and the woman he called Aurora was essential to the mission. On the other hand, his relationship with her had to appear real. Wasn't that exactly what Cobra had been investigating? There was a part of him that also wondered if he wasn't staking his claim. He could feel Park's hand reach up and rest on the middle of his back. It felt good, natural. Did it mean something bathing? Or was she just playing her part? His thoughts were interrupted by Cobra's approach.

"Wolf, could I talk to you for a moment?" Cobra asked. His eyes shifted to Ward, then to Parks, and back to Wolf again. "Alone," he insisted.

Wolf seemed annoyed. "I suppose," he said. "Let's go outside."

They slipped out the barn door. When they were gone Ward pulled Parks close and leaned in, pretending to give her a playful kiss on the forehead. Instead, he whispered in her ear. "This could be it," he said. She patted him on the back to show her agreement.

"What is it?" Wolf asked.

"What are you telling them?" Cobra was agitated. Wolf's conduct was reckless. "You haven't even shared the details of the next attack with me. We don't know enough about these two. It's dangerous."

"I've told them only what they need to know."

"They don't need to know anything," Cobra said, "not yet, and maybe not ever."

"You're in no position to second-guess me," Wolf growled. "I've made my assessment of them and their usefulness to our cause. They have a role to play. That's the end of it."

We'll see about that, Cobra thought. Something about them didn't seem right—the way they just happened to show up, happened to be the perfect fit at the perfect time. If he was right, they would make a mistake. Sometime, someplace, they would make a mistake. And he would be there to catch it, and them.

"Are you confident that they've been thoroughly vetted?" Cobra asked. He knew that this was a touchy issue with Wolf but had to risk it.

"My contacts don't make mistakes," Wolf snapped. "Unless you have some specific evidence this conversation is over."

Cobra said nothing.

"That's what I thought," Wolf snarled. "Back inside."

Cobra was fuming. He wouldn't be treated like this. *I'll find your fucking evidence*, he thought.

CHAPTER 75

9:08 a.m., Monday, June 5, in United States Marshals Service custody, Oklahoma County Jail, Oklahoma City, Oklahoma

Combs and Maness entered the interview room with Assistant United States Attorney Katherine Delgado. They had coordinated their approach, with Delgado to play the hardass. Combs guessed that the role wasn't much of a stretch for her. She seemed the type. He liked that in a prosecutor. Most agents did. But he also knew that securing a defendant's cooperation required more than simply threatening to drop the hammer. It required subtlety, psychology, and often an appeal to a range of factors and emotions beyond simple self-interest. It was entirely possible that Oden would continue be a hard sell, despite the new information at their disposal. So be it. They had planned for that contingency, and each of them would do their parts. The end result would hopefully be an agreement to cooperate, with Oden purging her contempt by testifying in front of the grand jury.

Their subject and her attorney, Jimmy Roy Holloway, were already in the room. Holloway had arrived a half-hour earlier to advise his client on what to expect. He had an idea of what was to follow, but Combs knew that Holloway didn't know the half of it. Delgado had not shared the bombshell of Eric Harper's new love interest. They would save that morsel for if and when it was needed. Combs was interested to see if the stint in the Oklahoma County jail had alone been enough to soften her resolve. Most normal citizens, if you could call her that, couldn't handle any significant jail time. Oden, despite her mouthy attitude, struck him as too soft to hold out for the duration. In fact, he was surprised that she had lasted this long.

As he studied her now, seated at the long interview table, the strain of incarceration showed. She was pale, haggard, no longer the attractive young woman that he and Maness had encountered at the flower shop. In his estimation, she was already close to breaking. If not, the information on Harper would surely send her over.

As they sat across from Oden and her attorney, Delgado took the lead.

"Jimmy Roy," she said.

"What's this about?" Holloway asked, straight to the point. He made no attempt to introduce himself to Combs or Maness. That was fine with Combs. He had no interest in exchanging pleasantries with defense counsel.

"We'd like to see if your client has come to her senses," Delgado said.

Holloway chortled. "What makes you think anything is different?" he asked in his slow drawl. "Ms. Oden has given me no indication of any inclination to help the government, or that she has any information of value whatsoever."

A smirk appeared on Delgado's face. "Is that so?" she asked. "Then I guess she's prepared to sit here for the remainder of the grand jury's term? Is that right?"

Combs saw Oden fidget in her seat. She looked down. The old defiance wasn't there.

"For the sake of conversation, if my client was inclined to testify—and I am in no way implying that she is—I assume that the terms of your immunity offer would remain in effect. Is that correct?" Holloway inquired.

"Not that she deserves it," Delgado said, "but yes."

Holloway leaned over and whispered in Oden's ear. She whispered something back. Combs thought he noticed an almost imperceptible shake of her head.

"My client is not interested in testifying," Holloway announced. He started to pick up some papers and a notepad scattered on the table and put them in his briefcase. "I don't believe there is anything else for us to discuss."

Combs spoke up. "Oh, I think there is." He knew there was some risk in the approach he was about to take. If Eric Harper was not their man Oden would tell them to go fuck themselves and she would be lost as a witness. But they had nothing else, and Combs' instincts told him that Harper was the right guy. The plan was to start with the silhouette matching angle. Holloway and Oden didn't need to know that the results were inconclusive, and neither would know enough about the process to seriously challenge him.

"And you are?" Holloway asked.

"Special Agent Toby Combs. This is my partner, Ian Maness." Combs did not extend his hand. He continued.

"We subpoenaed Ms. Oden's phone records and obtained subscriber information for the numbers frequently called," Combs said. "We then interviewed these individuals. There was one in particular who caught our attention." He watched Oden. She immediately looked up. "During the interview this person appeared nervous...evasive." Holloway's brow furrowed. Combs had his attention.

"And who is this individual?" Holloway asked.

Combs smiled. "I'll get to that," he said. "We secured video footage of this individual following the interview." He paused for a moment, letting the tension build, then focused on Holloway. "The arsonists were caught on a surveillance camera at the Paxton Ford dealership."

Holloway adjusted himself in his seat. "I fail to see how this in any way implicates my client," he said. "It's my understanding that the arsonists wore ski masks and dark clothing and could not be identified."

"Are you familiar with a process known as silhouette

matching?” Combs asked.

“I’ve heard of it,” Holloway replied.

Combs thought this was bullshit. The technique was not well known. He went on.

“Experts at the FBI lab compared the video from Paxton Ford to the footage of the individual we interviewed. They determined it’s a match.” Combs could hear Oden inhale. She stared at him, waiting. “I believe that Ms. Oden is quite familiar with Eric Harper.” He paused, watching her intently. “That’s right,” Combs said to her. “We know that you loaned your van to him.”

The color washed from Oden’s face. She seemed to sense it, looking away from Combs’ stare and then down at the floor. Combs was now positive that Harper was their man. After a second, Oden tugged at Holloway’s jacket sleeve. He waved her off.

“This sounds like voodoo science to me,” Holloway said. “Show me the report.”

“This information was conveyed over the phone,” Combs said. It was true, but he did have the report.

“We’ll get the report to you,” Delgado said, looking at Combs. “But there is another piece of information that your client might be interested in.”

“Oh, and what is that?” Holloway asked.

Maness took his turn. “We have some additional video of Mr. Harper,” he said. “It appears that he has moved on from Ms. Oden.”

“I don’t believe it!” Oden blurted out.

“I assure you that it’s true,” Maness said.

“It can’t be,” Oden said, her voice pleading. Tears formed in her eyes. “He wouldn’t do that. I know him. I love him.”

Holloway put his hand on her arm. “This is an outrageous attempt to exploit my client’s emotions,” he exclaimed. “We have no interest in viewing your blatant invasion of Mr. Harper’s privacy and your obvious attempt to distort whatever it is that you think you saw. I should go to the press with this.”

“Oh, stuff it, Jimmy Roy,” Delgado said. “Do you want your

client to sit in jail, maybe get indicted? You're not going to the press and you know it. Let's cut the bullshit and—"

"I want to see it," Oden interjected. Holloway looked at her. She nodded her head.

"Play it," Holloway said.

Maness had brought a laptop for the occasion. He turned it to face Oden and Holloway then clicked the start button. Combs studied Oden as the video played. It first showed Harper and his new friend exit the bar, lovingly intertwined. Oden's mouth opened. The camera then followed the couple as they casually strolled to her apartment, kissed and entered. The heartsick look that had been on Oden's face only moments earlier changed to one of scorn. There was a fire in her eyes. She whispered something in Holloway's ear. He nodded, then looked at Delgado.

"The immunity letter is still in effect?"

"That's what I said."

Holloway turned to Oden. "Go ahead."

Oden took a deep breath, clenched her jaw, then spoke. "I'll tell you anything you want to know."

CHAPTER 76

8:46 p.m., Tuesday, June 6, Green Glow Cafe, Portland, Oregon

Ward and Parks entered the Green Glow. Earlier that day Wolf had called and asked to meet them. Ward assumed that it was about the denial of service attacks they had discussed on Saturday night. Not knowing when these were expected to occur, he had hastily arranged for a quick refresher course from the FBI's white hat hackers, Etherlord and Incubus. He and Parks had returned from San Jose just that morning after an intense two-day immersion in the techniques of the DoS attack. It was an open question as to whether phony attacks could be perpetrated on whatever targets Wolf identified, but the two of them would at least look like they knew what they were doing. When the time came for them to launch the attacks it would be a fluid situation, one hopefully timed to coincide with arrests.

"There he is," Parks said, pointing to a table where Wolf sat alone. There was no Fern, no Skye or Sequoia, and, thankfully, no Cobra. They approached.

Wolf rose to his feet as soon as he saw them. "Let's go for a walk," he said abruptly.

Ward and Parks exchanged a quick glance. "Can't we just talk here?" Ward asked. "Thought we might get a drink," he offered by way of explanation.

"Too many ears," Wolf responded. He jerked his head toward the door. "Let's go."

Ward's first thought was the conversation between Wolf and Cobra on Saturday night. Cobra had insisted on talking alone, outside. Did he know something? If so, this could be a setup. A careful agent always tried to maintain as much control over the situation as possible and going out onto the street right now was not maintaining control. It could be that Wolf, as he said, was simply concerned about eavesdroppers. It was impossible to tell. Ward decided that they had to play it out. He checked with Parks, who nodded her approval.

"Let's go," he said.

They walked out onto the street. Sunset approached. There was still light, but not much, not enough. They might have a chance if the shooter approached them directly. Their odds dropped to near zero if the shot came from a window or rooftop. Cruz and Royer were running surveillance and sat a block off, but there was nothing they could do to stop a determined killer. The deed would be done before they could intervene. It was an ever-present risk in the world of the undercover operative. There were no tactical teams nearby waiting to sweep in, no fleet of patrol units at the ready, no snipers providing cover. Steel nerve and acting skill were the tools of a lonely trade.

"The secret to our success," Wolf began, "is compartmentalization, strictly limiting operational details to those who need to know, and only when they need to know it."

Success, Ward thought. *What bullshit.* He remembered the dead firefighter, Andy Garner. Then he stopped, reminding himself to stay in character. "That makes sense," he said.

"That rule even applies within our cell," Wolf said. "The task I will ask of you and Aurora must stay between us. Do you understand?"

"Of course," Ward said.

"Agreed," Parks added.

"Good." Wolf was silent for a moment, as if pondering whether to take this final step toward bringing them into the fold. It was either that or he was allowing time for someone to get in place. Ward scanned the rooftops, studied the windows. He dropped a step behind so that Wolf wouldn't notice and glanced back over his shoulder to see if anyone was following. As he did he caught Parks doing the same.

"I have your targets for the DoS attacks," Wolf said.

Ward felt some relief but knew better than to become complacent. Wolf was clever. This could all be part of a plan to get them to drop their guard. He studied the terrorist, looking for any signs of an imminent assault. There were no furtive eye movements, no indicators that he was nervous or ready to flee. In fact, as he walked, head bent down, hands clasped behind his back, he appeared to be deep in thought, planning the tactical details of some larger, grander operation.

"What are they?" Parks asked.

Wolf turned to look at her as he continued walking. "The New York Stock Exchange," he replied. "Also several major government websites: House of Representatives, Senate, White House."

Ward felt a chill. "Not easy," he said, "But it can be done." In truth, he doubted that it could, particularly a mock attack on the stock exchange. For Wall Street, investor confidence was everything. He couldn't imagine any great willingness to go along with a staged hacking incident. But they had a bigger problem. He and Parks now had to find out what the Earth Martyrs Brigade had planned for New York and Washington, D.C., and when it was set to occur.

"There's more," Wolf said. "We also want to compromise the websites of several major power companies, including those of importance in operating the electrical grid."

Ward grew increasingly alarmed. What were these bastards up to? He knew that all of this involved much more than a denial of service attack. These website disruptions would merely coincide with something bigger, but what? He recalled the comments of several experts after the incident involving the substation in Omaha. They said that a coordinated series of such attacks around the country could bring down the entire grid. Should they arrest Wolf now, sweat him for the details? No, that wouldn't work. He wouldn't know the entire operational plan. Wolf had said it himself, compartmentalization. That was how these people worked. Besides, arresting Wolf or anyone else in the Portland cell would drive the other members of EMB further underground, make them more secretive, more dangerous. The best way to disrupt their plan, and their organization, was to stay put and play it out.

"That's a tall order," Ward said. "As you might imagine, those companies have some of the best network security available." He knew that wasn't entirely true. Sophisticated hackers tied to foreign governments had managed to access those networks. But Wolf didn't need to know that.

Wolf smiled. It was a relaxed, almost contented smile. "I'm sure you'll do your best," he said.

Ward wasn't sure what to make of the comment. It was almost as if the DoS attacks were a mere distraction. It made him uneasy.

"What companies?" Ward asked. He wanted to pass on as much information to Cruz and Royer as possible so that security could be stepped up at potential target sites.

Wolf put his hand on Ward's shoulder. "All in due course," he said. "We have several in mind. But things can change."

Parks gave it a try. "What about the timeframe?" she asked. "Even after we get the names, this will require some considerable prep work."

"Plans are being finalized," Wolf said. "Reconnaissance is taking place as we speak. You will have the information when you need it. Not before." He stopped and turned to face them. "Now, let's go back and get that drink."

CHAPTER 77

7:10 p.m., Wednesday, June 7, outside Boulder Outfitters, Boulder, Colorado

Combs checked his watch. It should be any time now. From surveillance they knew that Harper got off work at seven. He had yet to appear, but the fact that he had not yet emerged at ten minutes after was not unusual. Seven-fifteen had been his typical departure time since they had started watching him. It would be another ten to fifteen minutes before Combs would start to get nervous. There was no way Harper could have spotted them. They were eighty yards off in an adjoining lot. The patrol units that would assist with the stop were blocks away.

The goal was to make the arrest quickly, somewhere along Harper's route home, and immediately remove him from the scene. His car would be towed. They didn't want the attention that would come from an arrest at his workplace or residence. Coworkers and neighbors would talk. Even if not members of EMB themselves, they might say something to the wrong person, someone who could pass along news of the arrest to the organization. That could not happen, not before they had the chance to have a chat with Mr. Harper.

"There he is," Maness said.

Combs watched Harper emerge from the store and head toward his vehicle. He had a backpack slung over one shoulder. They would have to keep an eye on that during the stop. There was no telling what he might be carrying. Combs made a radio call to alert the locals that Harper was on the move, and to warn them about the backpack.

Harper hopped in his car. Within seconds he was headed out of the parking lot. Combs put the vehicle in gear. They would stay well back, radioing Harper's location. A marked unit would make the stop, ostensibly for some traffic infraction. It wasn't hard to come up with a viable pretext. Everybody exceeded the speed limit or failed to use their turn signal at some point on a given route. The key was to avoid raising the subject's suspicion any sooner than necessary. They watched as Harper exited right onto a city street. A few seconds later Combs swung out into traffic a good hundred yards behind him.

At the first stoplight Harper accelerated through a yellow light and turned left just as it changed to red. He hadn't bothered to use his signal. A patrol unit approaching from the opposite direction spun around on him and hit the lights and siren.

"That didn't take long," Maness said.

Combs grunted. He suspected that Harper was the kind of guy who didn't think the normal rules applied to him in any context.

Harper went about a quarter mile before finally pulling over. The marked unit stopped on the shoulder about fifteen yards back, the nose of the vehicle pointed at a slight angle toward the traffic lane. This was a safety precaution to partially protect the officer should a third vehicle make impact from behind. But Combs knew that it also provided better cover should the subject of the stop come out shooting.

Combs pulled off about fifty yards back and waited. Soon, a second patrol unit arrived and parked behind the first. A third followed. It was then that a uniformed officer emerged from each vehicle. They approached Harper's car, coming up on both sides, weapons drawn. Combs could see the first officer lean in the driver's window. There was a brief exchange. Seconds later Harper exited his vehicle, hands in the air. He was escorted to the second patrol unit where he was patted down, cuffed and placed in the rear seat.

"Showtime," Combs said. He and Maness exited and approached the officers.

"Give us a minute with him," Combs said to the corporal who had been first to respond.

"He's all yours."

They climbed in the front seat of the squad car.

"Hello, Eric," Combs said. "Remember us?"

A look of recognition swept across Harper's face, followed by what Combs thought was a glimmer of fear. It lasted only a second and was replaced with the same smug defiance that had been displayed during their initial encounter two weeks earlier.

"What the fuck do you two want?" Harper asked.

Combs smiled. "Nice to see you, too. We'd just like to chat."

"Fuck you."

"Thought you might say that," Combs said. It was reality-check time. He was going to enjoy this. "We had a nice visit with Linda Oden. She had a lot to say, at least after we showed her the video of you and your new girlfriend coming out of the bar last Thursday."

Harper laughed. "Okay," he said, still cocky. "Let's hear it."

Combs summarized what Oden had told them, including Harper's admissions to her about his involvement. It was when they got to the death of the security guard that the crack in the façade began to show. Harper let out breath, the smugness seemingly gone. But then he made one last attempt to rally.

"That's what she says. Big fucking deal. You have nothing to corroborate it."

Combs chuckled. "You ever heard of silhouette matching?" He described the process, embellishing the definitiveness of the results from the FBI lab. He let that sink in for a moment before delivering his final blow. "Oh, and it wasn't very smart of you to use your personal credit card on the route to Oklahoma City and back."

Harper hung his head.

Combs waited for some comeback. There was nothing. They were in the driver's seat. "There are some people who'd like to talk to you. What do you say we take a ride…K2?"

Harper looked up. He nodded.

Assistant U.S. Attorney Katherine Delgado had made the drive up from Oklahoma City. The Dallas SAC, Jack Olin, and two of his agents were also present. Things were moving quickly. The word from Main Justice was to try to get Harper talking as soon as possible. A team was en route from D.C., but she was authorized to make the offer.

Delgado waited for Harper to be brought into the interview room first. She wanted to make an entrance. It heightened the impact. As they waited, she turned to Olin.

"Do you know if he's been Mirandized?" she asked.

"I don't believe so," Olin replied.

Delgado considered that. A suspect had to be read their rights, waive them and agree to talk prior to any custodial interrogation. Otherwise, any statements made in response to questioning could not be used in court. Harper was definitely in custody. He was not free to leave. The problem was that reading a suspect their rights often induced them to clam up. And while it was true that any voluntary, spontaneous statements he might make were legally permissible, whether in custody or not, it was always dicey to rely on that theory in court. Judges were often inclined to find interrogation, even when it didn't exist.

"We need to advise him of his rights," Delgado said.

"Agreed," Olin replied. "I'd be happy to do the honors."

Just then, Special Agent Toby Combs entered the room. Delgado recognized him from the Oden interview. Agent Maness was with him.

"He's here," Combs said.

"Okay," Delgado replied. "Let's go."

They entered the interview room. Harper was seated at the

table, an officer standing on either side of him.

"Mr. Harper, I'm Assistant United States Attorney Katherine Delgado. This is Special Agent in Charge Jack Olin. I believe you know Special Agents Combs and Maness."

Harper jerked his head in acknowledgement.

Delgado took the chair immediately across from Harper. She turned to Olin. "Read him his rights."

"You have the right to remain silent," Olin said. "If you give up that right, anything you say can, and will, be used against you in a court of law. You have the right to an attorney, and to have an attorney present during any questioning. If you cannot afford an attorney, one will be appointed for you."

Delgado leaned forward and looked into Harper's eyes. "Now," she said, "let's talk about how you avoid the death penalty."

CHAPTER 78

8:38 a.m., Thursday, June 8, New York Stock Exchange, 20 Broad Street, New York, New York

Frog sipped his latte as he studied the comings and goings on Broad and Wall Streets. It was his third day of surveillance, monitoring area foot traffic, looking for that peak moment when impact would be maximized. He jotted some notes using his own code. If apprehended they would be meaningless to anyone who might read them, indecipherable scribbles. He would use the notes later to identify the best path in, the perfect location, and the exact timing.

Of course, he had also assessed security, which appeared to be lax. The situation was exactly what they had hoped for. Black, wrought-iron fencing surrounded an area extending out approximately twenty feet from the front of the building. It ran down the block. A white tent with transparent plastic sides sat at the entrance. It served as a security checkpoint and was staffed by NYPD officers and private guards, none of whom paid him the least bit of attention. They seemed complacent, inattentive. He watched them from nearby structures, or while casually strolling by, always careful to stay in a crowd. That wasn't difficult. It was New York City. There were people everywhere, millions of them. It was easy to disappear in their midst. The whole city was a crowd, a huge, filthy, polluting crowd. He hated it, hated everything about it.

An enormous American flag was displayed across the Roman columns that supported the sculpted pediment. The inscription engraved just below those carvings announced the *NEW YORK STOCK EXCHANGE*. It was an iconic image, one that for him symbolized corporate greed, corruption, and the plunder of Mother's resources. There could be no better place to make their statement. Wall Street, and the entire nation, would shudder with fear in the aftermath.

Frog drained the last drops from his latte and tossed the cup in the trash. He had what he needed. The report would be drafted and passed through channels to those who would utilize it. He looked up at the street marker that read *WALL ST* and smiled. The Earth Martyrs Brigade would soon deliver Mother's vengeance.

CHAPTER 79

2:31 a.m., Friday, June 9, Cos Cob Substation, Greenwich, Connecticut

It was a significant facility, one that when taken down would impact electrical service over an enormous area. She had heard that others were conducting similar surveillance at two dozen additional sites scattered up and down the East Coast. No one had told her, but the goal was clearly much more than a blackout for this section of Connecticut, it was disruption of the entire grid.

Cheetah knew that it could be accomplished. What had happened in Omaha showed the vulnerability of the current infrastructure. Experts said at the time that a coordinated series of similar attacks could cause a total system failure. She imagined the chaos that would ensue. America would be brought to its knees, the folly of relying on their filthy energy sources exposed. People would have to understand that the old ways were better, more reliable. For her, the goal was a return to a simple, agrarian lifestyle, one in which people lived in harmony with nature. That was the goal of the Earth Martyrs Brigade, and the reason she had joined the battle.

Cheetah had observed the site for most of the last two days, studying the flow of workers, trying to assess what security was in place. There were numerous transformers at the site. She documented the location of each, noting the best locations from which to fire, carefully mapping the area so that the assault team could be in and out as quickly as possible.

In that regard, there was quick access to Interstate 95 which was only a block away. The snipers could escape north into New England or south into the New York metropolitan area where they could blend into the masses. A vehicle exchange would be set up at a discrete location to assure that they avoid detection. They could discard their weapons in one of the numerous bodies of water that lined the route, including Cos Cob Harbor itself. There was also the possibility that they could arrive and leave by water. It seemed risky, but it would allow for easy disposal of evidence. The harbor led out to Long Island Sound. If a boat exchange could be arranged it might be the way to go.

Cheetah made some final notations and then began the trek back to her vehicle. It was parked in a residential area on the other side of the interstate so as to minimize the risk of detection. As she marched along her mood grew buoyant. An overwhelming sense of pride accompanied the completion of her task. Though her role was small, she had played a part in an event that could save the planet. "For Mother," she whispered.

CHAPTER 80

9:42 a.m., Friday, June 9, Dirksen Senate Office Building, Washington, D.C.

The weapon was composed of sixteen separate pieces, all plastic. They would not come in at once. A few small batches would be smuggled in and assembled later, onsite. He assumed by the assassin but did not know. Plastic tools would be used. They had also been manufactured by a 3D printer. It was all amazing. The truly critical piece of the puzzle, however, was just newly available. After years of experimentation, plastic ammunition was a reality. It would change everything.

It was Panther's job to bring in the first several pieces, to test the process. Others would follow. He did not know how many or when. It didn't matter. It was his task to forge the path, to assure that they would not be detected in their sacred mission. A phone call had been made earlier in the week. Posing as a constituent, he had easily secured permission to visit a certain senator's office. Panther took delight in the fact that the particular member of Congress whose office had been exploited was a notorious friend of Big Oil.

As he approached the metal detector Panther reminded himself to breathe, stay calm, appear casual. The component pieces, along with a small amount of adhesive tape, were in a plastic baggie that was wedged in an area where no member of the

Capitol Police would be inclined to put his or her hands. From what he could see of those who went before him there was little reason for concern. Most in line moved through quickly. Those who set off the detectors were subjected to nothing more than a quick sweep of a security wand to pinpoint whatever errant metal object had cause the alert. Forgotten pocket change appeared to be the most common culprit. Panther had been careful to remove anything that might set off an alarm.

"Good morning, Officer," Panther said as he placed his watch, belt, keys and cell phone in a plastic tray. He smiled pleasantly. "Gonna be a hot one out there today."

The guard looked up and grunted. "You got that right." He motioned for Panther to move forward.

As he walked through, Panther held his breath, some instinct telling him that it might make a difference. In his mind he knew this wasn't true, but he did it anyway. He became increasingly anxious. Did it show? Did they see the sweat? He could feel the moisture on his upper lip, sitting there, signaling his deception. He stared straight ahead, determined not to make eye contact with anyone at the checkpoint. *Casual*, he thought, *unconcerned*. He waited for the alert to sound. There was no reason for that to happen, but he was suddenly sure that it would. There was nothing.

Panther retrieved his items from the tray. He quickly put on the belt and watch, slipped the phone and keys into his pockets, and then walked down the hall. He could feel his heart pounding as he struggled to maintain composure, forcing himself not to look back over his shoulder. He strode forward, purposeful, businesslike, but not in a rush. His goal was Room 366. It was there that hearings were held before the Senate Committee on Energy and Natural Resources.

The various parts that would form the weapon would be hidden in a nearby restroom, perhaps taped under a sink or hidden in a ceiling tile. It was up to him to find the best spot. Those who followed would add to the collection until everything necessary was in place. The most difficult piece would be the roofing nail that was needed as the firing pin. Given the amount of restoration and maintenance that was constantly underway at the Capitol complex it was believed that one could be obtained on site. If not, it would be brought in via body cavity, the smuggler simply forced to take his or her chances.

Close to Room 366 he found a men's restroom. Panther went in. Someone was in one of the stalls. He entered another and undid his pants, careful to prevent the plastic baggie from dropping to the floor, or worse. He pretended to use the facilities, holding the bag of gun parts between his knees, patiently waiting for the man next to him to leave. It seemed to take forever. Panther began to wonder if the man was all right. Then he heard the rustling of what sounded like the pages of a newspaper being turned. He shook his head. The man was sitting there reading the paper. As Panther waited, pants around his ankles, he heard others enter and leave. He used the time to study the ceiling. It appeared that removing a tile and hiding the items there would not be possible. He would have to look for other options.

Finally, after what seemed like an hour, the newspaper reader got up, exited the stall, washed his hands and left. Panther quickly pulled up his pants, retrieved the tape from inside the plastic bag and stepped from his stall. He would have to act fast. Traffic through the restroom had not been heavy but was significant enough to warrant concern.

He looked around the room. The area under the washbasin seemed the most likely hiding place. Panther dropped to one knee and looked underneath. He was in luck. There was enough space there to secure the bag without detection. Panther quickly taped it in place. He stood and moved around the room, observing the basin from different locations. The package was not visible from any normal angle. He doubted that security was so thorough as to check there. Satisfied, he left the men's room and headed for the exit, anticipating the moment when his efforts would come to fruition.

"For Mother," Panther whispered as he pushed through the doors and stepped out into the sunlight.

CHAPTER 81

3:58 p.m., Saturday, June 10, SmartPark Garage, 4th and Yam-hill, Portland, Oregon

Wolf had summoned them again. This time the meeting place was a parking ramp in the middle of the city. Ward's antennae were up. Why this place? Was Wolf trying to avoid someone, like Cobra? Or was the reason more sinister? Ward wondered how many hits had taken place in just such a location. He circled the block for a second time as he and Parks studied their surroundings and watched for Wolf's vehicle. They were to meet at four o'clock, and Ward planned to let Wolf arrive first so that he couldn't pull in and block off their exit.

"Anything?" Ward asked.

"Nope."

Cruz and Royer were parked just over a block away, next to the Multnomah County Circuit Court. They could be onsite in seconds. That was great, unless he and Parks were already dead. Ward felt the comforting weight of the weapon wedged in his ankle holster. He studied Parks, suddenly aware of how badly he wanted to keep her safe. Having your partner's back was one thing, but this was something different, the kind of thing they warned about.

Parks looked at him "What?"

"Nothing," Ward said. He turned his eyes back to the street.

They drove in silence until Parks spoke. "There he is." She

pointed at the intersection ahead. Wolf's van was passing through.

Ward slowed to allow Wolf time to pull into the garage before turning to follow him. He wondered if there was anyone in the van with him.

"Let's do another lap, give him time to park."

They circled the ramp one more time and then pulled in, climbing up through the levels until spotting Wolf's van. He had already exited. No one else was present, at least outside the vehicle. Ward debated whether to stop immediately behind him and block off his exit. No, that would set off alarm bells. Instead, he pulled into the adjoining spot. As soon as the Prius was parked Wolf opened the rear driver's side door of the vehicle and got in the backseat. Ward's hand quickly slid toward the gun strapped to his ankle. He saw Parks do the same. They both spun around to face Wolf. Instinctively, Ward's gaze went to the terrorist's hands. Seeing no weapon, he focused on the eyes. They gave away nothing.

Wolf nodded his greeting and got straight to the point. "As I mentioned before, the key to our operational success is compartmentalization. Only the two of you need to know the particulars of your task."

Ward began to relax, his hand moved away from his gun.

Parks spoke up. "You mentioned DoS attacks on several power companies. I take it you have additional details?"

"I do." He handed her a piece of paper. She looked at it, her face inscrutable, and then handed it to Ward.

"In addition to the specific targets discussed at our last meeting," Wolf said, "we want you to launch denial-of-service attacks on the websites associated with these targets."

Ward studied the list jof energy companies. He believed that all of them operated in the northeast. It was clear that the Earth Martyrs Brigade did, in fact, plan an attack on the power grid.

"It's an ambitious list," Parks said.

"I have confidence in you...both of you."

"If we knew what else was planned we would have a better idea of which online services to target," Parks said. "It could narrow our focus, improve the chances for success."

"And help maximize the impact," Ward added.

Wolf was silent for a moment, studying them. Was he considering it? Or had they gone too far. Ward held his breath. He shot a quick glance at Parks, who showed nothing.

"Again," Wolf said, "compartmentalization."

"Understood," Parks said quickly. "It makes sense."

"Now," Wolf said, "About the timeframe. The cyber-attacks on the New York Stock Exchange and government websites will occur at 9:30 a.m., eastern time, this Wednesday."

Ward felt his pulse accelerate. There wasn't much time. He began to catalog the things they needed to do as soon as they got out of there.

"As for the power companies," Wolf continued, "those attacks need to occur between 1 and 2 a.m., eastern time, on Thursday."

"Then that's when they'll happen," Ward said.

Wolf leaned forward. "I'm sure they will." He placed a hand on each of their shoulders. "For Mother."

"For Mother," Parks said.

Ward nodded solemnly. "For Mother."

As soon as Wolf was safely distant Ward called Cruz.

"What's up?"

"I've got dates, and more target info." Ward summarized what they'd learned.

There was no immediate response from Cruz. "Fuck me," he finally said.

"Yeah."

"I'll get the word out. We need to meet, now."

"We're on our way."

CHAPTER 82

5:02p.m., Saturday, June 10, The Biscuit, Portland, Oregon

Ward pulled in behind the apartment building and parked. He checked the rearview. A car drove past the alley entrance but kept moving. Did it slow down, or was that just his imagination? There had been no time to swap the Prius for another vehicle on the way there. He didn't like to breach protocol on these things, but they had to act fast. The route to their safe house had even been less circuitous than usual. Still, neither of them had seen any sign of a tail.

Parks was out of the car first. She strode toward the door, not waiting for Ward to catch up. He jumped out and scrambled after her. Once inside, they stepped into the elevator and rode up. Halfway to the loft Ward realized that he hadn't given a thought to the old rattletrap or his claustrophobia. He was too focused on the mission. They both were. He looked over at Parks. She paid him no attention, staring at the floor of the elevator cab, lost in thought. Ward knew that, like him, she was desperately trying to formulate their next move.

The old beast clanked to halt on the top floor. They stepped off and quickly entered the loft. Cruz and Royer were already there, seated at the table, pounding away at their laptops.

"What took you so long?" Cruz asked.

"I had to stop periodically and send up flares," Ward said. "You know, make it really easy for them to follow us."

Cruz chuckled. Royer did not. "Let's get to it," he said.

Ward and Parks sat. Royer went first.

"Tell me again everything that Wolf said." His fingers were poised over the laptop, ready to type.

Ward described the encounter as Royer tapped away at the keyboard. When Ward was done, Parks slid the list of additional targets across the table. Royer picked it up and examined it. He let out a low whistle, then resumed typing, periodically referring back to the list.

"They clearly want to bring down the grid," Cruz said.

"No question," Ward agreed. He turned to face Cruz. "Can we even arrange this many bogus DoS attacks in such short time?" he asked. "And even if it's logistically possible, is there any way these power companies or the New York Stock Exchange would go along with it? I'm thinking about the panic that would ensue from even the appearance that they've gone down."

Cruz shook his head. "I'm not even sure about the House and Senate websites," he admitted. "The White House takedown has already been arranged. They were very cooperative. But I can't imagine the executives at these companies agreeing to this."

Ward slumped back in his seat and ran his hand through his hair. "We need a plan, people."

The room was silent. Even the clicking sound from Royer's keyboard had stopped as he considered their predicament. Finally, Parks spoke.

"We've investigated a lot of computer phishing cases," she said, looking at Royer. "And how do they lure people to provide their personal and financial information?"

Royer smiled. "They direct the victims to phony website that looks like the real thing."

"Exactly," Parks said. She turned to Cruz. "Who says we have to take down a real website?"

"I like it," Cruz replied.

"I imagine our friends Etherlord and Incubus could be of great assistance in such an endeavor," Ward noted.

"Definitely," Royer agreed. "I'll inform them that they'll be working this weekend. You two ready for another trip to San Jose?"

"Absolutely," Parks replied.

"We should go back to our apartment first," Ward said. "We'll leave from there on foot and meet you a few blocks away, make sure we're not followed."

Royer nodded. "I'll call you when we're close." He was quiet for a moment, staring at the floor, contemplating something.

"What is it?" Ward asked.

"I think we need to increase surveillance on members of the Portland cell. I know it increases the chances of being detected, but right now we have to use everything at our disposal to find out what these bastards are up to." Royer looked at Ward. "What do you think?"

"I was going to suggest it myself."

A half-smile crept onto Royer's face. He nodded once at Ward. "I'll call for reinforcements."

Cobra sat a block down the street from where he had seen them stop. From his location he could make out the faded wording of a weathered sign painted on the building—*The Butler Biscuit Company*. It appeared to be an old factory or warehouse that had been converted into apartments. While he watched there had been little traffic, odd for five o'clock in the afternoon. The building showed no signs of having any tenants. And he wasn't aware of any movement toward this part of town. A search of an apartment finder app on his phone found nothing else for sale or rent in this area. More importantly, it showed that this building had multiple vacancies.

They had been in there for twenty minutes. What the hell were they doing? Something wasn't right.

CHAPTER 83

7:01p.m., Sunday, June 11, Logan International Airport, Boston, Massachusetts

FBI Special Agent Frank Quinn sat on the opposite side of the concourse, ostensibly reading the Sunday edition of the *Boston Globe*. In reality, he was waiting for the passengers to disembark through Gate B-24. The United flight from Chicago's O'Hare Airport had arrived a few minutes earlier. He once again pulled up the images of the suspects on his phone. There were three of them, two men and a woman. They had traveled from Portland to Chicago where they caught a connecting flight to Boston. The IDs used to book the flights and pass through the TSA checkpoint at Portland International had been covertly examined and run through the system. Not surprisingly, they were bogus. According to Homeland Security they were also impressive, the fake driver's licenses indistinguishable from the real thing.

Word was ATF had flipped an EMB member in Colorado who put them onto the group's source for phony credentials. The informant claimed that the guy was a real artist who had forged hundreds of documents for them, including passports. That was a problem, one that would be dealt with later. For now, they needed to stay on this crew and figure out what the hell they were up to.

A buzzer sounded as the door to the ramp opened. Quinn pretended to read the paper, watching, waiting for them to come through. Two additional agents were posted nearby, within his line of sight. Several others were waiting outside the airport in their vehicles, ready to tail the suspects whether they stayed together or split up.

The first passengers began to disembark. Quinn didn't see them in the crowd. He glanced again at the images on his phone. They shouldn't be hard to spot. Two dozen more followed. There was no sign of them. Another twenty spilled into the concourse, but still nothing. Quinn started to become concerned. Had there been a mistake in Chicago? That didn't seem likely. They had been observed boarding the plane. Did they alter their appearance during the flight? Their carry-on bags had been checked, with nothing suspicious noted. And it would be difficult to carry the makings of a good disguise on your person, let alone get through security with it. They had to be on the plane.

Quinn looked toward his colleague, in line at a coffee stand some sixty feet away. The other agent raised his eyebrows, inquiring. Quinn shook his head, *not yet*. He turned back. It was then that the first of them emerged. It was the one known as Wolf. The others were right behind him. Quinn gave the signal. He waited for them to pass before rising from his seat.

The terrorists moved quickly through the terminal. Quinn and another agent dropped in behind them, at varied distances. A third stayed twenty yards ahead of them, listening to his colleagues through a small earpiece. The group moved first to baggage claim, where only two small pieces were claimed. They then traveled out of the airport and across Interstate 90 to the rental car center. Each of them secured a vehicle. That would complicate things, but Quinn was certain there were adequate resources in place to track all three. He alerted the agents stationed in their vehicles to be ready to move. One of the pursuit teams would pick him up.

Wolf drove away from the rental center and headed south. The woman, Fern, followed close behind. But the third terrorist, the one known as Cobra, drove west into Boston. Quinn was in the tail vehicle assigned to Wolf. Their briefing that morning disclosed that Wolf was the head of the Portland cell, and possibly part of EMB's command structure. Quinn would stick with him until told otherwise.

Wolf and Fern drove south out of the Boston metropolitan area on Interstate 93. They eventually made their way to Interstate 95, one of the major American north-south corridors, and headed down the coast. At that point, Quinn knew that they could be headed anywhere. But there were two possibilities that raised the most concern: New York and Washington, D.C.

CHAPTER 84

2:37 a.m., Monday, June 12, Ward's undercover apartment, The Hawthorne District, Portland, Oregon

The gentle nudge immediately woke him. Ward opened his eyes to see Parks standing there. Was this the midnight visit he had fantasized about? Even in an oversized T-shirt she looked spectacular. He wasn't sure what to do. Should he reach up for her? Did she want him to follow her back to her room?

"Don't get any ideas," she said, seeming to sense his thoughts. There was the hint of a smile.

Ward's fantasy crashed as abruptly as it had begun. Then he noticed the cell phone in her hand.

"What is it?" he asked.

"That was Royer. He just heard from the Boston office."

Ward sat up. She sat next to him, close, their bare legs pressed together, shoulders touching. He could smell her hair, feel her warmth. Momentarily distracted, he forced himself to focus.

"And?"

"Wolf and Fern are doing surveillance on electrical substations in New Jersey."

Ward nodded. It wasn't a complete surprise. "Well," he said, "at least we've identified some would-be targets."

"There's one other thing." Pause. "They lost Cobra in Boston."

"And you think…"

"He's checking our cover stories."

CHAPTER 85

10:08 a.m., Monday, June 12, The Cabin, Yellowstone Cell Site of the Earth Martyrs Brigade, somewhere outside Yellowstone National Park

The intensity in his dark brown eyes pulled her in. His ever-present smile was confident, but gentle, even soothing. There was a love that flowed from him to those who truly believed. Rain could feel that love now flow to her. It washed over her in waves. She began to understand the spellbinding power of Ocean that others had described.

It was difficult to believe that she was at The Cabin, the home of the Yellowstone cell. Most had only heard of it. Few knew its location, fewer still had been there. The experience was surreal. She was entranced by the place, by him, yet her thoughts, her purpose, had never seemed more clear. He held her hands as he looked deep into her eyes. It felt as if he had entered her mind and was now talking to her in a dream.

"My beloved Rain, it is you who Mother sends as her messenger. Through me, she has chosen you above all the others, chosen you to be her most important disciple. It is you who will deliver her message to the greedy capitalists of Wall Street that their exploitation of our Earth will end. When the revolution comes, it will be your actions that lit the fuse."

Ocean stroked her face as he continued. "You have been blessed with a sacred mission. Your selfless act will be spoken of for generations. It will change the course of history." He pulled her into an embrace. "Your courageous sacrifice will save the forests, the mountains, the seas. All of Mother's creatures will live on because of you."

She wanted to do this for him, for Mother. It was so others could survive, so Earth could survive. And, it was immortality.

CHAPTER 86

6:20 a.m., Pacific Time, Wednesday, June 14, Portland Cell Site of the Earth Martyrs Brigade, somewhere outside Portland, Oregon

The barn would not have been Ward's first choice as a location from which to launch their cyber-attack, but Wolf had insisted on it. A more neutral spot would have been preferred, one with fewer members of the Portland cell present. Still, Cruz, Royer and a significant tactical unit were close by, ready to move in if needed. And a rural setting would lessen the attention that might come from a raid.

It was nine-twenty, eastern time. The DoS attacks on the bogus websites would occur in ten minutes. Laptops were set up, four of them, one for each target: House of Representatives, Senate, White House, and the New York Stock Exchange. Etherlord and Incubus had worked their magic, creating phony sites that were indistinguishable from the real thing. Even the URLs, the web addresses for the fakes, were close to the originals.

Ward had been a bit surprised to learn that Ralph Holgate, the eighty-seven-year-old owner of the farm, even had internet service. He was just as surprised to learn that a wireless connection was available in the barn. According to Wolf, Mouse had figured out a way to boost the signal from Holgate's residence. The discussion had prompted Ward to ask what was to prevent Holgate, a known early riser, from walking in on their little operation. It was explained that a trip out of town had been arranged for the old farmer, something about an organics convention. Ward hoped that was the real reason for Holgate's absence, not something more ominous.

Wolf had met them earlier that morning and let them in. It had been an unpleasant surprise to find Cobra there with him. Cobra's presence was troublesome. Not only was he clearly armed, but as the morning progressed he seemed to be watching them more closely than usual. Had he learned something in Boston? If so, had he shared it with Wolf? There didn't seem to be any change in attitude toward them from the cell leader, but he was characteristically inscrutable. Neither of them said a thing about the trip to the east coast.

Another problematic development was the arrival of Seqouia and Skye. Why the hell were they here? Given the group's mantra about compartmentalization, their presence seemed odd. What was their need to know? What role was there for either of them in this assignment? Ward couldn't think of one. It was a bad sign, and yet another reason for he and Parks to be extra cautious. Even so, the Earth Martyrs Brigade was about to launch something big. And whatever it was, their presence was critical to stopping it. Law enforcement resources had been quietly beefed up at every possible target, but there was still a lot that was unknown. Because of that, they had decided to make one final push for more information, with Parks to take the lead, and now was the time. He looked at her. She caught the sign.

"Since we're just about to launch, could we learn a little more about what else is planned?" Parks asked nonchalantly. "We might be able to tailor the attack for more impact."

Wolf said nothing. He remained impassive. Ward grew concerned. He glanced at Cobra, who moved closer, clearly interested in where this was going.

"I see no reason to share any additional details," Cobra said, looking at Wolf. "They do not need to know."

Wolf studied Cobra, and then turned his stare to Parks. "I agree," he said.

Parks looked at Cobra, then Wolf. "Fair enough," she said, and dropped it.

Cobra seemed unsatisfied. "I have a few questions," he announced.

"About what?" Parks asked.

"Last Saturday," he said, "your trip to an empty apartment building in an abandoned warehouse district."

Parks glanced at Ward, then turned back to Cobra. "You were following us?"

"You seem concerned." He moved closer. "Why were you there so long? Were you meeting someone, law enforcement perhaps?"

"That's ridiculous," Parks said, ostensibly annoyed. "We're looking for a bigger apartment, simple as that." She shook her head. "You're paranoid."

"Am I," Cobra asked? "Then why the circuitous route to get there? Were you concerned about being tailed?"

Parks opened her mouth to reply, but Ward beat her to it. "We were driving around the neighborhood, seeing if it's an area where we might want to live. That's it." He turned to Wolf. "Can we get back to the task at hand?" he asked angrily. "It's seven minutes to launch. We don't have time for this bullshit."

Wolf shot Cobra a stern look. "No more distractions. Understood?"

Cobra smirked. He didn't answer.

"Let's get on with it," Wolf said.

Ward and Parks sat with their backs to the group so that everyone could watch them work. Ward typed in the URL for the bogus New York Stock Exchange website. The display that popped up was virtually identical to the real thing. He repeated the process for the phony White House page. Parks did the same for the House and Senate sites. They then switched to black screens and began to type in code. Soon they were ready.

"Just say when," Ward announced.

Wolf smiled and looked at his watch. "Forty-five seconds," he said. When the time drew close he began a countdown. "Seven, six, five, four, three, two, and…" He pointed at Ward. "Now."

Ward tapped the *enter* key on one laptop, and then another. Parks did the same. Code began to furiously scroll down each screen, eventually starting to slow, and then stop. Ward typed in the URL for the fake Exchange website and hit enter. He did the same for the White House site. Parks followed suit. Symbols appeared indicating that the computers were trying to process the requests. But after approximately thirty seconds of trying to access the websites messages began to pop up on each: *website is currently unavailable.*

Wolf rested a hand on Ward's shoulder. "Good work. Mother is pleased." He placed the other on Parks' back. "Soon you will understand the significance of your efforts here today."

"It seems we have a problem."

Ward turned to see Cobra staring at his smartphone.

"I just pulled up the New York Stock Exchange website," Cobra announced. He showed the display to Wolf, then began to type in another search. "And here is the White House page, fully operational."

Wolf turned to Ward. "Explain," he demanded.

"I'll explain," Cobra said, studying the laptops. "The websites they are trying to access are fakes. The addresses they typed in are phony. It's a staged attack. All they've done is crash some bogus sites."

Wolf's face turned dark. They were exposed. Ward saw Parks tap the screen on her phone. She had preloaded a text to Royer containing the signal for the tactical team to come in. They would move fast, but it would be a matter of minutes not seconds. Ward's hand inched toward the gun in his ankle holster, a .40 caliber Glock Model 27.

"Take them," Wolf ordered.

"Gladly," Cobra said through gritted teeth.

He reached for his weapon, but Parks had hers out first. "Drop it," she said, her gun trained on Cobra's torso.

As Ward raised his weapon Sequoia's giant hand came from nowhere and wrapped around his wrist with crushing force. Sequoia jerked Ward's arm up and back, almost dislocating his shoulder and causing his chair to topple over. Ward crashed to the ground, losing the grip on his gun. He scrambled for it. Parks turned to help. As she did, Cobra smashed his weapon against her temple. Ward saw her slump to the ground.

It was then that Sequoia grabbed the overturned wooden chair and raised it above his head, aiming to bring it down on Ward's skull.

"Dan, no!" Skye screamed at Sequoia. He turned toward her.

Ward used the distraction to his advantage. He hooked his legs on either side of Sequoia's, locked his heels, and then jerked his body to the right. The move instantly threw the big man off balance, causing him to plummet backwards. Unable to catch himself, he took the full brunt of the impact on the back of his head. Sequoia was badly stunned, but not completely out. He moaned in pain. Ward jumped to his feet, weapon in hand.

"Put the gun down!" Cobra spat, his weapon raised and ready.

Ward glanced to the right. Wolf stood four feet away, seemingly paralyzed. It was a split-second decision. He dove sideways, behind Wolf. It had the desired effect. Cobra hesitated. Ward fired, dropping Cobra with one shot, center chest.

Wolf seemed to regain his bearings. He dove for Ward, who had no time to swing his gun toward the terrorist and get off a shot. The weapon was pinned between them as the two men wrestled for control. They rolled across the floor, one on top, then the other. There was a shot. The Portland cell leader stared into Ward's eyes, the wicked smile returning to his face. "You cannot stop us," he said. Then his breathing grew shallow, his eyes began to droop. "For Mother," Wolf muttered. The eyes flickered, and then closed. He slumped onto Ward, lifeless.

Ward shoved him off. Parks stood ten feet away, her weapon aimed at the dead terrorist, blood streaming from a nasty cut at her temple. "You're welcome," she said.

Skye was the only cell member left standing. She rushed to Sequoia, kneeling at his side. He began to get to his feet.

"Stay on the ground!" Parks yelled. "Face down, hands behind your head! Now!"

Sequoia hesitated.

"Do it, Danny! Please!" Skye begged.

Sequoia slowly rolled onto his stomach and laced his fingers together behind his head.

Ward grabbed Skye and pulled her away from Sequoia. "We need to know everything you know, right now!"

"I, I…"

"Don't tell them anything!" Sequoia growled.

Parks put her foot on his neck. "Shut the fuck up!"

Ward grabbed Skye by the shoulders and looked her in the face. "I don't think you believe in the violence, the killing."

Skye shook her head. She opened her mouth, but nothing came out.

"Please help us stop this," Ward implored. "Murdering people does not help your cause. You know that," he insisted.

Skye nodded, now crying. "They haven't told me much," she said. "Some of it I just overheard, bits and pieces."

"Tell me," Ward said.

"There's a Senate hearing this morning, something about drilling on federal lands."

"What else?" Ward asked.

"The New York Stock Exchange." She covered her face. "Something is supposed to happen, right before the start of trading."

It was then that the tactical unit exploded into the barn. Cruz was out front, Royer right behind him.

"It's under control!" Ward yelled over the noise.

Cruz held up his hand and gave the signal for them to stand down.

Ward jogged to him. "We've got some information!"

CHAPTER 87

9:21 a.m., Eastern Time, Wednesday, June 14, Dirksen Senate Office Building, Washington, D.C.

Owl reached under the washbasin. The pieces were there, as promised. He had smuggled in the remaining components and was now prepared to assemble the weapon and carry out his mission. He removed the bags that had been placed there by his colleagues and retreated to the stall to begin his work.

He would have to act fast. The secretary of the interior was scheduled to testify before the Senate Committee on Energy and Natural Resources at nine-thirty. He would advocate for drilling on federal lands, a crime against Mother that EMB could not abide. A statement had to be made, and he would be the messenger. Owl knew that he might not survive but was prepared to take that risk.

The assembly took only a few minutes, the plastic gun now loaded and ready. It was bulky, but Owl was certain that he could keep it hidden until the moment came. Several rounds of ammunition had been smuggled in, but there would likely be no time to reload. There was only one shot. He would have to make it count. Owl looked at the weapon in his hand and smiled. It was time to change history.

* * *

Capitol Police Officer Devon Jacobs stood his post just outside Room 366. The full Committee on Energy and Natural Resources was about to be gaveled into session. The issue for today's hearing was expanded drilling for oil on federal lands. Witnesses were making their way to their seats. The crowd of onlookers was substantial, given the subject matter, but not unusually large. At last night's briefing they had been told to keep their eyes open for environmental activists. The events of the last few months had everyone on edge and security had been beefed up.

He scanned the crowd for anything that looked like trouble. Nothing seemed out of the ordinary. That was good. He had other things on his mind, like attending the Washington Nationals game that night and proposing to Naomi. Nationals Park had been the scene of their first date. He had managed to obtain tickets for the exact same seats they sat in that night. Jacobs hoped that didn't tip her off. She was smart enough to pick up on that sort of thing.

As the hearing began Jacobs entered the room, closing the doors behind him. The witnesses were sworn in. Attention was focused on the secretary of the interior, Nolan Campbell, who was reading from a prepared statement.

"This Administration believes that energy independence is critical to our national security and that drilling for oil on federal lands is an important part of the equation for achieving and maintaining that independence," Campbell said. "The reserves present on these lands are substantial and can be extracted safely with little impact on the environment."

Jacobs' earpiece crackled. A message came through: "We have received intel that the Earth Martyrs Brigade may attempt an attack at the Energy and Natural Resources Committee hearing. The exact nature of the threat is unclear. Keep alert for anything unusual. Additional personnel are on the way."

Just as the message ended he saw it out of the corner of his eye. The man reached in his jacket and pulled out something white, oddly shaped. Jacobs focused. He had seen pictures of this during training, a plastic gun, manufactured by a 3D printer. He drew his weapon.

"Drop the gun!" Jacobs yelled.

There were screams from the crowd. People dove to the ground or scrambled for exits. Secretary Campbell was shoved to the floor by two of his aides. Jacobs was jostled by those pushing for the door but kept his balance. The gunman turned toward him.

"Drop the gun, now!" Jacobs ordered.

Two shots rang out. The gunman dropped to his knees, and then fell sideways. Jacobs rushed toward him. He secured the man's weapon and then reached down to check his pulse. He was dead.

It was only then that Jacobs checked himself over. When he brought his hand up from his stomach it was covered in blood. He radioed for assistance just before things started to go dark.

CHAPTER 88

9:23 a.m., Eastern Time, Wednesday, June 14, New York Stock Exchange, 20 Broad Street, New York, New York

Officer Ray Amato studied the pedestrians passing by, the tourists snapping photos, the homeless asking for a handout. He had been on the security detail at the New York Stock Exchange for almost four months now and every morning looked the same. It was hard not to become complacent. Seven years with the NYPD. This was not why he joined. Still, he reminded himself, as he did every morning, that this place was a major league target. Diligence was required, especially at this time of the day. Trading would start in a few minutes. Any sort of attack right before the Big Board opened would be catastrophic.

Amato walked along the fence that formed a barrier along the front of the building. He exchanged greetings with a few tourists, never letting his guard down or forgetting why he was there. The most innocuous-looking individual could be the one who did something. He kept eyes open for any unusual behavior, suspicious movements, abandoned packages—anything that seemed out of the ordinary. Nothing caught his eye. He turned and started back toward the security checkpoint. As he did a voice came through his earpiece. It was his sergeant on the radio: "We just got information that the Earth Martyrs Brigade has an attack planned for the Exchange! Our intel says today, right before the start of trading! I need everyone on maximum alert now! Backup is on the way!"

Amato raced back to the checkpoint. His eyes swept over the crowd. It was then that he saw her, approaching slowly, an almost peaceful smile on her face. Something wasn't right. He held his hand up in warning.

"Stop right there!" Amato ordered. His hand moved to his weapon. She kept coming.

Other officers saw what was happening and rushed over. They drew their weapons and formed a perimeter around the woman, at the same time yelling at the crowd to move back.

"Stop where you are and put your hands above your head!" Amato demanded.

Her movement slowed but did not stop. Her hands remained at her sides.

Damn it, Amato thought. He did not want to shoot this young woman. She began saying something. Her voice was soft, the words almost a chant: "You will deliver her message to the greedy capitalists of Wall Street that their exploitation of our Earth will end. You will save the forests, the mountains, the seas. All of Mother's creatures will live on because of you."

She was Earth Martyrs Brigade. Suddenly, Amato knew how this was going to end. She reached toward her waist. He fired.

She slumped to the ground and fell back, arms spread, her hand never finding what it was reaching for. Amato approached, his weapon still aimed at her chest. He kneeled down and checked for a pulse. There was none. The other officers gathered around them. Amato opened her jacket and lifted the loose-fitting shirt a few inches, exposing her waist.

"Does she have a gun?" one of the others asked anxiously.

"No," Amato said. He recognized the device strapped around her waist from his two tours in Afghanistan. It was a suicide vest. "But we're gonna need the bomb squad."

CHAPTER 89

3:26 a.m., Eastern Time, Thursday, June 15, electrical substation, Trenton, New Jersey

FBI SWAT team leader Chad Herren waited patiently. His crew had been in place for almost three hours. They were almost certain that this substation was an intended target. The terrorist Fern had been observed conducting surveillance on the location three days earlier. She had since returned to Oregon, where agents were watching her every move.

He looked at his watch. It was now three-thirty in the morning. Was it possible that EMB had cancelled the Trenton operation? That didn't seem likely. There were reports of arrests at substations throughout the northeast from northern Virginia up to Boston. Clearly, they were going through with the attacks, despite the events of Wednesday morning. Of course, there was the possibility that this particular assault team had gotten wind of those arrests and bailed out, but that also seemed unlikely. All SWAT units had been instructed to isolate the terrorists and prevent communication during the course of the operation. That, the fact that EMB operated in semi-autonomous cells, and their emphasis on compartmentalization made him think that an event here was still probable.

Two substations had been successfully taken out by the group, one in Greenwich, Connecticut, and another in Baltimore. Blackouts had ensued. Fortunately, they were brief. The power companies, alerted to the possibility of widespread attacks, were set up to quickly reroute electricity through other channels. Herren knew that a crash of the grid was now unlikely. What he didn't know, and what the FBI didn't know, was how many other substations might still be threatened.

Herren peered through his night vision goggles, searching the areas where Fern had been observed during her reconnaissance. His eyes moved from one spot to the next. Various nocturnal creatures appeared in his sights, but no terrorists. Then he saw something, a movement. One appeared, then another: two black-clad individuals moving fast and low. Herren signaled the others on his team, alerting them to the terrorists' location. He crept forward, watching their direction, anticipating the spot where they would set up to fire. His crew moved in from various angles, forming a perimeter around the assailants. Herren could see from their actions that the SWAT team had not been spotted. He moved closer. When he was fifteen yards away he whispered the command into his microphone: "Now."

SWAT team members rose on all sides, their assault rifles trained on the terrorists.

"Drop your weapons!" Herren barked.

One of the assailants spun toward him, firing wildly. "For Mother!" he screamed.

Herren's crew opened fire. Bullets thudded into the terrorists from all angles, jerking their bodies one way and then another until the threat was terminated. When the shooting subsided Herren stepped forward. He nudged the assailants with the barrel of his rifle. It was clear that both were very dead. It was then that he felt the pain in his chest. The bullet had entered just under his collarbone.

"Fuck. I'm hit."

CHAPTER 90

5:32 a.m., Mountain Time, Friday, June 16, The Cabin, Yellow-stone Cell Site of the Earth Martyrs Brigade, outside Yellowstone National Park

The cooperators had begun to talk, aiming to save themselves. It always happened, even with a bunch of zealots like these. That is what led them here, to a modest cabin on the outskirts of Yellow-stone National Park, and to the man his followers referred to as Ocean. Toby Combs studied the place. It was hard to believe that this was the epicenter of a terrorist organization that had fright-ened a nation.

Sunrise was in ten minutes. They would go in well before that. The ATF Special Response Team was in place and ready to make entry. Combs had been invited to join them. He wanted to look the leader of the Earth Martyrs Brigade in the face as his failed movement came to an inglorious end.

It was almost time to go. Everyone moved into place. A schematic of the structure had been drawn by one of the informants. Flash grenades, also known as flashbangs, would be launched into both bedrooms and the living room. The intense explosion of light and noise they produced would disorient anyone inside, leaving them temporarily blind and deaf. They were highly effective and greatly reduced the chances of any resistance.

The team leader started his countdown, then signaled for the flashbangs. They were tossed through the windows. The sound was deafening. A brilliant flash of white light beamed through each window, illuminating the countryside. The Special Response Team burst in, swarmed through the living room and into the bedrooms. They found him on the floor in a fetal position, hands over his ears, eyes clenched shut. Combs walked up and stood over him. So, this was their great leader. He suppressed the urge to spit.

Combs gave the terrorist a few minutes to reorient, then kneeled down and introduced himself. "I'm Special Agent Toby Combs, ATF. And you are under arrest."

Combs snapped on the cuffs, nice and tight, thinking of Andy Garner as he did so. This was for the dead firefighter and all the others who had died because of this piece of shit. No chance to cooperate would be offered. That came from the top. They didn't need his help. The only thing this asshole would be offered was a lethal injection. He rolled Ocean onto his back so that he could look him in the face as he read him his rights.

"You have the right to remain silent," Combs began. "If you give up that right, anything you say can, and will, be used against you in a court of law. You have the right to an attorney, and to have an attorney present during any questioning. If you cannot afford an attorney, one will be appointed for you. Do you understand these rights?"

Ocean smirked. "Your precious rights will mean nothing when Earth has been destroyed by fools like you."

"I need you to answer my question," Combs insisted through clenched teeth. "Do you understand these rights?" He fantasized about putting his boot in the terrorist's face.

"I understand," Ocean said. "You are the one who does not understand.

"We'll call that good enough," Combs said. He signaled to the others. "Get this piece of shit out of my sight."

CHAPTER 91

6:30 p.m., Wednesday, July 12, CBC News, New York, New York

The recorded introduction began: *From New York, this is the CBC Evening News, with Bryson Daley.*

As the writing on the teleprompter began to scroll Daley started to read. "Good evening. Our lead story tonight concerns the latest chapter in a federal investigation that we have been following here at CBC News for the past three months. Authorities today announced the indictment of dozens of members of the Earth Martyrs Brigade, an organization accused of committing numerous acts of domestic terrorism to further their environmental agenda. For the latest, we turn now to CBC Justice Department correspondent Aaron Raines who has been tracking today's developments."

"Good evening, Bryson," Raines said. "In a statement issued this afternoon federal prosecutors announced the sweeping indictment of the alleged eco-terrorists on criminal charges that include murder, arson, conspiracy, use of destructive devices, violations of the Animal Enterprise Terrorism Act, and violations of the Racketeer Influenced and Corrupt Organizations Act, better known as RICO. Sources tell us that numerous state charges are also likely. The Earth Martyrs Brigade, also known as EMB, is accused of a long list of terrorist attacks. These include the arson of the Silver Trail Casino in Stateline, Nevada, in which one firefighter lost his life, the sabotage of numerous electrical substations around the country in what was apparently an attempt to crash the power grid, the burning of a Ford dealership in Oklahoma City, the destruction of a research lab at Southern Illinois University, the assassination of Pittman Petroleum CEO C. Robert Titus, and a sniper attack on the Keystone XL Pipeline that killed numerous workers. Their reign of terror seems to have culminated with the recent attempted suicide bombing at the New York Stock Exchange this past June 14th, the same day that one of their members attempted to assassinate Secretary of the Interior Nolan Campbell as he testified before the Senate Committee on Energy and Natural Resources."

"I understand that the indictment includes some notable characters, and at least one prominent individual," Daley said.

Raines nodded. "That's right, Bryson. The indictment states that the group's alleged leader, Duane Larkin, was known to members as *Ocean*. In fact, all of those charged in their true names are also charged under an alias. Most of these seem to involve some sort of nature theme, Sequoia, Fern, Firefly, Troll, Mink, Spider, as well as many others. We are told that, in an attempt to protect their identities, the members operated exclusively under these aliases. Their real names were generally not known even within the organization. The most notable name in the indictment, however, belongs to an individual without an alias, someone who is well known in this country and throughout the world. Gordon Cline, the founder and president of the Green Earth Alliance, and one of the nation's most revered environmental leaders, stands accused of funding the Earth Martyrs Brigade and its activities."

"Simply astonishing," Daley said.

"It is," Raines agreed. "CBC News has attempted to contact Cline's attorney but has received no response. We also reached out to senior management at the Green Earth Alliance. No one there was willing to comment at this time."

"We will continue to monitor developments in this important story," Daley promised. "Thank you, Aaron."

"You're welcome. This is Aaron Raines, CBC News, the Justice Department."

CHAPTER 92

10:53 a.m., Saturday, July 15, the Garner residence, Zephyr Cove, Nevada

He had called twenty minutes earlier to make sure that it was still a good time. Erin Garner sounded tired on the phone but insisted that he was welcome to stop by. Ward knocked softly. A beautiful young woman answered the door. She smiled pleasantly, but there was an unmistakable hint of pain. Ward suddenly felt immensely guilty about his presence, a reminder of the terrible events of three months earlier. Why had he come? Had he done it for Andy Garner, for his family, or for himself?

"Please, come in," Erin said. She gestured for him to step inside.

Ward entered. "I'm sorry for bothering you," he said. "But it was important to me that we meet."

"It's no bother," Erin replied. "Besides, you mentioned on the phone that you had come down from Montana. How could I say no to someone who had traveled so far?"

Ward smiled.

"Would you like some coffee?" Erin asked.

"Sure, if you have some made."

"I do." She directed him to the kitchen table, then went to retrieve two mugs. Ward studied the room, his eyes settling on a picture of her and Andy in happier times. It made him think about Maria, and then about Rowan Parks. During the hectic aftermath of the shootout at the farm they never really got a chance to say their goodbyes.

Erin returned with the coffee. Ward took in the aroma, and then took a sip. It was fresh. She had made it just before he arrived.

"I apologize for being so late in paying my respects," Ward said.

"It's okay," she replied. "You mentioned on the phone that you're with ATF. Tell me, how did you know Andy?"

"I didn't, really."

Erin looked puzzled.

Ward explained. "I was involved in the investigation of the Earth Martyrs Brigade. That's why it has taken me so long to come by." He briefly summarized the operation, downplaying his own role. "I felt that you had a right to know."

Her eyes moistened. She reached over and took his hand. "Thank you."

Ward looked down, feeling guilty. He hadn't come for thanks. Others had given so much more, some losing their lives while trying to stop the terrorists. They deserved the gratitude. Then, his thoughts were interrupted by the concerned voice of a young boy.

"Mommy, are you sad?"

Jake had entered the kitchen and seen the tears in his mother's eyes. Ward could not even imagine how difficult it had been for them both, how many times they had both cried.

Erin forced a smile. "I'm okay, honey." She reached out to Jake and pulled him onto her lap. "This is Special Agent David Ward," she said. "He helped catch the bad guys who hurt Daddy." A tear rolled down Erin's cheek.

Ward struggled to maintain his composure.

Jake got off his mother's lap and came over to Ward. "Can I give you a hug?" he asked.

"You sure can," Ward said. He embraced the little boy, never feeling more certain about the importance of his mission.

EPILOGUE

7:16 p.m., Friday, July 21, Lolo, Montana, just south of Missoula

Ward stood on his back deck, looking out at the Bitterroot River as it rolled through the Montana landscape. He had always considered himself something of an environmentalist. Still did, even after dealing with the zealots of the Earth Martyrs Brigade. As with other such groups he had infiltrated, he was fascinated by their cult-like mind-set, the detachment from reality. Any rational person could see that EMB's actions would alienate the public and only hurt the cause of legitimate environmentalists. Yet, the members were blind to this. They were at war. And for them, it was a holy war.

Ward had heard that contributions to the Green Earth Alliance had dried up since Gordon Cline's role with EMB was exposed. In fact, a number of established environmental organizations had reported a decline in donations. Those who advocated and worked for a cleaner planet and more sustainable living were being painted with the broad brush of extremism in the aftermath of the case. That was unfortunate. He was sure it would turn around, but when?

Ward took a sip of his beer. As he sat it back on the railing he heard the familiar call of his old friend, Jim McNeal.

"Dave, you comin' or not?"

Ward chuckled. He took another swallow and headed for the basement. As he walked through the living room he glanced at the spot where Maria's picture had once been. There was a pang of guilt at having removed it. But it was for the best.

"You guys ready to play or what?" Ward asked as he descended the stairs.

"There it is," McNeal said, feigning exasperation. "Every fuckin' time." He raised his hands. "We've been ready. Of course, you knew that."

Tommy Stafford shook his head, playing along. "No commitment to the band. None."

Ward smiled at the comforting ritual. It was good to be with his friends. He plugged in the cord connecting his guitar to the amplifier and flipped on the power switch. As he slipped the strap over his shoulder he heard footsteps upstairs. Normally, the sound would have caused him to grab his weapon. But not this time.

She came down the steps carrying pizza and beer. Ward smiled at her presence. He felt lucky.

"Gentleman," Ward announced, "I'd like you to meet Special Agent Rowan Parks."

"Howdy, boys. Anybody need a beer?"

ACKNOWLEDGMENTS

In writing this novel I developed an even greater appreciation for the men and women who work to keep us safe from terrorism, foreign and domestic. The challenges they face are extraordinary, their sacrifice great, their constant vigilance remarkable.

I gratefully acknowledge the many friends in law enforcement who contributed to this work. I want to extend a special thanks to Cliff Cronk and Mike Jaraczeski. Their insight gave this story a realism far beyond anything that I could have achieved alone. Any mistakes that remain are solely my own.

Thank you to Claire Gerus, whose guidance has been invaluable; to my wife, Karen, who continues to encourage and support me in more ways than I can count; to our children, who think it's cool that their dad writes stories; to my editor, Mark Terry, who made this book vastly more readable; and, finally, to Lance Wright and everyone at Crimson Gate Books.

JOEL W. BARROWS is an Iowa district court judge who regularly oversees both criminal and civil trials. Prior to his appointment to the bench he was a practicing attorney for nearly twenty-three years; the last eighteen of those spent as a state, and then federal, prosecutor. As an attorney, Joel regularly argued before the United States Court of Appeals. His cases have been as diverse as white collar crime, environmental crime, cyber-crime, child exploitation, narcotics and firearms offenses, immigration crimes, bank robbery, health care fraud, public corruption, civil rights offenses and threats against the President, and have included many high profile prosecutions. He has traveled extensively in Central America. He lives with his family in eastern Iowa along the banks of the Mississippi.